# MOTHER OF WINTER

# MOTHER OF WINTER

## BARBARA HAMBLY

A DEL REY® BOOK

BALLANTINE BOOKS • NEW YORK

A Del Rey® Book
Published by Ballantine Books

Copyright © 1996 by Barbara Hambly

http://www.randomhouse.com

Hambly, Barbara.
Mother of winter / Barbara Hambly.—1st ed.
p.   cm.
"A Del Rey book."
ISBN 0-345-39722-3
I. Title.
PS3558.A4215M68   1996
813'.54—dc20                                96-2768

Manufactured in the United States of America

First Edition: October 1996

10  9  8  7  6  5  4  3  2  1

*For Robin*

# Contents

THE NORTHERN ICE

SNOWY MTNS.

shilgae

Karst

Gae

FELWOODS

PLAINS

Sarda Pass

Dare's Keep in Darwath Vale

GREAT

Arrow River

Brown River

Black Rock

Penambra

GETTLESAND

THE ROUND SEA

LKETH

D'haalac

Zenuuak

Khirsrit

Mountain of Saycot

Lake of Nychee

Xyam (The Mother of Winter)

Christine Levis

# MOTHER OF WINTER

# Prologue

In the moonstone dawn, the lone rider dismounted at the top of the steps, passed through the black square open eye where the doors would one day be, and halted on the edge of shadowed abyss. The woman who lay on the obsidian plinth in the chasm's midst knew by the shape of his shoulders and back, by the way he carried his head, who he was; there was in any case only one person he could be. The wind that brought the smell of the glaciers down to her funneled past him through the passageway and carried on it the stench of blood.

When he stepped clear of the gate's collected gloom, she saw he was covered with it, as if he had lain down in a butcher's shambles. Some of it she knew was his, all mixed with the nigrous grease of torch smoke; there was also mud on his bare left forearm where he had fallen or been thrown from his horse, and on his bare knees above his boot tops, as if he had knelt in gore-soaked earth—to raise someone in his arms, perhaps.

The great clean-hewed pit of the foundation lay between them, deep as the cliffs that surrounded the Vale, and filled with the night's last shade. The plinth that rose through it, nearly to the level of the ground, was circled by half-made levels and support pillars like the greatest trees in some primordial iron forest, dwarfed to fragility by the chasm's sheer size. The machines that fused the black stone walls, insectile monsters of crystal and meteor iron, stood quiescent on platforms in the scaffolding; smaller slave-crystals and drones floated in the air between like exhausted stars, and here and there great sheets of wyr-web flashed softly in the nacreous light. Where the stairways and catwalks joined and crossed between the greater platforms, sleeping figures could be seen, lying where they had collapsed within the rings and spheres of silver dust, dried blood, smoke and light that trailed off the fragile plank flooring to float like sea-wrack on the air.

He looked down to meet the woman's eyes.

Depleted by last night's Great Spell, she propped herself up with her hands and coughed, feeling twice her sixty years. As the man picked his way across the spiderweb lines of bamboo and planking, descended ladders and stepped over gaps that fell away into a thousand feet of gloom, she saw that he, too, moved carefully, holding to the ropes and stopping now and then to stand half bowed over, gathering strength.

"It's all right," she said, when he looked down from a ladder at the intricate patterns woven on the plinth's circular top. "The spells are accomplished, such as they are. Stay between those two lines and all will be well."

He was a respecter of such things. Not everyone was these days. He looked around him again, and she wondered if, from the plinth, he could see what she saw: the whole of the future edifice called forth in those ghostly traceries, as if the fortress already existed, wrought of starlight and future time.

Every Rune, every circle, every sigil and smoke-trace had been placed individually, by her hand or the hands of those who slept all around her huddled in the lee of the Foci, broken by what they had done.

And to no avail, she thought. To no avail.

She asked him, "Are they dead?"

He nodded.

"All of them?"

"All."

It was not the worst thing she had ever borne, but in some ways more painful than the knowledge that the world's end was coming sooner than anyone had reckoned. She had loved many of those who died last night.

"You should have asked our help."

He was unshaven under the filth; even the ends of his long hair, by which he was nicknamed at Court, were tipped with grue. "It was the only chance you had, of raising the power to do this." He had a voice like gravel and clinkers in an iron pan. "The locking point of sun, moon, and stars, you said. The time of greatest power." He swallowed, fighting pain. "It was worth what it cost."

She folded her arms across her breasts, bare beneath the midnight wool of her cloak. The morning was very cold. Below her the murmur of water was loud where springs had been broached in the rock. The smell of wet earth breathed up around them. Far down the Vale where the trees grew thick at the head of the pass, birds were waking.

"No," she said. "For we failed. We put forth all our strength, and all our strength was not enough. And all this—" The movement of her hand took in the half-raised walls, the silent machines, the chasm of foundation, the whisper of water and of that half-seen skeleton of light. "—all this will pass away, and leave us with nothing."

Her head bowed. She hadn't wept for years, not since one night when she'd seen a truth too appalling to be contemplated in the color of the stars. But her grief was a leaden darkness, seeming to pull them both down into the beginning of an endless fall. "I'm sorry."

BOOK ONE

# FIMBULTIDE

# Chapter 1

"Do you see it?" Gil Patterson's voice was no louder than the scratch of withered vines on the stained sandstone wall. Melding with the shadows was second nature to her by now. The courtyard before them was empty and still, marble pavement obscured by lichen and mud, and a small forest of sycamore suckers half concealed the fire-black ruins of the hall, but she could have sworn that something had moved. "Feel it?"

She edged forward a fraction of an inch, the better to see, taking care to remain still within the ruined peristyle's gloom. "What is it?"

The possibility of ghosts crossed her mind.

The five years that had passed since eight thousand people died in this place in a single night had been hard ones, but some of their spirits might linger.

"I haven't the smallest idea, my dear."

She hadn't heard him return to her from his investigation of the building's outer court: he was a silent-moving man. Pitched for her hearing alone, his voice was of a curious velvety roughness, like dark bronze broken by time. In the shadows of the crumbling wall, and the deeper concealment of his hood, his blue eyes seemed very bright.

"But there is something."

"Oh, yes." Ingold Inglorion, Archmage of the wizards of the West, had a way of listening that seemed to touch everything in the charred and sodden waste of the city around them, living and dead. "I suspect," he added, in a murmur that seemed more within her mind than outside of it, "that it has stalked us since we passed the city walls."

He made a sign with his hand—small, but five years' travel with him in quest of books and objects of magic among the ruins of cities populated only by bones and ghouls had taught her to see those signs. Gil was as oblivious to magic as she was to ghosts—or fairies or UFOs for that matter, she would have added—but she could read the summons of a cloaking spell, and she knew that Ingold's cloaking spells were more substantial than most people's houses.

Thus what happened took her completely by surprise.

The court was a large one. Thousands had taken refuge in the house to which it belonged, in the fond hope that stout walls and plenty of torchlight would prevent the incursion of those things called only Dark Ones. Their skulls peered lugubriously from beneath dangling curtains of colorless vines, white blurs in shadow. It was close to noon, and the silver vapors from the city's slime-filled canals were beginning to burn off, color struggling back to the red of fallen porphyry pillars, the brave blues and gilts of tile. More than half the court lay under a leprous blanket of the fat white juiceless fungus that surviving humans called slunch, and it was the slunch that drew Gil's attention now.

Ingold was still motionless, listening intently in the zebra shadows of the blown-out colonnade as Gil crossed to the edge of the stuff. "It isn't just me, is it?" Her soft voice fell harsh as a blacksmith's hammer in the unnatural hush. "It's getting worse as we get farther south." As Gil knelt to study the tracks that quilted the clay soil all along the edges of the slunch, Ingold's instruction—and that of her friend the Icefalcon—rang half-conscious warning bells in her mind. What the hell had that wolverine been trying to do? Run sideways? Eat its own tail? And that rabbit—if those were rabbit tracks . . . ? That had to be the mark of something caught in its fur, but . . .

"It couldn't have anything to do with what we're looking for, could it?" A stray breath lifted the long tendrils of her hair, escaping like dark smoke from the braid jammed under her close-fitting fur cap. "You said Maia didn't know what it was or what it did. Was there anything weird about the animals around Penambra before the Dark came?"

"Not that I ever heard." Ingold was turning his head as he spoke, listening as much as watching. He'd put back the hood of his heavy brown mantle, and his white hair, long and tatty from weeks of journeying, flickered in the gray air. He'd trimmed his beard with his knife a couple of nights ago, and resembled St. Anthony after ten rounds with demons in the wilderness.

Not, thought Gil, that anyone in this universe but herself—and Ingold, because she'd told him—knew who St. Anthony was. Maia of Thran, Bishop of Renweth, erstwhile Bishop of Penambra and owner of the palace they sought, had told her tales of analogous holy hermits who'd had similar problems.

Unprepossessing, she thought, to anyone who hadn't seen him in action. Almost invisible, unless he wished to be seen.

"And in any case we might as easily be dealing with a factor of time rather than distance." Ingold held up his six-foot walking staff in his blue-mittened left hand, but his right never strayed far from the hilt of the sword at his side. "It's been . . . Behind you!"

He was turning as he yelled, and his cry was the only reason the thing didn't take Gil full in the back like a bobcat fastening on a deer. She was drawing her own sword, still on her knees but cutting as she whirled, and aware at the same moment of Ingold drawing, stepping in, slashing. Ripping weight collided with Gil's upper arm and she had a terrible impression of a short-snouted animal face, of teeth thrusting out of a lifted mass of wrinkles, of something very wrong with the eyes . . .

Pain and cold sliced her right cheek low on the jawbone. She'd already dropped the sword, pulled her dagger; she slit and ripped and felt blood and intestines gush hotly over her hand. The thing didn't flinch. Long arms like an ape's wrapped around her shoulders, claws cutting through her sheepskin coat. It bit again at her face, going for her eyes, its own back and spine wide open. Gil cut hard and straight across them with seven-inch steel that could shave the hair off a man's arm. The teeth spasmed and snapped, the smell of blood clogging her nostrils. Buzzing dizziness filled her. She thought she'd been submerged miles deep in dry, living gray sand.

"Gil!" The voice was familiar but far-off, a fly on a ceiling miles above her head. She'd heard it in dreams, maybe . . .

Her face hurt. The lips of the wound in her cheek were freezing now against the heat of her blood. For some reason she had the impression she was waking up in her own bed in the fortress Keep of Dare, far away in the Vale of Renweth.

"What time is it?" she asked. The pain redoubled and she remembered. Her head ached.

"Lie still." He bent over her, lined face pallid with shock. There was blood on the sleeves of his mantle, on the blackish bison fur of the surcoat he wore over that. She felt his fingers probe gently at her cheek and jaw. He'd taken off his mittens, and his flesh was startlingly warm. The smell of the blood almost made her faint again. "Are you all right?"

"Yeah." Her lips felt puffy, the side of her face a balloon of air. She put up her hand and remembered, tore off her sodden glove, brushed her lips, then the corner of her right eye with her fingertips. The wounds were along her cheekbone and jaw, sticky with blood and slobber. "What was that thing?"

"Lie still a little more." Ingold unslung the pack from his shoulders and dug in it with swift hands. "Then you can have a look."

All the while he was daubing a dressing of herb and willow bark on the wounds, stitching them and applying linen and plaster—braiding in the spells of healing, of resistance to infection and shock—Gil was conscious of him listening, watching, casting again the unseen net of his awareness over the landscape that lay beyond the courtyard wall. Once he stood up, quickly, catching up the sword that lay drawn on the muddy marble at his side, but whatever it was that had stirred the slunch was still then and made no further move.

He knelt again. "Do you think you can sit up?"

"Depends on what kind of reward you offer me."

His grin was quick and shy as he put a hand under her arm.

Dizziness came and went in a long hot gray wave. She didn't want him to think her weak, so she didn't cling to him as she wanted to, seeking the familiar comfort of his warmth.

She breathed a couple of times, hard, then said, "I'm fine. What the hell is it?"

"I was hoping you might be able to tell me."

"You're joking!"

The wizard glanced at the carcass—the short bulldog muzzle, the projecting chisel teeth, the body a lumpy ball of fat from which four thick-scaled, ropy legs projected—and made a small shrug. "You've identified many creatures in our world—the mammoths, the bison, the horrible-birds, and even the dooic—as analogous to those things that lived in your own universe long ago. I hoped you would have some lore concerning this."

Gil looked down at it again. Something in the shape of the flat ears, of the fat, naked cone of the tail—something about the smell of it—repelled her, not with alienness, but with a vile sense of the half familiar. She touched the spidery hands at the ends of the stalky brown limbs. It had claws like razors.

What the hell did it remind her of?

Ingold pried open the bloody jaws. "There," he said softly. "Look." On the outsides of the gums, upper and lower, were dark, purplish, collapsed sacs of skin; Gil shook her head, uncomprehending. "How do you feel?"

"Okay. A little light-headed."

He felt her hands again and her wrists, shifting his fingers a little to read the different depths of pulse. For all his unobvious strength, he had the gentlest touch of anyone she had ever known. Then he looked back down at the creature. "It's a thing of the cold," he said at last. "Down from the north, perhaps? Look at the fur and the way the body fat is distributed. I've never encountered an arctic animal with poison sacs—never a mammal with them at all, in fact."

He shook his head, turning the hook-taloned fingers this way and that, touching the flat, fleshy ears. "I've put a general spell against poisons on you, which should neutralize the effects, but let me know at once if you feel in the least bit dizzy or short of breath."

Gil nodded, feeling both slightly dizzy and short of breath, but nothing she hadn't felt after bad training sessions with the Guards of Gae, especially toward the end of winter when rations were slim. That was something else, in the five years since the fall of Darwath, that she'd gotten used to.

Leaving her on the marble bench, with its carvings of pheasants and peafowl and flowers that had not blossomed here in ten summers, Ingold bundled the horrible kill into one of the hempen sacks he habitually carried, and hung the thing from the branch of a sycamore dying at the edge of the slunch, wreathed in such spells as would keep rats and carrion feeders at bay until they could collect it on their outward journey. Coming back to her, he sat on the bench at her side and folded her in his arms. She rested her head on his shoulder for a time, breathing in the rough pungence of his robes and the scent of the flesh beneath, wanting only to stay there in his arms, unhurried, forever.

It seemed to her sometimes, despite the forty years' difference in their ages, that this was all she had ever wanted.

"Can you go on?" he asked at length. Carefully, he kissed the unswollen side of her mouth. "We can wait a little."

"Let's go." She sat up, putting aside the comfort of his strength with regret. There was time for that later. She wanted nothing more now than to find what they had come to Penambra to find and get the hell out of town.

"Maia only saw the Cylinder once." Ingold scrambled nimbly ahead of her through the gotch-eyed doorway of the colonnade and up over a vast rubble heap of charred beams, shattered roof tiles, pulped woodwork, and broken stone welded together by a hardened soak of ruined plaster. Mustard-colored lichen crusted it, and a black tangle of all-devouring vines in which patches of slunch grew like dirty mattresses dropped from the sky. The broken statue of a female saint regarded them sadly from the mess: Gil automatically identified her by the boat, the rose, and the empty cradle as St. Thyella of Ilfers.

"Maia was always a scholar, and he knew that people were using fire as a weapon against the Dark Ones. Whole neighborhoods gathered wherever they felt the walls would hold—though they were usually wrong about that—and burn whatever they could find, hoping a bulwark of light would serve should bulwarks of stone fail. They were frequently wrong about that as well."

Gil said nothing. She remembered her first sight of the Dark. Remembered the fleeing, uncomprehending mobs, naked and jolted from sleep, men and women falling and dying as the blackness rolled over them. Remembered the thin, directionless wind, the acid-blood smell of the predators, and the way fluid and matter would rain over her when she slashed the amorphous, floating things in half with her sword.

They picked their way off the corpse of the building into a smaller court, its wooden structures only a black frieze of ruin buried in weeds. On a fallen keystone the circled cross of the Straight Faith was incised. "Asimov wrote a story like that," she said.

" 'Nightfall.' " Ingold paused to smile back at her. "Yes."

In addition to her historical studies in the archives of the Keep of Dare, Gil had gained quite a reputation among the Guards as a spinner of tales, passing along to them recycled Kipling and Dickens, Austen and Heinlein, Doyle and Heyer and Coles, to ease the long Erebus of winter nights.

"And it's true," the old man went on. "People burned whatever they could find and spent the hours of day hunting for more." His voice was grim and sad—those had been, Gil understood, people he knew. Unlike many wizards, who tended to be recluses at heart, Ingold was genuinely gregarious. He'd had dozens of friends in Gae, the northern capital of the Realm of Darwath, and here in Penambra: families, scholars, a world of drinking buddies whom Gil had never met. By the time she came to this universe, most were dead.

Three years ago she had gone with Ingold to Gae, searching for old books and objects of magic in the ruins. Among the shambling, pitiful ghouls who still haunted the broken cities, he recognized a man he had known. Ingold had tried to tell him that the Dark Ones whose destruction had broken his mind were gone and would come no more, and had narrowly missed being carved up with rusty knives and clamshells for his pains.

"I can't say I blame them for that."

"No," he murmured. "One can't." He stopped on the edge of a great bed of slunch that, starting within the ruins of the episcopal palace, had spread out through its windows and across most of the terrace that fronted the sunken, scummy chain of puddles that had been Penambra's Grand Canal. "But the fact remains that a great deal was lost." Motion in the slunch made him poke at it with the end of his staff, and a hard-shelled thing like a great yellow cockroach lumbered from between the pasty folds and scurried toward the palace doors. Ingold had a pottery jar out of his bag in seconds and dove for the insect, swift and neat. The roach turned, hissing and flaring misshapen wings; Ingold caught it midair in the jar and slapped the vessel mouth down upon the pavement with the thing clattering and scraping inside. It had flown straight at his eyes.

"Most curious." He slipped a square of card—and then the jar's broad wax stopper—underneath, and wrapped a cloth over the top to seal it. "Are you well, my dear?" For Gil had knelt beside the slunch, over-whelmed with sudden weariness and stabbed by a hunger such as she had not known for months. She broke off a piece of the slunch, like the cold detached cartilage of a severed ear, and turned it over in her fingers, wondering if there were any way it could be cooked and eaten.

Then she shook her head, for there was a strange, metallic smell behind the stuff's vague sweetness—not to mention the roach. She threw the bit back into the main mass. "Fine," she said.

As he helped her to stand, there was a sound, a quick, furtive scuffling in the slate-hued night of the empty palace. The dizziness returned nauseatingly as Gil slewed to listen. She gritted her teeth, fighting the darkness from her eyes.

"Rats, you think?" They were everywhere in the city, and huge.

Ingold's blue eyes narrowed, the small scars on the eyelids and on the soft flesh beneath pulling in a wrinkle of knife-fine lines. "It smells like them, yes. But just before you were attacked, there were five separate disturbances of that kind in all directions around me, drawing my attention from you. The vaults are this way, if I remember aright."

Since her coming to this world in the wake of the rising of the Dark, Gil had guarded Ingold's back. The stable crypt opening into the vaults had been half torn apart by the Dark Ones, and Gil's hair prickled with the memory of those bodiless haunters as she picked her way after him through a vestibule whose mud floor was broken by a sea-wrack of looted chests, candlesticks, and vermin-scattered bones. An inner door gave onto a stairway. There was a smell of water below, a cold exhalation like a grave.

"When the vigilantes started hunting the city for books—for archives, records, anything that would burn—Maia let them have what he could spare as a sop and hid the rest." Ingold's voice echoed wetly under the downward-sloping ceiling, and something below, fleeing the blue-white light that burned from the end of his staff, plopped in water.

"He bricked up some of the archives in old cells of the episcopal dungeon and sounded walls in the vaults to find other rooms that had been sealed long ago, where he might cache the oldest volumes, of which no other known copy existed. It was in one of these vaults that he found the Cylinder."

Water lay five or six inches deep in the maze of cells and tunnels that constituted the palace vaults. The light from Ingold's raised staff glittered sharply on it as Gil and the old mage waded between decaying walls plastered thick with slunch, mold, and dim-glowing niter. The masonry was ancient, of a heavy pattern far older than the more finished stones of Gae. Penambra predated the northern capital at Gae; predated the first rising of the Dark thousands of years ago—long predated any memory of humankind's. Maia himself came to Gil's mind, a hollow-cheeked skeleton with arthritis-crippled hands, laughing with Ingold over his own former self, a foppish dilettante whose aristocratic protector had bought the bishopric for him long before he was of sufficient years to have earned it.

Perhaps he hadn't really earned it until the night he hid the books—the night he led his people out of the haunted ruins of their city to the only safe place they knew: Renweth Vale and the black-walled Keep of Dare.

Before a bricked-up doorway, Ingold halted. Gil remained a few paces behind him, calf-deep in freezing water, analyzing every sound, every rustle, every drip and dull moan of the wind, fighting not to shiver and not to think of the poison that might be in her veins. Still, she thought, if the thing's bite was poisoned, it didn't seem to be too serious. God knew she'd gone through sufficient exertion for it to have killed her twice if it was going to.

Ingold passed his hand across the dripping masonry and murmured a word. Gil saw no change in the mortar, but Ingold set his staff against the wall—the light still glowing steadily from its tip, as from a lantern—and pulled a knife from his belt, with which he dug the mortar as if it were putty desiccated by time. As he tugged loose the bricks, she made no move to help him, nor did he expect her to. She only watched and listened for the first signs of danger. That was what it was to wear the black uniform, the white quatrefoil emblem, of the Guards of Gae.

Ingold left the staff leaning in the corridor, to light the young woman's watch. As a mage, he saw clearly in the dark.

Light of a sort burned through the ragged hole left in the bricks, a sickly owl-glow shed by slunch that grew all over the walls of the tiny chamber beyond, illuminating nothing. The stuff stretched a little as Ingold pulled it from the trestle tables it had almost covered; it snapped with powdery little sighs, like rotted rubber, to reveal leather wrappings protecting the books. "Archives," the wizard murmured. "Maia did well."

The Cylinder was in a wooden box in a niche on the back wall. As long as Gil's hand from wrist bones to farthest fingertip, and just too thick to be circled by her fingers, it appeared to be made of glass clear as water. Those who had lived in the Times Before—before the first rising of the Dark Ones—seemed to have favored plain geometrical shapes. Ingold brushed the thing with his lips, then set it on a corner of the table and studied it, peering inside for reflections, Gil thought. By the way he handled it, it was heavier than glass would have been.

In the end he slipped it into his rucksack. "Obviously one of Maia's predecessors considered it either dangerous or sacrilegious." He stepped carefully back through the hole in the bricks, took up his staff again. "Goodness knows there were centuries—and not too distant ones—during which magic was anathema and people thought nothing of bricking up wizards along with their toys. That room was spelled with the Rune of the Chain, which inhibits the use of magic . . . Heaven only knows what they destroyed over the course of the years. But this . . ." He touched the rucksack.

"Someone thought this worth the guarding, the preserving, down through the centuries. And that alone makes it worth whatever it may have cost us."

He touched the dressings on the side of her swollen face. At the contact, she felt stronger, warmer inside. "It is not unappreciated, my dear."

Gil looked away. She had never known what to say in the presence of love, even after she'd stopped consciously thinking, *When he finds out what kind of person I am, he'll leave.* Ingold, to her ever-renewed surprise, evidently really did love her, exactly as she was. She still didn't know why. "It's my job," she said.

Scarred and warm, his palm touched her unhurt cheek, turning her face back to his, and he gathered her again into his arms. For a time they stood pressed together, the old man and the warrior, taking comfort among the desolation of world's end.

They spent two days moving books. Chill days, though it was May and in times past the city of Penambra had been the center of semitropical bottomlands lush with cotton and sugarcane; wet days of waxing their boots every night while the spares dried by the fire; nerve-racking days of shifting the heavy volumes up the crypt stairs to where Yoshabel the mule waited in the courtyard, wreathed in spells of "there-isn't-a-mule-here" and "this-creature-is-both-dangerous-and-inedible." The second spell wasn't far wrong, in Gil's opinion. On the journey down to Penambra she had grown to thoroughly hate Yoshabel, but knew they could not afford to lose her to vermin or ghouls.

Sometimes, against the code of the Guards, Gil worked. Mostly Ingold would send her to the foot of the stairs from the stable crypt, where she listened for sounds in the court as well as watching the corridor outside the cell where the books were. He left his staff with her, the light of it glistening on the vile water underfoot and on the wrinkled, cranial masses of the slunch. What they couldn't load onto Yoshabel, Ingold rehid, higher and drier and surrounded by more spells, to keep fate and rats and insects at bay until someone could be sent again on the long, exhausting journey from Renweth Vale to retrieve them.

In addition to books—of healing, of literature, of histories and law—they found treasure, room after room of Church vessels of gold and pearl and carven gems, chairs crusted with garnets, ceremonial candleholders taller than a man and hung with chains of diamond fruit; images of saints with jeweled eyes, holding out the gem-encrusted instruments of their martyrdom; sacks of gold and silver coin. These they left, though Ingold took as much silver as he could carry and a few of the jewels flawless enough to hold spells in their crystalline hearts. The rest he surrounded with Ward-signs and spells. One never knew when such things would come in handy.

They took turns at watch that night. Even in lovemaking, which they did by the glow of the courtyard fire, neither fully relaxed—it would have been more sensible not to do it, but the strange edge of danger drew at them both. Now and then a shift in the wind brought them the smells of wood smoke and raw human waste, and they knew there were ghouls—or perhaps bandits—dwelling somewhere in the weedy desolation along the canals. Gil, her face discolored and aching in spite of all Ingold's spells of healing, fell asleep almost at once and slept heavily; wrapped in his fur surcoat, Ingold sat awake by the bead of their fire, listening to the dark.

This was how Gil saw him in her dream the second night, when she realized that he had to die.

They had made love, and she dreamed of making love to him again, in the cubicle they shared, a small inner cell in the maze of cells that were the territory of the Guards on the first level of the windowless Keep. She dreamed of falling asleep in the gentle aftermath, her smoky dark wilderness of hair strewed like kelp on the white-furred muscle of his chest, the smell of his flesh and of the Guards' cooking, of leather oil from her weaponry and coat, filling her nostrils, smells for which she had traded the car exhaust and synthetic aromatics of a former home.

She dreamed that while still she slept he sat up and drew the blankets around him. His white hair hung down on his shoulders, and under the scarred lids his eyes were hard and thoughtful as he looked down at her. There was no gentleness in them now, no love—barely even recognition.

Then he began, while she slept, to work magic upon her, to lay words on her that made her foolish with love, willing to leave her friends and family, her studies at the University of California, as she had in fact left all the familiar things of the world of her birth. He lay on her words that made her, from the moment of their meeting, his willing slave.

All the peril she had faced against the Dark Ones, all the horror and fire, the wounds she had taken, the men she had killed, the tears she had shed . . . all were calculated, part of his ploy. Taken from her with his magic, rather than freely given for love of him.

Her anger was like a frozen volcano, outraged, betrayed, surging to the surface and destroying everything in its path. Rape, her mind said. Betrayal, greed, lust, hypocrisy . . . rape.

But he had laid spells on her that kept her asleep.

She would not be free of him, she thought, until he was dead.

She woke and found that she had her knife in her hand. She lay in the corner of the bishop's courtyard, fire between her and the night. Yoshabel, tethered nearby, had raised her head, long ears turning toward the source of some sound. Ingold, his back to the embers, listened likewise, the shoulders of his robe and the mule's shaggy coat dyed rose with the embers' reflection. Gold threads laced the wet edges of the slunch bed, the leather wrappings of the books. Somewhere a voice that might have been human, half a mile or more away, was blubbering and shrieking in agony as something made leisurely prey of its owner.

*Good,* she thought, calm and strangely clear. *He's distracted.*

Why did she feel that the matter had been arranged?

The blanket slid from her as she rose to hands and knees, knife tucked against her side. In her bones, in her heart, with the same awareness by which she knew the hapless ghoul was being killed for her benefit, she also knew herself to be invisible to the stretched-out fibers of Ingold's senses, invisible to his magic. If she kept low, practiced those rites of silence the Guards had taught, she could sever his spine as easily as she'd severed that of the thing that had torn open her face.

*His fault, too,* she thought bitterly, surveying the thin fringe of white hair beneath the close-fit lambskin cap. *His doing. His summoning, if the truth were known.*

*I was beautiful before . . .*

She knew that wasn't true. Thin-faced, sharp-featured, with a great witchy cloud of black hair that never would do what she wanted of it, she had never been more than passably pretty, a foil for the glamour of a mother and a sister whose goals had been as alien to her scholarly pursuits as a politician's or a religious fanatic's might have been.

The awareness of the lie pulled her back—pulled her fully awake— and she looked down at the knife in her hand.

*Jesus,* she thought. *Oh, Jesus . . .*

"Ingold . . ."

He moved his head a little, but did not take his eyes from the dark of the court. "Yes, child?"

"I've had a dream," she said. "I want to kill you."

# Chapter 2

"Once upon a time there was a boy . . ." Rudy Solis began.

"Once upon a time there was a boy." Altir Endorion, Lord of the Keep of Dare, wriggled his back against the side of the big chest-bed to get comfortable and folded his small hands, the low glare of the hearth's embers shining in his speedwell-blue eyes.

"And he lived in a great big palace . . ."

"And he lived in a great big palace."

"With lots of servants to wait on him and do whatever he asked."

The blue eyes closed. Tir was thinking about that one. He had long black lashes, almost straight, and his black forelock, escaping from the embroidered sheepskin cap he wore, made a diacritical squiggle between cap rim and the drawn-down strokes of his brows. In thought like this he seemed older than five years.

"He went riding every morning on horses by the river and all his servants had to go with him," Tir went on after a moment. "They'd all carry bows and arrows, except the boy's servants had to carry the boy's bows and arrows for him. They'd shoot birds by the river . . ."

His frown deepened, distressed. "They shot birds that were pretty, not because they wanted to eat them. There was a black bird with long legs wading in the river, and it had a little crown of white feathers on its head, and the boy shot at it with his arrows. When it flew away, the boy told his servants, 'I would that you take this creature with net and lime,'" his voice stumbled over unfamiliar words, an antique inflection, "'and bring it to me, for I will not be robbed of my . . . my quarry . . .' What's quarry, Rudy?" He opened his eyes.

"Quarry is what you catch when you go hunting." Rudy gazed into the hearth, wondering how long it had been since black egrets had haunted the marshlands below the royal city of Gae. A hundred years? Two hundred? It was part of his wizardry to know, but at the moment he couldn't remember. Ingold could have provided the information out of his head, along with a mild remark about junior mages who needed their notes about such things tattooed on their arms—along with their own names—for lagniappe. "Sounds like a mean boy to me, Pugsley."

"He was." Tir's eyes slipped shut again, but his face was troubled now, as he picked and teased at the knot of deep-buried memories, the recollections of another life. "He was mean because he was scared all the time. He was scared . . . he was scared . . ." He groped for the thought. "He thought everybody was going to try to hurt him, so they could make somebody else king and not him. His daddy's brothers, and their children. His daddy told him that. His daddy was mean, too."

He looked up at Rudy, who had an arm around his shoulders where they sat side by side on the sheepskin rugs of the cell floor. Even the royal chambers of the Keep of Dare were mostly small and furnished simply with ancient pieces found in the Keep, or with what had been hewn or whittled since the coming of the remnant of the Realm's people. The journey down the Great South Road, and up the pass to the Vale of Renweth at the foot of the still higher peaks, had been a harsh one. Those who'd gone back along the route the following spring in quest of furnishings thrown aside to lighten the wagons had found them not improved by a season under mud and snow.

"But why would being scared all the time make him be mean?" Tir wanted to know. "Wouldn't people be nastier to him if he was mean?"

"If they were his daddy's servants, they couldn't be mean back," pointed out Rudy, who'd learned a good deal about customary behavior in monarchies since abandoning his career as a motorcycle painter and free-lance screw-up in Southern California. "And maybe when he was mean he was less scared."

Tir nodded, seeing the truth of that but still bothered. As far as Rudy could ascertain, Tir didn't have a mean bone in his body. "And why would his daddy's brothers want to be king instead of the boy? Being king is awful."

"Maybe they didn't know that."

Tir looked unconvinced.

As well he might, Rudy thought. Tir remembered being king. Over, and over, and over.

Most of what he recalled today would be of more interest to Gil than to himself, Rudy reflected. She was the one who was engaged—between relentless training with the Guards and her duties on patrol and watching the Keep's single pair of metal doors—in piecing together the vast histories of the realms of Darwath and its tributary lands; its relationships with the wizards, with the great noble Houses, with the Church of the Straight God, with the southern empires and the small states of the Felwood and the distant seaboard to the east. She could probably figure out which king this mean boy who shot at netted birds had grown up to be, and who his daddy was, and what politics exactly had caused his uncles to want to snuff the little bastard—no loss, by the sound of it.

Except that if that boy had not grown up and married, he would not have passed down his memories with his bloodline and eventually have created the child Tir.

And that would have been tragedy.

The wizard in Rudy noted the details remembered about the palace, identifying flowers in the garden, birds and beasts glimpsed in the trees, picturing clearly the place that he himself had only seen in ruins. But mostly what fascinated him were the workings of that far-off child's life and family, how cruelty had meshed with cruelty, how anger had answered angers formed by fathers and grandfathers; how constant suspicion and unlimited power had resulted in a damn unpleasant little brat who quite clearly worked hard to make everyone around him as miserable as he possibly could.

No wonder Tir's eyes were a thousand years old.

"Rudy?" A tousled blond head appeared around the doorway after a perfunctory knock. "M'lord Rudy," the boy hastily amended, and added with a grin, "Hi, Tir. M'lord Rudy, Her Majesty asks if you'd come to the Doors, please. Fargin Graw's giving her a bad time," he added as Rudy reached for his staff and started to rise.

"Oh, great." Fargin Graw was someone whose nose Rudy had considered breaking for years. "Thanks, Geppy."

"May I go play with Geppy, Rudy?"

"Yeah, go ahead, Ace. If I know Graw, this'll take a while."

With Geppy and Tir pelting on ahead of him, Rudy walked down the broad main corridor of the royal enclave—one of the few wide halls in the Keep not to have been narrowed millennia ago by the owners of cells breaking walls to cadge space from the right of way—and down the Royal Stair. Someone had taken advantage of the draught on the stair and stretched a clothesline across the top of the high archway where the stair let into the Aisle, the black-walled cavern that ran more than three-quarters of the Keep's nearly half-mile length. Rudy ducked under the laundry, scarcely a wizardly figure in his deerskin breeches, rough wool shirt, and gaudily painted bison-hide vest, his dark hair hanging almost to his shoulders. Only his staff, pale wood worn with generations of hand grips and tipped by a metal crescent upon whose sharpened points burned blue St. Elmo's fire, marked him as mageborn.

The Aisle's roof was lost in shadow above him, though pin lights of flame delineated the bridges that crossed it on the fourth and fifth levels. The glasslike hardness of the walls picked up the chatter of the launderers working in the basins and streams that meandered along the stone immensity of the open floor; some of them called greetings to him as he passed.

Fargin Graw's voice boomed above those homier echoes like flatulant thunder on a summer afternoon.

"If we're supporting them, they'd damn well better earn their keep!" He was a big man—Rudy could identify his silhouette against the chilly light that streamed through the passageway between the two sets of open Doors while he was still crossing the last of the low stone bridges over the indoor streams. "And if they're not earning their keep, which I for one can't see 'em doing, then they better find themselves a useful trade or get out! Like some others I could name sitting around getting fat . . . There's not a man in the River Settlements who doesn't get out in the fields and pull his stint at guarding—"

"And boy, after all day in the fields, they must be just sharp as razors on night-watch." Rudy hooked his free hand through the buckle of his belt as he came out to join the little group on the Keep's broad, shallow steps, blinking a little in the pallid brightness of the spring sun.

Graw swung around angrily, a brick-faced man with the fair hair not often seen in the lands once called the Realm of Darwath, perhaps five years older than Rudy's thirty years. Janus of Weg, commander of the elite corps of the Keep Guards, hid a smile—he'd lost warriors twice due to the inefficiency of Graw's farmer militia—and the Lady Minalde, last High Queen of Darwath and Lady of the Keep, raised a hand for silence.

"Rudy." Her low, sweet voice was pleasantly neutral in greeting, as if he had not spoken. "Master Graw rode up from the Settlements with the tribute sheep today to hear from your own lips why there hasn't been further progress in eliminating slunch from the fields."

Rudy said, *"What?"* In three years, slunch in the fields—and in huge areas of meadow and woods, both here in Renweth Vale and down by the River Settlements—had become an endemic nuisance, indestructible by any means he or Ingold or anyone else had yet been able to contrive. It would burn after a fashion but grew back within days, even if the dirt it had grown upon were sown with salt, soaked with oil of vitriol at any strength Ingold could contrive, or dug out and heaped elsewhere: the slunch grew back both in the dirt heap and in the hole. It simply ignored magic. It grew. And it spread, sometimes slowly, sometimes with alarming speed.

"How about asking me something simple, like why don't we get rid of rats in the Keep? Or ragweed pollen in the spring?"

"Don't you get smart with me, boy," Graw snapped in his flat, deaf man's voice. "You think because you sit around reading books and nobody makes you do a hand's turn of work you can give back answers to a man of the land, but . . ."

Rudy opened his mouth to retort that until the rising of the Dark, Graw had been a man of the paint-mixing pots in Gae—his wife and sons did most of the work on his acres down in the River Settlements, by all accounts, as they'd done here in the Vale before the nine hundred or so colonists had moved down to the river valleys to found settlements three years ago. But Alde said, still in resolutely friendly, uninflected tones, "I think what Rudy is trying to say is that there are some problems, not amenable to any remedy we know, which have been with us for thousands of years, and that slunch may turn out to be one of them." The glass-thin breeze from the higher mountain peaks stirred tendrils of her long black hair, fluttering the new leaves of the aspen and mountain laurel that rimmed the woods, a hundred yards from the Keep on its little mound. "We don't know."

"The stuff's only been around for three years," pointed out Rudy, upon whose toe Alde had inconspicuously trodden.

"And in those three years," Graw retorted, "it's cut into the fields we've sweated and bled to plant, it's killed the wheat and the trees on which our lives and the lives of our children depend." One heavy arm swept toward the farms downslope from the Keep, the fields with their lines of withe separating one plot holder's land from the next. Like purulent sores, white spots of slunch blotched the green of young wheat in three or four places, the wrinkled white fungus surrounded by broad rings of brown where the grain was dying.

Graw's mouth clamped into a settled line, and his pale tan eyes, like cheap beads, sliced resentfully between the slim black-haired woman beside him, the young wizard in his painted vest, and the heavy-shouldered, black-clothed shape of the Commander of the Guards, as if he suspected them of somehow colluding to withhold from him the secret of comfort and survival.

"It's sickening the crops, and if the River Settlements are sending wheat and milk and beasts for slaughter up here to the Keep every year, we're entitled to something for our sweat."

"Something more than us risking our necks to patrol your perimeter, you mean?" Janus asked thinly, and Graw scoffed.

"My men can do their own patrolling! What the hell good is it to know about saber-teeth or some bunch of scroungy dooic ten miles from the nearest fields?" He conveniently neglected to mention the warning the Guards had brought him of the White Raiders last winter, or the battle they and the small force of nobles and men-at-arms had fought with a bandit company the autumn before. "But if our labor and our strength are going out to support a bunch of people up here at the Keep who do nothing or next to nothing . . ." His glance slid back to Rudy, and from him to Alde's belly, rounded under the green wool of her faded gown.

The Lady of the Keep met his eye. "Are you saying then that the Settlements Council has voted to dispense with sending foodstuffs to the Keep in return for patrols by the Guards and advice from the mages who live here?"

"Dammit, we haven't voted on anything!" snapped Graw, who, as far as Rudy knew, wasn't even on the Settlements Council. "But as a man of the land whose labor is supporting you, I have the right to know what's being done! Not one of your wizards has come down to have a look at my fields."

"The slunch is different down there?"

"Thank you very much for coming to us, Master Graw." Minalde's voice warmed as she inclined her head. As Graw made a move to stride toward the Keep, she added, with impeccably artless timing, "And I bid you welcome to the Keep, you and your riders, and make you free of it."

He halted, his jaw tightening, but he could do no more than mutter, "I thank you, lady. Majesty," he added, under the cool pressure of that morning-glory gaze. He glared at Rudy, then jerked his hand at the small band of riders who'd accompanied the herd of tribute sheep up the pass.

They fell in behind him, bowing awkward thanks to Alde as they followed him up the shallow black stone steps and vanished into the dark tunnel of the Doors.

Rudy set his jaw, willing the man's hostility to slide off him like rain.

In a sweet voice trained by a childhood spent with relentless deportment masters, Minalde said, "One of these days I'm going to break that man's nose."

"Y'want lessons?" Janus asked promptly, and they all laughed.

"Why is it," Minalde asked with a sigh, later, as she and Rudy walked down the muddy path toward the Keep farms, "that one always hears of spells that will turn people into trees and frogs and mongrel dogs, but never one that will turn a . . . a lout like that into a good man?"

Rudy shrugged. "Maybe because if I said, 'Abracadabra, turn that jerk into a good man,' there'd be no change." He shook his head. "Sheesh. I've been around Ingold too long."

She laughed and touched his hand. His fingers fitted with hers as if designed to do so at the beginning of time. The farms—which, contrary to Graw's assertions, were in fact the chief business of the Keep, and always had been—were far enough from the walls that wizard and lady could walk handfast without exacerbating the sensibilities of the conservative. Everyone knew that the Keep wizard's pupil was the lady's lover and the father of the child she carried, but it was a matter seldom mentioned: the religious teachings of a less desperate age died hard.

"You're going to have to go down there, you know," Alde said in time.

"Now?"

Their eyes met, and she rested her free hand briefly on the swell beneath her gown. "I think so," she said matter-of-factly. "It's the second or third time he's been up here, demanding that something be done about slunch. He has a lot of influence in the Settlements, not with the nobles, but with the hunters, and some of the farmers. If he broke away from Keep rule, he'd probably turn bandit himself. The child isn't due for another two months, you know."

Rudy knew. Though he'd helped to birth dozens of babies in the five years he'd been Ingold's pupil, the thought of Alde being brought to bed while the master wizard was still on the road somewhere terrified him.

With Alde, it was different.

The Lady of the Keep. The widow of the last High King. Tir's mother.

The mother of the child that would be his.

The thought made him shiver inside, with longing and joy and a strange disbelief. He'd be a father. That child inside her—inside the person he most loved in the whole of his life, the whole of two universes—was a part of him.

Involuntarily—half kiddingly, but half not—he thought, *Poor kid. Some gene pool.*

And yet . . .

Under the all-enveloping bulk of her quilted silk coat she barely showed, even this far along. But she had the glowing beauty he'd seen in those of his sisters who'd married happily and carried children by the men who brought them joy. Ingold had early taught him the spells that wizards lay upon their consorts to keep them from conceiving, but she had pleaded with him not to use them. Nobody in the Keep talked about their lady carrying a wizard's child, but even Bishop Maia, usually tolerant despite the Church's official rulings, had his misgivings.

"It can't wait till Ingold gets back?"

"It's only a day's journey." He could hear the uneasiness in her voice, see it in the set of her shoulders and the way she released his hand to fold her arms around herself as she walked. "Much as I hate to agree with anything that man says, he's right about slunch destroying crops. Unless the harvest is better this year than last, our stores will barely get us through next winter."

"It was a bad year." Rudy shifted his grip uneasily on the hand-worn smoothness of his staff. "Last winter was rough, and if Gil was right about the world getting colder, we're in for a lot more of them."

Beyond the shaggy curtain of pines, the Snowy Mountains lifted to the west, towering above the narrow valley, the glittering cliff of the Sarda Glacier overhanging the black rock. Far up the valley, St. Prathhes' Glacier had moved down from the peaks of the spur range called the Ramparts, a tsunami of frozen diamond above the high pastures. Edged wind brought the scent of sterile ice and scraped rock with the spice of the spruce and new grass. It wailed a little in the trees, counterpoint to the squeak of Alde's sheepskin boots in the mud and the purl of the stream that bordered the fields. The mountains may have been safer from the Dark, Rudy thought, but they sure didn't make good farmland.

Cows regarding them over the pasture fences moved aside at Rudy's wave. He clambered over the split rails and helped Alde after, not liking the lightness of her frame within its faded patchwork of quilting and fur. Spring was a time of short rations. Even with last year's stored grain and the small surplus sent up from the Settlements, everyone in the Keep had been on short commons for months. Crypt after crypt of hydroponics tanks lay in the foundations deep beneath the Keep, but Rudy didn't have to be a technician to know they weren't operating as effectively as they could be. In any case, grain and corn had to be grown outdoors, and in the thin soil of the mountain valley, good arable was short.

The withy fences around the slunch in the west pasture had been moved again. The stuff had almost reached the stream. Past the line of the fences the grass was dying; the fences would have to be moved farther still. Three years ago, when slunch first started growing near the Keep, he and Ingold had agreed that neither humans nor animals should be allowed to eat it until they knew exactly what it was.

And that was something neither of them had figured out yet.

Short meadow grasses stirred around his feet, speckled bright with cow-lilies and lupine. There were fewer snakes this year, he noted, and almost no frogs. The herdkids waved to him from the other side of the pasture fence and choused the Settlements' tribute sheep into the main flock. He spotted Tir's bright blue cap among them, beside Geppy Nool's blond curls. Geppy's promotion to herdkid—with the privilege of sleeping in the byres and smelling permanently of dung—had consumed the smaller boy's soul with envy, and for several days Tir seriously considered abdicating as High King of Darwath in favor of a career in livestock supervision.

"Damn crazy stuff." Rudy waved back, then ducked through the hurdles that made up the fence. Alde followed more clumsily, but kept pace with him as he walked the perimeter of the rolling, thick-wrinkled plant—if plant it was. Sometimes Rudy wasn't sure. He'd never found anything that looked like seeds, spores, roots, or shoots. Slunch didn't appear to require either water or light to grow. It just spread, some six inches high in the middle of the bed, down to an inch or so at the edges, where wormlike whitish fingers projected into the soil bared by the dying grass.

Rudy knelt and pulled up one of the tendrils, like a very fat ribbon stood on its edge. He hated the touch of it, cold and dry, like a mushroom. By the tracks all around it there were animals that ate it, and so far neither the Guards nor the Keep hunters had reported finding dead critters in the woods . . .

But Rudy's instincts shrank from the touch of it. Deep inside he knew the stuff was dangerous. He just didn't know how. He squeezed it, flinching a little at the rubbery pop it gave before it crumbled, then wiped his hands on his soft deerhide trousers. With great effort Ingold had acquired enough sulfur from a dyer's works in Gae to manufacture oil of vitriol—sulfuric acid—and had tried pouring that on slunch. It killed it but rendered the ground unfit for further use. And the slunch grew back within three or four weeks. It was scarcely worth the risk and hardship of another trip to the ruins of Gae for that.

"Do you think that thing Maia described to Ingold—the Cylinder he found in the vaults at Penambra—might hold some clue about the slunch?" Alde kept her distance. The dark fur of her collar riffled gently around her face, and the tail of her hair made a thick sable streak in the colors of old gowns, old curtains, and old hangings that had gone into her coat.

"It might." Rudy came back to her, uneasily dusting the sides of his breeches and boots. "Ingold and Gil haven't found zip about slunch in any archive they've searched so far, but for all we know it may have been common as daisies back before the first rising of the Dark. One day Pugsley's going to look up at me and say, 'Oh, we always dumped apple juice on it—shriveled it right up.' And that'll be that."

Alde laughed, and Rudy glanced back at the cold, thick mass behind them, inert and flaccid and yet not dead. He said, "But we better not count on it."

The sun had slipped behind the three great peaks that loured over Sarda Pass: Anthir, the Mammoth, and the Hammerking. The air above glacier and stone was still filled with light, the clouds streaked crimson, ochre, pink, and amber by the sunset, and the eternal snowfields picked up the glory of it, stained as if with liquid gold. Like a black glass rectangle cut from the crystallized bone of the mountain, the Keep of Dare caught the reflection, burning through the trees: a fortress built to guard the remnant of humankind through the times of darkness, until the sun should shine again.

Looking below it, beyond it, to the scant growth of wheat and corn in the fields along the stream, the white patches of slunch and the thinness of the blossom on the orchard trees, Rudy wondered if those ancient walls would be protection enough.

*Just my luck. I make it to the world where I belong, the world where*

*I have magic, the world where the woman I love lives—and we all starve to death.*

*It figures.*

"The range of my tribe lay at the feet of the Haunted Mountain, between the Night River and the groves along the Cursed Lands, and northward to the Ice in the North." The Icefalcon slipped his scabbarded killing-sword free of his sash, set it where it could be drawn in split instants, and shed vest and coat and long gray scarf in a fashion that never seemed to engage his right hand. "Never in all those lands, in all my years of growing up, did I hear speak of this slunch."

Only a few glowstones dispersed white light in the Guards' watch-room. Most of the Guards' allotment of the milky polyhedrons illuminated the training floor where Gnift put a small group of off-shift warriors—Guards, the men-at-arms of the Houses of Ankres and Sketh, and the teenage sons of Lord Ankres—through a sparring session more strenuous than some wars. Hearthlight winked on dirty steel as the incoming shift unbuckled harness, belts, coats; ogre shadows loomed in darkness, and across the long chamber someone laughed at Captain Melantrys' wickedly accurate imitation of Fargin Graw feeling sorry for himself.

Rudy sighed and slumped against the bricks of the beehive hearth. "You ever ride north into the lands of the Ice?"

The young warrior elevated a frost-pale brow in mild surprise. "Life among the tribes is difficult enough," he said. "Why would anyone ask further trouble by going there?"

"People do," said Seya, an older woman with short-cropped gray hair.

"Not my people."

"Well," Rudy said, "slunch is obviously arctic—at least it started to show up when the weather got colder . . ."

"But never was it seen near the lands of the Ice," the White Raider pointed out logically. His long ivory-colored braids, weighted with the dried human finger-bones thonged into them, swung forward as he chaffed his hands before the fire. Like all the other Guards, he was bruised, face and arms and hands, from sword practice. It was a constant about them all, like the creak of worn leather harnesswork or the smell of woodsmoke in their clothing. "Nor did our shamans and singers speak of such a thing. Might slunch be the product of some shaman's malice?"

"What shaman?" Rudy demanded wearily. "Thoth and the Gettle-sand wizards tell me the stuff grows on the plains for miles now, clear up to the feet of the Sawtooth Mountains. Why would any shaman lay such a . . . a limitless curse?"

The Icefalcon shrugged. As a White Raider, he had been born paranoid.

"As for foods that will grow in the cold," he went on, settling with a rag to clean the mud from his black leather coat, "when game ran scarce, we ate seeds and grasses; insects and lizards as well, at need." Constant patrols in the cold and wind had turned the Icefalcon's long, narrow face a dark buff color, against which his hair and eyes seemed almost white. Rudy observed that even while working, the Icefalcon's right hand never got beyond grabbing range of his sword. All the Guards were like that to a degree, of course, but according to Gil there were bets among them as to whether the Icefalcon closed his eyes when he slept.

"Sometimes in days of great hunger we'd dig tiger-lily bulbs and bake them in the ground with graplo roots to draw the poison out of them."

"Sounds yummy."

"Pray to your ancestors you never discover how yummy such fare can be."

"We used to eat these things like rocks." Rudy hadn't heard Tir come up beside him. Small for his age and fragile-looking, Tir had a silence that was partly shyness, partly a kind of instinctive fastidiousness. Partly, Rudy was sure, it was the result of the subconscious weight of adult memories, adult fears.

"They were hard like rocks until you cooked them, and then they got kind of soft. Mama—the other little boy's mama—used to mash them up with garlic."

The Icefalcon raised his brows. He knew about the heritable memories—an old shaman of his tribe, he had told Rudy once, had them—and he knew enough not to put in words or questions that might confuse the child.

Rudy said casually, "Sounds like . . ." He didn't know the word in the Wathe. "Sounds like what we call potatoes, Ace. Spuds. What'd that little boy call them?"

Tir frowned, fishing memories chasms deep. "Earth-apples." He spoke slowly, forming a word Rudy had never heard anyone say in the five years of his dwelling in this world. "But they raised them in water, down in the tanks in the crypt. Lots and lots of them, rooms full of them. They showed that little boy," he added, with a strange, distant look in his eyes.

"Who showed him, Ace?"

Melantrys, a curvy little blonde with a dire-wolf's heart, was offering odds on the likelihood of Graw finding a reason not to send up any of the hay that was part of the Settlements' tribute to the Keep come July—betting shirt-laces, a common currency around the watchroom, where they were always breaking—and there were shouts and jeers from that end of the room, so that Rudy had to pitch his voice soft, for Tir's hearing alone.

Tir thought about it, his eyes unfocused. He was one of the cleanest little boys Rudy had ever encountered, in California or the Wathe. Even at the end of an afternoon with the herdkids, his jerkin of leather patches and heavy knitted blue wool was fairly spotless. God knew, Rudy thought, how long this phase would last.

"An old, old man," Tir said after a time. He stared away into the darkness, past the lurching shadows of the Guards, the stray wisps of smoke and the flash of firelight on dagger blade and boot buckle. Past the night-black walls of the Keep itself. "Older than Ingold. Older than Old Man Gatson up on fifth north. He was bald, and he had a big nose, and he had blue designs on his arms and the backs of his hands, and one like a snake like this, all the way down his head." Tir's fingers traced a squiggly line down the center of his scalp, back to front. Rudy's breath seemed to stop in his lungs with shock. "And it wasn't a little boy," Tir went on. "It was a grown-up man they showed. A king."

It was the first time he had made the distinction. The first time he seemed to understand that all the little boys whose memories he shared had grown up to be men—and after living their lives, had died.

Rudy tried to keep his voice casual, not speaking the great wild whoop of elation that rang inside him. "You want to go exploring, Pugsley?"

"Okay." Tir looked up at him and smiled, five years old again, rather solemn and shy but very much a child ready for whatever adventures time would bring his way.

"They won't thank you, you know," the Icefalcon remarked, not even looking up from his cleaning as they rose to go. "The know-alls of the Keep—Fargin Graw, and Enas Barrelstave, and Bannerlord Pnak, and

Lady Sketh. Whatever you find, you know they shall say, 'Oh, *that*. We could have found that any day, by chance.' "

"You're making me feel better and better about this," Rudy said.

The White Raider picked a fragment of dried blood out of the tang of his knife. "Such is my mission in life."

*It's him!* Rudy thought as, hand in hand, he and Tir ascended the laundry-festooned Royal Stair. *It's him!* For the first time, Tir's memories had touched something that lay verifiably in the original Time of the Dark.

The old man with the big nose and the bald head and the tattoos on his scalp and hands was—had to be—the Guy with the Cats.

Records did not stretch to the first rising of the Dark. Gil and Ingold had unearthed archives dating back seven hundred years at Gae; two of the books salvaged from the wreck of the City of Wizards were copies of copies—said to be accurate—of volumes two thousand years old. The Church archives the ill-famed and unlamented Bishop Govannin had carried from the broken capital contained scrolls nearly that age, in dialects and tongues with which Ingold, for all his great scholarship, was wholly unfamiliar. When the mage and Gil had a chance to work on them, they had arrived at approximate translations of two or three—at least two of the others Gil guessed had been copied visually, without any knowledge of their meaning at all.

But in the Keep attics above the fifth level, in the hidden crypts below, and in the river caves up the valley, they had found gray crystalline polyhedrons, the size and shape of the milk-white glowstones: remnants of the technology of the Times Before. And when Gil figured out that the gray crystals were records, and Ingold learned how to read the images within, they got their first glimpse of what the world had been like before that catastrophe over three millennia ago.

The Guy with the Cats was in two of the record crystals.

The crystals themselves were magic, and readable only through the object Rudy described to himself as a scrying table found hidden in an untouched corner chamber of the third level south. But less than a dozen of the thirty-eight were *about* magic, about how to *do* magic. Even silent—neither Rudy nor Ingold had figured out how to activate the soundtrack, if there was a soundtrack—they were precious beyond words. Magic was used very differently in those days, linked with machines that Ingold had tried repeatedly—and failed repeatedly—to reproduce in the laboratory he set up in the crypts. But the crystals showed spells and power-circles that were clearly analogous to the methods wizards used now. These Rudy and Ingold studied, matching similarities and differences, trying with variable success to re-create the forgotten magic, even as Gil studied the silent images in the other stones to put together some idea of that vanished culture and world.

On the whole, Rudy guessed that their conclusions were about as accurate as the spoofs written in his own world about the conclusions "scientists of the distant future" would draw about American motels, toilets, and *TV Guides.*

But in the process, he and Gil had come to recognize by sight a bunch of people who died about the time of the Trojan War.

They had given them names; not respectful ones, perhaps, but convenient when Gil noted down the contents of each crystal.

The Dwarf.

Mr. Pomfritt—named less for his resemblance to a long-forgotten character in a TV show than for his precise, didactic way of explaining the massive spiral of stars, light, and silver-dust that funneled, Ingold said, a galaxy-wide sweep of power into something kept carefully out of sight in a small black glass dish.

The Bald Lady.

Mother Goose.

Scarface.

Black Bart.

And the Guy with the Cats.

And now Tir said that the Guy with the Cats had been in the Keep. That meant whoever that old mage was, he'd been of the generation that first saw the Dark Ones come.

The generation that fought them first. The generation that built the Keep.

"The little boy got lost here once," Tir confided in a whisper as they wound their way along a secondary corridor on third south. Night was a time of anthill activity in the Keep, as suppers were cooked, business transacted, courtships furthered, and gossip hashed in the maze of interlocking cells, passageways, warrens, and bailiwicks that sometimes more resembled a succession of tight-packed villages than a single community, let alone a single building. Rudy paused to get an update on Lilibet Hornbeam's abscess from a cousin or second cousin of that widespreading family; nodded civil greetings to Lord Ankres, one of the several noblemen who had survived to make it to the Keep—His Lordship gave him the smallest of chilly bows—and stopped by Tabnes Crabfruit's little ill-lit workshop to ask how his wife was doing.

Tir went on, "He was playing with his sisters—he had five sisters and they were all mean to him except the oldest one. He was pretty scared, here in the dark."

*What little boy?* Rudy wondered. *How long ago?* Sometimes Tir spoke as if, in his mind, all those little boys were one.

Him.

"They sent a wizard up to find him?" Rudy was frequently asked to search the back corners of the Keep, or the woods, for straying children.

They ascended a stair near the enclave owned by Lord Sketh and his dependents, a wooden one crudely punched through a hole in the ceiling to join the House of Sketh's cells on the third level with those on the fourth. Warm air breathed up around them, rank with the pungence of cooking, working, living, drawn by the mysterious ventilation system of the Keep.

One more point for the wizards who built the place, Rudy thought. However they'd powered the ventilator pumps and the flow of water, most of them still worked. He and Ingold had never been able to ascertain that one to their satisfaction. They'd found the pumps, all right, and the pipes and vents like capillaries through the black walls, the thick floors, but no clue as to why they still worked.

A young boy passed with two buckets of water on his shoulders, accompanied by a henchman wearing the three-lobed purple badge of the House of Sketh—Sketh was notorious for thinking it owned the small fountain in the midst of the section where most, but not all, of its servants and laborers lived. Alde suspected they were charging for access, but couldn't prove it.

"Uh-huh," Tir said. "There were three wizards in the Keep then, an old man and a lady and a little girl. The girl found the little boy."

"So these were different from the guy who showed the King how to find the potatoes."

Tir thought about this. "Uh-huh. That was . . . I think the King was before. Way before." It was the first time he'd identified anything resembling a sequence to his memories. Eldor—Tir's dead father—had had some of Dare of Renweth's memories, toward the end of his pain-racked life; according to Ingold, few others of the line had. Ingold deduced that the wizards who built the Keep had engineered such memories into certain bloodlines to make sure of their preservation, but it was never possible to predict who would remember what, or when.

The boy frowned, fighting to reach back into that barely comprehended darkness, and they turned a couple of corners and cut through a quarter-cell somebody had chopped into a corridor: Tir still leading, still pursuing old recollections, matching in his mind the way the Keep had been three thousand years ago against the shortcuts of his current experience.

"There's stairs way back there but we can go up here," he said, pointing down another hall.

Here, toward the back of the fourth, many of the fountains had failed. The cells were inhabited by the Keep's poorer folk, who'd received less productive land in the division of arable allotments or whose birthrate had outstripped what they were assigned; those whose land had been damaged by slunch or whose livestock had sickened and died; those who had sold, traded, or mortgaged first their land, then their time and freedom, to the wealthier inhabitants who had food to spare. Many of the cells, lying far from the stairways or the bridges that crossed the Aisle, weren't inhabited at all. Around here the air smelled bad. It was all very well to be living in a place whose ventilation pumps were still operative after three thousand years, but over the millennia, as Rudy put it, somebody had lost the manual. When a pump broke, it stayed broken.

Rudy hadn't mentioned it to Alde, but he lived in fear that a lot of this stuff would all give out at the same time, as the internal combustion engines of his experience generally had. *And then Shit Creek won't even be the phrase for it,* he thought uneasily.

Toward the back of the Keep the corridors lay straighter, too, for no one had lived here long enough to alter the walls. The darkness seemed denser away from the pine-knot torches, the lamps of smoking grease, and the occasional glowstone in its locked bracket of iron.

The stairway Tir led him to was at the back of the fourth, a deserted area smelling of the rats that seemed to spontaneously generate in spite of all the purging-spells he or Ingold could undertake. Without the blue-white glow that burned from the head of Rudy's staff, the long corridor would have been as lightless as the crawl spaces behind Hell. A smoke-stained image of a saint regarded them gloomily from a niche at the stair's foot: St. Prool; Rudy recognized her by the broken ax she held in her hands.

He'd never figured out, when Gil told him the story, why God had broken the ax in half *after* ol' Proolie got the chop. The blood line around her neck was neatly drawn in red, like a sixties choker.

The stairs themselves were rough plank, almost as steep as a ladder. Tir darted ahead, feet clattering on the wood, and Rudy cast his magic before him so that a ball of witchlight would be burning over the child's head when he got to the top.

He himself followed more slowly, thrusting his glowing staff-head up through the ragged hole in the stone ceiling to illuminate the cell above. The magelight was bright, filling the little room and showing Rudy, quite clearly when he came up level with the floor, the thing that stood in the cell's doorway.

It was a little taller than his knee, and, he thought—trying to summon the image of it in his mind later—a kind of dirty yellowish or whitish-yellow, like pus except that there was something vaguely inorganic about the hue.

It had a head but it didn't have eyes, though it turned the flattened, fist-sized nodule on its spindly neck in his direction as he emerged. It had arms and legs—afterward Rudy wasn't sure how many of each.

He was so startled he almost fell, lurching back against the stone edge of the opening in the floor. He must have looked away, grabbing for his balance on the ladder, because when he looked back it was gone.

"Tir!" Rudy lunged up the last few rungs, flung himself at the door. "Tir, watch out!" He almost fell through the doorway, the blast of light he summoned flooding the corridor, an actinic echo of his panic and dread.

He looked left, then right, in time to see Tir emerge, puzzled, from another cell door perhaps fifty feet down the hall.

There was no sign of the thing he'd seen.

# Chapter 3

"**S**tay there!"

Tir looked scared—by the panic in Rudy's tone as much as by anything else—and held on to the jamb of the doorway in which he stood, while Rudy summoned all the light he could manage. By that brilliant, shadowless wash Rudy checked every cell for fifty feet down the corridor, quick looks, loath to turn his back on the passage or on the other empty black openings. Most cells here were bare, scavenged long ago of everything remotely useful—boxes had been stripped of their metal nails, old barrels of their strapping, even the curtains or the rickety shutters that in other places in the Keep served to cover the openings. Here and there Rudy found a cell crammed, disgustingly, with the waste and garbage some family on five north thought Minalde's quaestors wouldn't notice.

Rudy stretched his senses out, listening, trying to scent above the overwhelming garbage stink. But his concentration wasn't what it should have been. Thinking back, he recalled no odor connected with the creature, nor any sound, not even when it fled.

"Maybe it's a gaboogoo," Tir surmised, when Rudy returned to the boy at last. "They're sort of fairy things that live in the forest and steal milk from cows," he added, with the tone of one who has to explain things to grown-ups. "Geppy's mama tells neat stories about them."

Some of Ingold's lore concerned gaboogoos, and they almost certainly didn't exist, though legends of them persisted, mostly in the southeast. But in any case, according to most of those legends, gaboogoos were humanoid: blue, glowing, and "clothed as richly as princes," a description that made Rudy wonder where they and similar fairy folk purchased size minus-triple-zero petite doublets and gowns. *Same place superheroes order those nonwrinkle tights from, I guess.* On the other hand, of course, he hadn't believed in dragons, either, until he'd been attacked by one.

"Whatever it is, it sure as hell isn't supposed to be here." Rudy looked around him uneasily, then down at the boy again. As the first shock and alarm wore off, the implications were coming home to him. Something was living in the upper reaches of the Keep. Something he'd never seen, had never heard of—which probably meant *Ingold* had never heard of it, either. The old man had sure never mentioned weird little eyeless gremlins to him. And that meant . . .

Rudy wasn't entirely sure what it did mean, except that it meant big trouble somewhere. "I think it's time we got you home, Ace." He took Tir's hand.

"But you said it was smaller than me," Tir protested. "And it didn't have a mouth or teeth or anything. And I want to see it. Maybe it's got a treasure."

"Maybe it's got claws," Rudy said firmly, leading the way back toward the cell where the steps descended. Oddly, he couldn't remember whether it had or not. "Maybe it's got great big long skinny fingers to strangle you with."

*Maybe it's got a big brother. Or lots of big brothers.*

"But what about the . . . the earth-apples, the potatoes?" Tir pronounced the word carefully, and with a good imitation of Rudy's clipped California accent. "If you've got to go to the River Settlements with Master Graw tomorrow, we won't be able to look for them for days."

"If they've kept for a couple thousand years, they'll keep for another three, four days." Rudy glanced behind him at the corridor as they entered the cell where the stair led down. His concentration had not been up to maintaining the full white magelight for more than a few minutes, and it had faded and shrunk around them until it was once more two smoky stars on the points of the metal crescent that topped his staff. "Besides, I'll be damned if I'm leaving this place till I figure out what's going on, Master Graw or no Master Firetrucking Graw."

He held the staff down through the hole that led back to the fourth level, to make sure the cell below was empty and safe, and watched Tir carefully as the boy climbed down. In the few seconds that took, he also managed to glance over his shoulder at the cell doorway behind him seven or eight or maybe ten times.

He hadn't realized how much, in the past five years, he had taken for granted the safety within the walls of the Keep.

"**Y**ou're sure it wasn't an illusion?" Ingold asked a short time later.

Rudy considered the matter, propping his shoulders against the dyed sheepskins, bison pelts, and pillows of knit-craft and leather that made homey the pine-pole bench in the big workroom on first south that he and Ingold shared.

"I dunno," he said at length. He tilted the scrying crystal in his hand so that the older wizard's image, tiny but clear, shone more brightly in the jewel's depths. By the look of it, the old man was in a ruined villa at Willowchild, four or five days' journey from Renweth Vale.

The sight filled him with relief. He didn't feel capable of dealing with what he'd seen earlier that evening—or what he thought he'd seen.

"I'm usually pretty good at spotting an illusion," he went on slowly. "And this didn't feel like one." At the other end of the bench, Alde curled up like a child, her feet tucked under her green wool gown and her long black hair loosened for sleep, as it had been when he and Tir had come in to tell her what he had seen. Despite the lateness of the hour—the Keep was settling into somnolence around them—the boy was wide-awake, watching Rudy's end of the conversation with vivid interest.

"It didn't have a sound or a smell to it. Pugsley and I were looking for stuff the old guys hid . . . And hey, you know what? The Guy with the Cats, from the record crystals? He was the one Tir remembered seeing in the Keep all those years ago! He described him perfectly. So we know when he lived! But Tir didn't see squat, did you, kid?"

"Not squat," the boy affirmed. Though he had demonstrated an almost preternatural ability to separate the formal intonations of proper speech from the combination of peasant dialect and barrio slang that Rudy and most of the herdkids spoke, Alde rolled her eyes.

"Hmm," Ingold said and scratched a corner of his beard. Rudy had been half hoping the older wizard would say, *Oh, THOSE eyeless, rubbery, mysterious critters*, but at least he hadn't blenched, clutched his heart, and cried, *Dear God, stay together and barricade the doors!* either.

"Well, we can't rule out that it was an illusion," Ingold finally said. "And considering the stringency with which the Guards protect the Doors, and the spells of Ward written over the steps, the doorposts, and the inner and outer doors themselves, it's difficult to see how something could have gotten in, though of course that doesn't mean it didn't. The Ward captains at the back end of the fifth aren't going to like it much— Koram Biggar and Old Man Wicket and the Gatsons have been raising chickens illegally up there, and never mind what it does to the rat population of their neighbors' cells—but I think you need to have the Guards make a thorough sweep."

He considered the matter a moment, his sharp blue eyes distant with thought, then added, "Tell them to take dogs."

The Guards swept that night. And the Guards found nothing. It was after midnight when they began their search, and it was not a popular one. They swept the fourth level and the fifth, back away from the inhabited regions around the Aisle, where the corridors lay straight and cold and uncompromising far from the water sources and curled tight and thick where they had been, or still were, perhaps. They questioned those who lived there about things seen or smelled or found, and heard no word of strange droppings, or food missing, or odd or unwarranted smells.

Not that one could tell in some places, Rudy reflected dourly, and there was trouble, as Ingold had predicted, with the Biggar clan, and the Browns, and the Gatsons, and the Wickets, and others who resented being taken to task for their disregard of Keep health regulations. "Hell, it ain't botherin' no one!" protested Old Man Gatson, a sour-faced patriarch whose family occupied the least desirable tangle of cells on fifth north—least desirable because there was no waste disposal for many hundred feet.

"What about the people who live directly underneath?" Janus of Weg demanded, disgusted and exasperated at the sight of the stinking, swarming boxes and jars heaped up in an abandoned cell. "Who get your cockroaches?"

"Pah," the old man snarled. "It's Varkis Hogshearer that lives underneath and he can have my cockroaches—and what they live off, too! Twenty-five percent he charged me for the loan of seed wheat—*twenty-five percent!* He's lucky I don't—"

"That'll be enough of that," the commander snapped, while Rudy and the Icefalcon drifted silently down the corridor toward the empty darkness beyond the Gatsons' warren, listening. Up here, away from the thick-settled regions of the Keep, Rudy sensed the ghosts of old magic in the smooth black stone of the walls. Magic that had defeated the Dark Ones; magic that turned the eyes of ordinary folk aside. Magic that did things Rudy could not identify. But he could feel it as he might feel cold or heat, a kind of magnetism, a tingling in his fingertips or a sense that someone stood quite close beside him whispering words in a language he could not understand.

Wizards had raised the Keep. Their laboratory still existed, deep in the crypts near the hydroponics chambers. Of the great machines that had been made and stored there, nothing remained but scratches and stains on the floor—what had become of them, Rudy hated to think. Smaller, largely incomprehensible equipment of gold and glass and shining tubes of silver had been found, hidden when the old mages themselves had vanished. Echoes of their spells lingered in places: in addition to selected cells in the Church sector, where no magic whatsoever would work, there was a cell on second north where Rudy's powers, and Ingold's, were sometimes magnified, sometimes disturbingly randomized, so that spells had different effects from those intended, and a Summoning would frequently result in the appearance of something appallingly other than that which had been called. Ingold had found a three-foot-long section of corridor on fifth south where he could speak in a whisper and Rudy, if he stood at a particular spot in the third level of the crypts, could hear every word.

There was a room in the crypts that would kill any animal, except a cat, that walked into it—including the one human being who had tried it—and a corner of what had been a chamber on third south where from time to time letters would appear on the wall, smudgily written in light as if traced with someone's fingertip, spelling out words not even Ingold understood. The corner had been bricked off from the main cell in a subsequent renovation—the main cell itself was currently used as a store-room.

So why couldn't the Guy with the Cats have guarded his bewitched potatoes with visions of little eyeless gremlins?

Rudy didn't think so, however.

Arms folded, he probed at the sunless silence, listened deeply into the chambers all around him and down that empty hall, tracking the footfalls of the Guards as they carried their torches and glowstones from doorway to doorway. Grimy streaks of yellowish light marked flea-ridden curtains or shutters with broken slats. Skinny men and women, feral children with hungry eyes, came to the doors of cells, resentful at being waked and asked, "Any food missing? Anything disturbed, prints . . . Cats afraid? Any places the children have spoken of as wrong, or odd?"

"No, sir . . . No, sir. Why, my Jeddy, she been all over this level like it was her own warren. She'd have let me know soon enough if there was suthin' amiss in the corners in the dark. You tell the man, Jeddy."

The statue of an enormously plump saint in a chalky, yellowy-white robe smiled beneficently from a niche between two tallow candles, and Rudy felt uneasy, filled with a sense of looking at clues he did not understand.

Ingold sat for a long time after Rudy ceased speaking—after Gil presumed that Rudy had ceased speaking, for she could hear nothing of what Ingold heard when he used the scrying crystal—turning the two-inch shard of yellowish quartz over and over in scarred, thick-muscled fingers, firelight honeying the white hairs that dusted their backs. Outside the villa's crumbling walls Gil could hear the far-off ululations of wolf-talk, and nearby, Yoshabel the mule stamped and laid back her ears, her eyes green-gold mirrors of brainless malice.

Waking to the sound of Ingold's voice, Gil had for a time been so overwhelmed with rage at him, so filled with the conviction that the throbbing agony in her face and all the sorrows in her life were his doing, that she had had to close her hands around a broken projection of marble in the packed earth near her blankets and stare at the dim pattern of firelight among her knuckle bones until the anger went away.

For no particular reason, she thought of Sherry Reinhold, the beautiful blond, tanned, aerobics-perfect classmate who'd been one of the few to be friendly with her in high school. Sherry had become an airline stewardess and had married a dentist and acquired a house the size of one of the smaller campus buildings. Meanwhile, Gil herself was still struggling with the poverty and frustration of the UCLA graduate program in medieval history.

She remembered Sherry sitting across from her at the Bicycle Shop Café in Westwood, saying, "I don't know why I do it. I don't even like the taste of alcohol. I know getting drunk isn't going to solve anything, or help anything, or do anything but screw me up worse. And then I'm sitting there with eleven empty glasses in front of me telling some man I've never seen before my telephone number and the directions to my house." That had been after the divorce. "It's like the words 'Oh, have another one' come out of the empty air, not connected to anything—not the past or the future or anything real—and it's the rightest and sanest and most sensible thing in the universe. I have to do it."

*Kill him. Kill Ingold.*

The rightest and most sensible thing in the universe.

She closed her eyes. Wondered what she had dreamed—about her mother and sister?—that had made her at once angry and convinced that nothing she would ever do would bring her happiness again.

Though she had spoken to him of the dreams, of the terrible urgings that swamped her mind, he had refused to bind her hands. "You may need your weapons, my dear, at any moment," he had said. "And I trust you."

"You shouldn't." They were standing under the dying sycamore tree in the courtyard where she had first been attacked, looking down at the ripped sack that lay on the ground. It contained what little was left of the thing that had attacked her, torn down and chewed by vermin as if no spells had been placed upon it, as if no Wards had ringed the tree.

"Then I trust myself," he had said, picking up the maggotty hindquarter and stowing it—and the remains of the original bag—in another sack pulled from Yoshabel's numerous packs. "Whatever it is that is driving you to assault me, if it can quicken your timing and get you out of the lamentable habit of telegraphing your side lunges, I'd like to meet it."

He'd smiled at her—with Ingold as one of her swordmasters, she could take on almost any of the other Guards and win—and Gil responded to his teasing with a grin and a flick at him with the pack rope. Even that small and playful assault he'd sidestepped as effortlessly, she knew, as he would have avoided a lethal blow.

"Thoth?" she heard Ingold say softly now. "Thoth, can you hear me? Are you there?"

She turned her head and looked. A slice of amber light lay across one scarred eyelid and down his cheekbone, refracted from the crystal in his hand. His brows, down-drawn in a bristle of fire-flecked shadow, masked the sockets of his eyes.

"Has that ever happened before?" she asked. "Before last week, I mean?"

He raised his head, startled, "I'm sorry, my dear, did I wake you? No," he answered her question, when she signed that it didn't matter. "And the troubling thing is, I've frequently had the sensation that Thoth—or one of the other Gettlesand wizards—is trying to signal me, but for some reason cannot get through."

He got up from his place by the fire, crossed the room to her, a matter of two or three steps only. The former library was one of the few remaining chambers with four walls and a roof, though the wooden latticework of the three wide windows had been broken out. Wickering ember-light revived the velvety crimson memory of the frescoes on the wall, lent renewed color to the faces of those attenuated ghosts acting out scenes from a once-popular romance.

She curved her body a little to make room, and Ingold sat beside her, still turning the crystal in his hand. "I had hoped," he went on quietly, "that if Rudy could get through to me I would be able to get through to Thoth, but that doesn't seem to be the case. There's only a deep sense of . . . of pressure, of heat, like a river far beneath the earth. Like a rope pulled taut and about to snap." He put the crystal away and sat silent for a time, gazing at the broken window bars and toying one-fingered with a corner of his beard.

"What did Rudy have to say?"

Ingold told her. At his description of the thing Rudy called a gaboogoo, she was seized with the flashing sensation of familiarity, a tip-of-the-tongue impression that she had seen such a thing, or dreamed about it, but the next instant it was gone. Her dreams had been strange, and even deeper than the urge to hurt Ingold, to destroy him, was the reluctance to speak to him of the things she saw in them . . . And indeed, when she tried to frame those bleak, fungoid landscapes of pillowlike vegetation, the amorphous, shining shapes that writhed through it or flopped heavily a few feet above its surface, the very memory of those visions dissolved and she couldn't recall what it was that she had seen.

And so it happened here. When Ingold paused, raising his eyebrows at her intaken breath, her words jammed in her throat, like a stutter, or like tears that refused to be wept, and she could not remember whether she had dreamed about such a thing or not. She shook her head, embarrassed, and was deeply thankful when Ingold only nodded and said, "Interesting."

And she thought, almost as if she heard a voice saying it in the back of her mind, *It will appear at the window.* She didn't know what it was, but she automatically checked her hand's distance from the sword that lay next to her blankets and mentally triangulated on where Ingold's back would be when he turned his head. Her mind was starting to protest, . . . *like Sherry Reinhold . . .* when Yoshabel threw up her head and squealed in terror.

Ingold swung around; Gil came out of her blankets like a coiled spring, catching up the scabbarded blade and drawing in a single fluid, killing move. She had a dim awareness of something large and pale clinging to the lattice with limbs more like pincers than claws, of a round fanged mouth where no mouth should be and of a wet flopping sound, all subsumed by the vicious calculation of target and stroke. She wrenched the blade around and drove it into the dirt with a chop that nearly dislocated her wrists, hardly aware that she cried out as she did so, only knowing afterward, as she stood shaking like a spent runner with her hair hanging in her eyes, that her throat hurt and the painted walls were echoing with an animal scream.

Ingold was already moving back toward her; she rasped "No!" and fell to her knees, sweating, the wound in her face radiating a heat that consumed her being. There was an interim when she wasn't able to see anything beyond her own white-knuckled hands gripping the sword hilt, was conscious of nothing but a wave of nausea, but he must have used the moment to stride to the window. In any case, he returned instants later. The thing outside had vanished.

"Are you all right?"

His voice came from a great distance away, a dull roaring like the sound within a shell. Though her eyes were open, she saw for a moment a vision of red laced with tumbling diamond fire. Then he was holding her, and she was clinging to the coarse brown wool of his robe, her face crushed to his shoulder, gripping the barrel chest and the hard rib cage to her as if they both floated in a riptide and she feared to be washed away.

"Gilly . . ." He whispered her nicknames. "Gillifer, beloved, it's all right . . . it's all right."

The desire to pull out her knife and shove it up between his ribs drowned her in a red wave, nauseating her again. She locked her hands behind his back, fighting the voices in her mind. Then the rage ebbed, leaving in its wake only the wet shingle of failure and utter despair.

As Rudy suspected, Graw's urgent demand that something be done about slunch meant that patches of it had developed in his fields and pastures—which happened to lie on the best and most fertile ground in that section of the Arrow River bottomlands. Though the sun had long since vanished behind the Hammerking's tall head when the little party reached its goal—what had once been a medium-sized villa, patched and expanded with log-and-mud additions and surrounded by what Rudy still thought of as a Wild West–style wooden palisade—Graw insisted that Rudy make a preliminary investigation of the problem.

The villa and fort were Graw's homestead, and everyone in them a member of the red-haired man's family, an outright servant, or a small-holder who had pledged fealty in exchange for protection. Three of the nobles who had made the journey to the Keep from Gae had established such settlements as well, populated both by retainers and men-at-arms who had served them before the rising of the Dark, and by those farmers who sought their protection or owed them money.

Even had Gil not filled Rudy in on their own world's Dark Ages, he'd have been able to see where that practice was leading. It was one reason he'd acceded to Minalde's pleading, in spite of his own unwillingness to leave the Keep with the gaboogoo question unanswered. That, and the white look around her mouth when she'd said, "It's only a day's journey." The livestock at the Keep would need hay from the riverbottoms to survive the winter. Not all the broken remnants of the great Houses were particularly mindful of their vows to Alde as the Lady of the Keep.

She didn't need more problems than the ones she already had.

"Now, when you folk up there started putting all kinds of rules on us instead of letting us go our own way," Graw groused in his grating, self-pitying caw, "I had my doubts, but I was willing to give Lady Alde consideration. I mean, she'd been queen all her life and was used to it, and I thought maybe she did know more about this than me." He shoved big rufous hands into the leather of his belt as he strode along the edge of the fields, Rudy trailing at his heels. The split rails of the fences had been reinforced with stout earth banks and a chevaux-de-frise of sharpened stakes, heavier even than the ones around the Keep wheat fields that discouraged moose and the great northern elk. This looked designed to keep out mammoths.

"I did ask why we were supposed to send back part of our harvest, and everybody said, 'Oh, shut up, Graw, it's because the Keep is the repository of all True Laws and wonderful knowledge and everything that makes civilization—' "

"I thought the vote went that way because you were taking Keep seed, Keep axes and plows, and Keep stock," Rudy said, cutting off the heavy-handed sarcasm, vaulting over the fence in his host's wake.

Graw's face reddened still further in the orange sunset light. "Any organism that doesn't have the courage to grow will die!" he bellowed.

"The same applies to human societies. Those who try to hang on to all the old ways, to haggle as if the votes of ten yapping cowards are somehow more significant than a true man of the land who's willing to go out and do something—"

"When did this stuff start to grow here?" Rudy had had about enough of the Man of the Land. He halted among the rustling, leathery cornstalks, just where the plants began to droop lifeless. They lay limp and brown in a band a yard or so wide, and beyond that he could see the fat white fingers of the slunch.

"Just after the first stalks started to come up." Graw glared at him as if he'd sneaked down from the Vale in the middle of the night and planted the slunch himself. "You don't think we'd have wasted the seed in a field where the stuff was already growing, do you?"

Rudy shook his head, though he privately considered Graw the sort of man who'd do precisely that rather than waste what he wanted to consider good acreage, particularly if that acreage was his. *Silly git probably told himself the situation wouldn't get any worse.* "So it's gone from nothing to—what? About twelve feet by eighteen?—in four weeks? Have the other patches been growing this fast?"

"How the hell should I know?" Graw yelled. "We've got better things to do than run around with measuring tapes! What I want to know is what you plan to do about it!"

"Well, you know," Rudy said conversationally, turning back toward the fence, "even though I've known the secret of getting rid of this stuff for the past three years, I've kept it to myself and just let it grow all over the fields around the Keep. But I tell you what: I'll tell you."

"Don't you get impertinent with me, boy!"

"Then don't assume I'm not doing my job to the best of my ability," Rudy snapped. "I'll come out here in the morning to take a good look at this stuff, but—"

Voices halooed in the woods beyond the field, and there was a great crashing in the thickets of maple and hackberry along the dense green verge of the trees. Someone yelled, "Whoa, there she goes!" and another cried, "Oh, mine, mine!"

There was laughter, like the clanging of iron pots.

Rudy ran to the fence, swung himself up on the rails between two of the stakes in time to see a dark figure break from the thickets, running along the waste-ground near the fence for the shelter of the rocks by the stream. Two of Graw's hunters pelted out of the woods, young ruffians in deer leather dyed brown and green, arrows nocked, and Graw called out, exasperated but tolerant, "Oh, for heaven's sake, it's only a damn dooic!"

It was a female—mares, some people called them, or hinnies—with one baby clutched up against the fur of her belly and another, larger infant clinging hard around her neck, its toes clutching at the longer fur of her back. She ran with arms swinging, bandy legs pumping hard, dugs flapping as she zigzagged toward the tangle of boulders and willow, but Rudy could see she wasn't going to make it. One hunter let fly with an arrow, which the hinny dodged, stumbling. The smaller pup jarred loose as she scrambled up, and the other hunter, a snaggle-haired girl, laughed and called out, "Hey, you dropped one, Princess!"

The bowman fired again as the hinny wheeled, diving for the silent pup in the short, weedy grass.

The hinny jerked back from the arrow that seemed to appear by magic in the earth inches from her face. For an instant she stared, transfixed, at the red-feathered shaft, at the man who had fired and the wriggling black shape of the pup: huge brown eyes under the heavy pinkish shelf of brow, lips pressed forward like pale velvet from the longer fur around them in an expression of panic, trying to think.

Graw muttered, "Oh, for heaven's sake," and whipped an arrow from the quiver at his belt. He carried his bow strung, on his back, as most of the men in the Settlements did; nocking and firing was a single move.

Rudy reached with his thought and swatted Graw's arrow as if it had been a stinging fly. At the same moment he spoke a word in the silence of his mind, and the bowstring of the male hunter snapped, the weapon leaping out of his hands and the nocked arrow, drawn back for another shot, jerking wild. The man cursed—seventy-five pounds of tension breaking does damage—and the hinny, gauging her chance, slipped forward, grabbed the pup by one foot, and flung herself in a long rolling dive for the rocks.

"You watch what you're goddamn doing!" Graw bellowed, snatching Rudy by the shoulder and throwing him backward from the fence. As he hit the ground, Rudy could hear the girl hunter screaming and the retreating, furious rustle of the streamside laurels as the hinny made good her escape. Breath knocked out of him, he rolled, in case Graw were moved to kick him, and got back to his feet, panting, his long reddish-black hair hanging in his eyes. Graw was standing foursquare in front of him, braced as for a fight: "Go on, use your magic against me!" he yelled, slapping his chest. "I'm unarmed! I'm helpless! I'm just trying to protect our fields from those stinking vermin!"

Rudy felt his whole body heat with a blister of shame.

Ingold had taught him what he had to do next, and his soul cringed from it as his hand would have cringed from open flame. The man was hurt, and Rudy was a healer.

Turning his back on Graw, he slipped through the stakes in the fence and strode up the broken slope toward the hunter who lay among the weeds. The buckskin-clad girl knelt over him, her wadded kerchief held to his broken nose. Both raised their heads as Rudy approached through the tangle of hackberry and fern, hatred and terror in their eyes; before he got within ten yards of them the girl had pulled the hunter to his feet, and snatching up their bows, both of them fled into the green shadows of the pines.

The shame was like being rolled in hot coals. He had used magic against a man who had none and who was not expecting an attack. He had, he realized, damaged the position of wizards and wizardry more by that single impulsive act than he could have by a year of scheming for actual power.

Ingold would have something to say to him. He didn't even want to think about what that would be.

He stood still, feeling suffocated, hearing behind him Graw's bellowing voice without distinguishing words beyond, "I shoulda known a goddamn wizard would . . ."

Rudy didn't stay to hear what Graw knew about goddamn wizards. Silently he turned and made his way down the rough, sloping ground to the fence, and along it toward the fort as the half-grown children of the settlement were driving in the cattle and sheep from the fields. The long spring evening was finally darkening toward actual night, the tiger-lily brilliance of reds and golds above the mountains rusting to cinnabar as indigo swallowed the east. Crickets skreeked in the weeds along the fencerow, and by the stream Rudy could hear the peeping of frogs, an orchestral counterpoint to Graw's bellowed commentary.

*Well*, he thought tiredly, *so much for supper.*

He was not refused food when the extended household set planks on trestles in the main hall to eat. What he was offered was some of the best in the household. But it was offered in silence, and there was a wariness in the eyes of everyone who looked at him and then looked away. The bowman whose nose he'd broken sat at the other end of the table from him, bruises darkening horribly; he was, Rudy gathered, an extremely popular man. Rudy recalled what Ingold had told him about wizards being poisoned, or slipped drugs like yellow jessamine or passion-flower elixirs that would dull their magic so they could be dealt with, and found himself without much appetite for dinner. The huntress' eyes were on him from the start of the meal to its finish, cold and hostile, and he heard her whispering behind his back whenever he wasn't looking.

After the meal was over, no one, not even those who were clearly sick, came to speak to him.

*Great,* Rudy thought, settling himself under a smoky pine torch at the far end of the hall and pulling his mantle and bison-hide vest more closely around him. The women grouped by the fire to spin and sew had started to gather up their things to leave when he approached, so he left them to work in the warmth, and contented himself with the cold of the far end of the hall. *I guess this is why Ingold makes himself so damn invisible all the time.* It didn't take a genius to realize that from fear like this it was only a short step to bitter resentment. *Especially with little Miss Buckskin helping things along with her mouth.*

Ingold—and Minalde—would have to put in weeks of P.R. and cleanup over this one.

From a pocket of the vest he took his scrying stone, an amethyst crystal twice the width of his thumb and nearly as long as his palm, and tilted its facets toward the light.

And there she was. Alde, cutting out a new tunic for herself by the light of three glowstones, working carefully around the unaccustomed bulk of her belly—smiling a little and reaching up to adjust the gold pins in her hair, final jeweled relics of the wealth of the High King's realm. Tir and Geppy Nool and a little girl named Thya made cats cradles of the wool from the knitting basket, and Thya's mother, Linnet—a slim brown woman of thirty or so who was Alde's maid and good friend—knitted and talked. The black walls of the chamber were bright with familiar hangings; Alde's cat Archbishop stalked a trailing end of yarn, dignified lunacy in his golden eyes.

Uneasy, Rudy tilted the crystal, calling to being in it the corridors of the fourth level, and the fifth; picturing in his mind the chalky little gremlin he had seen.

But there was nothing. No sign of the creature anywhere in the Keep. That didn't mean it wasn't there. The Dead Cells in the Church territory and some of the royal prisons were proof against Rudy's scrying—there were other cells as well from which he could not summon an image.

But it was hard to believe that the eyeless critter, whatever it was, knew where those were.

*Whatever it was . . .*

On impulse he cleared his mind and summoned to his thoughts the image of Thoth Serpentmage, Recorder of Quo: shaven-headed, yellow-eyed, hawk-nosed, brooding over broken fragments of pottery and scrolls in the patched, eroded Black Rock Keep in Gettlesand, the scribe of the wizards of the West.

But no image came. Nothing showed in the crystal, where a moment ago he'd seen the distant reflection of Minalde and Tir and the room he knew so well. No wizard could be seen without that wizard's consent, of course, but a wizard would know, would feel, the scrying crystal calling to him. And Rudy felt only a kind of blankness, like a darkness; and below that a curious deep sense of something . . . some power, like the great heavy pull of a tidal force.

He shook his head to clear it. "What the hell . . . ?"

After a moment's consideration he called in his mind the image of the mage Kara of Black Rock, wife to its lord, Tomec Tirkenson. But only that same deep darkness met his quest, the same sense of . . . of what? he wondered. Foreboding. Power, spells . . . a breathlessness fraught with a sensation of crushing, a sensation of movement, a sensation of anger. Anger? Like a river under the earth, the thought came to him . . .

And yet there was something about it that was familiar to him, that he almost knew.

Why did he think of California?

One by one he summoned them to mind: red-haired, beautiful Ilae; shy Brother Wend; Dakis the Minstrel, who could herd the clouds with the sound of his lute; and even Kara's horrible old mother, Nan—all the wizards who had taken refuge in the Keep of Gettlesand, when five years ago they had been exiled from Renweth by one of the stupider orders of the fanatic Bishop Govannin, now mercifully departed.

It was the same. It was always the same.

With an automatic reflex Rudy shook the crystal, as if to jar loose molecules back to their proper place. Delighted shrieking from the center of the big room drew his attention. The settlement children were playing some kind of jump-out-and-scream game. Rudy looked up as they scattered, in time to see a child hidden beneath a bench brandishing a homemade doll above the level of the seat. "It's Mr. Creepy-in-the-Woods! Mr. Creepy-in-the-Woods is gonna get you!"

The children all screamed as if enveloped by goblins.

With its long stalky arms, its minute legs—with its tassled, beaded bud of an eyeless head swinging wildly on a spindle neck—Mr. Creepy-in-the-Woods was the tiny twin of the thing Rudy had seen in the Keep.

# Chapter 4

In the country of Gil's dreaming there was light without sun. The sky had a porcelain quality, shadowless and bone-colored; the earth was the alien earth of her fleeting visions. Slunch padded the ground to the horizons, save in one direction—she wasn't sure which, for there were no shadows— where treeless mountains thrust up like dirty headstones. Far off, something leaped and cavorted drunkenly in the slunch. Closer, the vision she'd had at the window lattices repeated itself, a curling lozenge of flabby flesh, heavy pincers projecting from what looked like an enormous mouth at the front, gliding like a hovercraft over the surface of the ground.

In the stillness an old man was walking, leaning on his staff, and with some surprise Gil recognized Thoth Serpentmage, who had been recorder for the Council of Wizards at Quo. *What's Thoth doing on another planet?* she wondered as the old man paused, straightened his flat, bony shoulders and scanned the horizon with those chilly yellow eyes. *He's supposed to be in Gettlesand.*

Thoth struck out with the point of his staff, impaling something in the slunch at his feet. He reversed the staff, holding the thing where he could see it stuck on the iron point: like a wet hat made of pinkish rubber, covered with hard rosettes like scabbed sores. From his belt he took his dagger, scabbard and all, and with the scabbard tip reached to touch one of the rosettes. At that, all of them dilated open at once, like filthy little mouths, and spat fluid at him, gobbets of silvery diamonds that left weals on his flesh as if he had been burned with acid.

Thoth dropped staff and creature alike with a silent cry of pain and disgust. Overhead, dark shapes skated across the white sky, the flabby hovercraft thing pursuing a red-tailed hawk with silent, murderous speed. While she watched, it seized it with its pincers and hurled it in a cloud of bloody feathers to the earth.

*That isn't another planet. That* is *Gettlesand.* She smelled something cold and thin, as if someone who had neither nose nor taste buds were trying to counterfeit the scent of watermelon. Somewhere she thought she heard a trail of music, like a flute being played far beneath the earth.

The children had several names for Mr. Creepy-in-the-Woods. They, like Tir, called him a gaboogoo, but they used the term interchangeably with *goblin* and *fairy.* "They're too ugly for fairies, *stupid*," Lirta Graw declared, at which one of the smaller kids, a boy named Reppitep, started to cry. Reppitep had seen one, on the high wooded slopes above the fields, just within the line where the trees grew thick. He'd been gathering kindling.

"He's probably lying," Lirta said, and tossed her red head. "Anyway, his mother's a whore. I wouldn't be scared of no stupid gaboogoo. And Daddy says there's no such thing."

"Your daddy probably said that about the Dark Ones," Rudy said. Lirta's mother herded all the children away, glancing back furtively at him over her shoulder.

His sleep that night, in a corner of the hall on a straw pallet, like most of the men of the household, was filled with imageless dreams of breathless, weighted anger, a pressure that seemed to clog the very ether. Sometimes he thought he saw the plains and deserts of Gettlesand, felt the arid sunlight and smelled dust and stone and buffalo grass on the slopes of its jutting, scrub-covered black mountains. At other times he dreamed of California, as he hadn't for years. Dreamed of lying in his bed in his mother's crummy apartment in Roubidoux, feeling the whole building shake as the big trucks went by on the broken pavement of Arlington Avenue outside.

Something was going on, something that troubled him deeply. He didn't know what.

At dawn he went out to have another look at Fargin Graw's slunch.

Graw went with him, grousing that members of the River Settlements Council—which he had resigned in annoyance when they wouldn't accept his leadership—were antiquated holdovers of a system designed to keep down "true men" like himself, as though the elderly Lord Gremmedge, who had pioneered Carpont Settlement five miles farther downriver, were an impostor of some kind.

Rudy had heard the same at the Keep, with variations. Technically, everyone at the Keep held their lands through Minalde, just as, technically, they were her guests in a building that belonged to Tir. But men of wealth like Varkis Hogshearer and Enas Barrelstave spoke of cutting back the power of the queen and the little king, and giving the Keep and its lands outright to those who held them—one of whom was, coincidentally enough, Enas Barrelstave himself. There was also a good deal of feeling against the nobles, like Lord Ankres and Lord Sketh, and the lesser bannerlords, some of whom had arrived with more food than the poor of Gae and had parlayed that into positions of considerable power, though Rudy had noticed there was less of such talk when bandits or Raiders threatened the Keep. Most of the great Houses had never lost their ancient traditions of combat, and even ancients like Lord Gremmedge proved to be an asset on those few occasions when it came down to a question of defending the Vale.

For the most part, the lords looked down on men like Graw, on Enas Barrelstave—who had built up a considerable landholding of his own, although he was still the head of the Tubmaker's Guild—and on Varkis Hogshearer—and no wonder, in the latter case, thought Rudy dourly. In addition to being the Keep moneylender, earlier that spring Hogshearer had somehow gotten word that the only trader from the South to come north in six months was a few days off from the Vale. He'd ridden down to meet the merchant and had purchased his entire stock of needles, buttons, glass, seed, plowshares, and cloth, which he was currently selling for four and five times what the southern merchants generally asked. No other trader had appeared since, though Rudy scried the roads for them daily.

As Rudy expected, the slunch in Graw's fields was pretty much like the slunch everywhere else. It was almost unheard of for slunch to spread that fast, and he suspected that the patch had been there—small but certainly not unnoticeable—when Graw planted the seed.

Nonetheless, he checked the place thoroughly, on the chance that a slight variation would show him something he and Ingold had missed.

It didn't, however.

Slunch was slunch. It seemed to be vegetable, but had no seed pods or leaves or stems, and Rudy wasn't sure about the function of the hair-like structures that held its blubbery underground portions to the soil.

There was no visible reason for the vegetation all around the slunch to die, but it did.

Worms lived in it: huge, sluggish, and, Rudy discovered, weirdly aggressive, lunging at him and snapping with round, reddish, maggotlike mouths. "Yuckers," he muttered, stepping back from the not-very-efficient attack and flicking the thing several yards away with his staff. "I'll have to trap one of these buggers before I start for home."

A regular earthworm, swollen and made aggressive by eating the slunch? Or some species he'd never heard of or that had never heretofore made it this far south?

Ingold would know. Ingold's scholarship, concerning both old magical lore and natural history, was awesome—there were times when Rudy despaired of ever living up to his teacher.

But when he tried to contact Ingold, after Graw finally left him alone around noon, he could see nothing in his crystal. He shifted the angle to the pale sunlight that fell through the blossoms of the apple tree under which he sat, a thin little slip of a thing in an orchard surrounded by a palisade that would have discouraged a panzer tank division; let his mind dip into a half-meditative trance, drifting and reaching out. They'd be on the road, he thought, but there was a good chance they'd have stopped for a nooning. *Ingold . . .*

But there was nothing. Only the same deep, angry pulling sensation, the feeling of weight, and heat, and pressure. And underneath that, the profound dread, as if he stood in the presence of some kind of magic that he could not understand.

"C'mon, man," Rudy whispered. "Don't do this to me." He cleared his mind, reordering his thoughts. Thoth of Gettlesand: he might have an answer, might indeed know what was going wrong with communications. Might know what that nameless feeling was, that haunting fear.

When no image came, he called again on the names of every single one of the Gettlesand mages, as he had last night. Failing them, he summoned the image of Minalde, whom he saw immediately, a small bright shape in the crystal, standing by the wheat fields in her coat of colored silks, arguing patiently with Enas Barrelstave about the placement of boundary hurdles.

Worried now, he tried again to reach Ingold.

"Dammit." He slipped the crystal back into its leather pouch and returned it to the pocket of his vest. The day was mild, warmer than those preceding it and certainly warmer here in the bottomlands than in the high Vale of Renweth. Maybe summer was finally getting its act together and coming in.

*About goddamn time.* He didn't think the Keep could stand another winter like the last one.

Clear as a little steel bell on the still air, he heard Lirta Graw's voice, bossing someone about. Yep, there she was by the open gate of the log stockade, with a pack of the settlement kids. In a couple of years she'd be as obnoxious as Varkis Hogshearer's daughter, Scala, an overbearing, sneaky adolescent who spied and, Rudy suspected, stole. He wondered if there were some kind of karmic law of averages that required the presence of one of those in every group of thirty or more kids. There'd certainly been one in his high school.

He watched them from where he sat in his miniature fortress of sharpened stakes and apple trees, listened to their voices, as he watched and listened to the herdkids at the Keep and the children who tagged at their mothers' skirts by the stream when they did laundry. Partly this was simply because he liked kids, but partly—and increasingly so in the last year or two—because, like Ingold, he was watching for someone.

Waiting for someone to show up.

"The Dark Ones knew that magic was humankind's only defense against them," Ingold had said to him one evening when he and Rudy had gone out to locate Tir during the first flush of the boy's livestock supervision phase. The Keep herdkids, under the command of a skinny, towheaded boy named Tad, had been bringing in the cattle from the upper pastures; Rudy had known Tir should be safe enough with the older children, but the boy was then only four, after all.

"They attacked the City of Wizards, destroying nearly all its inhabitants; they knew me well enough to come after me." The old man frowned, leaning on his staff—a mild, unassuming, and slightly shabby old maverick, reminding Rudy of any number of overage truckers or barfighters he'd known in his Southern California days. "And in the past five years the fear has been growing on me that the Dark Ones—among all the hundreds of thousands of men, women, and children that they killed—sought out also the children born with the talent for wizardry. The next generation of wizards."

Rudy said, "Oh, Christ." It made sense.

Talent or propensity for magic usually manifested in very small children, Ingold had told him—five and younger—and then seemed to go underground until puberty. In the past five years, Ingold had kept a close eye on the children coming of age.

Not one had shown the slightest bent toward magic. Tad—eldest of the herdkids—had elected himself a kind of lab assistant to Ingold in the wizard's chemical and mechanical endeavors, but had no apparent thaumaturgical gift. He just loved gadgets, spending all his free time in helping them adjust the mirrors that amplified the witchlight in the hydroponics crypts. So far, there had been no one. Rudy wondered how long it would be.

The children straggled off toward the thin coppices of the bottomlands, carrying kindling sacks. They'd have to collect more wood in the Settlements, he thought. Even though the nights here were less chill than in the Vale, the sprawling stone villa didn't hold heat the way the Keep did. His eye followed them, Lirta Graw—sackless, as befitted the Boss's Daughter—striding ahead, and the little fair-haired child Reppitep in the rear, struggling to keep up.

As they disappeared into the cloudy green of hemlock and maples along the Arrow, Rudy turned his eyes back toward the slopes behind him; the rising glacis strewn with boulders and threaded with silvery streams, and above that the dense viridian gloom of the high forest.

*Where the trees grew thick,* the children had said. That was where several of them reported they'd seen Mr. Creepy-in-the-Woods.

It was an hour's steady climb to the edge of the trees. As he picked his way through fern and fox-grape up the rust-stained rocks of the streambed, Rudy wrapped himself in progressively thicker veils of illusion. He'd learned the art of remaining unseen from Ingold, whom he nicknamed— not without reason—the Invisible Man. Three years ago the first bands of White Raiders had made their appearance in the valley of the Great Brown River, tracking the spoor of elk and mammoth driven by cold from the high northern plain, and one still sometimes found their Holy Circles on deserted uplands. The thought of being the messenger elected to carry a letter written in pain to the obscure Ancestors of the tribes made Rudy queasy.

Moose and glacier elk raised their heads from grazing to regard him mildly as he passed, under the magically engineered impression that he was some harmless cousin of the deer tribe. Farther up the slopes, where the erratics left by the last glaciation poked through a tangled chaparral of brush, fern, and vines, a saber-tooth sunning itself on a slab of rock rolled over and looked at him, and Rudy hastily morphed the spell into *I'm a saber-tooth, too—but smaller and milder and definitely beta to your alpha, sir.* The huge, sinewy beast blinked and returned to its nap, surprisingly difficult to see against the splotchy gray-gold stone.

Wind breathed from the high peaks, carrying on it the glacier's cold. Rudy shivered.

As carefully as any hunter, he worked the line of trees above the waste and pasture. Among the short grasses and weeds, he found mostly the tracks that he expected to find: half a dozen different sorts of deer, rabbits and coons, porcupines and weasels, voles and wolves. On the bark of a red fir he saw the scratchings of a cave-bear, higher than his head. Hidden carefully under the ferns of the denser woods were the droppings of a band of dooic, and Rudy wondered momentarily whether that poor hinny had made it safely back to her pals. Once or twice he came upon tracks that made him pause, puzzled. Rabbit spoor that hinted of movement no rabbit would have made—no rabbit in its right senses, anyway. Wolverine pugs from the biggest, weirdest damn wolverine he'd never hope to run across.

But nothing that would qualify as Mr. Creepy-in-the-Woods.

The sun curved toward the harsh white head of the Hammerking, barely visible above the Rampart Range's broken-topped wall. A redstart called, Rudy identifying the almost conversational warble; farther down the long slope of rock a lark answered from the olive velvet of the pasture. Deep silence filled the earth, save for the eternal roaring of the wind in the pines. The sound seemed to wash away Fargin Graw's grating voice and the petty small-town politicking of the Keep. Rudy felt himself relaxing slowly, as he did when he went on his solitary rambles in the Renweth Vale in quest of herbs or minerals or just information about what the edges of the woods looked like on any particular day.

He was alive. He was a wizard. Minalde loved him. What else mattered?

He came clear of the trees and settled himself with his back to a boulder at the top of a long slope of blackish rock peeled and scrubbed by the passage of long-ago ice. *Due back any day*, he thought, without any real sense of that event's imminence. Below him, at the distant foot of the slope, the squalid congeries of villa and stockade, outbuildings and byres, lay surrounded by moving figures in the dull browns and greens of home-spun, going about their daily tasks. Still farther down the silver-riffled sepia line of the Arrow, other stockades could be made out among the trees: square log towers and tall, spindly looking watch-spires like masts. The squat stone donjon of Wormswell. From up here he could see the wheat fields and the stockaded orchard of Carpont, the next settlement over; a small group of half-naked men and women were clearing a drainage ditch.

*Not bad.* For people whose civilization had collapsed out from under them in the wholesale slaughter of most of the world's population by an incomprehensible force of monstrosities not terribly long ago, they'd recovered pretty quickly.

*Not that they had a choice,* he reflected, closing his eyes, the sun comforting on his lids. *Who does have a choice? You recover and get a place to keep the rain off you, you plant some food, you get over the pain, or you die.* Many of those people had come from the ruins of Penambra to unfa-miliar northern lands. Many were city folk, clerks, or Guildsmen unused to the scythe or the plow. Probably not a whole lot of them were comfortable being outside at night, even after five years. But they were managing.

He sighed, closing more tightly around himself the veils of illusion as he took out his scrying crystal once more. He let his mind dip toward the half-trance state from which most magic was worked.

But all that he felt in the depths of the crystal was the grinding of that anger, the pressure of some deep, otherworldly rage.

*Ingold, dammit, where'd you go? Pick up the phone, man!*

Had something happened to them? Now, there was a scary thought. Ingold was a tough old dude, and Gil was nobody Rudy would want to fool with, but there were White Raiders wandering in the valley, and ban-dits scavenging what they could from the ruins. A year and a half ago the merchant who'd brought Ingold the sulfur had told them that some Alketch princeling, banished by the upheavals in the plague-riddled South, had marched up the Great Brown River with a mid-size army, intent on conquest of the empty plantations and devastated acres of what had been the southernmost of the High King's realms. Ingold had kept an eye on them by scrying crystal for about a month. Then one morning he'd tuned in to see only a campful of corpses.

True, Rudy reflected, turning the facets of his stone toward the fading sunlight, they didn't have a wizard's ability to make themselves look like scenery, but still . . .

Rudy looked up to see a gaboogoo standing three feet in front of him.

It was as tall as he was, reaching for him with hands like animate rope.

Rudy screamed, grabbed his staff from the rock beside him and slashed with the razor-edged crescent at the slick, whitish knotwork of the thing's wrist. The hand fell onto his knee and clenched on like a machine of iron and cable, even as Rudy leapt to his feet and backward, cutting and slashing at the bloodless and undeterred thing that came at him with other hands outstretched.

It was fast. Rudy scrambled back, hacking at it and feeling the horrible grip of the severed hand shift its clutch on his leg, working its way up his thigh. He whipped the dagger from his belt with his free hand and slashed the leather of his trousers, pulling a great chunk of the buckskin loose, crawling hand and all. He hurled the thing as far as he could and spun to meet the gaboogoo again, slashing this time at the bobbing cluster of nodules on its head. They scattered like asparagus in a mower, and the thing kept coming on—*Well, they* might *have been sensory organs, dammit!*—and Rudy cut a third time, half severing the skinny, bobbing head from the stalk of the neck.

Movement on the ground caught his eye. The hand was creeping determinedly toward him over the rock.

*Feet, don't fail me now.*

Rudy bolted.

He plunged upslope and into the trees, wondering if the gaboogoo would be hindered at all by the forest. He dodged and plunged over fallen pines gross with ear-shaped orange fungus, and leaped the fern-clogged tangle of a stream. Here in the higher woods, little undergrowth hampered his flight, only the yellow pine-straw that slithered beneath his boots. He ducked back along the slope with the intention of circling toward the settlement again but saw something palely gleam ahead of him in the gray-green twilight beneath the trees.

He flattened to a spruce trunk and had another look. It was a second gaboogoo. A little smaller than the first but still sizable. Rudy counted at least four arms—with this one's bobbing nodules not confined to its head, it was somewhat hard to tell what was what. There seemed to be other growths on it as well.

Cloaking spells notwithstanding, it was coming in his direction.

The tag line of an old movie floated through Rudy's head—"*Who* are *those guys?*"—but it did nothing to diminish the terror that had him by the throat. He headed upslope again.

The going was tougher, the ground now very steep. Above the trees the sun had slipped behind the high glaciers of the Rampart Range, and the light between the hoary spruces and lodgepole pines was like translucent slate-colored silk. His boots skidded on rocks and pine-straw as he climbed, the gloom all around him striped now with white birch and gray aspen. The birds had gone silent.

The quality of the wind changed above the timberline. It howled over the split domes of rock and tore at Rudy's long dark hair, cutting through the sleeves of his woolen shirt as if he wore nothing, pouring through the gaping hole in his trouser leg like a carnivore ready to strip the meat off his bones. The small plants of the subalpine snatched at the invisible torrents of air like the wasted hands of the starving. Dozens of streams ribboned the lichenous rock up here, and behind a cracked spur of blue-black granite Rudy saw the terrible lavender wall of the glacier itself, a bled-out sapphire the size of the world.

Rudy thought, almost calmly, *I'm going to freeze to death.*

Below him, something white was working its way among the dwarf-willow and hemlock.

Shivering uncontrollably now, he headed northwest along the face of the slope, wondering if he could get past his pursuers and head down the Arrow Gorge. Something inside him whispered he was kidding himself, but he kept moving anyway. He didn't want to think about what would happen if he stopped.

He couldn't put from his mind the recollection of that white, spider-fingered hand inching over the rocks in his direction. He wondered if it was still trying to catch him.

*I'm invisible, dammit!*

Or unnoticeable, which was as close as wizards could get.

But unnoticeable by what? He seemed to hear Ingold's voice in his mind. To elk you look like a deer, to saber-tooths you look like one of themselves. To bandits he'd look like a tree, and to White Raiders—who could probably pick any individual tree out of a nursery lineup and give the coordinates of where it stood on the mountain—he'd look like a weasel or an owl or something that had business up there.

But to a gaboogoo?

*What* is *a gaboogoo?*

Having no idea what shape their perceptions took, Rudy had no key to their minds—if they had minds—no paradigm with which to tailor illusion. He had no idea what they were.

Except ugly, mean guys who were after him.

Rudy kept moving.

He counted four of them as the afternoon light darkened, the rutilant glare of the sunset illuminating the white beds of slunch that lay, hundreds of feet long sometimes, over the rocks. The gaboogoo whose head he'd half severed had managed to lose it entirely but didn't appear to notice. Like its hand, way back down the mountain, it kept on. The two others Rudy glimpsed among the columned pines below him weren't as big, but seemed subtly different in configuration—one of them appeared to be moving on all fours. Or all sevens, or whatever. Rudy didn't see whether it had a head or not.

He was genuinely scared. Years of living rough had given him a great deal of stamina, but as the gory sunset faded, Rudy was racked by profound shivering. In theory he could Summon heat, as he could Summon light, but he wasn't good at that particular Summoning and didn't think he could keep up his concentration while on the move. The vest of painted bison hide that kept him warm in the windless hollows by day wasn't going to be enough as temperatures plunged. He knew that. And the gaboogoos were working him like wolves, keeping their distance, tiring him out. Under the open crater in his trouser leg Rudy's thigh was black with bruises, a horrible tribute to the strength of that bloodless grip.

*Well, Ingold old buddy, I think we can safely deduce that no, these buggers aren't illusions.*

*And Jesus Christ, they're in the Keep!*

He had to get out of this. Had to get word back to Minalde, somehow, to sweep the Keep and sweep it now!

But even if there had been another mage at the Keep he could communicate with, he'd dropped his scrying stone during the gaboogoo's first attack. He spared a quick stay-put spell for it—problematical at this distance, but scrying crystals were good about that kind of thing.

Ingold's words about the Dark knowing that magic was humankind's only defense came back. Maybe these guys knew it, too.

Who *were* they? And what the hell did they want?

Dead wizards. Rudy looked down at the bruise on his leg again. *That* part of the agenda was pretty unambiguous.

And as the wind numbed his fingers, his ears, and his feet, he had the increasing feeling they were going to get what they were after.

Dark wrapped itself over the slopes. Rudy crouched, trembling, against a boulder, tucking his hands into his armpits to warm them. To his left a U-shaped canyon curved between rocky walls, scattered with boulders and dotted with sheets of water, runoff of the glacier that blocked the way at the farther end. To his right, downslope, he could see all four of his pursuers now, shining dimly as the slunch that blanketed the lower slopes seemed to shine. Out across the falling black carpet of trees he could make out the Great Brown River where the Arrow flowed into it, dull snakes of orange-gold under the flammeous moon. Five little spots of jonquil light showed him where the Settlements lay among the trees. Black clouds were moving in overhead, and his breath, paining his lungs, poured from his lips in streams.

He'd been on the move since slightly after noon, with nothing to eat or drink.

*A fire-spell*, he thought—not to warm himself, but to fight. *Fire or lightning.* He wondered if others would come, conjured a strange vision of them emerging like cheap plastic toys from a mammoth Cracker Jack box concealed somewhere in the trees. *"A big surprise in every pack."*

But he couldn't go farther. He knew that.

When he looked again, there were only three gaboogoo.

Rudy glanced automatically over his shoulder, half dreading the sight of the thing coming at him from up the glacier canyon. But there was nothing visible to his mageborn sight, and when he looked back, there was only one. While he watched, it, too, faded away into the night.

*Oh, come on, you expect me to believe that one?* Rudy shifted his weight uncomfortably. *Why don't you just point down and say, "Oh, look, your shoe is untied?"*

His hands were so cold now he could barely grip his staff. His legs were numb and aching, his chest burned, and he had to fight the growing urge to say screw it and to crawl under the rocks to sleep.

Eyes flashed in the darkness. Rudy sprang to his feet, staggering with cramp. He'd been nearly dozing.

*Eyes?*

It was a dooic.

Even at this distance, and in the piercing cold, he could smell it, if he reached out only a little with his senses—the rank pong of an omnivore. It was an old male, the brown hair of its arms, back, and chest graying to frost, its fanged muzzle nearly white. It was small, probably born wild, though there were dooic in the river bands who'd been born in captivity and trained to simple tasks like cutting sugarcane and digging in the mines, who'd escaped with the coming of the Dark.

This one was standing on its short, bandy hind legs, and through the darkness Rudy could swear that in spite of his spells of conceal-ment—which he had never relinquished throughout the day—it was looking at him.

*Can't be,* he thought, puzzled and scared. *Unless those things have somehow . . . What? Robbed me of power? That couldn't happen . . . Could it?*

He didn't know.

But the dooic definitely saw him. It lumbered a few strides back toward the dark wall of the trees, then turned again, raising its face toward him. Retreated again and turned . . . Retreated and turned. Rudy could see the glint of its tusks in the dimness, smell the stink of it, and he wondered if the creature associated him in its mind with those jerks in the settlement who had tried to shoot that poor hinny yesterday, or if it was merely hungry.

He listened and scanned the edge of the woods, but could neither see nor smell any other dooic near. They hunted in bands and would bring down and slaughter a human being if they could, but Rudy knew that even without magic he could probably deal with a single attack. *Man, I don't need this,* he thought tiredly, shifting his grip along the haft of his staff. *See me tomorrow, pal, I've had a lousy day.*

With a grunt, the dooic dropped to all fours. A moment later it settled to its knees and did something with its hand above a small pool of meltwater caught in the hollow of the rock.

And Rudy felt, strangely, the swift glimmer of something that almost seemed to be magic, like a drift of anomalous scent in the air.

*MAGIC???*

The old dooic moved away again, using its long forearms for speed, the whitish flesh beneath its fur a mottled blur as it reached the edge of the trees. It turned, staring upslope at him again, waiting.

Cautiously, ready for anything, Rudy came forward. Where the dooic had knelt by the meltwater, Rudy bent down—one eye still on the trees—and looked into the water.

In it he could see the pallid, fungoid shapes of the gaboogoo, as if in a scrying stone, moving away through the thick darkness of the woods.

"Jesus H. Christ on a bicycle." Clouds overhead covered the moon, but as a wizard Rudy could see clearly, and the tiny pool had definitely been ensorceled to show the gaboogoo departing. Rudy half recognized the woods through which they passed, downslope and to the north in the hardwoods of the lower forest, toward the Arrow River gorge. By the way they moved, he could tell they were following something, tracking something other than himself.

Movement at the edge of the woods made him swing around, ready for a fight, and he saw that a second dooic had joined the first, a female by the flat pale dugs protruding through the body hair, with an infant clinging to her belly and another on her back. Male and hinny turned at once, ran a few steps back into the trees, then turned again, waiting for him. This time Rudy could almost see the flickering of magic—not human magic, but magic of some sort—that trailed from the old male's fingers as it beckoned him impatiently to follow.

# Chapter 5

*Cast from my fist, shining in the sky,*
*  Brown wings lift and carry you from me.*
*With earthbound hooves I trace the road you fly . . .*

"Gil?" Gentle and uninsistent, the word seemed to come, not from Ingold, but from some darkness in her mind, the thought taking shape in the abyss of a bottomless well. Holding to the poem as to a lifeline in terrifying darkness, Gil managed to nod, to let him know that she heard, but she could not speak.

In a sense, she was still aware of the broken stone walls of an old stable around them—the house to which it had been attached consisted these days of a couple of charred walls overgrown with birch saplings—the rusted black scrollwork of the manger near her head. The smoke of the fire Ingold had built in a corner stung her eyes; she heard the far-off howl of wolves and the soft, restless blowing of Yoshabel's breath.

But it was as if all those images, that awareness, came to her down a cable from the bright surface of water through which she was slowly sinking, swimming deeper and deeper toward a lightless and terrible depth. As Ingold's spells drew her farther into the dark, her mind gyred back to images of the UCLA campus in Westwood, to the words of poems—Donne, Villon, Minalde's favorites Kaalis and Seredne, whom she, too, had come to love. Anything to avoid the fear that she sensed lay at the foundation of her dreams.

His magic was like the warmth of the fire, reassuring her with his measureless calm.

"What do you see, Gilly?" he asked. "What do you see?"

The wide lake upon whose stone verge she stood steamed like a cauldron in the air's cruel chill. In contrast to most of her dreams, Gil felt the cold and smelled the sulfurous tang of the waters: the jewel-indigo of enormous depths, an almost perfect circle miles across, ringed by a toothed wall of high lava escarpments. Steam drifted across a verge of reddish-black basalt, smeared near the shores with garish lichens—purples, golds, virulent reds. A volcanic cone, she thought. And above her a second volcano reared, infinitely tall, crowned with ice. All things, she knew—she didn't know how she knew—were ice-covered beyond the rim of those encircling cliffs.

Something crawled across her foot. It was another of the blubbery hat-shaped things Thoth had found. Like odd slugs with their calcined rosettes, they were creeping everywhere on the few yards of basalt beach that separated the sharp rise of the crater rims from the night-blue waters to her left.

Things like small scorpions, armed but legless, tails upcurled, floated above the steaming waters. The only sound was the groaning of the wind in the rocks.

"What do you see, Gil?"

She could not say.

An entrance squinted at her in the rock wall of the secondary cone, black, deadly; a tunnel into the mountain's ice-locked heart. She could feel the cold on her face as she stepped into the rift, and knew that the volcano, huge and ancient, had a core of ice. In the rock chamber where the tunnel to the ice began there was a statue: cut of black basalt, a man sitting in a chair and gripping with one hand the collar of a dog. The bearded face was stylized, but even so it held an expression of profound sadness, and the sculptor had forgotten or chosen not to cut pupils in the staring eyes.

The anachronistic image seemed to float, detached, in a lake of white ground fog that surged utterly soundless around Gil's knees.

Gil knew full well that this world filled with ice and silence had never been trodden by foot of man.

Ingold's voice came to her, very far away now, asking something, she did not know what. In any case, she could not have answered him. Even the memories of who she had once been seemed to have slipped beyond immediate recollection; whom she was seeking here, why she had come. Cold smoke flowed from a crack in the rock at the top of a flight of stone-cut stairs, and a smell of wet sweetness, sugary and attenuated. Gil followed, drawn by music she thought she had heard once before: music and the murmur of half-heard words.

They were speaking her name. How did they know her name?

At the top of the stair she looked down at her hands. She drew her dagger and slid the blade along her palms—the pain shocking even in the dream, but she could not help herself.

The voices grew clearer in her mind and she thought, *My blood knows my name, and they are a part of the poison that's in my blood.*

They were telling her Ingold had caused her that pain, but even in her dream she knew that wasn't true. As she walked deeper down the crack in the ice, the tension in her chest grew, the terrible anxiety tightening.

Looking down, she saw the dark bones of the rock, and through them, like horribly shining ropes, lines of tension and power in the ground, coursing into the earth.

Her blood dripped down onto the ice, hot against her cold fingers. Looking back over her shoulder, she thought she could see Ingold standing in the crevice that led to the surface of the ground, unable to cross its threshold. It was Ingold as he actually was—sometimes a glowing core of magic light, sometimes the arrogant, red-haired princeling who had caused the last of the great Gettlesand wars. Her lover. Her friend. The other half of her life. He held out his hand to her, but he could come no farther, and she could no longer hear his voice.

The singing filled her ears, and she followed.

The singers knelt in a world of lightless color, their magic shining into the ice of which the chamber was composed and reflecting back, allowing her to see. Glowing smoke surrounded them, rising from the fumarole in the chamber's heart; not the smoke of volcanic heat, but the smoke of cold, for the chasm was filled with something that wasn't lava, wasn't water—something gelid, thick, clear as diamonds, something that moved in slow glutinous waves with the stirrings of that which dwelt within.

The singers were wrought of jewels. They were making magic, performing a rite over and over again in the flat space before the chamber's door; a rite they had performed for eons, until the hard black stone of the floor had been worn into a pit, filled thick now with slunch. Every now and then something crawled out of the slunch: wriggling pale arthropods with masses of tentacles where their heads should have been or those flat, raylike, pincered flying things that she had seen chasing the hawk.

She couldn't see the singers clearly, but she knew they were calling her name. The blood that ran down off her fingers dripped into the slunch and began to crawl in thin red snakes in their direction, glittering with jeweled diamond flecks. The jewel things raised their heads, blue-fire gazes surrounding her. There was a profound cold stirring in the slow-throbbing pool.

"Gil, come back."

It would rise out of the lake, she thought. The ice-mages knew her name already. They would give her name to the thing in the pool, the thing that knew all names, and it would know her.

"Gil, come back now."

She had a dreamy sense of wanting to scream, watching her blood wriggle toward the ice-priests, who extended long hands down to gather it in; watching little whitish spiderlike blobs wriggle up out of the slunch, watching the slow emergence of the thing in the pool.

"Gil!" She felt his hands on her arms, very strong and warm. "You have to come back now. Can you follow my voice? You have to come back."

*I have to go back. I have to go back and kill him.*

She drew her knife again, her blood sticky all over its leather-wrapped hilt. She wondered if she killed herself in this dream whether she'd really be dead. Then they couldn't make her hurt him.

*Or maybe,* she thought, *they could.*

"Can you follow my voice?" She heard it then, the buried urgency under the calm tones. He was scared.

Her mouth felt as though it had been shot up with lidocaine. She managed to say, "Yes."

He led her out of the cavern by the hand. She felt his hand in hers but couldn't see him—something that sometimes happened in dreams—and once they were out of the cavern, past the stone room with the statue of the Blind King and the dog, on the lichen-grown basalt beside the great, cold lake, she felt him spring upward, flying, drawing her by the hand to fly after him.

In her dreams she could fly, if he was holding her hand.

They drifted upward a long way, through black waters again, heading for the light. Looking down, she could see the deep blue crater of the vast lake, like an open eye: the monster volcano beside it, dead and full of ice. It seemed to her she could still smell that sugary odor, still hear the singing of the ice-mages behind her, and the poison in her blood whispered the echo of that song.

Then there was only dark.

"What is it?"

He was kneeling in front of her. She sat on a broken chunk of stone in an old stable in the valley of the Great Brown River, cold to her marrow. "What did I do to my hand?" She withdrew it from his grip to look. Though the heel of her left hand ached as if it had been cut—and cut deep—there was no wound on the flesh.

"Are you all right?"

Why was he scared? His hands were warm on her frozen ones and there was both concern and fear in the sea-blue brightness of his eyes.

She made herself nod, though she didn't feel all right. She felt nauseated and exhausted, as if she had run for miles; her palm hurt like the dickens, and the unhealed bite on the side of her face throbbed as if the flesh had reopened and bled.

"I couldn't reach you." He pushed her hair away from the side of her face, quickly traced spell-marks over her cheek, her shoulder, her arm, warming the tracks of nerves and blood. "You slipped from me. I was afraid I wouldn't be able to bring you back in time."

"In time?" She was still groping in her mind, wondering what the hell she'd say to him if he asked her where she had been all that time, what she'd seen. She couldn't remember a thing, except that she'd been cold.

"We have to go. Now, at once, if we're to reach safety. I don't know—even now I can't be sure—but I think there's an ice storm on its way."

"Here? This side of the mountains?" She added an expression she'd picked up from the Guards, almost as an afterthought, for in that first moment she was too shocked to feel fear. She should, she thought reasonably, have been panicking. "I take it there isn't a cellar on the premises?"

"Not one deep enough. But we're only eleven miles from the old *gaenguo* at Hyve."

Only a few years ago Ingold couldn't have predicted an ice storm more than ten minutes in advance. But sketchy as it was, Gil's knowledge of air-pressure systems had aligned with one of the demonstrations in the record crystals, allowing Ingold to formulate—theoretically, at least— more advanced symptoms of warning.

Ice storms being a phenomenon of the far north and the high plains, his theory about the changes in the temperature, pressure, and smell of the air that heralded one remained untried, but lack of hard evidence about a subject had never stopped him from making eerily accurate long-shot guesses. In any case, Gil would have been willing to run eleven miles and hide in the deepest hole she could find on the old man's bare word, even were an ice storm—a pocket Götterdämmerung and Fimbul Winter rolled into one—not involved.

"Is that deep enough?" Gil had been to the place a few years earlier. The old chamber of sacrifice had been used at various times as either a dungeon or a wine vault, depending on the political circumstances of the surrounding countryside.

"I think we're going to find that out," the wizard replied mildly, and pulled on his mittens. "Are you able to start loading the mule? I have to reach Rudy at the Keep, warn him to get everyone—and the livestock—inside. I'll help you in a moment . . ."

"Ingold, I got my face cut up, not my arms broken." She breathed hard, fighting a wave of dizziness as she stood, and wondered at the flash of some half-recalled vision of her own blood creeping in two trails through the slunch . . . Creeping where? She looked at her palm, surprised anew to find it whole. Why surprised?

"What about the Settlements? Can they flash a message that compli-cated down from the watchtowers?" She pulled the Cylinder from its hiding place in Ingold's blankets, stowed it in her own jacket, pulled tight her sash and twisted her dark, crazy hair back from her face with a thong. "It's not a standard message. I mean, they won't have a code for it. There's never been an ice storm this side of the mountains, has there?"

"One last year, north of Gae but still this side of the mountains." He angled his scrying stone toward the fading embers of the fire.

Yoshabel, sensing that somebody was going to make work for her, bared her yellow teeth and snapped at Gil, who hammer-handed her hard in the side of the face.

"I don't want any lip from you, cupcake. You'll thank me for this."

"You underestimate our girl, my dear." Ingold tilted the crystal, the reflection darting over the scars around his eyes, the straggle of his knife-trimmed beard. "Even if she did know we were saving her life, she wouldn't thank us in the least. The word-code is longer, but they should have time to reach the caves on the mountainside."

*This shouldn't be happening.* Gil slung a blanket and a saddle buck over Yoshabel's back. *An ice storm—that's like getting hurricane warnings in Kansas City!*

Only hurricanes didn't kill everything aboveground.

Ingold was silent, bowed over his crystal, listening, Gil thought, to the turning of the air over the far-off mountains, to the pressure shifts, the unseen colors of the livid night. She worked quickly, thankful they always hobbled the mule when they made camp for the night. Balked of breaking Gil's shin with her foot, Yoshabel settled for lashing her across the face with her tail and puffing her belly as big as she could with air.

"Don't give me that." Gil drove her knee hard into the animal's gut. Even with Yoshabel's usual complete noncooperation, years of practice had made Gil very quick at saddling up, and the terror of the coming catastrophe added to her speed. She expected Ingold to come help her, at least with the loading of the books; dizziness returned twice as she worked, swift waves of it that swiftly passed, leaving her holding on to the wall and gasping. The second time it happened, she looked past her shoulder and saw the old man still bent over the fire, the crystal an arrowhead of flame in his hand.

"Rudy, are you there?" His voice was hoarse with strain. "Are you there?"

*Oh, cripes.* The vision of the Dead Cell deep within the Keep flashed across her mind, where the wizards had been imprisoned by Bishop Govannin when she decided to make the Keep conform to her version of the Straight Faith. It was ridiculous to think anything of the sort could happen with Minalde ruling the Keep, but Gil knew the stresses pregnancy put on a woman's health; knew, too, that in the event of a power struggle among the nobles or even the wealthier merchants, anything might happen.

Getting rid of the wizards at this point would be an utterly lunatic thing to do. As a historian, Gil had read accounts of greater lunacy than that, and she knew exactly how quickly power could shift.

She finished roping down the sacks, then crossed to the fire at a run. Loading had taken ten minutes. Even at a fast walk it would be more than two hours before they reached the eroded artificial hill where the Big House at Hyve had stood. God knew what they might meet on the way.

"Ingold, we have to go."

He didn't stir. His eyes were wide, staring into the crystal, willing Rudy to appear.

"Ingold, we have to get out of here. If you haven't reached him by now you're not going to."

Flèches of refracted brightness chased across cheekbones and eye sockets as he raised his head. "They'll die." He spoke as if waked from a dream, half disoriented with shock. "I think the winds are going to strike somewhere between here and Sarda Pass. Even if they aren't torn apart by the blast, the cold—"

"What's preventing you from making contact?"

He shook his head, anguish in his face, the horror of a man whose power has made him responsible for everyone and everything around him. She saw all the dead whose deaths he had been unable to prevent: his parents, the people he had grown up with in the long-vanished principality of Gyrfire. His student Lohiro, and a woman he had once loved. All the blood-dabbled, shrunken corpses in the streets and courts and alleyways of Gae when the Dark arose.

Tir's father, who had been Ingold's student, patron, and friend.

"What about shape-shifting?" Gil forced her voice to a rationality she was far from feeling. "Can you do that? Into something like a peregrine? Something that's fast and big enough to take the regular night cold for a couple hours? I think I can get to Hyve by myself."

The haunted look in the blue eyes turned to alarm—at the thought of leaving her to make her own way through the hostile dark of the countryside, Gil was certain, rather than at the hideous risk involved in changing shape and flying under the descending hammer of the coming storm. He hesitated, knowing already he'd have to leave her to her own devices, have to do as she suggested . . .

"I'll be all right." She added, "It's not like you have a choice." Thirty percent of the mages who tried shape-shifting didn't survive the first attempt, but she knew herself to be speaking the literal truth. In the absence of communication by scrying crystal, there was no other way for the warning to be given, for the lives of the herdkids, every man, woman, and child of the Settlements—the stock—to be saved.

She could see the calculation fleeting behind his eyes, gauging not the hideous stresses to body, mind, and the ability to use magic, but only how those stresses might best be circumvented. "No," he said at length. "No."

He rose in a single lithe move and made his way half at a run down the brick walk between the marble-faced stalls, shedding as he walked the heavy bearskin surcoat, the rough brown mantle, his face set like stone. Gil, at his heels, felt a sudden blowback of heat, as if she had stepped from the icy night into a summer afternoon: spells gathered around him for protection from the outer cold. Brown leaves in the corners of the broken carriage chamber whirled with the wind of warm air meeting cold, and as Ingold pulled off his boots, laid down his sword belt with a soft ringing of metalwork on brick, fog billowed around him, fraily lit from within by the blue galaxy of magelight above his head.

He slammed open the crazy stable doors, stepped through into the night, naked and shrouded with swirling cloud. Gil stepped into that core of heat and smoky brilliance, clasped him hard to her: "Watch out," she whispered.

"I always do, my dear." His long white hair lifted in the stirring of the magical warmth, his white beard surprisingly soft against her face, while the muscles of his bare arms were like rock. "Guard the Cylinder," he said. In the chaos of dark and mist, he seemed little more than a voice, strong arms, eyes that could have been summer stars. An old scar like a time-dimmed furrow marked the point of his shoulder; there was a bump where his collarbone had been broken long ago.

"If I don't return, send for Thoth or Kta or one of the powerful mages, for at all costs we must find out what it is and what it does. My child—"

Their lips met, the passion seldom spoken between them like unexpected flame: the fierce, cold, scholarly woman and the man who feared loving as he feared neither death nor foe.

She stepped back from him, like stepping through a door into the cold again. Ghostly streams of vapor whirlpooled around him as he lifted his arms and spoke in his great deep broken voice the True Names of the stars. Though she had heard the mages speak of it, Gil had never seen shape-changing; because of its terrible dangers, it was not anything she had ever thought she would see.

But now she watched, her fear of the ice storm all but submerged in wonder. The mists blew thicker, the light within them stronger, fiercer, lancing out in hard beams to outline the leaves of the blowing oak trees. The core of heat that surrounded Ingold thinned, condensed with the inward turning of his concentration as he drew power from his bones, his flesh, from the molecules of his blood. Lines of strain gashed his face as he called on his deepest reserves of power to change his own essence, the inner armature of his self, into something other than human.

Lightning flowed, cold and blue around him, dimming as the heat dimmed, until the power was only a fugitive sensation, like the attenuated whisper of spider-silk in sunlight. The vapors braided themselves into an upward-moving helix in which Ingold was no more than a half-guessed shape, arms upraised, head thrown back, foxlight luminous in his long hair. Gil seemed to hear the beating of wings, as when she had stood in the plaza in front of Royce Hall at UCLA and flocks of pigeons had taken to the air around her; she could almost smell feathers, the thin, coppery tang of blood.

Back inside, Yoshabel brayed, furious and scared, sensing the magic that charged the darkness. *Great,* Gil thought. *You have a hissy about Ingold and you can't sense the ice storm that's going to turn you and me into Swanson's frozen entrées. So much for animal instinct.*

The fog whispered with an inner pulse of light, and all around her stone and wood and the madly whipping leaves of the trees seemed to answer with a shimmer of that which was not light.

Gil raised her hand a little, knowing he was beyond seeing her, and thought, *Don't die . . .* Within the numinous coil she saw him move. The air changed, a wave of heat utterly unlike the spells of warmth, the dreadful heat of atomic matter altering shape and nature. The column of mist itself stretched skyward, a dozen feet, two dozen, lightless levin-fire incandescent around it. Then Ingold cried out in pain or triumph. The cloud seemed to collapse from within: the vapor poured earthward and streamed away in all directions, swirling over her feet.

The trees gave one final shudder and were still.

Ingold was gone.

Gil walked to the place where he had been and knelt to feel the earth. It was warm under her hand. A peregrine feather lay on the imprint of the mage's naked feet.

The night was suddenly very cold.

In her travels with Ingold, and her explorations of the countryside with the Icefalcon of the Guards, Gil had encountered *gaenguo* before. Millennia ago, victims had been bled to death in those deep pits and caves beneath the earth. But memory is long, even when not unpleasantly refreshed by the reappearance of allegedly extinct horrors. Gil did not think she'd find bandits, White Raiders, or wandering gangs of Alketch mercenaries taking refuge anywhere beneath the ground. Most people in the Keep couldn't even be brought to go willingly into its crypts.

As she hastened through the black trees as swiftly as she dared, her fear increased with the very stillness of the windless night, for there was no way of telling how long it would be before the butcher winds hit. None of the other wizards—with the possible exception of Kta, who wasn't precisely a mage anyway—considered Ingold's theories about predicting ice storms more than a few minutes ahead at all practicable. (Gil did not doubt the accuracy of his prediction for a moment.)

She felt as if she walked with an unseen arrow aimed at her back. Worse. She had survived arrow wounds.

The sacrificial mound at Hyve was protected by old cellar doors, which Gil herself had closed and barred two or three seasons back when she first explored the place. It stank of foxes, causing Yoshabel to balk and back and refuse to enter, and Gil dragged brutally on the bit, in no mood for another tantrum. Two hours and more had gone by since Ingold vanished into the light-laced fog.

*Any time*, she thought. *Any time.*

Her hair prickled on her nape.

A rock ramp led from the slab-roofed upper chamber beneath the hill to the corbeled one far below. Gil kindled a horn lantern from the little firebox of smoldering moss on Yoshabel's saddle bow. It threw about as much light as a dying flashlight bulb on rough-cobbled stone walls, on the dark earth before her, puddled with damp, and on the lip of the pit. Gill knew that the pit was smooth at the bottom—that no stairway led farther down to the deeper realms that had been the Dark's.

There were only broken skulls, scattered bones. This had been the final refuge for those in the house on the hill above, the house that stood no longer. The Dark had come here, too.

Returning to the wall near the door, she hoped the place was deep enough to be safe from the coming nightmare cold, that the curves of the stone ramp would be sufficient to keep out the worst of the wind if the place took a direct hit. From the packs she pulled Ingold's robe and mantle, and threw his surcoat across Yoshabel's back, for which favor the mule tried to bite her again. Her back to the wall, Gil settled into as tight a ball as she could, drawing in on herself, pressing her face to the coarse-woven brown wool that smelled of old campfires, of herbs, of the subtle freshness of his flesh.

*Don't die.*

Two days' walk to the settlements. Two hours' flight for a falcon.

If the night's cold didn't kill it. If it wasn't brought down by some larger, fiercer creature, an eagle owl or a wolf. If it didn't forget that it had once been a wizard; if it remembered that there was a killing storm on the way; if it remembered how to transform itself back into a wizard again once its goal was reached.

It wasn't that mages died of trying the spell, Thoth told her once. Some did, of course, for the strain of transformation was appalling. But many more simply continued their lives as animals, the memory of human magic, human faces, human families sliding from their small, intent animal brains. The most adept at transformation were the most in danger, it was said. There'd been at least four such dwelling in Quo when the City of Wizards was destroyed.

Gil had come from California—had turned down the chance to go back—to be in this world with him. She had accepted then that if he died—when he died—she would continue in this world without him. It was her world, now and forever.

Her face hurt her again, and she looked down at her hand, trying to recall why it pained her so sharply and what made her remember the blood running down her palm to drip into the slunch. There were dim images of a mountain with a core of ice, of a deep lake, blue as a jewel . . . of things like animate gems that looked at her and knew her name. Troubled by the recollections, she took from her jacket the leather wrappings that held the Cylinder.

It weighed heavy in her hand. Without crack, without bubble, without shadow or flaw; its surface wasn't even pitted, and it had to be old, three thousand years, four thousand, maybe more. There was no way to tell. It gleamed in the smudgy lantern light as if oiled. Beyond the shadow of a doubt it was the product of magic, the product of the wizards who lived in the Times Before. Everything she had seen of this world before the Dark's last rising had a decorated quality: the walls half timbered or ornamentally bricked, turreted and frilled with statuary and screens. The furniture was carved with flowers and beasts, the clothing— at least that of the rich—elaborate with trapunto and knotwork and embroidery. Of the Times Before, only the Keep itself remained, slick and enigmatic and black, a featureless rectangle immensely huge; the Keep, and the crystals of light and images, likewise smooth and unblemished by eons of time.

And this?

She turned it in her hand, seeking vainly for a flaw or a scratch or a clue. A communicator? A power-core? The leg of a footstool? Rudy would be able to feel magic in it, to touch it and sense something beyond its age. Ingold and Rudy both teased Gil about her complete lack of any sense of magic, her inability to feel it: odd, Ingold had once said, in someone who understood it so well.

She thought about him, staring into the depths of the glass core, but saw only the distorted image of her own hand closed around it and the tiny reflection of the lantern's flame. Now, that was something they could use—a device that permitted communication of those who were not mageborn. A telephone.

He had left her alone.

The pain grew more intense, and she felt exhausted and nauseated, worse than ever before. Sword across her knees, she curled tighter within his robes, staring into the darkness that seemed to collect so thick in the buried chamber, above the mouth of the pit. Wherever he was, she thought, she was with him. Dead or alive, whatever the voices whispering in her brain told her.

There were other voices answering them, unanswerably.

. . . *thy sweet love remembered such joy brings*

*That I would scorn to change my state with kings.*

She felt the ice storm hit, far above her, as if all the world had been tipped over the edge into the pit of Fimbul Winter, the dark beyond the Norse Götterdämmerung, the cold that would see no spring, as if all the earth were sinking like a shipwreck through blackness to cosmos' end.

# Chapter 6

"**L**ook, guys, it's not that I don't appreciate the hospitality, but you gotta admit it's getting a little thick in here."

Rudy Solis started to rise, and George—the old dooic whom Rudy had decided bore a more than superficial resemblance to a comedian in his own world of that name—darted four-legged to the hole that led to the long and twisting passageway to the outer world, sat down in front of it and bared his yellowing tusks. It was a ritual gesture—at this point Rudy didn't really think George was going to bite him, though the discolored fangs were darn good for a guy that age—but he understood what it meant and backed to the wall again.

"Okay. I'm cool. So what the hell do you want?"

None of the dooic in the cave had laid a hand on Rudy, or come near him. There were perhaps a dozen of them, a small band as dooic went, mostly the wiry, dark-furred variety, though one or two of those with graying muzzles were large enough and scarred on the wrists and back in such a way that Rudy guessed they had been domestic slaves before the rising of the Dark. They huddled at the far side of the low-roofed, sandy-floored chamber around a fire that George had kindled by merely looking at the wood, in the age-old manner of wizards.

Rudy was still amazed. *I'll be buggered. Dooic have magic.*

He could not have been more surprised if he'd learned the same thing about tree frogs.

He settled down to watch the movements of the band. With one worried dark eye still on Rudy, George moved away from the entrance again, to admit three or four more of the tribe, who hauled after them dead branches and chunks of half-rotted logs. These they stacked in a corner of the cave. The cave itself, though wide and deep, was only about five feet high at its tallest, tapering at the back to little more than a horizontal crack that vanished into darkness, and the whole place reeked of carrion, smoke, and dooic. Not, Rudy thought, the place where he'd planned to spend the night, but it beat hell out of a slunch bed between the timberline and the glacier, with rubbery eyeless mushroom-critters dropping by for tiffin. For company he supposed it had a few points over Graw's great hall.

On the other hand, it was the opportunity of a lifetime to study a dooic band close up. He'd tried on other occasions, in the Vale of Renweth, but dooic were elusive as foxes in the woods—and if some of them could use magic, it was no wonder he'd never been able to sneak up on them. Despite the fact that dooic would occasionally slaughter and devour lone travelers, he felt no threat. Unless George was a hell of a lot stronger wizard than he appeared to be, his own magic should protect him from concerted attack—and anyway, they'd shown no disposition to gang up on him. George had lured him here with a trail of magic, of signs traced in light in the dark air, and Rudy had followed out of a combination of intense curiosity and the knowledge that Ingold would smack him with his staff if he passed up the chance.

They wanted him here.

Had they asked him to dinner to thank him for saving the life of the hinny with the two babies? Did they think that action had made him responsible for her and them? Was she going to end up his wife, in the best tradition of pulp adventure tales?

*Er—none for me, thanks.*

He could see her among the others in the corner, pups in tow, eyes gleaming in the almost impenetrable smoky darkness of the cave, but she had made no move to approach him; he'd christened her Rosie after a girl he'd gone to high school with. The other mares he labeled Mom, Margaret Dumont, Alice the Goon, Gina, Cheryl, and Linda, *and two days from now I won't recognize a single one of them . . .*

George, who'd gone over to the wood-bearers—all of whom moved easily on all fours, under the low pitch of the roof—now turned, as if he'd heard a noise from the passageway. He glanced back at Rudy and grunted something, accompanied by a swift, complicated gesture with his hairy, short-fingered hands. Rudy must have looked blank, because George caught the attention of another male with a piglike squeal, made another gesture, then ran, apelike on his knuckles, to the passageway and vanished into the dark. The other males made a flurry of gestures among themselves, incomprehensible to Rudy but speaking clearly of consternation and fear—why fear? Then four of them ran to sit in a row across the entrance, watching Rudy intently with those surprisingly human eyes.

"I get it," Rudy said. "Sit tight, right?" As he spoke he showed his hands, palms out, empty, then thought, *Oh, good. They communicate by gestures, and I've just told them all their mothers wear army boots.* He noted how the males were sitting, arms not wrapped around their knees, but crooked at the sides, hands palms down upon the drawn-up knees. He hunkered himself carefully into the same position.

They'd have shut the gates at the settlement hours ago. Whatever was going on up here, it would be an interesting night, provided they didn't expect him to share the dead rabbits and voles a couple of them had pulled out from behind rocks. He was starving, but even from here he could tell supper had passed its sell-by date quite some time ago.

Everyone in the cave seemed to be listening, tense and on edge; the males across the doorway jumped at sounds, gestured, and signed to one another. At one point one of them went into the passageway, clearly to check and see if George was on his way back.

The gaboogoos? Rudy wondered. Had the old dooic gone to chase them off again? And if so, how?

More logs were heaped on the fire. The cave grew uncomfortably warm and phenomenally odiferous. Huge shadows humped and jittered over the low walls as the dooic moved about in the ruddy light; now and then a couple would sit down and begin to groom each other, but it never lasted long. Whatever was happening, it was bothering the whole group.

In time the old one returned, carrying something in his enormous hands, and Rudy thought, *Did Mom send him to the local SuperGrocery for something fresh for dinner?*

The bird the old dooic was carrying was not only fresh, but alive. It stirred, trying to shift bloody feathers and bating feebly with its head. As George brought it near, Rudy saw the hard gold eye, the hooked beak of a peregrine falcon, and thought, *Nice rock-throwing if you could bring one of those down, pal!*

Or had something else wounded it, leaving it bleeding on the rocks below the caves? In that case, how had the old dooic located it in the dark? George held it carefully, hands wrapped gently around the bloody wings, rocking a little and muttering. The bird was either still stunned by whatever had brought it down or calmed by the dooic's spells. It did not fight, but glared around with feral topaz eyes in the near-dark.

*What was a peregrine doing flying after nightfall, anyway?*

Silence deepened in the cave.

Then George handed the peregrine to Mom and hunkered close to the fire. A moment later Rudy felt the magic of a Summoning of some kind—heat?

It radiated from the close-curled, gray-furred body as if old George had turned himself into a stove. Coupled with the warmth of the fire, it was nearly unbearable, but the entire band crowded close around. Rosie the hinny scurried over to Rudy and caught his hand, trying to draw him toward the group. He followed, though the smell of the steaming group was Olympian.

*This better be good.*

Rudy turned, halfway to the group, at the sudden shriek of wind in the passageway. Rosie dragged on his hand, fear in her eyes—the wind flung back Rudy's long hair, the cold striking hard and sudden and sharp enough to stab his sinuses like a knife. The wind's voice rose, screaming in the turnings of the rock, as if a cyclone, a hurricane, the end of the world were taking place outside.

The real cold came.

And Rudy knew.

*Oh Christ, it's an ice storm.*

He stood numb as Rosie plunged back into the safe warmth of her family. For a moment Rudy felt only astonishment at the coming of such a phenomenon, out of place and season.

And then: *The Settlements!*

It was too late. Knowledge of what an ice storm's winds would do to even such stout constructions as the old stone villas, the tree-trunk walls, ripped his heart like a bayonet. Walls ruptured, roofs jerked away, humans and animals flung like rag dolls in a lawn-mower—he'd seen the ruins on the plains of Gettlesand. . . .

Old George grabbed him, dragged him with horrifying animal strength back into the close-mobbed dooic, as if he genuinely feared Rudy would go dashing out into the storm.

But Rudy only thought, *Oh, Jesus! Oh, Jesus!* over and over, knowing there was nothing he could do. They were dead already— frozen, pulped, and dead.

Cold rolled into the cave like the waters of doom. The dooic crowded tighter around the fire, around the old male whose spells had saved them from other peril before.

*The Keep!* Those black walls had resisted the anger of the Dark and and would, he thought, resist the fall of the mountains themselves. But the crops would be killed, the crops they'd broken themselves all spring to plant, the crops that were their only salvation. Every head of livestock in the byres outside the Keep would perish of the outer-space cold even if they weren't dashed to pieces by the howling funnel of the wind.

And the herdkids with them.

Rudy screamed, *"No!!!"* barely aware that he had made a noise, then curled against the rock of the wall and buried his head in his arms.

Like tornadoes, ice storms struck and passed quickly. Rudy lay listening to the mad howl of the wind, every contraction of his heart telling him that the children he'd seen questing for firewood under Lirta Graw's command, the hunter whose nose he had broken, were dead now, their bodies sieved through the smashed palisade and the meat flash-frozen where it lay. So much for human plans, human aspiration, human love . . . So much for anyone we love or hate or who just has their own annoying agenda.

He shut his teeth hard against tears.

In time he stirred, turning his concentration to his own spells of Summoning heat. The repetition of the words, the drawing of the power, took his mind temporarily from the pain. These dooic, huddled around their meager fire, had saved his life, maybe because he'd saved Rosie's and maybe because old George knew he was a wizard and could help them out—he didn't know. But he owed them. So he snuggled closer into the fetid congregation, noting in surprise that Mom and some of the younger hinnies were wrapped in badly cured, flayed deerhides, under which they held the cubs close to their bodies, the first evidence he'd seen of dooic using implements more complicated than a rock. Though of course, he thought, the domesticated ones had worn clothing in servitude and may have thought that was a good idea to bring back to the tribe.

In time the wind died. The cold grew deeper, the freezing air flowing in . . . *Damn, it must have come down just about on top of us.* And on the Settlements. *Jesus, Jesus, Jesus.* Still in old George's hands, the injured peregrine stared around the circle with mad yellow eyes.

Only when his mageborn perceptions told him a crippled dawn was creeping up to warm the mountainside did Rudy wrap a deerhide over his shoulders for extra warmth and scramble, on hands and knees, up the low-roofed passageway to the surface of the ground again. The tunnel was slippery with ice, and absolutely black—at the top he found twenty or thirty feet of snow blocking the entrance. He gouged at it with the steel crescent of his staff, Summoning heat around the metal, so that melt-water ran down to soak his torn and filthy trousers.

The world was a ruin in the violet gloom of snow-light and morning: pines snapped, branches stripped, birds spattered dead against the rocks. He saw what might have been gulls, though so badly damaged it was hard to tell—God knew how they got there. From a livid bank of cloud over-head a few funnels still dipped earthward, then retreated again, miles away. Five feet in front of the cave mouth a boar had been skewered on the blasted shards of an oak tree, frozen to USDA Choice.

George and Mom emerged behind him, the graying female holding another deerskin around her, both peering uneasily, trading hand-signs, quick and small and silent. Rudy was barely aware of them. His mind felt erased. He was aware that he was looking at the end of the world, the beginning of Fimbul Winter indeed—the Ultimate Notification from the Great Darwinian Bureau in the Sky that said, "We regret to inform you that you have been selected against." He couldn't take it in.

There'd be no crops, either at the Settlements or the Keep. Last night would have iced them where they stood. No animals left at all.

Everyone in the Settlements—some nine hundred people—was dead.

Everyone at the Keep would starve.

George yowled a warning and flung up his hand. Underfoot the mountain moved, a hard, sharp twitch, then a few seconds of stillness, followed by a long slow roller-coaster sensation, as if they all stood on the belly of some monstrous anaconda as it swallowed a couple of deer.

"Chill out." Rudy caught his balance against the sprawled, up-lifted roots of a broken tree as the old dooic and his mate clung to one another, looking for someplace to run. "It's a five-two, tops. I wouldn't even get out of bed for it back home." Like many Southern Californians, Rudy was adept at playing Guess the Richter with local earthquakes. By the time lag between the kicker and the roller, he judged that the epicenter was far off.

He picked his way through the smashed and uprooted trees, mortared together with snow frozen hard as concrete. Where the wind had scoured the snow away, weeds stood stiff, held upright by the water in their cells that had turned to ice, waiting for the touch of the sun that would let them lapse from pseudolife into brown and crumpled death.

There was a little patch of slunch on the rocks. Though snow lodged in its folds, it seemed perfectly healthy.

Rudy muttered, "Son of a . . ."

He stepped around the rock and stopped again. Toeless footprints marked the thin snow beyond. A little blown snow had dusted into them, enough for Rudy to calculate the timing: after the winds had ceased, but during the worst of the cold. He didn't even want to think about what the temperature had been.

Behind him he heard old George grunt, and Mom yammer in fear. Seizing his staff, Rudy ducked around the rocks, skidding on the hard snow-crust as he ran back to the mouth of the cave.

Ingold stood there, shivering and blinking, wrapped only in the flayed hide of one of the dooic's deer.

"I don't know what happened." The old man's voice was hoarse and hesitant, and he flinched as Rudy turned his mangled arm to the light at the mouth of the tunnel entrance, where they had taken shelter against the cold. Rudy had gone back to the deeper chamber to fetch firewood and kindled a small blaze in the tunnel, the heat reflecting back from the rocks. Outside, the virulent clouds were breaking, the sun beginning to melt the snow.

Ingold was unable to summon fire; unable, Rudy guessed, to summon heat or light or any of the small magics that were wizardry's second nature. He lay against the rock shivering with exhaustion, barely responding as Rudy examined the wounds on his arms and back, and on the back of his head. He looked as if he'd been attacked by maniacs wielding chisels and cleavers. The wounds reminded him of something that might have been inflicted by pincers, like an enormous lobster or a Roger Corman–sized crab. Not claws, he thought. Not teeth either, really.

And all the while he was marveling, *Ingold really did it. I'll be buggered. He actually turned himself into a goddamn bird.* It was something he couldn't imagine himself or anyone else even trying to accomplish. He was conscious of awe and an overwhelming wish that he'd been there to watch—to see it and to see how it was done.

But he only said, "Man, if that storm had hit while you were still on your way, you'd be dead meat!"

Ingold raised his head a little, brought up one hand to wipe at a gash over his brow. "I had to risk it. I couldn't reach you by scrying stone—"

"Couldn't reach me? I was tryin' all morning to get in touch with you, man! And Thoth, and the Gettlesand gang! Then I lost my crystal . . . I'll have to go back and look for it. But whenever I tried, I just got this . . . this . . ."

"Weight," Ingold said, his voice almost dreamy, as if he were slipping again into sleep. He tried clumsily to pull the deerskin back over the bare, freckled goose-flesh of his shoulders, hands almost unworkable with cold. "Anger. Magic deep in the bones of the earth. Which is gone now, incidentally," he added, rousing a little. "I expect that after the earthquake we should have no trouble reaching Thoth."

Rudy looked at him a little blankly, trying to work that one out. Mom emerged from the throat of the passageway to proffer an appalling double handful of what was almost certainly chewed leaves, and Rudy said, "Uh—thanks." He sniffed it—borage and willow, and he'd handled worse in five years—and passed a quick hand over it, feeling the magic already in it and adding his own spells of disinfection and healing. Ingold's mouth did not so much as twitch as Rudy spread the mess over the gaping, clotted wounds.

"So what the Sam Hill is going on?"

Ingold shook his head, pressed the side of his face to the rock of the wall, the long white bloodstained hair hanging down to half conceal his face.

Rudy said, "You gonna be okay for a couple minutes more? I gotta stitch this one."

The old man nodded and signed for him to go ahead. Rudy threaded up a needle with the toughest line of sinew in his belt kit and turned Ingold's shoulder so that his back took the direct patch of the in-falling morning light. Under blood and muck, the skin was crossed with the scars of old whip cuts, scores of them, white gouges that when fresh must have gone nearly to the bone.

"We can find your crystal and contact Thoth and the others in Gettlesand, later in the day." Ingold's voice was barely a whisper, though Rudy had laid on him every spell he could to dull pain. Anyone else— anyone who had no magic of his own to combat it—would probably have been in shock, and by the old man's coloring, he was pretty near it, anyway. He was shivering convulsively, fighting to steady his breath. "But our first duty lies in the Settlements. To burn them in death, since we could not save them in life."

Rudy gave Ingold his long woolen shirt and would have given him his trousers, too, if they'd have fit the wizard's stockier frame. The shirt came down to his thighs, and Ingold wrapped strips of deerskin around his legs and feet. Rudy cut him a staff from an oak sapling, and the two descended, like a couple of shivering beggars, through the ghastly silence of ruined woods covered with snow to the dead land below.

As they walked, Rudy told Ingold about the gaboogoos that had attacked him in the woods and how they had followed him despite every spell he had laid to throw them off the track; how he had found their spoor in the lee of rock still dusted with the snow that had fallen during the worst of the night. He spoke to take his mind off what he knew was waiting for them, to turn it aside from all those questions about what they were going to do now. About what they could do.

Long before they reached the Settlements, they found sheep, or parts of sheep, impaled on the broken trees, their wool brown clots of blood. The warming air melted the snow in patches, and the two men had to struggle to keep from slipping in the mud—Rudy kept a wary eye on Ingold and a hand ready to steady him should he fall, but though the older wizard's pain and exhaustion slowed him, he seemed to recover as the day went on. Rudy looked at the birds—eagles or bull owls—crushed against the trees like bugs on a windshield, and wondered again what it was that had caused those pincerlike wounds; what had struck Ingold down before he'd gotten to the Settlements.

Just before noon they passed the place where the storm funnel had touched down. The trees had been swept up by their roots and lay in a smashed heap against the mountain's first rising slopes, mixed with rocks, laurel shrubs, the carcasses of animals, and ice and snow. It was melting at the edges, and there was a great dirty pool of water and blood below the tangle, like a colossal beaver dam of matchsticked spruces and bones.

Barely a mile south of that unbelievable scour lay what was left of Fargin Graw's fortress. At one end of the imploded wreck the two wizards uncovered the bodies of Graw, his wife and sons, and most of the other members of his household, mashed by the fallen roof beams and lying in a lake of snowmelt and gore. The child Lirta, a few of the servants, and the hunter whose bow had broken his nose had been carried by the wind nearly a dozen yards and smashed against the wreckage of the stables, where their bodies mixed with the slow-thawing rummage of cattle and sheep. They found the boy Reppitep later in the afternoon, when the sun strengthened enough to melt some of the larger drifts.

"It will have happened very quickly," Ingold said as he and Rudy dragged the far-flung bodies to lie in what would be their pyre among the thatch.

Tears running down his face, Rudy yelled at him, "And that's supposed to make me feel better?"

Ingold replied wearily, "In time."

The old man insisted, to Rudy's rage and horror, on thoroughly looting the buildings, making a stack of kitchen utensils, clothing, plows, rake heads, needles, and harness buckles near the well. "Can't you show a little respect, for Chrissake?"

"No," the old man said, slowly pulling on a pair of somebody's boots. "Not in the circumstances."

*He transformed himself into a bird,* Rudy thought, watching him trying to wash some of the grime off with snow before dressing clumsily in a dark leather jerkin, baggy trousers, and a sheepskin vest Rudy remembered seeing on one of the hunters the night before last. *Done one of the most crazily dangerous acts of magic possible in the outside hope of warning these people.* It was only by sheerest chance and the wisdom of the dooic mage that he wasn't a bloody blot on the snow someplace now. And everyone here would be just as dead.

Rudy had to remind himself of that again when he saw the old man laboriously going through the corpses, removing knives from the men's belts and needles from the sewing still in the women's hands. When they passed the place where Rudy first met the gaboogoo, they had picked up his fallen scrying stone, half buried under snow, and now Rudy got up his courage to look into it and saw Minalde weeping as she struggled to drag wood to the pyre in front of the Keep on which they'd lined the bodies of fifteen little herdkids.

Rudy watched until he saw Tir, stumbling at her heels with an armful of kindling. For a horrible time, Rudy had feared that last night had been one of the many occasions on which Tir had sneaked out to spend the night with the other kids.

He let the image die. Once he'd ascertained Tir and Minalde lived, he didn't want to see anything else.

Mountain shadows stretched across them, blue and chill. Hating himself, Rudy went to the heap of garments Ingold was making where the gatehouse had been and found among them his own ramskin coat, its sleeves gay with painted flowers. The sky would remain soaked in summer light for hours. Looking up, he saw the air above the mountains streaked in peach and apricot, a phenomenal, overblown sunset such as Rudy had previously associated with the tackier variety of cowboy painters or photographs in inspirational magazines.

He whispered, "Wow," and Ingold, to whom he hadn't spoken since his bitter railings about respect, limped to his side.

"Come now, Rudy, don't tell me you're surprised."

"You're predicting sunsets now?"

"There was an earthquake this morning," Ingold said. His hand was pressed to his side, his gored face gray. "I thought it might have been triggered by the eruption of another volcano in Gettlesand."

"You're right," Rudy said. "That makes—what? Three this winter? What you got there, pal?" he added, nodding at the gory wad of sacking in the old man's hands. The limb of an animal—a rabbit? But no rabbit had claws like that—protruding from it at an awkward angle.

"I haven't any idea." Ingold stooped agonizingly and unwrapped the thing on the remains of the foundation by which they stood.

Rudy said, "Yike!" and took a step back, then came close again, staring. "What the hell *is* it?" In his own voice he heard the echo of a theme he'd been singing for days now, and looked across at Ingold, baffled and a little scared. "Where'd you find this thing?"

He gestured with his eyes. "Against the palisade." Only one wall of the palisade remained, the south one, into which the north wall and huge chunks of the old villa and outbuildings had been driven, a dune of wreckage. Stiffly, Ingold wrapped the carcass up again. His hands were swollen with the work he'd done, shifting timbers and grubbing for bodies under pools of half-frozen water, and the flesh around the cuts on the left side of his face was bruised nearly black. "I've noticed that—"

At the sound of some noise, he turned, and there was nothing stiff or crippled about the smoothness with which he suddenly had one of the dead farmers' shortswords in his hand.

Rudy turned to follow his gaze. There were figures in the road, dozens of them, faces glimmering pale in the gathering dusk. Someone called, "Who's there? Is anyone alive?"

Rudy recognized the voice. "That you, Yar?" He left the darkness by the gatehouse and strode down in the direction of the straggling line of newcomers. "It's Rudy and Ingold." He almost didn't need a mage's sight to recognize Lank Yar, the Keep's chief hunter, a drooping leather strap of a man who seemed, body and soul, to have been braided back together out of his own scar tissue following the rising of the Dark. Behind the hunter he identified others: Nedra Hornbeam, the matriarch of third level south, with her son and son-in-law; Lord Sketh, pushing fussily to the front with two or three of his purple-badged men-at-arms; several of the Dunk clan from second north with Bannerlord Pnak; Bok the Carpenter and half a dozen Guards under the command of the Icefalcon.

"They're dead here," Rudy said quietly. "They're all dead."

"Good God, man, we thought you were gone as well!" Bok strode forward and caught Rudy's arms in huge hands, then enveloped him in a hug that was like being hugged by an iron tree. "And Lord Ingold . . . !"

"Lord Ingold," Yar the Hunter said quietly, "who ought never have left the Keep to begin with this spring. Had he stayed where he belonged, these folk would have been alive, and the children of the herds, too."

He turned and walked away. Lord Sketh came over quickly, caught Rudy's hand in one of his own round moist ones, said quickly, "Ridiculous! Are you well, man?" There was scared relief in his eyes, desperate relief that the Keep would not, in the face of such catastrophe, be left wizardless as well. "What happened? Was it an ice storm, as the Icefalcon's been saying? We heard nothing, only opened the Doors this morn to a wall of snow."

"It was an ice storm," Ingold said softly. "And Yar is right. I should not have left the Keep."

They worked through the fevered sunset and long into full dark, under a moon that came up gibbous and crimson, like a dirty blood-orange, as if the grue that lay soaking into the ground had stained its golden light. Under Lord Sketh's orders, the hunters and volunteers and Guards dragged every horse, every head of stock, every deer, every boar, even the rats and rabbits and voles found crushed in the woods or mashed into the palisade, and made great thawing piles of them between

the ruined house and the heap of matchwood that had been the gates.
Rudy and Ingold laid spells of preservation on those dripping heaps, to
arrest and postpone decay once they should begin to thaw, and men and
women set to hacking the meat into chunks, to be carried up to the Keep.
Through a haze of blind exhaustion, of pain in his frozen hands and
toes, Rudy understood that this meat was all the Keep would have to live
on, summer, winter, and into the following spring.

And he could already see that it wasn't going to be enough.

While the meat thawed, Lord Sketh ordered a pyre built of broken
timbers and the drying thatch; they kindled it an hour before dawn.
The smell of the smoke was a vast, oily cloud over the charnel house of
wet bones, ice-beaded meat, and glittering heaps of salvaged harness
buckles and shoes. Lank Yar, more practical-minded, set parties to
building sledges to carry the meat, and racks on which to smoke it, and
the first group of bearers set off for the Keep with Fargin Graw's food
reserves and the news that the two wizards were alive just as dawn was
staining red the waters of the Great Brown River to the east.

Whuhen Rudy woke from exhausted sleep, Gil was there, her black hair
braided to keep it out of the blood, her face half masked in field dressing and more bruised even than Ingold's. She looked exhausted, sick,
and deeply worried, and no wonder, Rudy thought. Some distance away
he could see Ingold at work cutting up a sheep neatly as a butcher, and
like a butcher soaked and spattered with blood from head to foot; he
would answer if someone spoke to him, but he seemed, as Rudy knew
he would, to have taken Lank Yar's words completely to heart.

At least it was too early for ants or flies to have commuted in. *Thank
God for small favors.*

"I was worried about you, punk." Gil sat down next to him and
handed him a bowl of gruel and a dried apple. They'd almost certainly
come from the settlement store. Rudy thought about the people who
should have been eating them for breakfast and felt nearly sick.

"I wish I could say the same about you, spook." He was too hungry
and exhausted not to eat, and once he began, he felt better. He had eaten
almost nothing yesterday and had worked cutting wood and hauling
bodies to the pyre until he was ready to drop. "But until that thing hit, I
was clueless, and when it did—" He paused and shook his head. "—I

didn't really think about any one person, I guess. Just, like, 'Oh, Jesus, no.' I guess I figured if you were with the old man, you'd be okay. Did you— did you see him turn himself into a bird?"

She smiled crookedly—with the wound on her face, she could hardly help it—and nodded. But she only said, "I thought Lord Sketh was going to propose marriage when I showed up with the mule. The orneriest, nastiest old bizzom in the Keep, and now she's the only domesticated beast of burden in the Vale. That'll learn Enas Barrelstave to argue against us borrowing the best instead of the worst critter when we go out scavenging. Sterile, too, of course."

"Oh, Christ," Rudy said. He hadn't thought of that—Gil was generally about two jumps ahead of him. "What're we gonna . . . ? I mean, what about plowing next spring?"

"Don't worry about it, punk." Gil got to her feet and swept the ruined settlement with a gaze as chill and silvery as the heatless sky. "We're gonna starve by Christmas."

"Most of it's still frozen," the Icefalcon was saying as Rudy and Gil came up to the shambles where Ingold was jointing deer and pigs with an ax. "We'll probably be able to get it up to the Vale before it begins to go off, but on foot it will be a slow trek. Warmer weather's coming," he added, glancing to the north. "There'll be flies."

"I'll do what I can about that," Ingold said. He looked like ten miles of bad road, and moved as if he'd been beaten with a stick. Rudy guessed he hadn't slept at all.

"I expect there'll be parties coming down to clear out Manse and Carpont today," the young Guard continued, one blood-gummed hand tucked into his sash. "We may need spells to prevent decay then. When we go up to the Keep tomorrow morning, one of you should remain."

"One of 'em should stay just to tell us if there's another one of those what'd you call, ice storms, on the way," Yobet Troop threw in, stopping nervously beside them with dangling bundles of frozen chickens yoked to his shoulders. He glanced at Ingold with frightened eyes, and then at the sky. "You'll do that, won't you, m'lord wizard? That's your job."

"Yes," Ingold said gently. "That's my job."

He added to Gil, when Troop and the Icefalcon had gone their ways, "Things aren't as bad as you might suppose. The storm affected an area perhaps fifty miles across, and beyond that there will be game, and fruits in abandoned orchards if we can get parties out there quickly enough, and nuts in the woods. The Icefalcon spoke to me earlier about leading a raiding party against the bandits around Penambra, who will have horses if nothing else."

"I bet they'll be real efficient raiders on foot," Gil said.

Ingold regarded her in mild surprise and mimed a dig through his pockets. "If you're willing to put money against the Icefalcon on foot in a contest with the average group of mounted bandits . . ."

"The hell I am," Gil said, with the first grin Rudy had seen out of her all day.

"And I'm sure Lady Minalde will send to Tomec Tirkenson in Gettlesand for livestock as well, provided we can haul hay up from the river meadows below Willowchild to feed them." Moving as slowly as an old man, Ingold limped to the stack of carcasses and began to drag free a deer. His hands fumbled their grip and Gil and Rudy hastened to help him; Rudy handed him the ax he'd been using, but after lifting it, Ingold set it down again, as if too wearied, for the moment, to go on.

"They're taking the mule, you know," Gil said, turning to the stump nearby, where several axes were stuck. It was the first time in years that Rudy had seen more implements than there were people. Gil judged her striking point on the carcass and buried the ax head just below the foreleg, bracing her foot and shoving to wrench free the ice-stiff limb.

"As well they must." Ingold looked across at Rudy. "Rudy, I'm counting on you to spell the books Gil and I brought from Penambra. I concealed them last night in the root cellar here. Between my peregrinations of the night before last and laying every fragment of magic I could summon on the meat last night and today, even should I get some rest between now and nightfall, I'm barely going to have the strength to do what I'll need to do."

Rudy didn't like the sound of that. Still less did he like the way the muscles of Ingold's jaw tightened when he hobbled slowly to the other side of the carcass, to help Gil reduce it to limbs and trunk.

"Every ward and guard you can summon," the old man went on without giving him time to reply. "Decay, water, fire, theft, insects, even notice by another wizard. Goodness knows how long it will be before someone can be sent to fetch them. Those books are some of the oldest that exist outside the City of Wizards, and some of them are copies of texts even older than that city itself. They may contain the answer to questions necessary for our very survival."

Warily, Rudy said, "You sound like you ain't gonna be around."

Ingold scratched the side of his nose, leaving a streak of slightly fresher blood in the grime. "Well, I do feel badly about that."

*Don't do this to me, man. Don't leave me to deal with this alone.*

"I should not go," Ingold went on, very slowly. "For Yar was right, you know. I was culpable for leaving as I did. For assuming that such a disaster would not befall."

"Who knew?" Rudy flung out his hands. "And who's gonna be dumb enough to say that it was our fault this happened? You can feel those things coming ten minutes ahead of time, tops; I can't feel 'em at all. Even before I feebed my crystal, I wasn't able to reach you. I still haven't figured out why . . ."

"You haven't?" Ingold appeared mildly surprised. "Be that as it may, it was my fault, and I am responsible. And I suspect that once we return to the Keep, there will be pressure brought to bear on both of us not to leave it again." He glanced over at Gil, then away.

"It isn't only for the sake of the art of wizardry itself that I've been searching for a mageborn child, Rudy. We desperately need more wizards at the Keep. We should never have gone from month to month, year to year, putting off sending for a few of the Gettlesand wizards . . . I've spoken to Thoth, by the way."

"You did?" Contact with the Gettlesand wizards—and the entire subject of the gaboogoos—had completely slipped his mind. "Did he say what happened? Why we couldn't get in touch?"

"He told me a number of extremely disquieting things, but no, he had no idea why communication by scrying stone was impossible. But I suspect that the night before last was not the first time that such a thing has happened. I haven't time to go into that now—maybe later, or more likely you can speak to him yourself. The important thing is that something very strange is going on—strange and appalling and, as far as I know, completely unprecedented."

"Well," Rudy said sarcastically, heaving up one severed hindquarter of the deer and manhandling it onto the nearby sledge for transport, "I'd kinda guessed that."

"You always did have a good, solid grasp of the obvious," the mage replied approvingly. "But I'm not sure you are aware how rare the *completely* unprecedented actually is: *never*-heard-of; beyond human experience. Gil's a historian. She knows the truth that was said by the Lord of the Sigils: *There is no new thing beneath the sun.* It's not just a wise platitude—it's the basis of all lore, all scholarship, all the method of magic.

"But these gaboogoos seem to be precisely that. And as such, they bear fairly close investigation."

Ingold straightened up and wiped the sticky gum of half-frozen blood from his hands.

"That's why magic won't work on them, huh?" Rudy said slowly. "Because we don't really know what the hell they are. They don't bleed, I'll tell you that. And if they sweat or smell or excrete or eat or spit, they do it damn inconspicuously. They sure walked through my spells of concealment like they were a cheesy plastic bead curtain."

"Precisely." Under the bloody grime of his overgrown mustache, Ingold's mouth was hard. "And the trouble is, it isn't just the gaboogoos. The creature that attacked Gil—almost certainly in concert with other beings that I did not see—was utterly unfamiliar to my lore or the lore of anyone I have ever read or spoken to. Last night the Icefalcon and his scavengers brought to me three other totally unknown animals, at least insofar as I could tell from the parts that remained. And there is no record—none—in the most ancient books or the tales of the most wide-ranging travelers, of what slunch is."

"Slunch?" Rudy blinked at the sudden reversion to the mundane . . . if it was mundane. His first reaction—slunch is slunch—was automatic and, he found on reflection a second later, rather unsettling. He'd gotten used to it. Everyone had. "I don't get it."

"Nor do I." The blue eyes glittered, very pale and very bright, against the gruesome dark of bruises, old blood, and filth. "And considering that I have spent the longer if not the better part of my sixty-eight years learning to *get it* in every conceivable and inconceivable situation, I find that fact, in itself, extremely unsettling. And therefore," he went on, turning back to the vast heap of frozen beasts for another to hew, "I am leaving you tonight, to seek an answer outside of and beyond the bounds of human experience. I am going to visit the Nest of the Dark."

# Chapter 7

It made sense. Rudy had to admit that.

The Dark had a hive consciousness, a single sentience cloned into millions upon millions of protoplasmic, magic-imbued cells. What any Dark One learned, they all then knew. Thus, what any Dark One at any time in the past had learned was remembered by all, down through the ages, from the deepest gulfs of infinite time.

When the Dark had invaded Ingold's mind—in a fashion that Rudy preferred not to think about—Ingold had been, for a time, in touch with the mind of the Dark and had gained as much understanding of it as any human could deal with sanely. Once they had broken his resistance and absorbed his consciousness into their thoughts, he had understood the essence of their reality and the shape of their magic.

As a wizard, Rudy knew that the structures of certain types of crystal could absorb and retain both magic and memory. The ancient sages of the Times Before had certainly been able to ensorcel the smoke-gray record crystals to hold images and information and goodness knew what else, and to feed them back through the great black scrying table.

Therefore it made sense that the collective memories of the Dark would have soaked into the rock walls of their Nest, memory that stretched back in an unbroken thread to the days of the white, shambling apes of the warm savannahs, when first the shamans of those frightened tribes had evolved the single most important trait for survival: the ability, at need, to call fire from cold wood. And it made sense that one whose mind had been in the mind of the Dark could draw forth those memories from the rock and know them again.

The whole idea still gave Rudy the creeps.

"I miscalculated the depth of peril in which we stood after the Dark departed—miscalculated it badly." Ingold wrapped his surcoat more tightly about him and shivered in the hard cold of the utterly silent dark. It was the hour, in spring, when birds first begin to call their territories, halfway between midnight and morning. Not even a stirring of wind in the pine trees broke the silence. In the ebony lake of the bottomlands below the ridge where the old man stood with Rudy and Gil, small spots of amber campfire-light glowed, and beyond them, sickly streaks and patches of moony slunch.

"With all you've told me about the way weather is made, Gil, I should have guessed that six volcanoes erupting in the past year or so would have some effect. Yar is right. I had no business leaving the Keep."

"Like hell," Gil said. Her face, and the white quatrefoil emblems of the Guard, were pale blurs in the thin flicker of magelight that floated before their feet, and Rudy heard the faint whisper of fabric as she hooked her left thumb under her sword sash and shook back her hair. "Who else would have gone after the books? Who else could have found them, or retrieved them, from Penambra? Who else would have known which ones were most likely to help us, somewhere down the line? You can't do everything."

"It's still my fault."

"Maybe," Gil said. Then she added, in a conversational tone, "So what makes you think these gaboogoos present a greater threat than the possibility of another ice storm? Even one that hits in the daytime, when everybody's in the fields?"

"Christ!" Rudy said, appalled. "Another one? Can we get clobbered again this quick?"

"Beats the hell out of me," the wizard replied, an expression he'd picked up from his two friends. "Ice storms are a little-studied phenomenon, due to the fact that those areas subject to them tend to be completely uninhabited—or become so in very short order. As for the gaboogoos . . ."

He frowned, and shifted the straps of his pack on his shoulders: barely more than a bedroll, Rudy thought uneasily. Ingold could have helped himself to the summer's stores of Fargin Graw's bins and granneries, Guards or no Guards; that he hadn't was a measure of his concern about what rations would be like in the Keep in a couple of months. It didn't make Rudy feel any better.

In time he went on, "Thoth tells me that three men in the Gettlesand Keep went mad about an hour before the volcano erupted in the north and tried to kill the wizards Dakis and Kara. When prevented from doing so, they turned their knives upon one another. I have no idea what, if anything, that has to do with the gaboogoo, or with the power along the fault lines of the ground that caused the scrying crystals to fail, or with the thing that attacked Gil. I need information."

His blue eyes glinted under their long white brows, catching the witchlight's foxfire gleam and the far-off sparks within the circle of the broken palisade. The pine trees on the slope above them whispered, a sound like a heavy sigh that quickly passed; Ingold's heavy mantle and the fur surcoat over it stirred and lifted with the movement of the wind, then fell still.

"I've told Lord Sketh I'm remaining to help with the butchering for another day or two, until my powers return to what they were. Yar would send someone after me if he knew I was leaving, and aside from the nuisance of evading them in the woods, I know they can't spare the workers. I trust the two of you to lend what verisimilitude you can to my story."

"The two of us?" Rudy said, surprised, and glanced over at Gil. He saw her gaze cross Ingold's and lock. Her eyes held a shuttered expression; Ingold's, a shadow of deepest concern. It was almost unheard of for the wizard to go into any kind of danger without Gil watching his back, and traveling with his magic only the bruised shadow of its former strength certainly qualified.

Gil only said, "I don't think it would be a good idea right now for me to go with him," and looked away.

Ingold touched her chin, drew her face around so that his eyes met hers. After a moment she stepped close to him, pressed her uninjured cheek to his shoulder while he folded her in his arms. Rudy heard him whisper, "All will be well, Gilly, my love. All will be well."

Her face was like stone, but after a moment her body relaxed and she nodded. They kissed, like a spell against darkness.

Then he gave Rudy a breathtaking bear hug, kissed Gil again, and melted into the dark like a great, battered brown owl. Gil shook her head and said, "If there were a war, Ingold would blame himself for the invention of gunpowder. Or swords, in this case. Let's go, punk. It's a long way up the mountain tomorrow."

Only a small crowd was gathered on the steps of the Keep when the second party of foragers from the Settlements came into sight from among the trees, but they set up a ragged cheer nevertheless. The watchers permanently posted on the Tall Gates, the ruined towers at the head of the pass to the Arrow River gorge, must have signaled the Keep that they were coming. Even at that distance, Rudy identified Minalde, small and slim in her many-colored cotehardie; the black-uniformed cluster of Guards and the crimson scarecrow that was Bishop Maia; the Lords Ankres and Pnak—and Lord Brig Canthorion, who still retained his title and honors in spite of the fact that with the collapse of civilization, he'd cheerfully abandoned his position as scion of the highest family in the land to become a farmer and move in with Nedra Hornbeam. That would be Lady Sketh on the end there, in her gown of very expensive crimson wool, and Lady Ulas Canthorion . . .

And that small, dark form clinging to Alde's side would be Tir.

The smell of wood smoke hung over the whole of the valley, blue and heavy. Beyond the Keep, in the fields where the early wheat lay withered now on the turned black soil, long rows of wooden racks had been set up over snaky mounds of wood, and most of the population of the Keep could be seen, butchering the carcasses of the herds as they thawed. Farther up the Vale, beneath the blue scarf of the mountain shadows, Rudy could see a small party emerging from the woods carrying bundles that he knew were the hacked-up quarters of something they'd found, and baskets of dead foxes, rabbits, birds.

Lord Sketh lifted his hand in a wave and pointed to Rudy—there was another cheer. As they came close to the steps, Rudy met Minalde's eyes and saw them filled with tears, relief, the ache to run down the steps and into his arms . . .

She compromised by walking down, holding out both her hands for him to clasp. Someone in the crowd yelled "Kiss her!" and was shushed by a shocked murmur from the religious conservatives; the look in her eyes, raised to his, was almost as good. She said softly, "When we opened the doors of the Keep—when we found the children frozen, the world dead . . ."

The harrowing work, the horror and grief of the past four days, were marked on her face in the chalky pallor of fatigue and the black-circled redness of her swollen eyes. Her hair was still braided up for work. Looking down, he saw her hands were blistered.

"God, the herdkids," Rudy whispered, sickened again with the grief he had felt pulling the child Reppitep's body out of the snow, with the hammerblow of realization he had felt in the dooic cave. "Was Geppy . . . ?"

She nodded quickly, and wiped her eyes. In a soft voice, still excluding those gathered on the steps, she said, "And Linnet's daughter Thya."

"Thya?" The child had been barely Tir's age. "What the hell was Thya doing . . . ?"

Linnet was standing among the Guards, at Tir's side, holding his hand. Her face was like something cut out of stone, grief gouged into it as with acid. She saw Rudy's eyes come to her, and she stared at him, cold, bitter, hating.

"She sneaked out to spend the night with the herdkids," Alde whispered. "You know they all did, all the children in the Keep, one time or another. Linnet knew. She said it wouldn't do any harm." She forced her voice steady with an effort. "Rudy—"

"How's Tir taking it?"

In her eyes he saw that she'd feared all along the moment he'd ask this; her silence hit him in the pit of his belly and the way she avoided his glance. Quickly, almost involuntarily, he raised his head in time to see the child turn and disappear between the legs of the Guards, into the dark of the Keep's great doors.

Tir came to the meeting of the Keep Council, held once it grew too dark outside for those butchering and hanging the meat to smoke to see what they were doing. He sat beside his mother wearing a face like a little ivory mask, saying nothing; his eyes were dry but haunted by loss and uncomprehending grief. It was one thing, Rudy thought, to remember deaths of other friends, in other lifetimes, that whole succession of "little boys" whose awareness he sometimes shared. It was another to wake up one morning and find all your friends dead.

Tir would not meet his eyes.

"The first thing that needs to be done is to take an inventory of what we have," said Nedra Hornbeam briskly. "That way we'll know—"

"And why is this the first thing?" Lord Ankres demanded. "My goats presumably remain my goats, in death or in life, to dispose of as I please."

Hornbeam's son Lapith, a young man of startling good looks and unsurpassed conversational dullness, spoke up. He and close to two dozen other non-Council members had crowded into the Council chamber to speak for their segments of the Keep, their families, their neighbors. "And I suppose all those people out there helping you smoke the remains of your goats are doing so out of the goodness of their hearts?"

"Of course we must pool our resources." Maia of Thran, like an ugly but amiable scarecrow in badly dyed ecclesiastical red, raised one crippled hand. "In the face of this catastrophe—"

"There's no 'of course' about it," retorted Varkis Hogshearer, one of the gate-crashers, a pale-faced, rather stoop-shouldered man who seemed, to Rudy's eye, to be a whole lot cleaner than anybody else in the room, and didn't walk as if he ached in every joint of his body from working—which, to do him justice, Lord Ankres did. "We have rights to our property . . ."

*And you'd just as soon nobody searched your cells,* Rudy thought, recalling the man's propensity for buying up anything he could from anyone who was in need. He was also fairly certain that the moneylender was one of the several, like Koram Biggar of the grubby tribe in fifth north, who had for years been keeping chickens illegally in the Keep. *I can see my request to shake down the upper levels for gaboogoos is going to go over like an ejector seat on a roller coaster.*

"Our first concern," put in Enas Barrelstave pompously, "is the whereabouts of Lord Ingold. Saving your presence, Master Rudy, you and not he should have been the one to stay at the Settlements with Master Yar. I must say that he has demonstrated throughout a complete lack of responsibility—"

"Ingold stayed in the Settlements because trying to get back in time to warn them about the ice storm wiped every gram of magic out of his body," snapped Rudy, who had had just about enough of the squabbling of the Council for one day. Between his return to the Keep just before sunset, and this Council, he had spent weary hours, first calling up the magic from his own heart and bones to lay spells of preservation and Bugs-Go-Away on the vast piles of thawing meat—the first flies had arrived that afternoon—and then awkwardly skinning the hunks and quarters to be smoked. Sodden with fatigue, his muscles knifed with pain every time he moved. The meat was just beginning to go off, too, and the smell of it, in his clothing and that of everyone in the room, was something he felt he'd never be free of.

"So he figured since I was in better shape, I could come back up here, while even if he couldn't work magic for a couple of days, at least he could sense danger on the way. So he stayed down there."

"He did not!" A lumbering, heavy form in an expensive blue dress shoved her way to the fore next to Hogshearer—the moneylender's daughter, Scala, a girl of fourteen with unwashed hair and piggy dark eyes. "He ran away!"

Hogshearer turned his head quickly, eyes eager—Rudy saw the interest flare in other eyes as well: Ankres and Lady Sketh. "Who told you that, girl?"

"One of the men." There was smug delight in her voice at being the center of attention. In her blue gown she looked, if not exactly clean, at least like she hadn't been working, either. "One of the men said he saw Ingold run away from the camp the night before they left, and he never came back."

Everyone began talking at once, waving their arms. Koram Biggar said, "By Saint Bounty, I told you wizards couldn't be trusted!" and Janus of Weg's voice, under the general yammer, growled, "Birch the lying little—"

"Is that true?" Minalde's voice, soft as silver bells, seemed to cut through the clamor, as if she spoke to Rudy and Rudy alone. Her eyes were deeply troubled.

Rudy didn't want to, but before those blue eyes, he could do nothing but nod. "He had his reasons," he said as renewed shouting rose like the roar of the sea. "And if you think heading out alone, without magic, into the river valley these days is safer than sticking with a bunch of armed guys in what's left of a fort, remind me never to go camping with *you*, pal."

"Then I suppose we need to ask," Bannerlord Pnak said quietly, "why he departed without coming here to our aid? And for that matter, why it was that he—and you, Master Rudy—survived, and everyone else at the Settlements perished?"

"Nice goin', punk." Gil raised her head from the scroll she was deciphering when, many hours later, Rudy finally returned to the workroom. She'd collected every glowstone in the place and grouped them around her on the big oak table in the middle of the room, and the upside-down light made her thin face skull-like and odd in its masses of unbound black hair. She'd bathed and gotten someone in the Guards to change the dressing on her hurt cheek, but the bruises all around the area still looked dark and angry. "You know Pnak and Barrelstave have been itching for years to put Tir under a Council of Regency—ever since Alde socialized seed wheat instead of letting people speculate in it. If they can discredit Ingold—"

"Don't start on me, spook." He dropped in the corner the bundle of his grubby traveling clothes he'd changed out of in Alde's rooms and went to stand beside her. "Lemme have a look at that."

She turned her face obediently, unmoving while he peeled back the dressing. The bruises were fading some, but the bite itself didn't look like it was healing. Malnutrition, Rudy thought. Spells of healing, even those of a master like Ingold, could only go so far without nutrients to work from.

Still, there was something about the discoloration that he didn't like.

"You manage to get in touch with Thoth?" she asked, and Rudy nodded.

The interview—after Alde had slipped into sleep in his arms, long after the shouting in the Council chamber was done—had troubled him, partly for the obvious reasons and partly with a kind of subconscious worry, a tip-of-the-tongue sense of something deeply wrong. The Gettlesand mage had looked as harried as it was possible for that sardonic, vulturine scribe to look, and although the sky beyond the windows of his rockpile hermitage—built against the outer wall of the old Black Rock Keep, for the wizards there did not as a rule sleep within the Keep walls—still held light, there had been an oddly blenched or faded appearance to the whole image, like a photograph badly exposed.

Thoth had disclaimed knowledge of gaboogoos—pronouncing the word in much the way a housewife might remove a dead mouse from the family casserole—but his yellow eyes had narrowed, and his spindle-knuckled fingers stirred in the gray sleeves of his robe. "The dogs have barked all around the Keep, night after night for a fortnight past," he said. "Gray and Nila, when they spoke to us for the last time from the slopes of the Devil's Grandmother, said they had seen some kind of creature there."

"Gray and Nila?" Rudy recalled the two women, part of the original Wizards' Corps in the war against the Dark. "What were they doing up on the Devil's Grandmother? Wasn't that the volcano that . . . ?"

"They followed the . . . the track, the spoor, of the power we sensed in the ground," Thoth said. "They were on the western slope of the mountain when it erupted. They spoke of things there, pale creatures that walked through Wards and illusion as if they were not there, whose tracks they found 'round their camp every morning."

Rudy shivered, remembering the ghostly shapes in the dark among the pines. He found himself hoping that wherever Ingold was, he was watching his back.

Hesitantly, because like everybody but Ingold he was a little afraid of Thoth, he said, "Could somebody—some wizard we don't know about—have been . . . I dunno, tapping the energy of the volcano, maybe? Drawing on it, the way Ingold or you would draw on the energy within the earth-lines or the stars?"

"Considering that he or she would have had to be directly on top of the volcano to derive benefit from such an exercise," the Serpentmage replied dryly, "such a source of power would have obvious limitations. And what wizard would be operating in the wilderness, without contact with human communities? Still," he added, tilting his head in a fashion that made him more than ever resemble some strange wise member of the buzzard clan, "it would not do harm to speak to Shadow of the Moon and ask him whether the shamans of the plains have heard aught."

The insectile fingers refolded themselves into another pattern. In the virulent light the old man's sunken features seemed skull-like, worn and weary under the bald curve of his brow. "It is an ill time," Thoth said at length. "The Raiders move down from the far north, and settlers from the Alketch have been plaguing our herds. They say fever and civil war ride unchecked through those countries, that famine rules on the Emperor's throne and the cities have become infernos of lawlessness, blood, and smoke. Tirkenson deems it too perilous to send cattle toward Sarda Pass to your aid. It were folly, he says, to waste the lives of our riders only to feed our enemies. Brother Wend and the Lady Ilae have agreed to journey to Renweth, that you may not be without magic. It is true that we have been remiss; someone should have gone to you long ere this. Will this serve?"

"Well, Alde may get back with you on the cattle." Rudy rubbed his chin, still smarting from the razor, and glanced over at Minalde's sleeping form. "But thank Wend and Ilae, and tell 'em they'll be more than welcome. You guys had any luck with finding mageborn kids? Ingold and I have been watching . . ."

He fell silent, remembering that the Keep was over a dozen children shorter than it had been a week ago.

Thoth shook his gleaming head. "We gave the Dark too little credit in that," he said softly. "I begin to wonder whether we do these . . . gaboo-goos, as you call them . . . enough."

*Another damn thing to worry about,* Rudy had thought as the crystal faded. *I'll have to hire a secretary to keep track of them.*

Standing now beside Gil in the deep late-night silence of the Keep, he remembered the conversation again, and his uneasiness returned. Walking back to the workroom through the ebon stillness, the images of the gaboogoos had returned to him, the tall, vicious, palely glowing monstrosities that had pursued him over the mountainside, and the little knee-high creature that had stood in the doorway of that room on fifth north, eyeless head turned in his direction as if it could, in fact, see.

"So who's this Saint Bounty?"

"Huh?" Rudy snapped back to reality. He realized she and Ingold had been gone for nearly two months. He'd kept them up on gossip and events, but there were always things he hadn't thought to mention. "Oh, him."

He moved aside one of the terra-cotta pots in which Ingold had been nursing seedling roses for years. Only two varieties had survived the downfall of civilization, and one of them didn't look any too robust. Rudy had been babysitting them all spring, feeding them little bits of stinking fish and conjuring miniature spells to keep them warm.

"His statues have been showing up all over the north half of the fifth level, around the Biggars and the Wickets and the other trailer-park types up there. I don't know who started it. Fat guy with a basket of food—just who you'd figure to get popular when we're all looking at starvation. You're the saint expert."

"Well, yes, I am." Her eyes were thoughtful, cold and very blue in the dazzle of the glowstones. "And I've never heard of the guy. I asked Maia. He said there was no Saint Bounty in the official calendar, nor was there any local saint of that name he knows about. And I don't like the color of his robe."

"His *robe*?" Rudy had gotten used to Gil's trick of fixing her attention on bizarre tangents, clues visible to a scholar that even a wizard might miss. It was one of the things she had in common with Ingold, who was popularly considered to be slightly mad. But even so . . .

"The iconography of saints is very stylized." Gil carefully rolled up the scroll she had been studying, tied it and carried it and her notes across to the big iron-bound oak cupboard. Rudy could see that her notes were almost entirely in the flowing bookhand of the Wathe, interspersed here and there with English, which neither of them used much anymore. "It's a teaching tool for the illiterate. There's a reason behind every image, every color, every *tchotchke* . . ."

"Gil-Shalos?" Shadow moved in the doorway that led through to the Guards' watchroom, the pale flower of a quatrefoil on dark clothing, and long ivory braids with dark fragments of bone woven into them, framing a narrow face. The Icefalcon came in, carrying something in a scrap of burlap through which dirty brown fluid had soaked. If the whole Keep hadn't been faintly redolent of salvaged carrion, Rudy would have had more warning of his approach. "I had to wrench these from the Council's regulators of meat. I trust you're sufficiently grateful."

"Kill anybody over it?" Gil carried it to the table.

"And have to clean my sword hilt again?"

Gil grinned and picked apart the wrappings.

"Yuckers," Rudy said.

"Up your nose, punk." She turned one of the hacked-off limbs thoughtfully. It looked like the front leg of a wolverine, but there was something badly wrong with the proportion of it: too long in bone, the claws widened into short spades. "You seen tracks of this one?"

The White Raider nodded, hand resting lightly on the hilt of his sword. "The whole valley went under snow during the storm, but I saw this track during the winter, though I never saw the things themselves. Perhaps three, maybe four, all told, in the Vale."

"Always near the slunch?"

The Icefalcon nodded. He looked little the worse for the climb up from the Settlements, nor for days of hunting the woods for storm-kills. He carried two or three fresh bruises, from that evening's training session. Rudy privately suspected he was an android.

"I told Ingold of it, during the snows." He folded his arms and looked down over Gil's shoulder as she sorted through the other objects in the cloth: paws and limbs, mostly, but there was the head of something that might have been a woodchuck.

Gil considered the remains for a moment more, then went to fetch the remains of the thing that had attacked her in Penambra from the cupboard where they were stored. Rudy glanced across the table at the Guard and asked, "That wasn't you who saw Ingold leave the settlement last night, was it?" If anyone had been able to see through the wizard's illusions, it would have been the Icefalcon, but it was very unlike that cold-blooded young killer to mention such a thing, and certainly not to the daughter of Varkis Hogshearer.

The Icefalcon shook his head. "His name was spoken among the men today on the way up the mountain," he said. He moved a glowstone out of Gil's tidy circle, making patterns of them around the sticky bundle and its horrid contents. "Many things were said of him, most of them stupid, but no one spoke of his leaving the camp."

"Then how the hell did—"

"What about insects in the slunch?" Gil came back to the table, set the crusted hempen wrappings of the Penambra thing down with a sodden thwack. "The slunch-worms don't seem to attack crops."

"I've seen them," the Icefalcon said. He had a very soft voice, light like a young boy's, and seldom spoke above a whisper. His silvery eyes were without expression as he studied Gil's face, but he asked, "Are you well? I'll be returning to the Settlements at dawn. Everything in Manse and Carpont will be well and truly rotting, but there will be seed grain at least, and metal, do we get there before bandits do. Will you be all right?"

"Fine." It was a lie. Rudy could see that and so could the Icefalcon, for the tall warrior put his hand to the uninjured side of Gil's face and turned it to the light.

He stood for a time, considering her, resembling a long-limbed pale cheetah but slightly less human. Then he turned to Rudy and said, "Look after her." He melted away into the shadows. At no time, Rudy realized, had he used his right hand or moved it out of reach of his sword hilt.

"I really am fine." Gil's voice was very small. She had turned her back on him, her head half bowed as she sorted through a revolting collection of animal parts with her dark hair half hiding her face. In her baggy, too-big black clothing, she had a fragile look, like an alley cat in a hard winter. There was a tension in her, too, as if she were perpetually braced, perpetually fighting something or ready to fight something; a look of pain, a series of lines around eyes and brows and mouth, that went past the wound on the side of her face.

Her tone returned to business almost with her next breath. "Have you had time to look at any of this?"

"In between my painting class and ballet practice, you mean?"

In the quick beauty of her grin he saw the shy girl peek out from behind the warrior's armor, then duck away to safety, again. As if half ashamed of appearing human, she turned her attention quickly back to the mess before her. "Ingold collected most of this during the salvage. The Icefalcon's helped me a lot in woodcraft, but you're the naturalist. Any of it look familiar?"

Rudy shook his head. "That's the whole problem, spook. Like the old man said, nobody's ever seen any of those critters before."

He stepped close to look, nevertheless, drawing his knife and scraping at the slimy meat. Under Ingold's guidance he'd boiled and disassembled and reassembled dozens of animal carcasses the way he used to break down cars, fascinated by the delicate interfitting of muscle and sinew and bone.

"I was a historian, not a biologist," Gil said, probing with her fingers. "But if you're an economic determinist, you pick up a little bit of science when you study stuff like climatology and demographics. Look at this one, the way it's put together. Look at the foot bones and the elbow joint."

"Weird." Rudy turned the limb over in sticky fingers. "You got the back foot of this thing?"

She produced it from another corner of the table, scraped to the tendons. He held it close to the clustered glowstones, then summoned a brilliance of witchlight around him as well. "I've never seen this kind of deformation in the center of the bone shank. Look, it's on every one of the long bones, from the radius right down to the carpals. But from the joints I'd say this was some kind of rabbit."

"That's what I thought, too." Gil perched on a corner of the table, wiped her hands on the corner of a rag. "Now, that furry slug thing Ingold found in the woods after the storm—when you skin it down and chop out the fat, you find leg bones. Here's the skull. It's really deformed, look here. Same texture as the long bones of the rabbit, but most of that deformation's cartilage. Look at the teeth."

"Ferret," Rudy said immediately. "Holy cow-pies." He set the greasy skull down next to the deformed rabbit feet. "But that takes thousands of years. Thousands of generations."

"Hundreds of thousands," Gil said. She crossed to fetch a basin and ewer from the sideboard, dunked her hands in the chilly water. The magelight showed up the harsh lines around her eyes, turned the bruises livid along cheekbone and chin. "Even with a really intensive program of selective breeding—like if you're trying to breed down to a teacup poodle—you're looking at fifteen or twenty years at the very least."

Rudy shook his head wonderingly. "Fifteen or twenty years' work for a teacup poodle. Some people need to get a life."

The wound made her grin lopsided, and it faded quickly.

"So you're saying . . . what? Somebody's breeding these things? Who the hell would do that?" He'd said that before, he thought. Recently. Gray and Nila, standing on the slopes of the Devil's Grandmother . . . The deep pulse of anger in the ground . . .

"It's not that simple." She touched one of the roses, came back to his side. "You feel the quake a few hours ago?"

He shook his head. A few hours ago he'd been in bed, half blind with exhaustion, Minalde weeping in his arms.

"It wasn't a big one." She nodded toward the scrying table. "Here in the Keep you could barely feel it at all. See if it was caused by another volcano someplace."

It took a long time. Hours—Rudy wasn't sure. Though it could not be used for communication, the scrying table's range was greater than a small stone's, and the images that stirred within the central crystal were larger, clearer, tiny landscapes that absorbed the mind. Using the table, scenes were visible to Rudy that would have been impossible to see in a smaller gem, people and places appearing sometimes without prior knowledge or any will of the scryer, displaying things unknown.

Staring into the glimmering depths, Rudy let his mind drift, first infinitely deep, then out across the arid wastes of Gettlesand and the burned-out, ash-white ruin of upland forest on the slopes of the Devil's Grandmother; over the Bones of God and the Sawtooth Mountains; then out to the Seaward Mountains, wreathed still by the limmerance of forgotten spells. He saw green icebergs floating in oceans the color of asphalt; endless continents of slow-moving glacial pack. Warriors rode in a fragile line below the white cliffs of glacier; islands smoked in the heaving sea. At last he saw in the south the tall cordillera of some unknown land, pale with drought and unwonted cold, plastered with unbroken miles of pus-colored slunch that stirred with uneasy, obscene movement. The trees on the mountainside were burning for miles, and dust and heat roiled skyward like the mushroom clouds of a holocaust of hydrogen bombs. The sky was black. Endless miles of tarry, starless, daytime black.

"Got it."

He looked up, aware for the first time that his head ached. Gil had tidied away the bones, save for two or three sets, and was making notes again. By the heap of wax tablets at her elbow, she had been doing this for hours.

"Somewhere way the hell in the south, maybe even on some other continent. Big. The ash-fall looks about the size of Texas."

The square, sensitive lips tightened to a single cold line. "That's how many this year? Six? Eight? That we know about?"

"Something like that."

"I wish I knew the statistical likelihood of that many volcanic eruptions in six months—or in thirty-six months, because the first couple of eruptions Ingold commented on were about three years ago. The summer before we found the first slunch up in Gae."

"Makes sense," Rudy said with a shrug. "Wherever it comes from, slunch is a cold-weather thing. The ice storm ripped it to hell at ground zero, but it didn't kill it. It was like you'd left a piece of plastic out overnight. Nedra Hornbeam tells me there's patches of it growing all the way down the pass now, little spots like that . . ." His fingers circled to something the size of a U.S. silver dollar. "She thinks the wind carried it, but I don't know."

Gil shook her head. "It's the cold, not physical seeding. And something else the Icefalcon told me: the tracks he's seen around the slunch, the really weird ones, are mostly rabbit—" She touched the aberrant bones. "—and ferret—" Her thin fingers brushed another. "—and wolverine."

Rudy was silent, filled with the sense he had so often in talking to Ingold, of following a dancing light over unseen ground in darkness. As if someone had handed him a pile of jigsaw puzzle pieces, which put together would form a message he really didn't want to read.

Around them the Keep was settled into the deep-night watch, when only the smallest sounds murmured in the black glass corridors: the light tread and harness-creak of a Guard's passing, the murmur of water in the pipes. The scurry of rats or the swift flick of a cat sliding serpentwise around corners in pursuit. Darkness filled every crevice, like a liquid filling up the whole Keep from the crypts to the attics where the pumps churned with eternal, sourceless power; darkness and the breathing of sleepers, though Rudy was conscious that many within those walls wept in their dreams.

"Rudy," Gil said softly, "trust me when I say this sounds as weird to me as it does to you. Maybe weirder, because I don't know enough about magic to know whether it can be done or not. I really hope I am crazy, because if I'm not, I think we're all in real trouble. And I may be crazy," she added, rubbing the bridge of her nose between thumb and forefinger, her forehead suddenly creased with pain. "I feel so . . . so strange lately."

She shook her head, pushing the strangeness—and whatever it implied—aside. "But be that as it may . . . Doesn't it seem to you that somebody or something is using magic to terraform the world?"

# Chapter 8

Two nights later Rudy dreamed about the Bald Lady.

He recognized her, as he'd recognized the Guy with the Cats, from the record crystals: a tall, thin woman in a plain sheath of white gauze that fitted her rangy form closely. Though it was nearly transparent and left her flat breasts bare, he found her no more erotic than a ghost might have been. Her head was shaved, as it was in the crystal's image, and, like the Guy with the Cats', patterned with a line of blue tattooing. She wore a dark blue cloak over her bare arms, and where her fingers curled around its edge, the blue lace of tattoo marked them like a glove.

She was walking in the Keep. There was no mistaking the black, sleek hardness of the walls, the uniformity of the square doorways. Rudy even thought he recognized one of the snail-shell spirals of stair that led to the crypts below. She walked haloed in the white splendor of glow-stones; once, she passed a fountain that sparkled with that clear radiance. She was alone. He thought there was no one else in the Keep, in all those vast black spaces—no one at all.

Her face was calm but filled with unutterable grief.

*She has the answer,* he thought. *The answer to the whole thing.* How he knew this, he didn't know, except that he knew it was true.

She had the key.

He thought he was standing at the foot of a stair—first level? Upper crypts? He wasn't sure, the Keep had changed too much over the years— watching her come down the spiraling steps toward him, her blue cloak moving around her, he saw there were tears in her eyes. Her face was the face of death borne alone.

*But she can't die, she can't go away!* he thought frantically. *She knows the answer to all this!* He tried to speak to her, tried to stop her, to ask her where she was going, but she passed him, and in the dream he could feel the warmth of her cloak contrasting to the cold of the air when

116

it brushed against his arm, and he could smell the cardamom and vanilla of her perfume.

She walked away from him, the glowstones picking up the midnight sheen of her cloak, the smooth line of her shoulders, the curve of her shaven head, as she vanished into the dark.

*R*udy. Ingold's voice spoke very clearly in his mind.

Rudy came awake at once. He'd been expecting this, and groped under his pillow for his scrying stone. Almost instinctively he knew it was early in the night, the Dancers, the Demon, the Star-Lord with his shining belt, not yet clearing the ice-tipped tusks of the Rampart Range. The witchlight he Summoned rested like a pale blue Tinker Bell on his hay-stuffed pillow, illuminating the scuffy patterns of the ancient brick wall that cut his own little half cell off the Guards' storeroom and seeming to impart a secret significance to the pattern of faded lights and darks of the quilt on his bed.

"I'm here, man."

"And I'm here," Ingold said. "By the Four Ladies."

Past his shoulder Rudy could just make out the weathered shapes of the standing-stones that dominated the high meadow at the top of the Vale, blue dolomite found nowhere in the mountains: three on their feet, one lying among them, dead of grief, it was said, for her child. Though the stars burned faint and yellow through the thin overcast, their light glimmered in firefly threads on the glacier's towering wall. "Can I bring you anything?"

"Just some food." His white hair hung in strings around his face, which was bruised black and gulched with strain. Rudy wondered when he'd last eaten or slept.

"I'm on my way."

Gil was tossing, breathing fast, in the narrow bed in Ingold's room, but she woke before Rudy could reach out to her with a spell of quiet. Her hand went to her sword and Rudy said quickly from the doorway, "It's me, spook," Summoning just enough witchlight so she could see him. Though he doubted that any Guard would comment on his slipping out of the Keep to meet Ingold, a couple of Lord Ankres' warriors and one of Lord Sketh's were in the watchroom as well—sarcastically rehashing

Lady Sketh's latest demands upon her hapless spouse—and Rudy didn't believe in handing anyone any more ammunition than they already had.

Gil rose and dressed without a word, while Rudy retreated to the workroom to wait for her. He stretched out his senses to pick up Melantrys' always hilarious imitations of Barrelstave's pontifications and Hogshearer's incessant whining, but it was clear even to him, from remarks the Sketh warrior made, that someone—probably Lady Sketh—had been twisting the interpretations of Ingold's motives and movements. "You got to admit, nine hundred people, near enough, died—and him the only one that survived?"

"He's a frigging wizard, you dolt. Of course he'd survive. And he's Ingold Inglorion. He'd survive if the Earth fell on his head."

"Then why didn't he save the others?"

Gil emerged slinging on a thick sheepskin coat over her black uniform. From a cupboard she took a satchel of the bread and meat that she'd been sequestering from her own meager rations—with contributions from Rudy and the Icefalcon—for two days now. Minalde had had her way, and placed all food and all seed in the Keep under guard; they were still fighting in Council about distribution, and Rudy knew for a fact that Varkis Hogshearer was the center of a spanking black-market trade. Rudy had checked and rechecked the hydroponics crypts—including Gil's suggestion about making sure the light there was full-spectrum—and it was obvious the yields were going to be too small to make much of a difference.

Another thing to worry about.

And Tir hadn't spoken to him since his return.

Only when they were out under the sable blanket of the night sky, Gil holding to Rudy's cloak, her drawn sword in her free hand, did Rudy ask, "You okay?" There was no need to whisper. A trace of glamour had gotten them past the door Guards, and the wide-flung patrols had reported no sign of Raider or bandit anywhere near the Vale as of twilight. They had shut the Keep doors behind them, and in a weird way the Vale felt safe—safe in the moveless pall of death that lingered there still, like the oddly sculpted cones of unmelted snow remaining where the woods' shadows lay thick. No owl hooted, nor cried wolf, coyote, or any living thing. Their bodies had all been taken up by scavenging parties— stripped, broken, smoked, and stored. Rudy's mageborn eyes made out the black ranks of pine and cottonwood above the path, limp heaps of cold-killed summer vegetation rotting around their feet.

"Nightmares." There was casual dismissal in Gil's voice.

"About that thing in Penambra?"

"Yeah." Her tone was cool, the way it was when she was in pain and didn't want to talk about it. She'd left off covering the wound in her face. It still wasn't healing. "Some. No. I don't know." In the stillness he could hear the creak of her boot leather, the swish of the satchel against the hide coat, the faint scrunching of his own boots on the pine mast underfoot. Wind breathed a soughing sound from the trees and then fell still. Before them, St. Prathhes' Glacier stretched in a pearly rampart, nearly two hundred feet high, poised between the black teeth of the rocks.

"Jewels," Gil said finally, but she sounded puzzled. "I dreamed about . . . jewels."

"You mean a treasure?"

"No. It was inside a jewel. Things that looked like jewels." The steady pressure of her grip on his cloak altered as her hand moved a little, a fumbling gesture, as if trying to express something she wasn't sure how to envision. "They hurt Ingold," she said after a long time. "These three . . . things. Made of jewels. They were playing the flute to the thing that sleeps in the pool. Now and then things would crawl out of the slunch in the pit in front of them. Blood . . ." She frowned, like a sleeper disturbed by incongruity but unable to wake.

"Are they up at the Nest?" Rudy pitched his words to be no more than a murmur in the dark, so as not to bring her away from the borderlands where she could still see down into her dream.

"I don't think so."

"In the Keep, maybe?"

She thought about that for a long time. "They're in this jewel," she said at last. "It's full of mist, and there's a statue there without any eyes, staring ahead into the darkness. But there's light where they are, only it isn't really light."

Light that was not really light flickered ahead of Rudy, a wizard's signal among the mourning humps of the stones. Five years ago Gil had shown Rudy the trail over which Ingold had led her from the Nest in what had once been a city of the Dark, and that trail was gone now, swallowed by St. Prathhes' inexorable advance. Great heaps of wanly glittering ice lay all along the glacier's feet, broken from the wall above, and all the ground between the Four Ladies and what had been the trail head lay under a sheet of water, milky in the night.

The miniature elfwood of dwarf alder that had grown hereabouts was dying. One end of the meadow was leprous with slunch.

"Ingold?" called Rudy softly. "You there, man?"

"As much of me as is left after coming over the glacier." What Rudy thought was one of the Four Ladies moved, and the frost he thought he'd seen dislimned itself into wispy hair and an unkempt beard. Ingold levered himself to his feet using his staff. Fingers and palms were bandaged, the rags that wrapped them crusted with blood. "Did you bring food?"

"You want an appetizer first, or the salad?" Gil handed him the satchel.

"Appetizer, please." Ingold limped painfully between the rocks, leading them to a hollow under the shoulder of a granite dome. He was soaked to the thighs from wading through the lake of meltwater; streaks of mud and niter mottled his robe. The hollow was about the size of a restaurant booth and only three or four feet high, and from its entrance the whole of the Vale could probably be seen by day. As it was, only the faintly glowing beds of slunch stood out in the darkness, islands in an iron sea.

The feeble witchlight on the tip of Ingold's staff brightened somewhat, to illuminate the little chamber. The wizard sank to the ground and opened the bundle Gil had brought. "I do hope there's an entire ox in here, with peppercorns and just the slightest suspicion of garlic," he said in a hopeful voice.

"Darn!" Gil smacked her forehead with the heel of her hand, as if she'd only just noticed, "you turned into a person again! I brought stuff for a falcon!"

"Gillifer, my dear," Ingold sighed with feigned patience, and held up the few scraps of what looked like road-kill, "you really need to write these things down."

"What kind of wine you want with that, man?" Rudy ducked low under the slope of the ceiling, dropped cross-legged at the old man's side and uncorked the small bottle of what was called Blue Ruin around the Keep.

"All of it in the entire world."

There was a time of silence.

At length Rudy asked, "The Dark tell you anything?"

The wizard's eyes glinted under scarred lids. "I didn't telephone them, you know." He leaned his shoulders carefully against the cold, dimpled rock of the wall, wiped the last bits of grease from his fingers, and examined the picked bones regretfully. Gil had managed to cadge an apple, one of the last from the previous winter. The wizard had devoured it core and all.

He sighed and rubbed the bridge of his nose, as if to massage away the ache of the old wounds. "It was more like . . . oh, sorting through diaries or looking through the record crystals, trying to piece together information for which there is no context. Like dreaming someone else's dreams."

Rudy said nothing. He had gone down into a deserted Nest once before the Dark Ones had departed from this world, and two or three times afterward, and the images he had carried back with him were those of endless caverns of limestone sheathed in the withered remains of brown moss, strewn with the bones of the Dark Ones' pitiful herds. Ceilings, walls, stalactites and stalagmites had all been polished silken by the crawling feet of untold numbers of the Dark, the rock discolored into a thousand hues of yellow and green and blue by the action of their body acids. He didn't like to think of the old man's mind leaving his body to walk into the places where the shapeless ones had left their memories.

Didn't like the thought of what form those dreams might take.

Almost as if speaking to himself, Ingold went on, "Part of the problem is that those we seek could not exist in the same world as the Dark. Like the Dark—or like the Dark in the end became—they were travelers, Void-walkers. As the Dark Ones eventually moved on to another world, so these came here, long before either the Dark Ones or humankind arose. The world was cold then, bitter, iron cold, nearly waterless and locked under sheets of ice miles thick. Strange things moved over the surface of its ground, or swam weightless in its air. Things that crystallized out of its few pools and streams or grew like sponges from the rock. A cruel world, but it suited Them."

He frowned, gazing out at the glimmering precipice of the ice and the dim speckle of reflected witchlight on the thread of the stream.

"How long ago?" Rudy's voice was almost a whisper, and Ingold shook his head.

"The Dark didn't know. The Travelers came and had their eons of dominion, and sank first into sleep and then into death when the Dark Ones' furthest ancestors were no more than grubs clinging to the hot volcanic vents on the ocean floors. The stars were different then, the sun weak behind a universe of dust."

His voice, rough-textured and deep, seemed far away, speaking of those dreams that were not his dreams, as if he were barely aware of the two friends who sat at his side. Perhaps, Rudy thought, he was not.

"This I . . . saw in dreams, lying on the rocks in the darkness. I don't even know whether what I saw was true or only what the Dark believed to have taken place. The awareness of the Dark is not like the awareness of humankind.

"The Dark were aware that the final remnant of all those things still existed, deep within caverns wrought of ice, beneath the bones of an eternal mountain. The Dark hated cold and kept their distance, but they heard the songs of Those Who Wait."

He shook his head, unfocused, gazing still into the alien dream.

"They sang of waiting, to the music of a chiten flute. Eternal sureness, treading a black eternal road, waiting for the world to become what it had been once again."

Rudy shifted uncomfortably on his hunker-bones. Wind made catfeet on the milky glacier lake and brought the smell of ice and high places. "And that's happening?"

"The current cold cycle has been enough to wake them up, anyway." Gil's voice chipped into the dense texture of the Dark Ones' dreams, her long, thin fingers twisting dark curls away from the unhealed mess of her cheek. Ingold's eyes opened, bright and present once again. "For whatever reason, Those Who Wait have decided to quit waiting."

"Gil's sort of figured out what's happening," Rudy said, and quickly outlined her theory of terraforming. "We think the gaboogoos have to be growing out of the slunch," he said at the end. "They disregard magic, the same way magic doesn't touch the slunch. Gil thinks that after animals eat it, slunch starts to metabolize them from the inside. But why the critters are mutating into the forms they are is beyond me."

"Is it?" Ingold blinked at him, appearing not in the slightest surprised. "I suppose it would be." He fell silent then, hands folded before his mouth, witch-blue shadows deepening in the lines of his face as he gazed back into the night, as if in the blackness he could see again the Dark Ones' dreams.

"You knew about that?" Rudy demanded, miffed.

"Of course I knew it. I saw it," Ingold said. "In the vision. In the Nest. I saw it, but it seemed . . . without explanation. Insane. I can't tell you how pleased I am to discover that I'm not mad. Trust you, Rudy, and you, my Gil."

He put out his hand and touched her wrist, and Rudy, who was looking in that direction, saw their eyes meet—saw the old man freeze. Ingold didn't flinch, but his eyes flared wide as he looked with shock and hurt and astonishment into Gil's face.

Rudy didn't know what Ingold saw there, as Gil returned the wizard's gaze. In the shadows her eyes were uncertain, maybe doubting what Ingold detected as well, but he saw her mouth alter, and she turned her face quickly aside. In Ingold's gaze there was, for a moment, only shock, as if he had stumbled upon some new and dreadful knowledge. For a moment, before the wizard also looked away, Rudy thought he could see that shock followed by a grief past bearing, and bitterest pain.

Gil said nothing. Her stillness was like a bent bow whose arrow aimed at a human heart. Maybe, Rudy thought—he did not know why—maybe her own.

Ingold drew breath to speak, but let the words leak away unvoiced. Whatever they were, they hung on the air, they and whatever he saw or thought he saw in Gil's face. It was a terrible silence, and Rudy, rather hastily, blithered into the breach.

"Uh—so where are these guys waiting? The Dark tell you that?"

There was a sleight-of-hand, a shift of expression, as if Ingold whisked away whatever he was feeling behind exasperation: "The Dark didn't *tell* me anything. They're not down there, you know." Rudy thought there was relief in his voice. "But yes. I know."

The white brows pulled down over his nose, and pain returned to the deep-scored lines of his face. "There's a mountain called Saycotl Xyam, the Mother of Winter; the last great peak of the Spine of the Serpent, the cordillera of the continent, that sinks into hills for a time and rearises as these mountains and the Bones of God in Gettlesand. Saycotl Xyam guards the plain of Hathyobar, the heartland of the Empire of Alketch, where the Emperor's city of Khirsrit rises on the shores of the lake of Nychee. They say the glaciers on its shoulders have never melted in all of human knowledge, in all of time. The mountain itself is said to have a core of ice, though none have been there to see."

"They're there," Gil whispered, and Ingold's eyes returned to hers. It seemed to Rudy that they both stared at the same thing, both looked into the same blue depths of jewel, understanding one another—what Ingold had seen in the Dark Ones' dreams and she in her own poison-tainted blood. Understanding to the cores of their souls.

"Yes." His lips moved; there was no sound.

"Three mages making images with the music of the flute."

"Yes."

"Their magic . . ." She started to say something else, then shuddered and averted her eyes, as if from something she could not bear to see. When she spoke again, it was only to say, "And you're gonna have to go down there, aren't you?"

He nodded. "Yes."

"The Alketch?" Enas Barrelstave puffed out his heavy cheeks and scowled solemnly, the high ruff of his shirt giving him the appearance of a very pink pudding balanced on an elaborately folded napkin. As the finer fabrics of the age before the Dark deteriorated with time, Gil had pointed out to Rudy how the hereditary nobles—the lords and bannerlords—had become more conscious of keeping the well-off commoners in the Keep from dressing like them; Barrelstave's shirt ruffles were drawing an angry glare from Lady Sketh, who had intruded herself into the Council as her husband's permanent "guest."

"I'm afraid that's out of the question."

"Out of the question?" Rudy's voice scaled up in disbelief. "We're talking about a . . . a force of magic that's going to destroy the world as we know it, and you're saying out of the question?"

"I still don't see how—even if such beings as you say Lord Ingold described to you do exist, for which I'd like to see a little more proof—" Lord Sketh began, and his wife dove in to finish his sentence for him.

"I still don't see how a volcano erupting in Gettlesand is any threat to us here."

"We have to have some priorities," Lapith Hornbeam added reasonably. All around the long pine conference table, flanked by black-drummed columns that ran the length of the big chamber, the various representatives of the Keep nodded agreement. "Yes, if there is such a problem, I agree that it has to be taken care of, but you must concede right now that it's more important to acquire stock. Parties can be sent downriver beyond Willowchild to gather hay, but my mother has come up with a plan—"

"I don't have to concede anything of the goddamn kind!"

"How does he know about these things in the Alketch, anyway?"

"It isn't that we don't believe him," added Philonis Weaver, of the second level north, a kindly woman who didn't look like she was going to survive the next frost, much less the next Ice Age. "It's just that there are critical things that we need now, things that only a wizard can provide. We need to have someone who can tell us if another of those terrible storms is on the way—"

"Oh, surely not!" Lady Sketh interrupted. "There's only been one of them, and now that it's over, and summer is approaching, it's unlikely there'll be another."

"I can goddamn guarantee you," Rudy said in exasperation, "that there's gonna be more ice storms, *and* no harvest, *and* nothing to eat, unless Ingold takes care of what's causing this!" He glared around the Council chamber, uneasily aware of the way Barrelstave's glance crossed that of Lord Sketh, and the speculative way in which both of them watched Tir.

"Well, perhaps you could inform Lord Ingold, when he returns," Lord Ankres said in his slow, dry voice, "that . . . when *does* he return?"

"I personally move," Bannerlord Pnak added angrily, "that when he does, he be reprimanded for deserting us in the first place. He has his responsibilities, after all—"

"Which he should have taken into account—"

"Second to that motion—"

"Now, my mother's plan—"

"Yikes and double yikes." Rudy closed the door to the Council chamber softly behind him and fell into step with Gil. The illusion he'd left in his place should keep most of them thinking he was still present for at least forty minutes if nobody spoke to it, and on their record it was unlikely anyone would.

"I take it they didn't think much of letting Ingold go south." Gil kept close to his side, sheltered by the umbrella of his illusions. They crossed through the white splotches of glowstone light and through inky shadow where those with business in the Keep jostled shoulders with them, unseeing.

"They're idiots!" Rudy remembered to keep his voice to a whisper, but his gesture nearly took the hat off Treemut Farrier, passing along the corridor with a basket of eggs. The Council had spent all day yesterday arguing about whether to expropriate and socialize all the illegal chickens that had survived the storm—eggs were being traded for everything from better-situated cells to sexual favors—and in the meantime the Wickets and Gatsons and Biggars had hidden their hens all over fifth level north. "If Ingold doesn't stop Los Tres Geezers down south from screwing with the weather, they'll lose everything to the next ice storm and we're gonna be under six feet of slunch by this time next year!"

"If Lord Sketh, or Barrelstave, can manage to turn the Guards or any sizable percentage of the Keep against Minalde while Ingold is away," Gil remarked, "you're going to be in trouble a lot sooner than that." She shifted the bundle under her cloak, heavier this time than last night—Rudy didn't want to know about how she'd gotten hold of that much food. "You've heard what they're whispering to the Guards—that Ingold could have stopped the storm if he'd wanted to. Or could have saved those kids. God knows what idiots like Biggar are putting around on fifth north."

The haunted look that had been in her eyes was more pronounced now, and she'd acquired a trick of looking at her hands, of feeling her wrist and elbow joints nervously, as if seeking something she didn't want to find. "It's easy now, because people are scared. Hell, I'm scared."

And she sounded scared, he thought. But not of the Fimbul Winter or the mages under the ice.

On the steps of the Keep they stepped aside in time to avoid being knocked over by Scala Hogshearer, storming away from an altercation with a couple of the other girls of the Keep. One of them was holding her wrist and shouting furiously, "She bit me! She bit me!" and the other collecting broken beads scattered on the steps; Rudy could only guess what that was all about. The day was a bright one, thin warmth returning to the shards of the spring. Nearly everyone was clearing the ruined wheat from the fields, preparing for a second sowing—late, but still just feasible in these upland fields.

That had been the topic for another heated discussion in Council—whether to sow the seed or hold it to feed the population through autumn and winter to come.

"And they've got no guarantee Ingold is right."

"Whaddaya mean?" Rudy demanded, furious. "Ingold saw that stuff!"

"Ingold *says* he saw it," Gil pointed out. "If you weren't a wizard yourself, would you believe him?"

"Hell yes!"

He said it because he had to, even though he knew he was wrong and dumb as the words came out of his mouth. She cocked a brow at him and said nothing. The bitten side of her face was toward him; he couldn't see whether the other side smiled.

Ingold was waiting in a copse of hemlocks just out of sight of the watchtowers at the Tall Gates. He looked better than he had last night, as if he'd gotten some sleep and the food had helped. "You were right," Rudy said as the old man sorted through the packs they'd brought: blankets, as much food as they could collect, a minimum of spare clothing, a few medical supplies. "Those yammerheads were talking about locking you up when you got back, trying to figure out goddamn 'securities' to make sure you didn't run off again."

"Precisely what I am doing." He straightened up and turned his head to survey the glassy black monolith of the Keep, visible through the trees. Men and women toiled in the fields, the lack of draft animals painfully evident. Apportionment of Yoshabel the Only Mule in the Vale was another matter much discussed in Council. Blue haze still hung heavy around the walls, from the smoking fires—even half-spoiled meat was still being brought up from Wormswell and Manse by the exhausted scavenging crews.

"Deserting them . . . for what could very well be a madman's fancy. Just because I'm able to work magic doesn't mean I'm not subject to hallucinations, you know," he added, seeing the look of uncertainty on Rudy's face. "Or deception by the Dark."

"Uh . . ."

"Somebody concerted those attacks on me," Gil said quietly. "And on you. Somebody is . . . talking to me. Whispering in my head."

Rudy saw between them that understanding again, blue gaze meeting blue, seeing the same thing. Silence hung on the air, deepening with unsaid words.

At last Ingold broke it, softly. "My child, were there a way I could . . . do without you on this journey . . . I would. As it is . . ."

"You can tell," she said, inaudible, her face like marble. "Can't you?" If it hadn't been Gil, Rudy would have sworn that tears silvered her eyes. "You can see it."

He looked away and nodded. "Yes. I—"

She went on, reaching out to touch his hand, her voice very low. "If I knew how to fight it, I would, Ingold. I swear I would. But the dream comes back to me, telling me to kill you."

Rudy gulped, shocked, and Ingold raised his head quickly, looking again into her face, almost as if he had expected her to say something different. She didn't see, for her own attention seemed to be fixed suddenly on her hands where they laced over the hilt of her killing-sword.

She only went on, her fingers probing at her wrist bones again, "I swear it won't happen. If it gets too bad, I'll let you know, so you can tie my hands at night. I'm all right in the daytime. But I've looked at it six ways from Tuesday and I think I need to be with you."

Still she didn't meet his eyes, and her voice was quick and a little breathless, as if this were something she'd memorized beforehand. "I'd stay here if I could. It's going to be hard, and sometimes I wonder if I'm this sure you'll need me because They want me to be. Because They want me to be the one standing behind you with a sword in my hand. But I swear to you I'll die before I'll let you come to harm."

Ingold was silent for a long time, studying her—two or three times Rudy saw him draw in breath to speak, but in the end he did not. At length he put a hand under her chin and turned her eyes to meet his. "No, my dear," he said softly. "I will always need you." He started to say something else; again Rudy had the sense of words stopped on his lips, and when he went on again, it was very different from the original. "Do you feel able to make the journey?"

Gil drew a deep breath, squaring her shoulders. Rudy saw suddenly by the tight lines around her lips that she was far from well. "I don't think either of us has a choice about that."

"No," he said. "No, I don't think we do. Rudy . . ."

He turned to clasp Rudy's hands, the warm, rough strength of his grip reassuring. "I wish I could help you," he said quietly. "Even if I'm not insane—and I have no assurance that the visions I've seen and those that plague Gil's dreams have the slightest connection with the truth—I'm aware that I'm doing you perhaps the greatest disservice of my life, but . . . as Gil says, I don't think any of us has any choice."

Rudy sighed. "And I wish I didn't agree with you, pal, but I do. And anyway, you know the spook's right more times than either of us."

Gil gave him the finger; Ingold smiled. The pain in his eyes did not lessen, and Rudy wondered suddenly what other vision might have come to the old man in the Nest of the Dark, what other truth he had learned that had fallen into place—Rudy could swear had fallen into place—when he touched Gil's hand.

"Two things are vital," Ingold said. "First, that you find these seeds, these earth-apples, that Tir spoke of."

"Hell, yes." Gil swiped at her eye with quick fingers bruised from sword practice, all her scholastic coldness upon her like armor again. "Potatoes completely revolutionized food production in the seventeenth century when they hit Ireland and Germany from the New World. If we can get hold of them—we'll be home free."

"More important even than that," Ingold went on, "is that you learn, as soon as possible, how the gaboogoos have gotten—or are getting—into the Keep. Even if I'm not mad, I'm not sure that I'm leaving you the easier task. Whatever waits for me in the ice beneath the Mother of Winter holds the key to what's happening here at the Keep. Of that I'm certain. But whether you'll be able to survive, whether you'll be able to protect the Keep and its people . . ."

"We'll get along," Rudy promised with an optimism he did not feel, and in Ingold's returning smile he saw that the old man wasn't fooled one bit. "Maybe things'll be tough here, but we'll kluge something together somehow. If you and I swapped places, I'd be sushi."

Ingold stepped close and embraced him as the son he had almost become, and Rudy had to fight not to think about what the hell would happen if the old man bought it down south.

"You watch your butt, man," he said again as they stepped apart. "With any luck, by the time you get back the whole Keep'll be ass-deep in french fries."

*If Tir ever speaks to me again,* he thought bitterly, remembering how Alde's maid Linnet had clung to Tir's hand, had glared her hatred at Rudy for not being there to somehow save her child.

He watched the sturdy old vagabond, the thin ramshackle woman, hoist their packs to their backs and move like wraiths into the twilight flutter of aspen-shadow that surrounded the rocks of the Tall Gates, and followed them with a spell of inconspicuousness. There was a faint oath as the watcher on the gates dropped his spear and bent down to pick it up while they crossed open ground; then Rudy turned back toward the black-walled fortress shining in the midst of the brown meadows, the only place he had ever really felt was his home.

*What if Alde goes into labor before he gets back?* he wondered desperately. *What if there's another ice storm? Or some other cocka-mamie thing I don't have the experience to watch out for? What if the gaboogoos turn out to be way weirder than even Ingold thinks? What do I do then?*

It was true Thoth had said that Brother Wend and Ilae—who must be nineteen or twenty by now, and Rudy shook his head at the thought: the girl he remembered was a child of fourteen—were on their way, but what if something went wrong?

*All I got to say is, there better be some kid in the Keep I can start teaching, because if anything happens, we're toast.*

He turned and looked back toward the crowding, gray-yellow shoulders of rock that guarded the pass, the crumbling stone watchtowers and remnants of wall visible among the trees. There was no sign of the old wizard or of the woman who would follow him, Rudy knew, to the end of creation.

He was almost at the Keep when a spate of people poured out of its great doors, as if the Keep Council had collected all its family members and minor supporters for a rally: Barrelstave and the Skeths, Koram Biggar and his squad of grubby fifth-level chicken farmers, Maia and Hogshearer and a lot of Hornbeams and Ankres' men-at-arms, all shouting, all waving their fists, all furious about something . . .

*Screw this,* Rudy thought and stopped in his tracks, deepening the cloak of illusion that had drifted around him and Gil all the way across the valley. *I don't need this now. Have your agent call my agent.*

But instead of parting to swarm past on either side, the mob stopped, too, and a shrill voice from within it screamed, "There he is!" Varkis Hogshearer's daughter Scala lumbered up to him, heavy chin jutting and malice in her squinty dark eyes. She yelled over her shoulder to her father, "I saw him meet old Ingold! I saw Ingold and Gil-Shalos run away down the pass together with a lot of food, like a couple of thieves . . ."

*She should talk,* Rudy thought—anybody that stout these days had to be a food-thief herself.

And then, as Minalde strode out of the group with genuine fury in her eyes, he thought, *Oh, crikey.* Shocked, he met the big teenager's red-faced gaze and realized what it meant, that she'd seen him through illusion and stealth. That she'd seen Ingold.

*This is who we've been watching for, these past five years.*

*This is the next mageborn in the Keep.*

BOOK TWO

# THE BLIND KING'S
# TOMB

# Chapter 9

Rudy saw the Bald Lady again, the night after Ingold left the Keep.

Her face was clearer to him in this dream, perhaps because he'd gazed into the crystal heart of the scrying table with his hand on one of the two record stones that held her images. Like all those forgotten mages—the Guy with the Cats; the Dwarf whose stubby fingers sparkled with a festival of jewels as she worked her incomprehensible cantrips with water and flowers; Black Bart, solemn and wise with a twinkle in his golden eyes—Rudy had come to know her well, and he wasn't surprised to find himself dreaming about her again.

In the earlier of the several crystal images, she was young, and in the others, only middle aged. It was strange to see her now so old. It was like viewing all the films of Katharine Hepburn, assuming that there were no changes in hairstyle to contend with, and that somewhere between *The Philadelphia Story* and *The Lion in Winter* Ms. Hepburn had visited Hell.

The Bald Lady was still unshakably beautiful, descending the long obsidian stair through clouds of glowstone light; still wrapped in her night-colored cloak, her bald head held at a proud angle; still weeping, soundless, giving nothing away as she walked. They were deeper in the Keep this time. Stone tanks lined the walls of the crypt where Rudy stood, water casting a crystalline moiré on the ceilings and across the strangely angled metal faces of machines wrought of wire and glass and what looked like hanging threads of tiny jeweled beads. Unusual, for the stark rectilineal design of the Keep, there were niches let into the wall of this chamber, four or five feet deep and the height of the tall ceiling; in a corner Rudy saw the black stone drum of a scrying table. Probably to read the tech manuals, he thought. She touched the machines, one by one, as she passed them, as if drinking in their soft-glowing power through her long fingers, crossed to trail her hand over the scrying table's surface before turning toward the crypt's inner door. There was pain and defeat in her shoulders, grief unbearable in the line of her back.

*Who are you?* Rudy cried, and dreamlike found himself unable to make a sound. In any case, the Bald Lady did not turn her head. *Where are you going? Where did you hide the answers?*

He reached out to catch her arm but could not touch her. The white glowstone light flickered in a tear as it slid down her face, and she pressed out of sight again into darkness.

# Chapter 10

The first village of the Alketch lands that Gil and Ingold entered burned to the ground within hours of their arrival. Gil gathered that such a thing wasn't uncommon these days in the territory that lay between the Penambra hinterland and the Kingdom of D'haalac-Ar, northernmost of the Alketch realms. But it wasn't an auspicious start.

"It's the end of the world," said the steward of the largest landholder in town, leaning in the doorway of the kitchen yard with an armload of shirts gathered to her bosom—she doubled as seamstress and brew-mistress of the house as well. "First it was the Dark, sent by the Lord of the Demons to divide the godly from those ungodly in their hearts. Since that time, it seems that demons have been loose in the land, what with the Golden Sickness, and famine, and the old Emperor and his son both dying and his daughter turning rebel and disobedient."

She shook her head wearily. "That has to be the work of demons, too." Gil guessed her age at forty or so, though it was difficult to tell because her hair was hidden by the caps and veils customarily worn by women in the south. She looked sixty, with the slackness of flesh of one who had been fat five years before.

"Now it's all armies on the march, Lord na-Chandros and General Esbosheth with his young king, as if him saying so could make the prince's concubine's little brother heir . . . *pfui!* And the bishop stripping the land of every standing man for troops, as if poor Father Crimael didn't have worries enough."

Father Crimael, Gil had deduced, was the head of the household, not only priest of the Straight God but the wealthiest man in the village.

After five years of seeing no one but the population of the Keep and its settlements—with occasional visits from peripatetic bands of mur-derers—Gil found it strange to encounter whole communities of people she'd never met. She hadn't realized she had become so insular. From the bench where she sat scouring rust from the harness buckles of every piece

135

of tack in the stables, she found herself marveling at the freestanding house of soft local brick and pink-washed plaster, even as she had found herself subconsciously offended at the fact that the humans of the household shared living space with pigs and cows as well as the usual Keep fauna of cats, dogs, chickens, and rodents. Odd to smell pepper and cinnamon in the steam that floated from the brick cookhouse on the other side of the court. Odder still to realize that not only was every female over the age of nine veiled, but to see their stares, to hear the catcalls and comments they had shouted at her because she was not.

The Dark had been here, that Gil could see. There were houses in the village that bore signs of extensive repair, and from conversation Gil understood that no one went out-of-doors after twilight for any reason whatsoever. But the scourge here and in all the Alketch lands was the political anarchy that had erupted in the wake of the Dark's rising. The Golden Sickness had followed that—she and Ingold had passed the rock cairns of the mass graves on the outskirts of the village that morning— fueled by years of famine as warm-weather crops like rice and millet failed. The steward's dress and zgapchin—the sacklike mob cap of country women—were faded to wan echoes of their original green and yellow, and the stables Ingold was currently cleaning would have accommodated a score of horses and cattle but bore signs of occupancy by only a few of each.

When Gil had suggested to Ingold that they earn food and shelter for the night by healing, as they'd done in the only other inhabited settlement they'd found, five days' walk north in the swamps of the delta, he'd shaken his head. "We're in the Alketch now, my child," he said softly. "Even herbalists are looked upon askance, be they not priests of the Church." The only spells he had used since coming out of the forested highlands of the border had been those of concealment from the armed bands, sometimes hundreds strong, that had passed them, harness jingling in the dry heatless afternoons, and the Spell of Tongues that enabled her to understand the gummy, circumlocutory borderland patois. In the negotiations for lunch, the priest-landlord's steward evidently hadn't even been aware that Gil wasn't using the ha'al tongue.

They were a brown race, here in D'haalac-Ar, with the blue eyes of the Wathe or sometimes the silvery irises of the true Alketch, and in the town square Gil had seen children with the white Alketch hair. According to Ingold, the color bar was stringently observed in the more civilized lands around Khirsrit, both by blacks and by whites. From behind the parched yellow rocks yesterday she had seen a marching force of them, gray eyes startling in the coal-dark faces, long plumes of white hair— or raven-black, there didn't seem to be anything in between—gathered up through the tops of red leather helmets, like panaches moving in the wind.

All were mounted—Gil hadn't seen that many horses together in years.

And all were men.

Gil tried to tell herself that that was why people stared at her— though goodness knew, living on the border they must have seen breeched and armed female bandits. She told herself that what was happening to her couldn't possibly be so far along as to show. Not yet.

But her hands strayed from the harness to touch her chin, her brow, her wrists, and the long bones of her hands. The changes couldn't be showing yet. Ingold had said nothing.

The conviction that she was mutating as the animals had mutated could even be illusion, like the pseudomemories that haunted her dreams and plagued even her waking hours now. Memories of rape at Ingold's hands; memories of his beating her, shouting names at her that it sickened her to recall—if it was recollection. Sometimes she could remember that it wasn't. Sometimes she couldn't tell, just as she couldn't tell whether or not her arms were growing longer, her fingers turning into spike-tipped horrors like the hands of the thing that had bitten her. She'd look in anything—she stared now into the polished silver pectoral of a martingale—trying to determine the truth.

But the truth eluded her. Sometimes it was impossible to focus her mind on her own image. Sometimes she thought she looked normal. Other times she found she could not remember what normal had been.

"Gil?" He stood in the stable doorway, soiled hay flecking his patched deerskin breeches and boots, his eyes filled with concern. "Are you all right?"

Was he staring oddly at her face? Her hands? *You can see it,* she had asked, and he had replied, *Yes.* What else, if not that?

She made herself sniff, and said, "I was just thinking that any kind of work is okay for a woman to do here, as long as it doesn't involve defending herself."

Ingold grinned and slipped his shoulders from beneath the yoke that held him to a sledgeload of equine by-products.

"My dear Gil, a woman's defense lies in not catching a man's eye and in trusting the saints." The wizard stretched his cramped shoulders and crossed to the bench where she sat, to drink of the water gourd at her side. "Just ask any man hereabouts."

He picked up his staff from the well head and sketched a word in the courtyard dust.

"That's *attes:* man. See this diacritical mark? It's an honorific, but it's always part of the spelling of the word. All men are Honored Men. *Tattesh:* woman. Literally, not-a-man or, more precisely, not-of-us, and as you notice, no honorific diacritical in sight."

"So we're here in an entire empire that thinks with its honorific diacriticals?" She cocked a wry grin up at him, and all was for a moment as it had been.

"More or less. See here: *pia'an.* Wizard. And *pjan:* demon." Every house bore hex signs against demons, as well as the customary bright-painted images of God's saints.

"Those two dots there mean nonhuman. You'll see them on the names of all animals except horses, falcons, and cats. The Emperor's horse, falcon, and cat all get honorifics, by the way, something none of his wives do. So one can mortally insult a pretender like our one-handed friend Vair na-Chandros simply by referring to his horse as *katüsh* rather than *kattush*—mortally for oneself, I mean."

"Get along to your work, old fool!" the steward called out, returning to the back door. "When Father Crimael gets back, he'll—"

She stopped. From over the courtyard wall came the sound of running feet, women's voices crying out. Then the fast thud of hooves, and men cursing, and a high, shrill child's shriek, "Soldiers! Soldiers!"

Gil dropped the harnesswork and grabbed her sword from the bench by her side; Ingold's was already in his hand. The wooden gate of the court blasted open under the weight of a horse, black and fully armored and ridden shoulder-first into the barrier, the man on its back gigantic in armor of bronze-lacquered bamboo. Ingold caught Gil's arm and fled through the still-room door—Gil could hear men shouting in both directions, the crash of furniture breaking, and the steward's shriek of helpless terror and pain.

They emerged into a shoving chaos in the town square, women holding their veils over their faces or their babies in their arms as they fled screaming, children underfoot like terrified piglets. Only a handful of men, most of them elderly, had been working the fields, and they were dying in pitched battle near the town fountain against three times their number of leather-armored soldiers. On the steps of the church, its curlicued facade a clutter of brilliant-hued statues and gilded sunbursts, a man in a red robe who had to be Father Crimael was shouting, beckoning the women and children who streamed past him into the blue-tiled sanctuary. Ingold tried to dodge down an alley and cut back as three horsemen rode at them, knocking into and almost falling over an elderly man fleeing a house with a bag of money in his arms. Gil cursed the miser as she and the wizard sprang up the church steps and into its shadows, the horsemen crashing after them, monsters of bronze and black.

Among the carnival house of tiny pavilion chapels, of sunken pits and spiral stairs and hanging lofts on a dozen different levels, women crowded, weeping, holding their children to them or shrieking their names. Down six steps and through a circular pit where a fountain bubbled softly, Ingold sprang, with Gil at his heels wondering how he knew where the back door was—and of course there was a back door that way, but though it stood open, it was jammed with frightened old men and women, pressing back as men in buglike black armor mounted the steps, weapons flashing. Ingold threw his shoulder against the door, and Gil, behind him, thought with sudden viciousness, *Shove him out . . . They'll cut him to pieces . . .*

She stepped back fast. People pressed her on all sides as she leaned her back to a twisted double pillar, fighting to breathe—for a moment her vision narrowed to a slim girl beside her, with Alde's morning-glory eyes staring at her over the stained gray cotton of a veil. By the time Gil's vision cleared, the girl was gone.

Hooves crashed behind her, booming within the church's fretted ceiling groins. Sunlight from the high windows fleered across armor, beaded plumes, the black captain's silvery eyes. Father Crimael, very young, came from among the refugees and stood before him, crimson robes faded but his clean-shaved head smooth as an egg, his face placid with the serenity of one whose reservation has already been phoned in to Heaven.

"Are you a heretic, then, to break the law of sanctuary, Captain Tsman-el?"

"We break no law." The bandit captain spoke the harsh c'uatal of the south. "We're here to collect tribute for His Lordship Esbosheth, regent for the true king. If a man can't pay it out of his goods, he owes what he can give, a woman or a couple of brats. We'll take those, saint-kisser."

"Then let Lord Esbosheth come here himself and make an accounting," the priest said steadily. "But any man who takes any living human from sanctuary is liable before God—not Lord Esbosheth, not the young king, but the man who himself performs the deed. You are liable before the Judges of the Straight Way, and the saints of God, and all the fires of Hell."

The captain grinned evilly. "Well, I can't have that, now can I? Can't let the Judges of the Straight Way and the saints of God be snickerin' bad things about me behind my back." He reined his horse around, its iron shoes ringing on the soft, pitted brick floor, so that he faced those who'd crowded through the door after him: dark faces, brown, and white, peering like demons from among a forest of ax blades and swords. "You boys heard the saint-kisser. Guess we'll just have to wait for volunteers to come out of their own free will."

The men laughed, and some of them called out obscenities to the women closest to them, or to the priest. Even before the captain had ridden his horse from the sanctuary and away down the front steps, Gil heard them dragging logs and brushwood to pile around the outside walls. She looked around quickly for Ingold, but there was an anger flaring in her, cold and deliberate—she knew the old man could get the two of them past the soldiers just by causing a couple of the horses to spook, but that wasn't what she wanted. Above her in a thick-carved shrine projecting from the wall she heard a girl sobbing, "I won't do it! I won't do it!" over and over; the babble of voices, soprano mostly and terrified, was growing louder as the heat-dance from the fires began to waver against the high windows and smoke poured in to roil in the ceiling's pendants and hammerbeams.

She wanted to kill them, those men in the square. Like the heat-dance the lying visions shuddered in her mind, hands holding her down—Ingold's hands. Angerless cold rose in her like a wave.

"Are you a bandit?" a voice beside her asked. "A robber?" The tone was that of one who seeks information only.

She looked around. It was the priest, Father Crimael.

"No. Just a woman who wants to travel without getting raped." She saw herself reflected in those light gray eyes, a thin, tall woman with a scar down one side of her unveiled face and hair like braided storm-wrack, a killing-sword in her belt and terrible knowledge in her eyes. If there was anything more, she could not tell it.

The priest didn't look more than twenty. He wore bright glass saint-charms around his neck and a strand of demon-scaring beads. "You're a northerner," he said, as if that explained it. "Will you help? We need every weapon. Your father, too, carries a sword—can he use it?"

"Just watch him." She looked around. They stood at the foot of a short flight of steps, leading up to a latticed window and the statue of St. Prathhes, recognizable by his attributes of crimson spell-rope, scourge, and poisoned cup. Like one of the wizards whom that most archaic of saints was said to have flogged, Ingold stood at the statue's feet, looking out the window, while below him in the round depression of a holy pit, men and boys took up candles and lampstands, handling them uncertainly, not sure how to use them as weapons.

"Ingold!" Gil called, but the old man made no response. He stood with head bowed, arms folded over his chest. The flames flickering outside emblazoned his scarred face and bloodied the white of his beard and the pale wool of his shirt. Smoke poured in through the window bars around him. She sprang up the stairs, Father Crimael at her heels, and called out again, "Ingold . . . !"

She reached the window just in time to see the fires die out of the blazing wood that surrounded the church. The Spell of Tongues gave her an accurate idea of what the captain and his officers said on the subject. *Interesting imagery, to say the least.* Tsman-el kicked the wood, thrust at it with his sword. Shouts from around the other side of the church indicated that the bonfires built there had gone out, too.

Ingold shifted his stance a little, drew a deep breath, but his scarred eyelids remained shut, only shifting a little with the movement of the eyes beneath.

Gil had to suppress the urge to laugh with angry delight. The bandits tried twice more to get the fires going again. They might just as well have been putting tinder and flint to bricks. On the second effort a man yelled, "Damn it, Captain, my fire-box has gone out!" Other troopers rushed to their saddles, where many carried fire-boxes of horn in which, with assiduous feeding on bits of moss and tinder, a couple of smoldering coals might be nursed along all day. The ensuing commentary was unedifyingly awesome.

"Who's the heretic now, eh, saint-kisser?" the captain yelled, swinging astride his black horse again and looking up at the young priest framed in the traceries of the window. Men were coming out of all the houses around the square, with sacks of seed millet, chickens, and the bleeding carcasses of pigs and pot-dogs slung over their shoulders. "Heretic and hypocrite as well, demons bugger you for a thousand years! Who gets to deal with the Judges now, and the saints, and the fires of Hell?"

"My, aren't the grapes sour today?" Gil remarked, watching the bandits ride past the church in a great choke of dust that glittered goldenrod in the slanting afternoon light. "Doesn't want to risk—"

The priest had gone. Ingold leaned his back against the striped pillars that flanked St. Prathhes' shrine, his eyes still closed, his breathing deep now and even. With his arms folded before his breast, he was closed in on himself, walled within his own private thoughts. The twisted images of her own mind gone, it occurred to Gil that he'd probably just saved almost as many people as had perished in the Settlements, if not from the quick murder of the ice storm, then from something slower, more wretched, more agonizing.

People were emerging from the church door. From her post at the window she could see them around the corner of the building, peer furtively about them to check if any soldiers remained, then scatter at a run to their houses. From between two houses that fronted the square, a young girl emerged, barely able to walk, her veil held in front of her face with both hands and her skirt torn and streaked with blood. A woman ran from the door of the church and caught the girl in her arms as she fell.

The priest's voice came soft to Gil's ears, asking, "Is it true?"

Ingold opened his eyes and looked at Father Crimael, who had come once more to the top of the little flight of steps. The sun fractured like blue topaz in his eyes. "Yes," he said at length. "Yes, it's true."

The priest's soft mouth tightened and he turned his face away. "They were right," he whispered, "who said that the Lord of Demons is subtle, and crueler than death. The holy place protected us from the horrors of war, but it could not guard us against Evil."

"What the hell . . . ?" Gil stared at that tormented young face, uncomprehending.

"I assure you," Ingold's voice cut in gently over hers, "none of the people protected within these walls by my magic owes the Evil One a thing. *I* quenched the fires, not they, and I did it solely because I would not see them harmed." A woman walked below the platform where they stood, going late out of the church; she carried a boy of two and led another, ten years old and pretty as a girl, by the hand. Ingold watched them, a kind of bitterness in his eye, as if he knew from terrible experience what happened to pretty boys as well as pretty girls, and not-so-pretty girls, and fairly ugly grandmothers, when soldiers sacked a town. "They have their lives and their freedom, to choose and find the good. Where lies the evil in that?"

There was sorrow in the young priest's face, as if he heard sentence of his own death. "All things that arise from Illusion partake of Evil," he said. "The Hand of Illusion lies upon it, and upon you, and now upon them by extension, and on this whole town."

He laid fingers like black velvet, workless and fine, upon Ingold's arm, and his eyes were pleading—Gil wondered for whose forgiveness. "I believe you meant only good, my friend. But the Lord of Lies has lied even to you, masking from your own eyes why you did what you did. Masking from you the stench of evil that touches all illusion, all magic, all things of his, no matter how they are meant."

In one of the houses close by the square an old man's quavery voice lifted, crying out in horror at what he found when he returned to his home. The priest's head moved, following the sound, and his face contracted with grief. "I must go to them." He raised his saint-beads to his lips. "Go now. I won't speak of this to them until sunset, by which time you can be far away. If this lies upon my soul for letting you escape after what you have done, so be it. I believe in my heart that you meant no ill. That you were deceived."

Gil was speechless, assembling the implications of what was said. It was almost easier to believe the whispered lies in her mind than that these people would believe that salvation from the wrong source would damn them all.

More cries went up from other houses in the town, weeping for those who had not made it to the church, or perhaps only for the fact that there was now no more seed and, like those in the Keep, they faced starvation.

Ingold said, "Thank you. It is kind of you, and that kindness should weigh something with God. Come, Gil."

The priest shook his head as they stepped past him, and he followed them down the pink sandstone of the steps. "If you are an agent of Evil," he said, "even an unknowing one, you know nothing of the Judges of the Way, or the saints, or the rule of the Straight God."

"Of all the bloody goddamn nerve!" Gil looked back at the village for the dozenth time. From the high hill it was small now in the discolored light. "You saved those people from being raped and tortured and sold into slavery, and he's going to 'let you go' out of the motherless goodness of his heart? I'm so overwhelmed at his generosity I think I'm going to faint! What would they have done? Burned you at the stake?"

The wizard smiled a little, as at an inner joke. "Well, since that would have been done with the same tinder I quenched around the church to save their lives, I think most of them would have girned at that. But did anyone in the town possess some kind of rune plaque or spell-ribbon or poison—yellow jessamine or passion-flower are what they use hereabouts—I'd probably have been in for a flogging at least."

He spoke lightly, but Gil had seen the marks on his back from long-ago manhandling by the then–High King; she had witnessed, also, the imprisonment and sentencing to death of all the wizards of the Keep by the Bishop Govannin of unpleasant memory. There were dozens of saints in the calendar like St. Prathhes, of whom nothing further was known except that he had been called "Killer of Wizards."

She was silent, treading the dusty way beside him, the dry glitter of the silvery olive leaves all around them, the world silent but for the scrape of insects and the dry rattle of geckos in the tangle of thorn and brushwood.

"The ability to use magic doesn't make a person good, Gil. It's a tool, like a knife, which can be used for good or ill. The Church has tradition-ally been the check upon wizards who use that tool for selfish ends or who sell it to further the greed of others. Given the nature of southern politics, it's no surprise that attitude has been popular hereabouts for centuries."

"Even if you saved their lives." She knew he spoke the truth. Brother Wend, Thoth's student, had undergone agonies of guilt before accepting that he was what he was.

"You know we've found evidence that the wizards who built the Keep, or their immediate successors, were destroyed or driven out," Ingold said. "It could have been politics, but politicians as a rule hang on to a few wizards even though they might throw out the ones that side with their enemies. Only fanaticism makes so clean a sweep.

"And indeed," he went on sadly, pausing at the crest of the hill, "I have no guarantee that poor Father Crimael—and Brother Wend, and all the others—aren't absolutely right. If there is an Evil One, a Lord of Illusion, he—or she—might deceive me so thoroughly that I think I am doing good by saving those people, when in fact I am putting them all in debt to the forces of Illusion, the powers of denial and lies. I wouldn't know the difference."

He shook his head, old doubt, old guilt, old horror a shadow on his face. "The same way I do not know whether the vision I saw in the Nest of the Dark Ones was correct; whether my quest is madness that will leave the Keep undefended to its doom."

Gil was silent. The subject of madness was a tender one with her, and she shied from it. The voices in her mind were quiet—only the thread of music remained, far back, and that odd, sweetish smell. She felt her wrist bones again, wondering if Ingold's silence about the changes she felt sure were taking place stemmed only from his punctilious politeness.

She felt strange and light-headed, and glad of the chance to stop and rest.

Ingold's face was averted from her. She knew there was something between them that ought to be said, but all that could be said had been said . . . And it would change nothing. The visions remained lodged like broken glass in her brain, scenes of ugliness and violence that she knew had never taken place. She was a threat to him, and to the success of this mad journey. It was reasonable, she thought, that he treat her as such and keep her at arm's length.

From here the village looked like someone had dropped a box of toy blocks, white and pink and mostly brown around the edges, ringed in a wide straggle of fences, corrals, sheds, and barns, the stream bright on one side, demon shrines making spots of red or blue in the corners of the fields, and the church a fantasia of color and gilt. Smoke blossomed from the roof of the church.

"Ingold . . ."

She pointed. As she did so, more smoke puffed, like exploding dandelions, from the roofs of two houses, then some sheds. She could see people moving around in the square, leading forth a few animals, but calmly, as if buildings were not taking fire all around them. Nobody seemed to be going for water. Nobody seemed to be warning anyone else. There were no horsemen, no soldiers, no flash of weaponry in the tiger-lily sunset.

The people themselves were firing the village.

"Atonement," Ingold said. He'd retrieved his dust-colored robe and brown mantle from Father Crimael's house; the sleeve was marked with spatters of the steward's blood. "And cleansing. Hoping that this will pay off their debt to the Lord of Demons, for saving their lives."

Gil could only stare. "They're idiots! Summer or not, it's damn cold around here at night! Most of them have kids. Even if they got run out of most of their food, to destroy their shelter, everything they own . . ."

"Most people are idiots about something, Gil." The old man sounded beaten and sad. "Only some of them behave like fools about liquor, or whatever drug they've chosen, or about scholarship, or training in war, or learning odd facts about the magical world, or their own personal power . . . or love." His voice hesitated over that last, and Gil turned her head quickly, trying to catch the look in his eyes.

His gaze, however, remained enigmatic, looking out over the valleys, and he kept his arms wrapped around himself, not offering her his hand. She thought, *He can't. He no longer trusts me.* Hatred for the ice-mages razored her, small and cold and perfect, beyond the murmur of their voices in her mind.

On the other side of the ridge they found a dead man in the crimson tunic of some military company pinned with an arrow to the trunk of a burned olive tree. Someone had already taken his weapons, boots, rations, and cut off a finger which presumably had sported a ring. There were bloody gouges in his earlobes where earrings had been. By the amount of blood around him, all of this had been done while his heart still beat.

Gil stood for a time looking down at him, smoke and blood-smell thick in her nostrils, listening to the cawing of the kites overhead. Ingold put his hand gently on her shoulder. "Welcome to the Alketch, my dear."

# Chapter 11

Needless to say, Scala Hogshearer's reaction to the realities of learning the craft of wizardry were precisely what Rudy's had been when he realized that she, of all the folk in the Keep, was to be his first pupil.

"Yuck! That's stupid! I won't do it!"

"Fine." Rudy took back the book she'd slammed shut, the *Black Book of Lists* for which Ingold had nearly lost his life in the giddily balanced ruin of the Library Tower of Quo. "Don't. See you." He turned away.

"You can't!" She grabbed his arm, twisting his sleeve. He was reminded of a girl he'd been to junior high with, the daughter of the owner of the biggest used-car dealership in San Bernardino. She'd always had the newest clothes, which never fit her, and the reddest lipstick on her pouting mouth.

"Papa says you have to teach me." There was spiteful pleasure in her voice. "He says the whole Council voted you had to, because I'm a wizard like you. So you have to."

Anger prickled through him like the heat of fever at the Council's self-important motion and vote. Rudy had been sorely tempted to tell the lot of them to go to hell—he'd teach whom he pleased. But from Hogshearer's smug hand-rubbing, he had looked across to Alde's white-faced grimness, and realized the seriousness of the danger in which Ingold had left them.

This girl was mageborn. The Keep would need her.

One day her magic might very well save Alde's life.

He still had to fight to keep his voice even and reasonable. "Great." He pushed the book back across the workroom table at her. "So learn."

"I want to learn something real!" She thrust it away again, the overblown rosebud lips puckering with scorn. "I want to learn something I can use."

"For what?" He was aware that his refusal to rise to her was driving her crazy. "To spy on Lala Tenpelts or Nilette Troop with their boy-friends, so you can tell their parents and get them in trouble again?"

"They were mean to me."

"Well, that sure justifies your behavior, doesn't it?"

She threw him a glare of smoldering rage. "They're selfish. They wouldn't let me wear their necklaces. And they're liars. They tell lies about me all the time." She wasn't looking at him now, pushing one stubby forefinger back and forth on the waxed wood of the old table. "But I showed them. Nilette's papa beat her when I told him about what she and Yate Brown were doing. He pulled her dress off her back and beat her with a strap."

"Spied on that, too, did you?"

She glanced up at him, ugly anger in the small, pouchy dark eyes. Even as a nine-year-old, when he'd first met her, she'd been unpleasant, stealing food from the general stores of the Keep and begging for things other people had, though her father was one of the wealthiest men in the Keep. It was now pretty clear how Hogshearer had learned about that merchant, earlier in the spring. For years the moneylender had been telling everyone that his only child would grow to be not only beautiful but brilliant.

"How'd you do it?" he asked, folding his arms and contemplating her across the table in the glow of the witchlight that he'd called forth to burn on the tips of the metal spikes which had long ago been driven into the walls. "In fire? In water? In a piece of glass?"

She looked as though she was about to say, *Wouldn't you like to know?* but thought better of it. "In fire," she said grudgingly. "All I have to do is look into fire, and I can see anybody in the Keep, anybody in the world."

"Fire's the easiest," Rudy said. It was, but he admitted to himself that he wanted to take the wind out of the little bitch's sails.

"It is not!"

"Okay," Rudy agreed affably. "I can see you know more about this than I do. But I'm telling you, Scala, learning magic is learning lists. Learning the True Names, the secret names, of everything, everything in the entire world. Every plant and leaf and pebble and animal has its own name, its real name. Learning the essence of these things, learning what they really are, gives you the power to Summon them, the power to command. I still have to memorize lists. *Ingold* still works on his lists. Until you learn that, you're just like everybody else."

Only hours after this conversation, Varkis Hogshearer cornered Rudy on one of the minor stairways to the fourth level. "You don't fool me one bit, Master Wizard!" he rasped, shaking a bony forefinger in Rudy's face. "You're prejudiced against my girl because she stands up to you for her rights instead of bowing down and licking your boots and the boots of that sly old man! Well, I'm letting you know right now that I won't have it! You want to keep all the knowledge to yourself, you and that—"

"Master Hogshearer," Rudy said tightly. "If I'm prejudiced against Scala—and I admit that I am—it's because she's bone lazy, she's a sneak, and a liar, and a spy; because she likes to get other people into trouble for her own amusement; and because she won't work. All those things make for a bad student."

"Don't think you can say that about my girl!" the merchant roared. "If there was any law in this Keep willing to go up against the likes of you, I'd put an injunction on you for saying that about her! You're all preju-diced—prejudiced by That Woman who thinks she can keep hold on everything in this community! Prejudiced by sheer jealousy of me! Well, now my daughter's got what you want, what you need, and I swear you're not going to keep her down!"

He stormed down the stair without waiting for a reply—back to the five-cell complex he'd traded and bargained several other families out of, where he and his wife and Scala lived in comfort with all the pots and pans, needles and pins, plowshares and hoe heads, bought from those who needed a little money or food and held until someone in the Keep was desperate enough to pay what he wanted for those unobtainable commodities.

Rudy sighed, leaned his shoulders against the coarse mix of plaster and stone behind him, and knocked the back of his head gently but repeatedly against the wall. *Ingold,* he thought, *you better be saving the world, because this sure ain't worth it if you're not.*

*Hell, I could be back at Wild David Wilde's Paint and Body Shop in Fontana. I'd have worked my way clear up to counterman by this time.*

*Nah,* he reflected on further thought of that alternate future, that alternate life. *By this time I'd have got some chick pregnant and be mar-ried with a coupla kids.*

And wretched, he thought. Wretched beyond contemplation or

guessing, with no idea what was wrong—only that there was something that he should be doing that he wasn't. That there was someone he loved to the marrow of his soul, who had not been born into that world.

Pain tightened hard around his heart at the memory of Minalde's cold anger—*And rightfully so*, he thought despairingly. Nobody knew better than he—except Alde—what a hell of a situation they were all in, facing starvation, facing the uncertainties of a world growing more hostile by the week with the inexorability of that pearlescent wall of ice creeping toward them down the valley. She must have been counting the weeks till the old boy got back.

And he'd aided and abetted.

*But I had to!* he argued silently. *Ingold had to be the one who went. Somebody had to go . . .*

*Yeah, right. There's these three old magic guys hiding under a glacier a thousand miles away, see, and they're gonna destroy the world in four or five years or so if they're not stopped.*

Even to Rudy it sounded like the kind of logic espoused by those who wore colanders on their heads to stop the Martians from reading their brains.

No wonder Alde was furious.

A soft voice said, "Rudy?"

He opened his eyes. She was standing next to him, blue eyes almost plum-colored in the grubby glare of the pine-knot torch at the head of the stairway. The shawl around her shoulders, which Linnet had knitted for her, made her look as frumpy and unstylish as that hypothetical shotgun bride back in Berdoo.

She was as beautiful as daylight and sun.

She said, "I'm sorry."

Rudy sighed, feeling as if the weight of the Keep had evaporated off his back. "Naah." He put his arm gently around her shoulders, and just the movement of her, the thankfulness with which she settled into place against his body, was everything he could have asked for in life, Hog-shearers and gaboogoos and the Fimbul Winter notwithstanding. "Christ, you have every right to be sore. It's your job to take care of everybody, and I helped Ingold screw you big-time. I'm glad you're not mad at me anymore, but for God's sake don't apologize to me for getting mad. I sure deserved it."

The worry passed from her eyes, and she rested her forehead

against his chest. "You didn't. Even Ingold doesn't, not really." The silence of the Keep closed them in; Rudy spared a residual spell to make anyone inclined to take this route from the fourth level urgently recall something they'd left back in their cell.

Her hair smelled of the sandalwood combs she arranged it with and the aromatics Linnet put in her soap.

Her arms tightened around his rib cage. "Those creatures under the ice you spoke of . . . they're real."

"I've never known Ingold to be wrong," Rudy said simply. "I don't think anybody ever has. It's in his contract or something."

The fragile bones of her, the too-thin flesh, rippled with a snort of laughter. "Eldor said to me once that Ingold got into more trouble with truth than most men did with error," she said, and after all these years it was possible for her to speak matter-of-factly the name of the man who had been her husband: someone she once knew, respected, and loved. "I didn't know Ingold in those days. He had a reputation for madness."

"I gotta admit," Rudy said, "this one sounds straight out of the super-market tabloids—our version of street-corner ballads," he added.

"That's Ingold." Alde nodded philosophically. "I heard some of the most astonishing things about him. He'd been at Court three weeks after my marriage before I realized who he was. I talked to him about roses in the gardens—I thought he was the gardener's uncle from Gettlesand. I expected Ingold Inglorion to be six and a half feet tall with burning red eyes glaring out from the shadows of a black hood."

She smiled a little, looking back at that timid sixteen-year-old in her sunny rose garden. Rudy took her hand, and they ascended the dark stairs together, their feet creaking hollowly on the rough-chopped planks that were little more than the rungs of a ladder. "I wish . . . well, I could have sent someone else with him. A party of Guards, not just Gil. She isn't well, Rudy. You saw that wound she took in Penambra. It shouldn't look like that."

*I'll die before I'll let you come to harm,* Gil had said, in the fawnspot shadows of the alders. Who'd guard Ingold against Gil?

He pushed the thought away. "I get the feeling we're gonna need everybody here before they get back," he said quietly.

Garunna Brown bustled past them, the slatternly matriarch of a whole web of kinship ties on fifth north. Rudy reached out a tiny spell to her sister-in-law Melleka, with whom she walked, so that Melleka said suddenly, "By Saint Bounty, I clean forgot to tell you about Treemut Far-rier and Old Man Gatson's stepdaughter . . ." The two women were too absorbed in their gossip to even notice Rudy and Alde, much less notice that they were holding hands.

*And anyway,* Rudy thought uneasily, *if someone could influence Gil's mind, why not the Icefalcon's? Or Melantrys'? Or Seya's or Yar's or anybody else's? A third party wouldn't have Gil's love to counter those commands.*

But it was true, he reflected, that a third party would not have all those years of instinctive trust to build on. Ingold would keep one eye on anyone else guarding his back.

"You did what you had to do, babe," he said softly. "I guess it's just karma that the kid who turned out to be mageborn is Scala."

"At least we know it now," she pointed out. "She isn't some private little tool of her father's, like a covered tile in a hand of *pitnak*. Tir asked me to find you."

Rudy stopped dead in the middle of the corridor. This part of the fourth level south was largely deserted on summer afternoons, its inhabi-tants working in the fields or scavenging the woods, or occupied in the water gardens in the crypts. To save fuel—even the pine knots that burned in clay or stone holders in the wall—the corridors up here were mostly dark. A whole generation of children lived here, who could run the labyrinthine passageways utterly without light. For Alde's sake he'd called a little flake of magefire to drift before them; it showed now the marks of strain around her mouth at her son's name.

Tir had not spoken to Rudy since his return, beyond a polite, "I understand." The boy would remain in the room with him if held by the dictates of good manners. It was a knife in Rudy's heart every time Tir wouldn't meet his eyes.

"He said," Alde went on, selecting her words with care, "that he has been thinking about these . . . these earth-apples, these potatoes. He thinks there's something about the northeast corner of the fifth level north. Far forward, he says, almost to the front wall of the Keep. He says he doesn't know clearly, but you might want to go there."

"And he thinks this'll help?" Rudy shut his mouth hard the moment the words were out, regretting the anger in his voice.

She averted her face from his shout, her beautiful, tender mouth motionless, trapped between her love for Rudy and her love for her son.

At length she said, "Geppy was his friend. Thya was his friend. All the herdkids were."

"For Chrissake, they were mine, too!" He almost yelled the words at her.

She didn't answer.

Rudy bowed his head, breathing hard. "I'm sorry," he said. "I'm sorry. But even if I'd been here, there was nothing I could have done."

"I know that," Alde said softly. "But you're the only father he knows, and a wizard. He feels that if you had been here, you could have done something. I think he'll realize differently, in time."

*Not if he keeps being looked after by Linnet*, Rudy thought glumly. *Not if he talks to the parents of those kids.* He had seen the way they looked at him when they'd pass in the corridors.

They stood silent for a time in the near-dark, her hands upon his waist and his on her shoulders, his head bowed so that their foreheads touched, not knowing what to say. Knowing there was nothing they could say. Far off someone called out, "Wrynna? Wrynna, are you home?" and rattled the makeshift shutters. Elsewhere a pair of cats snarled and swore at one another in age-old territorial dispute.

Rudy sighed and pulled Alde close, tasting the tang of betony tisane on her lips as he kissed her. "So," he said, "you wanna go hunt for spuds?"

Whichever of Tir's remote ancestors had seen or known anything about the western end of the fifth level north, he—and thus Tir—would not have recognized the place now. At some point in the Keep's long history, the place had become a tight-congested slum, cells subdivided off cells, corridors cut into rooms, minor rights-of-way carved through corners of other cells. Walls of dirty, desiccated wood or insufficiently plastered lath at once blocked and guided the way; pipes and conduits ran along the floors, or overhead, where water had been pirated from fountains. The place stank to heaven of rats and guano and abounded in statues of the smiling and ubiquitous Saint Bounty, adorned with stolen glowstones.

Rudy removed the glowstone from before a particularly refulgent image—there were limited quantities of the magic lights, far too few to let them be used as votives—and by its moony radiance studied the beneficent face, the tiny representations of woolpacks, fruits, hams, cheeses, eggs. "There anything wrong with that that you can see, babe?"

"Are you speaking theologically or aesthetically?" She considered it, tilting her head, her dark, heavy hair catching blue glints in the light. "I've never heard of Saint Bounty before this year—I mean, he's not a real saint—and Tir could model a better figure than that and has better taste in colors."

The foodstuffs represented were certainly garish, pinks and greens and reds and golds, like a lush photograph in a cookbook, and above the collar of his curiously chalky robe, Saint Bounty's round, beaming countenance looked rouged. Rudy wondered if that was what Gil had meant. "Maybe he's the patron saint of makeup? Like St. Maybelline in my world? Is that supposed to be a sheepskin he's sitting on?"

"It has to be," Alde said. "No one would portray a Holy One perched on a plate of pig entrails."

Rudy shook his head sadly. "You never can tell, babe. Might be spaghetti. Let's turn here. The original front wall's got to be behind all this mess someplace." He moved forward, sinking his mind into the listening trance of magic, and she followed, her hand in his like a trusting child's.

Most of the little patches and sniffs of magic Rudy had found lay along the outer walls, maybe because the rest of the immense building had changed so in the ensuing millennia. Better than witchlight, the glow-stone's radiance showed up the black mold on the plastered walls, the water stains of the pipes, the accumulated filth, packed hard and inches deep, on the floor of the narrow, crazy-house passageways. The smell was almost overwhelming. Many of the cells in this area had doors, Rudy noticed, solid plank structures shut tight in the old jambs. Most of the doors were new.

He brightened his own witchlight in addition to that of the stone. Strangely, it didn't help. Rats and insects went scuttling, but the grating sense of being watched, of being listened for, did not lessen; the sense that something dreadful was about to happen abated not one whit at the increased wattage. Rudy pushed gently on a door and was not surprised in the least to find it locked.

"They're poor folk," Alde said softly. "There may be a lot of thievery."

"Yeah. It was up on this level that I saw the gaboogoo."

He walked forward again, listening, feeling with his mind . . .

And there he was. The Guy with the Cats.

Not literally, of course. Not physically. Not even visually in the form of an image or vision.

But as surely as he knew his own name, Rudy knew the Guy with the Cats had been here, had worked some great magic here. The sense of him was as strong as if the old dude had stood on this spot yesterday.

Rudy halted immobile, reaching out to touch the wall, eyes shut, trying to call the ancient mage's image more clearly to his mind . . .

And realized there were people in almost every one of the rooms around them.

Alde started to speak, and Rudy held up a warning hand. He concentrated on the sound of all those thick-drawn breaths. On the hushed shufflings and pattings of moving flesh and moving clothing, behind those new locked wooden doors. The skitter of rat paws; a muttering voice asking something about Theepa's baby.

It was the middle of the afternoon. There was plowing, planting, foraging to be done—and in any case, who'd want to stay up here in the frowst?

"Koram Biggar says there's been illness here, since the ice storm," Alde said as he and she retraced their steps soundlessly through the twisting ways, Rudy marking dabs of invisible light on the walls, to guide him back to the place.

"There's always malingering here, if they think they can get the headman of the section to let them get away with it. Sometimes Old Man Gatson or Garunna Brown don't get off this level for weeks."

Alde frowned and paused to lean on the wall, her hand going to her belly while Rudy nearly swallowed his heart. *Ohmigod, she's going into labor, what am I going to . . . ?*

"I didn't like the smell up there," she said, a little apologetic, straightening up and walking on, leaving Rudy feeling both very silly and profoundly glad that he hadn't bolted down the corridor screaming for boiling water and towels. "I don't mean the whole place didn't smell like a privy," she added with her shy grin. "But there was a kind of underlayer of something. Something wrong. Unfamiliar."

Rudy frowned, trying to call it back to mind. "I wasn't noticing," he admitted at last, shamefaced. "I was just thinking about how bad the whole place stank. I'll watch for that when I go back there with the Cylinder."

"Will that show you anything?" She had released his hand, and even though she looked pale in the witchlight, she did not accept his proffered arm. They were down on the second level now, walking along the Royal Hall, one of the broad original corridors that stretched from the Royal Sector at the east end of the Keep almost to the front wall. Though everything was quiet here, too, the corridor passed through cells occupied by the House of Ankres and its henchmen, and Lord Ankres was conservative in his faith.

"I dunno." Rudy shrugged, hands tucked into his belt. "Can't hurt to try. Ingold has a whole list of words that came out of one of the oldest manuscripts that are supposed to be magic, but they were handed down phonetically, and nobody knows what they mean or what they go to anymore. He says they might be connected with machinery that's been lost."

"Like the hydroponics tanks?" she asked hopefully.

Rudy shook his head—it had been one of the first experiments he'd made with the Cylinder. The glass rod had vouchsafed no change. The tanks remained as inefficient as ever. *Figures*, he thought wryly. *The hardware's still here but somebody lost the manual. With our luck, when we find the thing it'll be in Japanese.*

"Do you think maybe Brother Wend and Ilae will be able to help when they get here?" Together they passed into the subdued bustle of the Aisle, the voices of the laundresses, the tailors, the flax-carders who worked there a gentle racket, like wind chimes in the flame-speckled dark.

"Maybe," Rudy said uneasily.

He'd contacted Wend yesterday via scrying crystal, at the young priest's camp somewhere among the Bones of God. Wend's hair and beard were a dark, matted mess, his soft, brown, cowlike eyes worried: "I don't know what it is," he had said, bending close to his own scrying stone, held within his cupped hands, "but something has been following us for three days. Ilae and I both have tried to identify it, tried to see it, to no avail." He'd glanced around; past his shoulder Rudy had seen Ilae, a thin red-haired young woman, fragile as she'd been as a witch-child taken in by the Wizards' Corps, nervously watching the pine trees that shut them into an emerald twilight.

"We lay awake, sleepless, all last night," Wend had continued, his voice low. "We have heard nothing, sensed nothing . . . except that there is something there."

*White Raiders?* Rudy had wondered at the time, but in his heart he knew that what was stalking the two young wizards across the empty wastes of Gettlesand wasn't anything as simple as that.

"We can't count on anything," he said now to Alde, as they passed through the half-deserted watchroom of the Guards. The big training room was dark, for there'd been a problem of glowstone theft lately, and Janus took good care to lock up the Guards' allotment. "And anyhow, Wend and Ilae aren't much more than novices themselves. If—"

He stopped on the threshhold of his workroom, rage searing him like a sudden electrical charge. For a moment he could not even speak.

"Goddamn little bitch," he whispered. "Sneaky lying *lagarta . . . !*" As if the words had released him from physical restraint, he strode into the double cell, to where the *Black Book of Lists* lay open on the table, a handful of its pages ripped out, the smell of ashes heavy in the stove. He ran his hand over the book, though he didn't need to. The echoes of Scala Hogshearer's spite and malice lay all over it like vomit. His voice rose in a furious shout, "I'm gonna break that friggin' little *puta's* neck!"

"No!" Alde grabbed him as he whirled for the door, putting herself in front of him, catching his sleeves, his vest. He rounded on her, panting with fury. She said firmly, "I'll go."

"This isn't your—"

"I'll go." The cornflower eyes flashed with sudden command. "You're angry." All the gentleness was gone from her now. Her face was the face of a queen who had seen the worst that Fate can give.

"God Christly damn right I'm angry" Rudy yelled. "Ingold risked his goddamn life to retrieve that book! Everything in it—"

"All the more reason I must speak to her, not you." She thrust him to the rough log chair, forced him to sit, and as she did so he thought, *Christ, this isn't any of her business! She should lie down . . .* Her face was pointy and white with exhaustion, and sweat stood out on her forehead beneath the soft black wings of her hair.

Another part of him thought, *She's right.* He knew if he saw his pupil now he'd cause an unforgivable breach, which the Keep absolutely and utterly could not afford. And furious as he was, he knew the book had been violated from teenage spite. He'd seen his sisters do that kind of thing all the time.

He watched the woman he loved as she crossed the big room to the door, her shadow reeling over the plastered walls in the glowstone's pallid light. There was a world of banked rage in the set of her back and shoulders—he wouldn't have wanted to be either Scala or her father at this moment.

In the door she turned. "She'll lie, you know," she said. "And her father will back her up."

Rudy sat for a long time in silence after she'd gone, struggling to calm his breathing, staring at the mutilated book. It was—thank God—the simplest of the early magic texts, and the lists it contained could be recompiled by Ingold and himself from memory—*in our copious spare time*, he reflected savagely. But he remembered Ingold, white and silent with shock and horror, crawling carefully under the precariously balanced weight of broken stone and tile to extract this book and two others from the wreckage of the library at Quo. He remembered all those long nights on the desert carrying it back, and the sense he had of the long years of magic and hope and effort that clung to its faded covers.

He couldn't even really wish Scala ill, because on her well-being might depend so much of the future survival of the Keep.

*The little bitch.*

He drew out his scrying crystal and calmed his mind enough to call Ingold's image to the stone.

And got nothing.

"Oh, Christ, don't give me that again."

He tried contacting Thoth, and then Brother Wend, with similar nonresults. In the open state of his concentration he felt, not the deep-flowing, angry pressure he had sensed before—the weight of magic along the earth's fault lines—but only a kind of hot heaviness on the fringes of his consciousness, a gray interference that would allow nothing through.

Rudy mumbled a scatological comment and put the crystal away. He gathered the *Black Book* up, made a search for possibly dropped pages near the hearth—there were none, of course—and took it to the big oak cupboard that filled most of one wall. It was still locked, and the spells of Ward and Guard still in place. Everything on the shelves was as he had left it. For a moment he had a horrible vision of Scala going through and smashing everything in her rage, as his sister Teresa had done when she threw out all of his sister Yolanda's makeup during that stupid business about who was going to date that dweeb Richard Clemente. But that didn't seem to be the case.

*Yet,* Rudy thought grimly. To Ingold's spells of Ward and Guard he added his own, woven specifically with Scala's name and image and the essence of her being. For good measure he placed the same Wards on the chest where Gil kept the record crystals, wrapped in their parchment indices.

Someday everyone in the Keep might have to depend on Scala Hog-shearer for their very lives.

He hoped he'd be dead by that time.

"Ah, Master Wizard," came Lapith Hornbeam's pleasant voice from the doorway. "I'm so glad I've found you in. About this idea my mother has, for locating stock . . ."

All in all, it was nearly twenty-four hours before Rudy returned to the fifth level and the magic of the Guy with the Cats.

# Chapter 12

As Alde had predicted, Scala denied having been anywhere near the workroom, and her father swore she had been with him and raged before the Council at Rudy's prejudice against his daughter. Rudy didn't think Scala would have the *cojones* to show up at the workroom that evening demanding a lesson, but she did. He blandly informed her that because some person or persons unknown had destroyed the relevant pages of the *Black Book of Lists*, he couldn't teach her anything whatsoever until Ingold returned and the pages could be copied from memory.

"You're lying," she yelled and kicked the leg of the table, making the glowstones jump. "You can teach me other things. You can teach me lots." Her heavy brows pulled into a scowl. "Other spells. Real spells."

"Like I told you, kid, *nothing* works unless you memorize the lists," Rudy said, though this wasn't strictly true. There were spells for things like starting fires, and reading the weather, that could be taught in the absence of the concepts of Names and Essence, but damned if he was going to turn the little snake into a firestarter. Scala went beet-red and threw a temper tantrum, hurling everything within reach to the floor— Rudy had taken care that there was nothing breakable on hand—then stormed away to fetch her father.

Rudy spent the rest of the afternoon trying to find time to go over every record crystal and every book of Ingold's meager library to see if he couldn't learn something that would increase the productivity of the hydroponics tanks. A comparison between the preliminary inventory of wheat and meat and the production rate of the tanks indicated an ugly hiatus right before the winter solstice. Coming back from the crypts themselves, Rudy passed a group of the Sketh henchmen in conversation with several of those farmers who owed allegiance, for one reason or another, to Lord and Lady Sketh—only after he'd passed them did he realize that they'd fallen silent at his approach and moved aside more than people customarily did to let him pass.

On his way back from walking in the high woods behind the Keep the following morning, Rudy had another go at contacting Ingold, and this time reached the old man without trouble.

"Yes, I can restore the pages from memory." Ingold rubbed the bridge of his nose with his fore-knuckle. There was a half-healed cut over one eye and a dirty bandage on his wrist, but he appeared cheerful and more or less rested, and the weather in the south seemed sufficiently warm for him to have put aside the bearskin surcoat he'd been wearing.

"I'll dictate them to her when I return," the old man said. "The penmanship exercise should make her regret her behavior, if she doesn't already. We'll have all the winter to work in."

Rudy shivered, for winters at the Keep were long. Even with spells to keep the area around the doors clear of snow, it sometimes lay up to twenty feet deep around the black walls. There was nowhere to go, and little to do except wonder whether the food would last and fight about trifles. Gil's reputation as a storyteller was not based on idle amusement but on a genuine need.

"In the meantime," Ingold went on, "teach her cloud-herding and the Summonings of things like water, and heat, and cold, and air. Those are all things that work in almost direct proportion to how well one does one's meditations. If she sloughs off on her meditation practice, she won't get results. With luck, by the time I get back she'll have learned a little self-discipline. And Rudy—" He half smiled ruefully. "—she's far from the most obnoxious student I've known of."

Rudy shivered again, as the old man's image faded.

Winter.

Looking up the valley, from where he sat at the edge of the woods, he could see the white horns of the St. Prathhes' Glacier. Below him, separated from the Keep by the pear and apple orchards Minalde's husband, Eldor, had ordered planted, years before the coming of the Dark—at least half of them dying, leafless, from the ice storm—the herdkids' ashes lay buried in the cemetery, along with the skeletons of their dogs once the meat had been boiled off them. From up here the wooden steles looked like Popsicle sticks thrust into the earth. Rudy saw their parents coming and going to the place quite often, when the unending work of replanting gave them time.

Through the hemlocks that grew at the southeast corner of the Keep, a small form was moving; even at this distance Rudy recognized Tir.

Altir Endorion, Lord of the Keep and High King of Darwath, he walked the path alone in his bright blue knitted jerkin. Rudy watched the boy go from grave to grave, standing for a few moments at each stele, tracing with his forefinger the carved letters of his friends' names.

Rudy's throat hurt, watching him. *I would have done something if I could.*

After a time the boy raised his head, and Rudy knew he saw him, a still figure in mottled brown and black among the mottled brown and black of rocks, lichens, and trees. Without a sign the child turned and walked back alone to the Keep.

Rudy gave him sufficient start to ensure that they wouldn't meet, then followed slowly. In the workroom he found no evidence that Scala had attempted to see him. He had taken to carrying the Cylinder with him at all times—though it weighed heavy in the pocket of his buffalo-hide vest—and sleeping with it under his pillow at night. From the cupboard he now took Ingold's list of spell-words and the various shapings of power seen within the record stones. By the quiet back corridors of the nearly deserted daytime Keep, he made his way up to the fifth level, the tangle of corridors and of rooms with their new-made doors shut tight.

The marks he had left on the wall, invisible to normal eyes, led him easily back to the place. Someone had replaced the glowstone in front of Saint Bounty; Rudy took it again, with a flash of irritation. The glowstones were supposedly reserved for the main junctions and stairways, and for those who had work inside, like spinning and weaving, though people were always swiping them. He suspected Varkis Hogshearer had a pile of them in his rooms, holding them for clandestine sale.

Rudy pushed the thought of the man away. The packed dirt on the floor here was so thick as to be uneven underfoot, like a forest path; the ceiling had been lowered at some time past to provide storage space overhead. Plaster and lath had fallen, leaving gaping holes. The smell was horrific, and, as Alde had said, there was something odd about it as well—sweetish, like a coloration that underlay everything else. He couldn't identify it.

It took Rudy a moment to realize that the soft snufflings, the whispered voices, were gone now. The doors that had been so tightly shut yesterday were ever so slightly ajar.

He reached with his staff, gently pushing. The leather hinges squeaked. Mageborn, he could see in the dark within. Only a squalid room, two-thirds of an original cell with a lowered ceiling, over half of it for loft space. He stepped inside. Filthy mattresses, the smell of fresh ashes and chamber pots. A box for a table, a really awful icon of Saint Bounty on the wall. A mouse regarded him insolently from a small pile of blankets and clothing in a corner.

The smell—with its undertone of oddness—was even stronger here.

Rudy remembered from his bar-fighting days how a drinking man's sweat carried the smell of alcohol, though he still couldn't identify this disturbing, sickly-sweet stench. He returned to the corridor, uneasy, and listened again. Nothing. In all the cramped rooms, the smelly hallways, the dry pipes, and crotted lofts around him. Nothing.

He didn't like it one Christly little bit.

The marks he'd left led him farther inward, to the place where the Guy with the Cats had worked the spell that caught his attention. The sense of it was strong, and Rudy, following it like a sound, came at last to the place where it was strongest, a half cell mostly lofted over, but with one wall still of the original black stone.

Here, he thought. He'd stood here.

He drew the Cylinder from his pocket and held it before him, opening his mind, breathing power into himself as if the magic of the air, the secrets of the dark earth, the pulse of the rivers that ran below the ground, all passed through him like white light. He formed the words in his mind without reference to the parchment in his belt. He hadn't realized how familiar they'd become to him, with all those readings.

Ancient words. Names of power. Half-guessed meanings and etymologies Gil had teased out from cognates and affixes.

Memory. Memory.

The Guy with the Cats was there.

Rudy was shocked, not at his presence—he knew he'd be there—but at his appearance. In the crystals Rudy had put his age at sixty or seventy, though with wizards it was difficult to tell. He was of a gene pool with which Rudy was unfamiliar, short and broad-faced, mouth and chin neat and small under a Durante hatchet of schnozz. In two of the spells he'd worked in the crystals—abstruse magics concerning machines of incomprehensible function—he'd worn a wig, blue-dyed wool dressed with gold, and in the third he'd been neatly shaven bald. Now his own hair grew long upon his shoulders, thin and white and held back with a couple of painted sticks, the serpent tattoo showing through the baldness on the forehead like a blue snake half hidden in colorless grass.

So thin was he, so worn, that Rudy almost didn't recognize him—probably would not, had they not both been mages. He looked like a man eaten from within by cancer, the marks on his hands shapeless where the flesh had shrunk. And older. Infinitely older.

Rudy looked around him. They were in a room, a double or triple cell extending to the front wall of the Keep. He could see the existing wood and plaster walls as well, not transparent or ghostly, but solid and real, though the other reality was just as visually clear. There were two or three other walls present that he knew immediately had been built and torn down in the interim, no longer there, but leaving echoes of what they had been.

Everything that had ever happened within these rooms was absorbed into the walls. Remembered, as if the Keep itself were a living thing. Rudy felt that he could hear all the voices just by touching them, and knew he didn't want to. Not ever.

"These are the last," the old man said. It had been so long since Rudy had spoken anything but the Wathe himself—or occasional English to Gil—that it came as a shock to hear something through the Spell of Tongues, the aural equivalent of the simultaneous vision of the walls. The record crystals were silent; Rudy had no idea what languages they spoke.

The old man sighed. "They laugh at me, Brycothis. With the storerooms heaped with food, they say I'm like a miser hiring guards to watch his gold when he's being fed and clothed and housed for free. But we've learned not to trust, you and I."

He laughed creakily, and Rudy looked around, searching for the one to whom he spoke. But there was no one. Because the old man was crazy? he wondered. Or because anyone who wasn't standing in this particular spot just wasn't visible to him? He had the strange impression that he'd grown suddenly tiny and was standing within the Cylinder on this spot, looking through it as through a window. He did not move as the old man walked forward, away from him—through all those intervening walls—to what Rudy knew was the front wall of the Keep.

He passed his hand along it, and Rudy could feel through his skin the power the old man used, the way he shaped it with his mind: a different way of concentrating power, a different sense of its plasticity and heft. A rectangular hollow opened in the wall; a panel slid aside where Rudy would have sworn no panel existed, to reveal a niche perhaps four feet long and two high. Rudy could not see how deep. The old man carried a wicker satchel over his right shoulder, and as he set it within, Rudy could see that it was filled with round black things like marbles. Some of them rolled out onto the stone floor of the niche.

The old man pushed them tidily back into the satchel and then made another pass of his hand. There was not even a whisper as the panel returned to its place, and no sign of a seam in the wall. The wizard tottered back to where he had originally been, a foot or so from Rudy's elbow, and made other gestures, signs of greater power; he held his hands and arms differently from the way Rudy had been taught, though the direction and the form of the gesture were the same.

Another wall appeared, in front of the actual Keep wall.

Illusion, and a very good one. The old man stood blinking at it for a moment, and Rudy could see on the curve of his forehead the glimmer of sweat. With a slight tremor in his illustrated fingers, the old man raised his hands again and drew breath; dark eyes closed, jaw set, drawing himself together for some final effort. He made a pass, a motion with his arms, drawing power . . . *from where?*

Rudy didn't understand its source, for it was nothing he had encountered before. But he felt the power come, flooding bright and sparkling into the old man's tired flesh. It was a spell such as Rudy had used when preserving the meat at the Settlements when his own power was exhausted, but as a wizard, he knew that its source was not the earth or the air, as he'd have known a tune was being played on a piano rather than a guitar.

The illusion of the second wall seemed to settle and solidify. For all time. For all who saw. It was a tremendous power-sink, a marvelous spell, like watching someone shape-shift or walk on water; the old man was trembling all over with fatigue when he was done. He whispered, "Thank you, Brycothis," and bowed his head.

Then he was gone.

It took Rudy four or five tries to work his way through the maze to the front wall of the Keep. He returned again and again to the place of the original vision, speaking the words of memory again and watching the scene through, observing, not the old man now, but the lay of the walls. Once he found the place where the niche had been, it took him a good deal of experimenting to work through the illusion of the false wall. He set his hands and his mind to make the gestures of Summoning, to call into himself the unknown power as the old man had, and the imaginary headline formed itself in his mind: *Wizard Zaps Self With Diabolic Death Rays Out of Past—Film at Eleven.*

*Or as my mother would say,* he thought wryly, *don't pick that up, you don't know where it's been.*

It took considerable tinkering with more orthodox forms of summoning power, but at length Rudy was able to set aside the illusion. It was a fairly simple matter then to open the niche beyond.

The black marbles were still there, scattered across the floor of the niche, which was about twenty inches deep in a wall that was, Rudy knew, almost fifteen feet through. Tinier seeds were scattered among them, like red-black beads. The satchel had perished, reduced to a scattering of desiccated fragments. The corners of the niche were filled with the skeletons and the droppings of mice. None of the marbles appeared to have been nibbled.

He picked one up. Deep within, he knew that it was food: ensorcelled, protected from harm and rot and circumstance, reduced at almost a molecular level to its true essence—a potato. And, Rudy sensed, turning it over in his fingers, definitely viable—if that was the term Gil used—if a way could be found to unravel the spells that had protected it for all these thousands of years.

Rudy drew a deep breath and let it out. *Completely revolutionized food production.*

*We might just make it.*

He picked out as many as would fit in the pockets of his vest, added a couple of the smaller seeds, and stepping back a little, spoke the spellword to slide the cover over the niche and settle the spells of illusion back into place. All he'd need, he thought, was Scala going into another snit and hiding these things. Or taking them to her father to sell back to the Keep for whatever concessions he could get.

God only knew whether he could get through the spells that had protected them, he thought, following the tracemarks of his magic back through the maze. That was damn big juju the old man had used, some of the strongest he'd ever encountered—he wondered again where the power had come from. Maybe Ingold could work it out.

If Ingold didn't buy it in combat against Los Tres Geezers.

Or wasn't stabbed in the back by Gil.

Or—

"Master Wizard!" a voice called out to him from around a corner, and he heard the frantic running of feet. "Master Wizard! Quick! The Lady Minalde . . . !"

Rudy whispered, "Jesus!" and began to run. "Where are you? Where . . . ?"

"Here!"

Rudy turned right, following the voice, damning the maze, and would have walked straight into the trap if he hadn't thought, *There's no reflection on the wall around the corner. The guy isn't carrying a light.*

It was a man's voice that had called him. And only children ran the maze lightless.

The next second a man's weight slammed into his back.

Rudy was already backpedaling, ducking, weaving, when the smelly weight of a blanket was thrown over his head, twisting away from where a knife had to be coming; and he was right, he felt the blade score along arm and shoulder instead of plunging into his chest. He struck, kicking, cursing, blinded by the thick folds of fabric; he threw himself backward against the man's weight and stumbled, fell, knocking his breath out of him, and when he tried to rise, the breath wouldn't come back.

He knew then that the dagger had been poisoned. Passion-flower, God knows where they'd gotten it . . . His mind swam, vision blurring in the darkness as he struck at the grabbing hands and kept moving, trying to pull the blanket clear. He'd dropped his staff—another knife went in, this one hard and deep, and the blood pouring out was a sickening lurch of weakness, a long sinking fall. He yelled, summoning lightning, the first spell he could think of, and through the blanket saw its purple-white blaze and heard someone scream.

Footfalls. Swimming dizziness. Gasping, he pulled the blanket clear and found himself in the corridor alone.

Rudy's first, immediate thought was that he could not afford to waste energy swearing. Poison distilled from the passion-flower—which grew in Penambra and some parts of Gettlesand but no farther north that he knew of—numbed the facility to work magic in small doses and was fatal in large ones. The roaring, buzzing grayness in his head, dimly similar to the sensation he'd gotten looking into the crystal when he last tried to reach Thoth, seemed to close in his senses. It was as if he could not remember how to summon power, could not remember what part of his brain to channel it to.

He took his hand from his side and looked at it. It was dark red, as if he had set it down in paint.

*Not good.*

Fumblingly, he gathered what magic he could still command, worked the spells against shock, against poison—healing of internal wounds. He didn't know if he was doing it right. The power was running out of him like his blood. His mouth felt dry and his whole body cold. The mousy, dirty smell of the floor, the stench of the cells around him, were overlain by a stink of charring, the dangerous ozone of lightning, and the coppery harshness of his blood. He only wanted to sleep.

Somewhere clothing rustled. The scritch of dirty hair slipping across shoulders as someone turned his head.

Rudy raised his head, blinking, and caught fleeting movement from the open door of a cell a few yards away. A foot pulled back from view.

They were in the cells all around him, watching. Waiting for him to pass out.

*"Tu madre,"* Rudy whispered, anger scalding him back to consciousness. He tried to rise and couldn't but managed to get to his hands and knees. When he crawled past the door, he turned to look within it— *Make my day*, hijoputa—but saw no one.

Whoever they were, they were hiding. But he heard them in the corridor behind him. Heard them shifting, slipping, moving through the cells in front of him as well.

Waiting.

*No*, Rudy thought, every breath a separate labor, like ripping trees out of iron earth. *No.* His vision blurred. At one time he thought he saw the herdkid Geppy Nool, and Linnet's little daughter Thya, running away down the corrridor from him; at another, indescribable little critters, like things from an Escher drawing, that scampered down the wall on spidery legs or ran lightly along the dirty floor in pursuit of a terrified mouse. He became very conscious of his heart, trying to contract with muscle that grew weaker and weaker. He couldn't seem to remember the spell to keep it going, couldn't find the power to make that spell work.

*You're the only wizard in the Keep. Alde's gonna die in childbirth if you buy it here.*

The anger at them, at those unseen watchers, flared anew. Her death would be on their hands. And they wouldn't care.

The smell of their clothing, their flesh, grew stronger in his nostrils. He heard the scrape of an elbow, the tap of a weapon, against the flimsy wall behind him. Barely able to turn his head, he saw them only as darkness within a growing darkness. An eye flashed, and then a blade.

*Dammit,* he whispered. *Damn it, damn it . . .*

He stretched out his hand, formed in his mind the words, the gestures, the Summoning that had been done by the Guy with the Cats.

It was like inhaling radioactive stardust, like a shot glass full of hyperdrive fuel. Rudy gasped, turned, flung lightning at the approaching shapes and heard one cry out and fall, smelled charred flesh as he scrambled to his feet, ran and staggered around another corner and down another passageway before he fell. There was a ladder down, not too far from here—he could see his own spell-marks on the wall, guiding the way. He tried to rise and fell again, though his flesh still tingled with the power he'd called. He poured it inward, blocking the effects of the poison as best he could. *C'mon, heart, do your stuff . . .*

In his hand he formed the illusion of a little purple fireball and set it on the floor. "Okay, Lassie," he said to it. "Go get the Icefalcon."

The fireball rolled away down the corridor in a trail of violet sparks.

Rudy listened behind him.

Nothing.

Slowly, he began to drag himself toward the stair.

# Chapter 13

He sat on plank scaffolding in a corner of the Keep . . .

*The Keep?*

Dawnlight surrounded him, dove-colored and chilly. But everything within him knew that he was in the Keep.

He seemed to be sitting at the outer edge of a maze of scaffolding, miles of it stretching away in both directions, thousands of feet along black glass walls that rose up unevenly against that orchid sky. He looked down and saw a chasm of shadow hundreds of feet deep, from which the spiderweb framework rose: planks and what looked like bamboo, rope bridges, all wreathed and woven with lines of magic. Machinery rested on some of the platforms, unfamiliar black shapes that glistened with cold crystal appurtenances in their circles of silver and smoke; more power-circles had been drawn on every jerry-built bridge and catwalk, their curves and lines reaching off into the twilight air to form a lace of unsupported magic.

And on every one of those platforms and bridges and catwalks, he could see the bodies of sleeping men and women, like sentries felled by plague. Beside one, two cats were sleeping, too.

*It is the Keep,* Rudy thought. *The Keep before it was finished.* And the woman who sat bowed, defeated, curled within herself on the black plinth that rose out of the center of the foundation—it was the Bald Lady. The scaffolding where he sat—he could feel the edge of the damp planks sharply against his thighs, smell the oil of the machine next to him and the heartbreaking cold—was close enough that he could see her face when she raised her head at the sound of hooves, close enough to see the stoic pain in her eyes at the sight of the man framed within the open square of what would be the Keep doors.

"Rudy?"

Alde's voice. She sounded scared.

As well she might, he thought.

He opened his eyes to a brief vision of her, sitting on the edge of the bed where he lay. Then he slipped back to find himself once more in the darkness of the corridor, with strange chalky creatures like legless scorpions rolling pillbug fashion down the dirty floor, and the dead herdkids standing in a row in front of him, hand in hand, watching him . . .

"Rudy!"

Pain went through his head as if it had been split with wedges, and he rolled over fast—someone barely got him a slop bucket before the tsunami of nausea hit.

"Well, there's a waste of good rations," remarked the Icefalcon's voice.

Rudy made a weary but universal gesture and after a moment ventured to open his eyes again. He was in his own small chamber. Somebody had brought in half a dozen glowstones, so the place was fairly bright, and about two-thirds of the population of the Keep seemed to have packed itself into the seven-by-fifteen cell. He revised the number downward to a score or so, including the Bishop Maia, Varkis Hogshearer and his repellent offspring, Philonis Weaver—who was one of the several nonmage Healers in the Keep patronized by those whose religious scruples kept them from consulting wizards—Lord and Lady Sketh, Koram Biggar, a whole squad of fifth-level-north types and another phalanx of Sketh and Ankres henchmen, and about half the Keep Council.

All of them were talking.

"Did you see them?" Biggar demanded. "Do you know who they were?"

"The Icefalcon found you near the Brass Fountain Stairway on the fifth north," Minalde said. "It's a deserted section; nobody Janus has questioned saw anything. It wasn't a . . . a gaboogoo, was it?"

"I tell you there's none such in the Keep!" Old Man Wicket snapped, and Biggar groaned.

"Don't tell me you're going to want the whole level searched again!"

"Who else would do such a thing?"

"Some I could name."

Rudy didn't see who in the back had made that remark.

Alde said quickly, "Whoever did it has to know that without a trained wizard in the Keep, the Keep itself is doomed."

"Doomed is what it is anyway, begging your pardon, lady." Bannerlord Pnak Nenion pushed his way to her side, with several of his third-level-north dependents. "I tell you, there will be no good in remaining in this place, not if we had a hundred wizards."

"And my daughter's trained," Hogshearer snapped. "Smart as a whip, she is—aren't you, Princess?—and picking up the Knowledge like she was taught from babyhood. Show them how you call fire. Show them, girl."

"But show them outside, please," Philonis Weaver said in her soft voice. "Outside the Keep entirely, if you would, dear. Look at me, Master Rudy. Are you seeing double?"

He shook his head. Her fingers rested on his wrist, cool and competent, then shifted to take the second, inner pulse. Weaver and two or three others in the Keep operated out of the long Church medical tradition, a combination of anatomical study, herbalism, and dream interpretation, which Ingold had learned and Rudy was learning: Weaver, though devoutly religious, was willing and happy to teach them.

She checked under his eyelids and pressed his nails and gave him a bitter draught of betony and a tiny breath of foxglove as a stimulant, and herded out everyone except Minalde, who remained sitting quietly on the edge of Rudy's bed.

As they passed through the door he saw Lady Sketh put an arm around Scala Hogshearer's shoulders and smile with toothy *noblesse oblige.*

The draught cleared Rudy's mind. He was able to lay spells of healing on the deep wound in his side, though he could tell there was no infection and that the internal bleeding had already been competently stopped. He could feel traces of the poison still in his system, but even that was below danger level.

He was naked to the waist—no real discomfort in one of the warm inner rooms of the Keep—with a bandage over the stinging wound on the back of his right arm and a mass of dressings and plasters bound on his side.

His head ached like a thousand hangovers and his mouth tasted like a peat bog.

"My vest over there, babe?"

She made a long arm for it, where it lay with his blood-soaked shirt on top of the chest. By the way she picked it up, he knew it still had the Cylinder in it and some if not all the ensorcelled potatoes. It clattered faintly as she set it down. "What on earth do you have in there?"

He fished in the pockets, found the Cylinder unharmed, and scooped out the glassy dark nuggets he'd retrieved from the niche. "The Spuds of Doom," he said.

Her blue eyes got huge. He'd told her what Gil had said about food and history—she knew the importance of what he'd found. She whispered, "Oh, thank God," and closed her eyes, all the tension in her body seeming, in that one moment, to ease. "Thank God."

"God and the Guy with the Cats." Rudy counted them quickly; all were there, as well as the smaller, unidentifiable beads. "I took enough to experiment with and left the rest where they were. I don't think there's a soul in the Keep but me who can get to them."

Her hands pressed over his. "Thank God. They've been talking about leaving the Keep, you know. In Council. Bannerlord Pnak and his people, mostly . . ."

"Leaving the Keep?" Rudy half made a move to sit, and immediately gave up the idea. "For where? Escorted by what army?"

"For the Alketch." Minalde's voice was shaky. "Enas Barrelstave wants us to throw ourselves on the mercy of the Emperor."

"Alketch is a war zone, and anybody who heads down there is just asking to end up dead or a slave."

"Master Barrelstave says our only source of that information is Ingold, who might very well be a lunatic. He says, why send someone with whatever wealth can be scraped up, to buy cattle and run the risk of being robbed, when we can go there . . ."

"Like we're not gonna be robbed wandering around in the wilderness on foot? We're fine here."

"That's what Lord Ankres said," Minalde sighed, and moved her shoulders, as if glad to be rid of some heavy yoke. "It was . . . ugly. And difficult. Koram Biggar said that as long as we've the wizards, we should be fine."

"*As long as we've the wizards.*" Rudy sighed and rubbed his temples. "Great. Thanks, Koram. Stick a target on my back, why don't you. When did he say this?"

"This morning," Alde said. Then she smiled and rubbed her hand gently across his chest, as if stroking a dog. "But if you think Enas Barrelstave would have you assassinated just to convince people of his opinion . . ."

"Naah." Rudy sighed. "Although, come to think of it, they'd have to dump me before they reached the Alketch because—according to Ingold, at least—they take a damn dim view of magic down there."

"It wasn't the gaboogoos, was it?" Her voice was a whisper.

Rudy shook his head. "Nope. It was definitely Our Side."

He slept, and woke, and slept again, and, waking sometime in the deeps of the night, tried to contact Ingold, to no avail. Whether this was the effect of the ice-mages' enchantments or a holdover from the poison, he wasn't sure—he could light a fire and summon illusion, but wouldn't have liked to bet his own or Alde's life on his ability to do more than that. He couldn't reach Thoth, either, nor Wend and Ilae. Wend's hushed, half-whispering voice echoed in his troubled dreams, and the way the little priest had kept looking over his shoulder as he'd said, *Something is there.*

Philonis Weaver returned to him in the morning with more draughts and commented on how well his side was healing, but the effects of the poison were slow to disperse. He would doze, waking sometimes to find Alde sitting quietly beside him holding his hand. Sometimes he would hear the soft tread of a Guard outside his door. She brought him books from Ingold's library, old scrolls and a whole sheaf of Gil's notes, and for hours he searched, looking for some mention of the power that had come to him on fifth north, or the spells by which he had called lightning, or the name Brycothis.

A day or two later the Icefalcon came in with the news that Banner-lord Pnak and about thirty-five of his adherents had departed, clandestinely and after helping themselves to considerably more meat and grain than the Keep could afford to lose. "By the look of things, it seems they attempted to take Yoshabel the mule as well," the White Raider added, setting down a fresh pitcher of water beside Rudy's bed. "An unwise decision, and in the event she is still with us. You should know, too, that Lady Sketh is much taken up with Varkis Hogshearer and his daughter, and has graciously deigned to receive them in her enclave."

"That's a change of heart," Rudy remarked. He folded together Ingold's oldest manuscript on Time and the alteration of States of Being, which he had propped against the wall beside him, and brightened the witchlight over his head for his visitor's sake, though in his heart he doubted that the Icefalcon really needed it. "I thought she didn't even speak to anybody who had less than eight different kinds of gingerbread on their House Emblem."

"You underestimate the ennobling qualities of a mage in the family," the Icefalcon replied. He'd just come from training, fingers bruised and bandaged and pale hair dark with sweat. "Master Hogshearer is received in many places in the Keep these days. I understand he's taken to promising his daughter's services, 'When my little Princess is the mage of this Keep.' I think only his knowledge that his little Princess hasn't actually learned a thing keeps him from putting a pillow over your face."

"I'm gonna friggin' kill the bastard," Rudy muttered savagely. "No wonder he and Scala have been in here twice a day asking me how I'm feeling and when can she start lessons again."

"You thought it was out of care for your health?"

"Yeah," Rudy snarled sarcastically. "And now you've broken my heart and I feel a setback coming on."

"I shall commit suicide from remorse."

"Your mother."

The Icefalcon bowed gravely. "Your horse." And departed.

That was annoying. But in the days that followed, various of the Guards and of Rudy's other friends in the Keep brought him news still more disquieting, news of rumor, of gossip, of whispers. "They're saying you should have refused to go down to the Settlements that day," Lord Brig informed him, leaning in the doorway of the cell with the dirt of the fields thick on his heavy sheepskin boots. "That you should have known, should have sensed danger coming . . ."

"Who's saying?" Rudy demanded, trying to sit up in the welter of notes and scrolls and codexes scattered over the counterpane, and His Lordship shook his head.

"Some laundresses, who heard it from one of the potters . . . The usual latrine chat. It's absurd, I know." He ran a hand over his dark tousle of hair. "Just thought you ought to know."

"I can see the argument with Ingold," Rudy said to Minalde when she came in later, exhausted and speechless with exasperation after a particularly contentious meeting of the Council. "Yeah, maybe he shouldn't go off scavenging every summer like he does, though if he hadn't, we'd never have gotten that oil of vitriol to experiment with for killing slunch. But why they should extend that to me . . ."

"Because you're here," Minalde said softly. "Because you're one of the things that keeps me in power. Because without you, an alliance between Lady Sketh and Lord Ankres might just prove strong enough to take control of Tir away from me."

She rested a hand on her belly protectively, and Rudy saw how thin it was, its rings abandoned when they no longer fit. He reached out and laid his own on hers.

"Lord Sketh is a cousin of mine, you know. He's started calling Tir 'cousin,' and telling him how he has to learn to be a man. If he can get Lord Ankres on his side, he has the position to step into regency, and control of the Keep."

"He can't do that, can he?" Rudy asked uneasily. "What's Lord Ankres got against you?"

Her hand moved gently over the child within her. "That I've given myself to a wizard. That I've violated Church law. It's one reason I've been so careful with you, Rudy. The child could be anyone's; no one can prove who the father is. Yes, everyone knows—but most people don't want to. Ankres has a very strong sense of what's proper. It's what has kept him loyal to me, but this has put his loyalty to the test. And now Lady Sketh is working on having an alternative mage, should anything happen to you."

But with all that, Rudy knew in his heart he couldn't stop teaching Scala whatever the girl could learn. He put her to memorizing the less devastating of the Runes—though they were all pretty dangerous—and noted uneasily that she'd acquired a string of what looked like real pearls around her unwashed neck, pearls he'd last seen on Lady Sketh.

"I can't learn these," Scala whined.

He set the notes aside, almost subconsciously putting them between his own body and the wall.

Scala threw the wax tablet down on the bed. "They're too hard."

Rudy opened his mouth to say, *Tough noogie, kid*, but something in those puffy, defiant eyes stopped him. *Cripes, old Varkis is probably all over her butt to learn something he can trade on*, he thought.

His voice was gentle when he said, "Magic's hard, Scala. It's hard for me. It makes me nuts when Ingold tells me to figure out something for myself." He reached out, trying not to wince at the pain in his side, and picked up the tablet from the faded quilt. "You know how he taught me the Runes? We were camped out one night in the desert—" And Ingold had been in the midst of his black depression after the destruction of

Quo, but Rudy suspected that hadn't affected his teaching style all that much. "—and he wrote out the whole cycle of them, all forty-seven, in a circle around the campfire. He didn't tell me what they were for and he didn't tell me to memorize them. He just assumed from then on that I knew them, and when he told me how to use one or another, I'd damn well better know what it looked like."

"Well, what if you didn't?" Scala demanded, fleshy mouth pursing into a pout. "What if you forgot? You can't help it if you forgot."

"Then I wouldn't know that piece of magic," Rudy said. "And I wanted to learn magic more than anything I've ever wanted in my whole life, except maybe . . ." He shook his head and let the sentence die.

"Except maybe for Queen Minalde to fall in love with you?" Her tone was juicy with spite, gossip glittering in her eye. Whatever he said, he guessed, would be spread to whoever she could tattle to in the morning.

He said simply, "Yes."

It was she who looked away, ashamed. "You're in love with her?" she mumbled at last.

"Scala," Rudy said, and she looked up at the sound of her name spoken in friendliness, "I didn't even know what love was until I saw her. C'mere."

He reached carefully to the little shelf above his bed and took from it one of the porcelain bowls that Ingold had brought back from one of his scrounging trips to Gae—with some trepidation, for there were very few of them in the Keep, and after the *Black Book* incident, he didn't trust her for a moment. "Here's something you can do with those words you have to memorize."

He taught her the True Name of Water and the simplest of Summonings. She had an attention span that would have embarrassed an eight-year-old, and her sweaty skin had an odd smell to it, unpleasant and yet vaguely familiar.

"You speak in your heart the True Name of Water, and at the same time you draw this triangle in the air over the bowl." The gesture was a simple focusing tool, but Rudy had needed such tools himself for nearly a year. Within the bowl, water beaded on the jadelike glaze. Eyes half closed in concentration, Rudy spoke the True Name again, reaching through the curtain of reality to the place where such things dwelt, scooping up a handful of water in his mind. The beads on the glaze turned to droplets and trickled to form a little pool at the bottom. Rudy doubted the girl was aware of the slight dryness of the air as moisture condensed out of it, though he felt his own sinuses prick.

Ingold had shown him how to separate water from wood, and from blood and milk as well.

It took about ten minutes for the bowl to fill to the brim. Scala breathed, "Wow."

"It's gonna be real slow at first," Rudy cautioned. He emptied the water into his bedside pitcher, wiped out the bowl with a corner of the sheet. "But if you practice the meditation every day, for as long as it takes a tallow candle to burn this far—" He nicked the one with which he'd demonstrated meditation and held her knuckles against it to make sure she had the measure correct. "—then in a couple of days you'll be able to make the water come faster."

"Meditate two knuckles' worth," Scala repeated faithfully, her brown eyes wide, and picked up the rune tablet and put it in the pocket of her woolen gown. It was new wool—an incredible luxury now that they had no sheep—and dyed a rather expensive shade of red.

*That ought to keep the little sneak busy,* Rudy thought. *And please Dear Old Dad and his new pals.* He wondered how long she'd stay interested.

The following day Rudy was on his feet, owing mostly to the importunities of Lapith Hornbeam, whose mother's vaunted idea for acquiring livestock turned out to be far from stupid. It was her suggestion to use a Summoning-spell. When Rudy explained that he'd already scried the Vale, and the pass, and the river valleys below for anything resembling stock, Hornbeam said, "Mother wondered if it were possible to somehow increase the range of your spells? Summon wild cattle or horses from Gae, for instance, or from downriver as far as Willowchild."

"I dunno," Rudy said. "Won't hurt to try. If any show up, we can feed 'em on local graze till we can get up a hay expedition downriver."

There was the usual fluster from Enas Barrelstave about "letting a wizard leave the Keep . . ." *Does he think I'm gonna abandon Alde to run after Pnak and his gang?* Rudy wondered. Meanwhile, Hogshearer assured everyone in sight that Rudy's departure didn't matter.

Rudy set out with Hornbeam and Hornbeam's mother and sister and brother-in-law—one of the Weffs from fourth south—and Lord Brig, with what passed these days in the Keep for a picnic lunch. He had just laid out the biggest circle he'd ever attempted, still shaky from exhaustion, when Thoth's voice rang clear and harsh in his mind:

*Look into your crystal, you stupid boy!*

His concentration on the circle shattered. Muttering, Rudy made his excuses and retired to the gray-silver aspen grove, plunked himself down cross-legged by the picnic hamper and pulled the scrying stone from his pocket. "What?" And then, "Christ, you okay, man?"

"I am alive," Thoth said. Blood streaked half his face, making his amber eyes stand out horribly from the bony shadow of brow ridge. "I suppose this qualifies as your okay." He put the inflection on the first syllable of the word, in the fashion of the north provinces of Alketch.

It would be barely light in Gettlesand. Behind the Serpentmage, Rudy glimpsed stone arches and a smoky brume of torchlight; the wizard stood in one of the rooms carved out of the original Aisle of Tomec Tirkenson's keep. Shadows milled, and balls of witchlight drifted overhead or clung to the metal points of the wall spikes, casting eerie reflections over strange murals that sprawled over every surface and pillar and flaring in the old man's eyes. Now and then Rudy saw the flash of weapons, or a banner of whiter, denser smoke.

"The Keep was attacked last night by the creatures you call gaboogoos," the mage said. "Not the Keep, precisely, but the cells of the mages, which as you know are built against its outer wall."

Rudy had seen the Black Rock Keep last year, about half the size of the Renweth Keep and badly decayed, its hard black stone shattered in many places and filled in with blocks—or occasionally rough-cemented boulders—of the local granite and sandstone. After their experience with the ill-remembered Govannin Narmenlion, the wizards of Gettlesand preferred not to sleep within the Keep itself, and Rudy could hardly blame them.

"Our hermitages are stout enough to resist all but the most terrible storm," Thoth went on, "but these creatures tore at the doors and windows as if no Wards, no spells of protection, had been laid on them at all. We were trapped within our cells until one of the herd-riders who also has an out-cell managed to slither through a ventilator into the Keep to warn them within."

"What is it?" Silua Hornbeam-Weff, bow in hand, came over to where Rudy sat staring into his crystal. Rudy waved her sharply away.

"They weren't alone," Thoth said quietly. "I've tried to warn Ingold, and cannot pierce this gray anger that fills the crystals. You must make the attempt, and take warning yourself. If he's in Alketch now, he'll—"

The crystal clouded over. Rudy yelled, "Son of a—" and shook it, then focused his own concentration, as if he were sending Thoth a message, trying to pierce the inner alignments of the stone, the dull, buzzing grayness that suddenly seemed to fill his perception.

"—changing," said Thoth's voice, dimly, in his mind, "but always there is that one fact." The image wavered back for a moment, the sharp, exhausted features, the chill amber eyes, the panic-filled torchlit darkness of the painted Keep's maze. "They only attack the mageborn, but they will kill whatever comes between the mageborn and themselves. In the distance, at the far side of the Great Slunch, our scouts have—"

The image faded again, and again Rudy sensed through the half trance of his listening the gray denseness, the heavy, angry heat. He waited. Once he thought he heard Thoth's voice say, "—slunch—" The image did not reappear.

*Changing,* Rudy thought. Who or what was changing? Those animals that had eaten the slunch? Or something else?

"Master Wizard?" Lapith Hornbeam called out from the side of the interrupted power-circle, drawn in powdered chalk mixed with bone-dust and Ingold's Penambra silver in the trampled mix of new green and dead yellow grass. "The day is drawing on, and you did say it would take time to complete the circle. Is all well?"

"Yeah," Rudy said. "Gimme another minute." It was a good bet he wouldn't be able to contact Ingold without a power-circle of some kind to raise the juice for it; whatever kind of interference the ice-mages were able to throw, it came and went, but right now it seemed to be pretty strong. Still, he made the attempt, and got nothing.

Later, after the circle was drawn—and at Lord Brig's suggestion he included deer and wild pigs in the Summoning-spell—he retreated a little distance from it and built a second circle, though the effort of that seemed to scrape the marrow from his bones, and sent out his mind across the distance between him and the Alketch, calling Ingold's name.

In the heart of his crystal he had a queer, quick flash of the old man's face, floured with dust and scabbed as if from minor battle, peering into the crystal, his lips forming what was clearly the word *Rudy?* without a sound. He seemed to be in a sort of hollow among towering, black, volcanic rocks shaded by withered tamarisks. Gil was just visible past his shoulder, slumped on a slanted stone, her head between her knees.

Then the image was gone.

# Chapter 14

Crowds always made Gil nervous. In five years of living in the Keep, of traveling in the depopulated lands the Dark Ones left, she'd forgotten how much she hated them.

"They can feel it," Ingold chided softly. "Your anger. And your fear of them." He put a hand on her waist, protective and comforting, and she felt some of her anxiety ease.

The Southgate quarter of Khirsrit—just within the massive complex of pale yellow blockhouses guarding the land road into Hathyobar—seemed to consist almost entirely of ruins: shattered churches, broken-backed mansions studded with demon-scares and some of the crudest statues of the saints Gil had ever seen, clapped-out warehouses lined streets whose paving-stones had long ago been mined for repairs. Gil had thought the stink was bad in the back corridors of the Keep. Here, night soil and garbage were out in the open, untrammeled by anything resembling Minalde's efforts at regulation. *No wonder they got hit with the plague!*

The surprise was that anyone was left alive at all. The moment she and Ingold were through the gate, children descended on them, goose-bumped and shivering in rags, whining for money, for food—not only children, but women in tattered zgapchins and stained and dirty veils, holding up babies like skinny grubs, displaying their scabs and their ribs. Men glowered from every stoop and wall and windowsill, thin men with hostile eyes.

"They feel your contempt of them," Ingold went on, in the wind-whisper murmur of scouts in an enemy land. "Open up to them instead of shutting down. They're only hungry and scared."

"Well, that makes seven hundred and two of us, then." Gil forced herself to relax and held out her own hand to a whining girl and said, "We're broke, too, friend—you know anybody we could kill around here for half a loaf of bread?"

The girl laughed at that, surprised, and said, "You c'n kill Uncle

Fatso the Moneylender!" Everybody hanging from the makeshift balconies, sitting against the rose-pink walls or under the dead and dying snarls of vines hooted approval. Another child yelled, "You c'n kill Hegda the Witch!"

"I'd give you a whole fresh cud of gum for this ol' man here!" shouted a young woman with no veil and no front teeth, either, jerking a thumb good-naturedly at the sleek man beside her, who laughed too whitely and pinched her breast.

Ingold nodded wisely and stroked his beard in an exaggerated mime of a wise old man. "I shall begin a list. I see there's much work of this kind here in town."

What they actually ended up doing for a little bread, wine, and cheese was hauling water nearly half a mile from a public fountain, then swabbing down the floors of a tavern in preparation for the dinnertime rush. The tavern was in the Arena district, slightly better off than the Southgate but still full of empty buildings and boarded-up houses marked with flaking yellow plague flowers. There seemed to be a little more money and a little more food hereabouts, but there was an edginess to everyone, an air of watching for advantage that scratched Gil's nerves.

"I suspect we're going to have to remain here until the fighting in the valley calms down," Ingold said, bringing over the gourd of sour wine to the table near the rear door that the tavern-keeper had grudgingly awarded them.

The city of Khirsrit sprawled in the gap between the arms of the mountains like a pearl in a pincer, built on the shores of the lake that filled the original crater, its waters a holy, unearthly blue. Beyond the patched carmine and yellow walls, crystal-etched even in distance, towered the snow-marbled black cone of the mountain Gil felt she recognized from unremembered dreams. She did not need to be told its name.

Saycotal Xyam. The Mother of Winter.

She had felt it in her sleep all the long way south, through the muddy and deserted coastal towns that made up the chief part of the wealth of the Alketch before tidal waves and plague destroyed them, across the savannah and over the overgrazed maquis of Alketch proper. Everywhere they had found villages in ruins, burned to their foundations by foraging armies, broken by the Dark Ones or by plague.

They had encountered no more armies, though, until they reached the Plain of Hathyobar. There, the vineyards of Kesheth were in flames, and only illusion brought them safely through the warring forces of Esbosheth, Vair na-Chandros, and a dozen minor warlords and gangster chiefs.

Now, all over the city, bells began to sound for evening prayers, ring speaking to ring in the complex mathematical permutations that differed from saint to saint. They'd washed in a stream in the hills last night but still looked like a pair of panhandlers, and Gil was getting thoroughly irked at the way both men and women stared at her unveiled face. She wondered if she would have felt the same had she not been scarred, wondered if they could see the mutations that she was positive were taking place. She'd checked a dozen times in the tavern-keeper's mirror, as she'd checked, obsessively, in every reflective surface she'd encountered on the way. There was no sign of change—*yet*, the voices whispered. She found herself wondering if the mirror could be wrong.

"It should not be long," Ingold added comfortingly.

"It better not be." Gil sopped her cheese-smeared bread into the wine. "We're out of money, and I don't think we can live on what we make hauling water and washing floors."

Ingold widened his eyes at her in mock surprise. "I thought you and I were going to go into the business of killing people for bread." He sipped his wine, then gazed at his cup doubtfully. "Some scheme will doubtless present itself. In fact, I only need . . . Ah."

Customers were coming in from the quick-falling, chilly dusk. Most seemed to be small-time street vendors and what looked like professional linkboys, but a group entered amid a great flaring of torches and noise: two men surrounded by unveiled women in thin, tight, bright-dyed dresses and face-paint—and incongruously elaborate necklaces of saint-beads—and male sycophants who aped the garments of the two principals. These consisted of high-cut trunks of gilded boiled leather—their fantastically jeweled codpieces entered the tavern well in advance of their wearers; high, gilded boots; short fur jackets and a good slather of body oil that probably didn't do much to cut the cold of the evening.

"Oh, be still my heart," Gil murmured.

"Gladiators," Ingold said, sounding pleased. "The two with the muscles, that is. The others will be—"

"Roadies and groupies," Gil said, with an odd sensation of delight at the predictability of human behavior. "In my world they followed rock 'n' roll bands. You mean with the whole empire coming apart at the seams, with civil war and golden plague and what-all else, people are still spending money on big-scale entertainment?"

"Oh, more than ever, I should imagine." Ingold's eyes narrowed with a professional's calculation. "Look at their jackets. Red, like our friend Esbosheth's men out in the vineyards—look, they've got the same emblems on the backs and sleeves. I should be surprised if the other teams haven't taken up patrons among the princes fighting for control of the empire. When I was here forty years ago, there were riots between supporters of the teams, killing hundreds sometimes, over the outcome of a bout. I'm extraordinarily pleased to see them."

"You know those guys?" With Ingold there was no telling.

"Not yet." The wizard finished his wine and stood. "But it's a comfort to know that some things haven't changed."

Instead of going over to the gladiators—who were behaving toward their groupies and the tavern staff about as Gil expected them to—he picked up his pack and moseyed out of the tavern, Gil soundless at his heels. Two streets from the tavern a public square fronted a low, broad, long building whose walls were vivid yellow and surrounded by porches of gaudily painted columns of plastered brick, garish with torchlight and the final lurid glare of the sunset. Crowds milled in the arcade and in the square itself, trampling up a cloud of dust that hung like smoke in the lamplight and grated in Gil's throat; pickpockets, prostitutes, drug dealers, and peanut vendors all seemed to ply their trades at the top of their lungs. Among the pillars topaz light flashed on bright silks, on gems real and phony, on embroidered veils, demon-scares that would choke a horse, silly hats, platform shoes with curly toes, on pomaded curls and bad wigs.

Ingold led the way through the forest of columns, Gil brushing shoulders with the bodyguards of the rich and the skinny gum-chewing beggar children. Around her, voices rose in chatter. Gil saw one young lady in yellow silk display to her friends the blood spattered on the side of her veil: "You think your seats were good? Our box was so close to the fighting that when the Gray Cat slit that Durgan's throat . . ."

They passed out of earshot, Gil's momentary anger at the girl folding itself away like a black kerchief into her heart. She'd slit throats herself and hadn't liked it. She clung to the back of Ingold's tattered robe and fol-lowed through an inconspicuous door that he found with the ease with which he always located doors. A big ugly guy with a broken nose and a club guarded it, but Ingold only moved a finger and the man sneezed so hard he stepped back out of the doorway and didn't see the old man and the girl with the scarred face slip past him into the blue dark of the corridor beyond.

Smoke from burning cheap oil and pine knots hung everywhere like a fog, and the place was rank with sweat and blood. Through an open arch Gil saw a young man in a butchery tunic bandaging a musclebound gladiator's cut thigh; through another, a couple of laborers in leather aprons and nothing else loaded bodies onto a sledge to the drone of an orchestra of flies.

Some of the bodies were women's, clad in skimpy bright-hued costumes, horribly battered and bruised. Some were children. Gil didn't even want to ask.

Ingold went straight to the office of the training director, a cubicle between the locker room and the staging area where gladiators waited to go into the ring. Despite the night's chill the big doors into the sanded arena were open, showing men and boys raking smooth the sand. Beyond the locker-room door Gil glimpsed rows of cramped chests and benches. Cheap terra-cotta and plaster saints ranged the locker tops, along with a couple of quite startling pornographic figurines. There were stone tubs at one end and a latrine trench along the wall. A lone gladiator, dolling himself before a polished brass mirror, yelled irritably, "What's that dame doin' here? Get her out!"

Gil ignored him.

Ingold looked through the narrow archway into the cubicle and said, "Sergeant?" and the man at the table there looked up, balding and heavy with a deceptive combination of fat and muscle. "I was told to come see you about a job as a swordmaster."

The man cracked the wad of gum he was chewing and took in the ragged, short-hacked white beard, the half-healed cut on the brow, the tattered and bloodstained wool robe kilted high under the sword belt, and the way the old man stood with his hand on the belt only a gesture away from the killing-sword's hilt. "Little old to be doin' this for a livin', ain't you, Pop?"

Ingold nodded humbly. "I'd be younger if I could."

The sergeant cracked his gum again. "Wouldn't we all." He got up, picked up the split wood training-sword that lay across his desk with an unthinking gesture: challenged, Gil guessed, he wouldn't even be aware he'd done it. His eye lighted on Gil and he seemed about to say something, then glanced at Ingold and changed his mind. Instead he raised his voice. "Boar? Your Majesty? Get a coupla lamps or somethin' out to the ring."

Ingold passed his audition, not to any surprise of Gil's. She'd sparred with him, both with the heavy training-swords used for his initial bout with Sergeant Cush and with live blades, such as Cush told him to use against first the Boar, then the King, and then both together while he and Gil held the torches . . . She knew he was good. She'd fought beside him against White Raiders and bandits and knew that the mild exterior was completely misleading: when he shucked off his holed brown mantle and rolled up the sleeves of his robe, she could see the awareness of this fact in Sergeant Cush's eyes, though it took the Boar and His Majesty longer to figure out what they were up against. The King, a White Alketch who kept his jewelry on and left his pomaded red-gold locks free during his bouts, was tall and outweighed Ingold by a good eighty pounds, and, Gil judged by the way he fought, was a bully in the bargain, seeking to wound in the face of the sergeant's order for control. Maybe seeking to kill.

Ingold got a scratched hand. His Majesty went to the infirmary. Gil made a mental note to stay out of that one's way.

In all, they spent four days at the St. Marcopius Gladiatorial Barracks, though it seemed longer at the time; it was better than hauling water. Despite the milling and shifting of warlord armies along the ring of lava cliffs that enclosed the Vale of Hathyobar, despite the burning of the farms there, the constant raiding parties, the smaller bands of town bullies scavenging for food in the countryside, Gil sensed that Ingold could have made his way to the Mother of Winter under cloak of illusion, had he chosen to.

He was waiting for something. So she made notes on the histories and customs of the southern lands, and helped him find pots in which to plant the roses that grew feral in the waste-grounds of the city, and slept at night alone with the whispering horrors of her dreams.

*I*'m *doing this wrong*, Rudy thought. The Cylinder weighed heavy in his hands, and he was dimly conscious of the way the witchlight shining through it fragmented into a starburst on the black stone rim of the scrying table on which his elbows rested. *This sure as hell is* not *what I wanted to see.*

He continued to look, fascinated nonetheless.

Tiny and very clear, the Keep of Black Rock was reflected in the heart of the Cylinder, like a toy seen through the wrong end of a telescope. At first glance Rudy had nearly stopped breathing with horror: Tomec Tirkenson's fortress was shattered, the black walls gouged and broken, the roof gaping to the cold blue desert sky.

Only at second look did Rudy realize that, though the shape of the Sawtooth Mountains in the distance remained the same, the land itself was different. The scrubby sagebrush and cactus had been replaced by taller, thinner thorntrees and eucalyptus. Grass grew more or less evenly on the barren soil, and brush and shrubs of all kinds clustered thick around the Keep's ruined walls. There was no slunch.

*The past?* Rudy wondered. The Cylinder sure as hell seemed connected in some fashion with memory, or what seemed to be memory. *Or the future?*

The scene changed to darkness, and through the darkness he saw her walking again, arms folded, blue-filigreed hands hugging her shoulders outside the midnight-blue cloak, white gauze floating loose around her slippered feet. She was deep in the crypts of the Keep now, passing through rooms he did not recognize: columns stretched from floor to ceiling like forests of wrought crystal that glimmered pale violet and green with her witch-fire; farther on, mazes of something that looked like twenty-foot spiderwebs, winking with lights—the work of an unimaginable magic, for purposes he could only guess. A crypt of water whose dark surface reflected, instead of the black ceiling overhead, a starry sky.

The woman passed her hands over the surface of the water and moved on.

*We failed,* she had said to the blood-covered man who had ridden up from his world's doom. *Our strength was not enough.* He thought of them together, in his vision of the unfinished Keep; the Bald Lady looking up with despair in her eyes, the bloodied, middle-aged warrior with his long hair hanging over his shoulders, who had just, Rudy knew somehow, lost everything he had.

*All this will pass away,* she had said, *and leave us with nothing.*

*I'm sorry.*

"Rudy?"

The tiny voice behind him almost didn't register. The words *In a minute, Ace* formed on his lips and froze there as he realized that what had once been a completely commonplace communication was now fraught with meaning.

He drew his breath and let the images within the Cylinder fold away on themselves. Let his thoughts settle and return home.

Another breath, for good measure.

Then he turned in his chair.

Small and clean in his shabby jersey and patched jerkin, Tir came into the workroom. His azure eyes were uncertain as they considered Rudy, and by the lines at the corners of his small mouth, he wasn't finding this easy. He was angry still and struggling to put it aside.

He carried a bundle in his hands.

"What can I do for you, Prince Altir?" Instinct told Rudy not to assume anything about Tir's visit, and Tir relaxed the smallest fraction at the formality of Rudy's attitude. *I understand you don't want to be my friend anymore and I respect your choice,* Rudy said, looking into the eyes of the child who had been like a son to him.

Tir's voice was stiff. "Rudy, I found this today in one of the rat traps. I thought you had to see it."

He set the bundle on the scrying table in front of Rudy and climbed onto the other stool to unwrap it. Rudy could see by the way the small hands worked at the dirty washrags that Tir didn't want to touch the thing inside.

"Yikes!" Rudy drew back hastily from what was revealed. "What the . . . ?"

Tir was watching him with grave eyes. A king's eyes, Rudy thought. A king who guessed his people were in danger and was checking the problem out with the local mage in spite of the fact that that mage had been responsible for the deaths of all his friends.

The rat was the size of a small terrier, and of a shape no rat had any business to be—a shape Rudy had never seen in a lifetime that had encompassed Wilmington wrecking yards and cities choked with the bodies of slain men.

His mind clicked to Gil's thin hands, scraping and picking at the collection of sticky and deformed bones. To the Icefalcon, showing him the slunch beds in the woods and the tracks around them. To the rubbery wastes of sickly herbiage that glowed in the twilight and the revolting sense of things bouncing and scuttling around their verges.

He whispered, "Friggin' hell."

Tir looked up at him, the distance he had set between them momentarily put aside in their shared responsibility for the inhabitants of this small, beleaguered domain. Rudy saw in his frightened face that he'd guessed already what was going on; that he was hoping he was wrong. But he wasn't.

Knowing it to be true, Rudy said, "There's slunch growing in the Keep."

# Chapter 15

Two girls from the fifth floor north found it: a deserted cell in one of the many waterless areas near the back wall, with slunch covering two walls and most of the ceiling. Rudy was interested to note, brightening the magelight above his head as Janus of Weg ordered his Guards to scrape the stuff down with shovels, that the organism had attached itself only to the partitions of wood and plaster that long postdated the building of the Keep.

"Pull down that ceiling," Janus ordered, squinting up at the rude beams that indicated a storage area jerry-rigged overhead. "Those walls have to come out as well. Biggar, send a couple of your boys down to the crypts for barrels . . ."

"On your authorization," the head of the Biggar clan said quickly. "I'm not having that thief Enas saying those barrels are charged to me."

"Seya, go with them," said Janus, who since the minor coup of the Keep Council had become very tired of details like this. "Tell Enas I'm asking for them and we've got authorization from Her Majesty. That suit you?" he added sarcastically, and the People's Representative of the fifth level north drew himself up, a greasy-haired, repellent man with a fleshiness sharply in contrast to the rather gaunt look that most of the Guards—and most of the people in the Keep—had these days.

"There's no need to be abusive," Biggar said. "I just like to keep these things clear."

"Tear down the whole thing." Janus had already turned back to his Guards. "Even what doesn't have the stuff on it. Rudy, what do we do? Burn it?"

Rudy straightened up. He'd been on one knee, studying the rat droppings that strewed the floor. Their size and configuration gave him a queasy feeling about what must be scuttling around the Keep.

"Ingold's got enough sulfur in the crypts to make vitriol." He came back over to the Guards, brushing off his hands. Caldern, the tallest, snagged a ceiling beam with a billhook and threw his weight on it; the whole thing sagged, and Rudy ducked aside as the skeletons and drop-pings of rats, plus an unspeakable rummage of disintegrated baskets, cracking brown rags, old dishes, and featherbeds rotted with rodent nests and insects came pouring down. Rudy could see slunch growing on the upper side of the false ceiling as well. "What a Christly mess."

The Guards moved by torchlight and glowstone through the fifth level and the fourth, their numbers augmented by the warriors and livery servants of Lords Ankres and Sketh and assorted volunteers. Rudy didn't like this latest development, because of a suspicion that was growing in his mind, but when he voiced his desire to limit the search to the Guards, Lord Sketh retorted, "So, have you decided to rule the Keep by yourself now, Lord Wizard?" Rather than subject Alde to yet another round of hair-pulling among the factions, he had held his peace.

But later in the day he spoke of it to her, when they stood together in the cold twilight on the Hill of Execution, watching the Guards pour oil of vitriol on the pitful of slunch and the still-squirming pieces of the one gaboogoo that Biggar's brother-in-law Blocis Hump had cornered and cut up in a back corridor on the fifth.

"Remember all those shufflings and whispering behind locked doors up in that area of the fifth that was supposed to be deserted?" he said qui-etly, turning his face aside from the acrid smoke that hissed up from the burning. "And what Gil said about not liking the color of Saint Motherless Bounty's robes?"

"I asked Maia about Saint Bounty," Alde said. "He said there is no such saint—not in the canon, anyway. But small villages did have their local saints, whom no one else had ever heard of."

"Maybe," Rudy said grimly. He made a move to lean his shoulders against the two iron pillars that crowned the hill, but at the last moment avoided their touch. He had been chained between them one cold winter night, and left for the Dark Ones—it was a memory that lingered.

"But I had another look at those statues, and I figured out what it is Gil didn't like about the color of Saint Bounty's robes. They're the same color as slunch. And the stuff he's sitting on, that looks like spaghetti or pig entrails or whatever? It also looks like slunch."

He cast a quick glance around, to see if any of the Ankres henchmen were near, and then, taking Minalde's hand, led her down the hill toward the narrow path that led around the south wall of the Keep and on to the higher ground, the orchards and the graveyard in the rear.

"I think there are people in the Keep who are raising slunch and eating it."

Alde drew back with an exclamation of disgust. "How could—" She stopped herself. In the five years of Gil and Ingold's career as scavengers in the decaying cities of the Realm, they had brought back tales of things far worse. Instead she said, "Janus and the Guards searched."

"Janus and the Guards and old Ankres' bravos and Sketh's guys and a whole squad of other folks, including people like Old Man Gatson and Enas Barrelstave who I *know* have caches all over the Keep of chickens and grain and meat swiped from the smoking racks. I'm betting there's corridors and cells around Lord Sketh's chambers that our people haven't searched; Barrelstave's, too. There could be anything there."

Alde drew her cloak more closely around her thin shoulders and walked at his side with bowed head, the chill glacier-wind flaying at the edges of her hair. "They're speaking about setting up a Council of Regency, you know," she said softly. "Lord Ankres and Lord Sketh— which actually means Lady Sketh—and Maia. There's a lot of unrest among their adherents, and among the general folk of the Keep. They say that you should not be so close to the governance of Prince Tir."

Rudy felt the hair of his nape rise. "Screw 'em," he said. "If they want a showdown with a wizard, I'll sure be glad to give 'em one."

"It's not that easy," Alde said. She had released his hand, and walked with arms folded, drawn in on herself. "I need Ankres, and I need Sketh—I need their men, and the power they wield. And I need the good-will of the Keep. And you can't seriously think of using your magic against those who have none. You have to sleep sometime, Rudy, and you know already there are those in the Keep who have the poisons that will rob a mage of his power."

He was silent, but his breath came hard, clouding white in the lurid, fading glare of the sunset. If he fought anyone, he knew, the loser would be Alde. She would lose Tir. Maybe, if the Guards put up a fight, if the factions chose up sides, they all might lose the Keep entirely.

As they approached the dying orchards, the graveyard with its steles that seemed to reach like the skinny fingers of buried hands to plead with some unfair god, he heard Varkis Hogshearer's voice: "Don't you fret about it, my lady. My girl's powers are growing every day. Why, in no time at all she'll be able to get you what you want . . ."

Rudy thought, among the gray boles of the withered trees, that he could make out the dark red gown and particolored veils he remembered seeing on Lady Sketh, down by the pit where they'd burned the slunch.

Slowly, he said, "So what do we do? Wait? Let the stuff keep growing in the Keep? I swear that's the reason I can't contact Ingold from inside the Keep—the slunch is interfering with magic in there, concentrating itself within the walls. What's it gonna interfere with next? The ventilators? The pumps?"

His mind went back to the Bald Lady, walking through what he would have sworn was some deep crypt within the Keep, passing the sparkling webs, the columns of crystal, the glimmering lights. Walking in magic.

*We have failed.* Sitting on her black glass plinth in the unfinished foundations, she had looked up into the long-haired warrior's eyes. *I'm sorry.*

But she'd been wrong.

She'd walked the halls of the Keep, weeping; passed through its crypts, deeper and deeper, tears running down her face . . .

*All of this will pass away.*

But it hadn't.

"We can't let the Keep go, Alde," he said softly. "No matter what Barrelstave and his fugheads say about moving downriver or resettling where it's warmer or making deals with whoever rules Alketch. No matter what kind of answer that idiot Pnak sends back, if he isn't playing postman to the White Raiders' ancestors by this time. No matter who we have to kill. The answer is there. The food is there. It was made as a shelter, to last for all of time. It's our only hope, if we can figure out . . . whatever it is we need to figure out."

They had reached the high ground, where the land steepened still farther toward the upper meadows and glacier streams. Westward the Keep reared, huge, black, slick, its half-mile bulk hiding the notch of Sarda Pass that led away into the west, hiding the knoll of execution itself.

Rudy recalled again being chained on that hill, the night the Dark had passed over the Keep in a silent, inky, inexorable river. The night Gil had killed Alde's brother in the moonlit snow. He still got the willies, being outside at night.

Now he thought about those pillars, that hill, the way they framed Sarda Pass like a gun sight if you stood on the steps of the Keep the way the bloodied warrior of his vision had stood.

*They had the whole lower meadow to build a hill on. Why put one there?*

The images came almost at once.

As before, it seemed to Rudy that he had grown tiny and was sitting within the Cylinder itself, rather than holding it in his hands where he knelt between the black pillars on the knoll.

It was night in his vision, a quarter-moon glistening like meringue on the glaciers, which were themselves no more than a thin rime above the coal backbone of the mountain walls. The grass that grew thick underfoot was diamonded with dew. The warmth of the night was almost palpable, warmer than the morning in which he actually sat, and he knew somehow that the scents of grass, of water, of the pine trees that grew thick over the floor of the valley, were drenching and heavy, like an exquisite drug.

Even the shape of the land was different. The whole Vale babbled with streams, bright and multifarious in the moonlight: streams and ponds and freshets where the big wheat field was now, fat with standing cattails and willows, wild grape, ivy. A sense of sleeping birds. The knoll had not existed then.

Where it would be, the grass had been scythed, burned over, and scattered with sand in a wide circle. Marshlights like will o' the wisp flickered in the tall sedges beyond the circle's bounds, delineating the Warden-spells of certain more ancient forms of the craft. A shape had been traced in the sand, three long lines, glowing circles knotted and interknotted with trackways—Roads, they were called in the oldest books, or Weirds. Flames burned where they crossed.

All this he saw as clearly as he still saw the Keep, the knoll, the wheat fields, and the present course of the stream. But the realities were equal, and for a time he did not know which was the dream and which present life.

The Bald Lady knelt in a protective circle only a few feet before him, but several yards down, at the old level of the ground. She was making the signs of what Rudy recognized as a dispersal, clearing up the ambient power from the air at the end of a rite. She wore a simpler version of the gauze sheath that she'd had on in his earlier visions, over it only a kind of sleeveless robe, also of gauze.

When she stood, the lines of multicolored light sinking back into the sand and the blue Warden-fires dying to coals, Rudy saw that she was young.

Younger than he was now.

She turned her head as at some sound in the deep woods of oak and hemlock, and a breeze Rudy could not feel lifted the gauze of her dress to a momentary, shimmering veil. Her straight, dark eyebrows dove in unalarmed puzzlement, and he followed her eyes to the thing that stood pallid and ghostly against the black trees.

His first thought was that it was a dooic. But the next second he saw that the thing was entirely human in shape, a naked, whitish, hairless grub raising tiny malformed hands to protect its huge eyes even from moonlight. It turned to flee, but the Bald Lady stretched out her hands, and Rudy felt the Word she laid on the warm night air: *Safety. Peace. Good.* The gentle strength of the spell was such that could he have done so, he would have stepped down out of the Cylinder and gone to her, too.

She gathered her gauzy clothes around her knees and waded through the summer lupine toward the newcomer.

She laid on words of trust at the white and pitiful thing—trust in her own strength, her serene power to protect—and watching her, Rudy felt his heart clutch up at the awareness of her own trust, the confident kindness in her step, the way she held out her hands. But as it stepped toward her, with its scratched, bloody hands, its tiny mouth gaping, huge eyes blinking helplessly—Rudy understood what it was.

It was a herd-thing. Of human descent, its race had been bred by the Dark Ones in their caverns below the earth, bred for thousands of generations as food.

Rudy sat for a long time between the black pillars of the knoll, thinking about what he had seen after the images were gone.

*Our strength was not enough,* she had said. *All this will pass away.*

He remembered her face, old and weary beyond words. Remembered the tears on her face and the fact that though she wept, she still bore herself like a queen.

And her secret was still there, whatever it was. Locked within the heart of the Keep.

He looked up, the night vision melting back to daylight, and saw

Scala, the Bald Lady's prospective successor, toiling sweatily up the knoll with the martyred air of one bearing an almost impossible burden for the good of all. He noticed again the unhealthy plumpness of her cheeks and neck, and the way her too-expensive crimson gown strained across the breasts and hips. *Food theft?* Or was Hogshearer holding something out for himself and his family?

A horrible vision flashed across his mind of Hogshearer having somehow found and broached the old food caches; of Scala disenchanting them; of everyone digging in and eating them instead of saving them for seed . . .

*Don't be ridiculous. If you can't get the things to quit being rocks, she sure as hell won't be able to . . .*

When she was ten feet away from him, Scala pulled back her arm and flung at him the thing she had in her hand. Rudy saw what it was the instant she released it and grabbed in a panic, barely saving it from breaking. "For Chrissake, Scala! We've only got a few of these things, and—"

"It doesn't work!" she screamed at him. "It's a stupid, crummy, worthless piece of trash and I don't care if it breaks! I'm doing it right! I know I'm doing it right!"

*Yeah, and you're talented and beautiful like your daddy says.* He stifled his anger, bit back his words, the little porcelain spell-bowl cradled protectively in his hands. "Yeah, but how smart is it to get mad at the bowl?" he asked gently, looking into the bloated, red, furious face. "Let me try." He held it cupped in his hands and spoke the Name of Water in his mind. "You been practicing your—"

"Of course I've been doing my stupid meditation!" she yelled. "Daddy makes me, hours longer than you said. And that doesn't work, either! It's stupid! You lied to me! Everybody lies to me!"

"It takes time, kid." Despite his knowledge that she was being used against him, he felt genuine pity for her, knowing what she had to be going through even without the Hollywood Father from Hell on her back. His high school math class was in his mind, his own voice asking the fascist numbskull at the blackboard to explain a proof: *Well, Señor Solis . . .* The mocking turn of inflection still stung. *You're using the same book everybody else is and nobody else seems to be having a problem? Now why do you think that is?* If he'd known why that was, Rudy wanted to say, he'd have known why he wasn't getting it. But he didn't understand even enough to know what he didn't understand.

The glassy porcelain of the bowl's interior was already running with droplets, pooling at the bottom. He emptied the water from the bowl, wiped it on a corner of his vest, fumbling for words. "Look, if you keep doing what you're doing, I swear to you, it'll come."

"That's easy for you to say!" She had turned her face from him, no longer shouting, but he could see the swollen cheeks mottled beetroot, horrible next to that bright gown.

"Magic isn't something that comes fast." He tucked the bowl carefully into the pocket of his vest, the Cylinder into another, and got to his feet. "God knows I don't know a whole lot about magic, about why somebody's born with the ability to change things in the physical world without touching them—about why it takes some people longer than others to get strong in it. When Ingold gets back—"

"Oh, him." She swung around to face him, her dark eyes ugly. "All he ever did was kill half the—"

And she froze, staring past his shoulder with shock and horror on her face.

Rudy ducked, zigzagged, grabbed her by the arms and thrust her ahead of him down the hill, knowing already what she had to see behind him and not waiting to look. Scala stumbled, trod on her train, and when he paused to catch her arm again, Rudy looked.

He'd known it had to be gaboogoos.

He hadn't expected these.

*The same ones mutated? New and Improved Mark III model?* He didn't know. Most resemblance to the original biped shape had disappeared, except for the long arms with their enormous, reaching hands, the long legs that started from the shoulder. The fishlike bodies were still covered with bobbles and pendules.

And they were big. Almost too big to be dealt with by a sword. The long legs covered twelve feet at a stride.

Rudy yelled, *"Run!!"* and shoved Scala ahead of him toward the Keep, turned back, raising his staff, and cried out the Word of Lightning, spotting for the place the creature would be because he did not know the creature's true name.

Ozone crackled, white light blinded, and Rudy turned and fled the bounding things that raced for him with such horrible speed. Something came scuttling like a flying bug from the woods and seized on his leg just as he turned and fired off another blast of levin-fire at the closest gaboogoo, hitting it this time, then slashing down with the razor crescent on his staff to carve off the thing that had fastened to his boot. It bled, whatever it was—he plunged down the hill and heard Scala scream as she fell. Turning back, he saw them on her . . .

. . . and springing over her without breaking stride as they came at him.

Scala screamed again, rolled into a fetal ball and clutched at her dirty hair. Rudy yelled the Word of Lightning again as the two remaining gaboogoos reached out toward him, and this time his aim was better, purple-white brilliance lancing the nearer gaboogoo like a javelin, hot tendrils splintering in all directions. The gaboogoo exploded, charred pieces flying; the other one didn't even stop. Rudy didn't stop, either, pelting toward the doors of the Keep as if the legions of Hell were at his heels—a fairly accurate description. Yelling and curses came from the woods, and someone fired an arrow at the gaboogoo—an exercise in futility, though it smacked into the thing as if it had been a hay bale—and from the tail of his eye Rudy saw Lank Yar and his hunters racing to his aid. He stumbled on the steps of the Keep and the Guards emerged from the doors at a run, swords like the hunger of doom in their hands.

"Inside!" Gnift grabbed him by the shoulders and hurled him through the doors as Rudy would have turned to fight. From the gate passage he saw the gaboogoo spring up the steps like a huge, deadly running bird. Guards, farmers, hunters closed upon it from three directions, hacking at the fungoid limbs. In its train ran other things, things from the woods, things that had once been animals and had the halfway, melted appearance of wolverines and rats. These things kicked and snapped at the Guards who tried to stop them, tried to slip past and come at Rudy, until the steps and the gate passage were runneled with blood and scattered with chalky, twitching limbs and gobbets. A gaboogoo's long-fingered hand crawled along the passageway toward Rudy like a determined spider no matter how many times Seya stomped and crushed the thing with her heel; the Guard finally bent and cut off all seven or eight fingers, which lay flexing like dying worms round the curling and uncurling palm.

Rudy clung to the doorpost of the inner set of gates. Lack of food made him light-headed, and the Word of Lightning had taken more out of him than he'd thought. His vision tunneled to gray, and he found himself staring fixedly at the remains of the mutant animal nearest him on the tunnel floor, something that might have started out as an eagle or a bull-owl, though mouth-armed tentacles dangled from its chest. The mouths were still champing as Melantrys kicked it away.

Shadow in the outer door. He forced the grayness aside, raised his head. Scala was sobbing, her face covered with grass stains and snot and tears of terror, holding in her arms the ostentatious masses of claret skirt that had tripped her and would have cost her her life if she hadn't . . .

*Hadn't what?*

"What'd you do, kid?" Rudy asked. He trod halfway down the passageway to meet her, led her back gently into the Aisle. "How'd you keep them off you?"

She shook her head, too upset to lie or posture or pose. "I didn't!" she sobbed. "They didn't keep off me! One of them stepped on me, look—"

"But they didn't kill you." Rudy looked out again onto the steps, where Guards were pushing and nudging the twitching remains down into a pile. He wondered how big a dent another tub of vitriol was going to make in the sulfur supply and whether someone could be sent back to Gae to look for more. *Which they'd carry here in their pockets?*

"Those things kill wizards, kid," he said, as Scala stared past him, fascinated and repelled. "They attacked the Gettlesand Keep in force; I think they've been following Wend and Ilae . . . They just stayed off you?"

She nodded slowly. A kind of smugness crept back into her face, a look of pleased calculation in her eyes, as she began to understand. "You mean I have some kind of magic I don't even know about? Something that keeps them off?"

"Looks like it," Rudy said. His arm slipped from her shoulders and he was suddenly conscious of a desire to slap her.

"You see!" Varkis Hogshearer pushed his way through the Guards, threw his arms around his daughter and hugged her close. "You see, Master Know-It-All! You've got to give her true teaching now!" He hugged his daughter convulsively tight, then looked back at Rudy with righteous fury in his pouchy eyes. "I knew my girl would put you to shame! She's the one who can defend against those things, the one who saved your life, *saved your life*, you understand, and maybe the lives of—"

"Just because they goddamm tripped over her doesn't mean she can kill them," Rudy retorted. "And she didn't save my life—she didn't do a damn thing! Those things kill wizards—"

"Are you saying my girl isn't a wizard?" Hogshearer bellowed in fury. "You're jealous, is all! Jealous of the power she'll one day have! You're seeking to keep her down!" He put his arm possessively around her, and the two of them pushed their way through the crowd in the Gate Passage, to where Koram Biggar and Lady Sketh were waiting for them.

"Of all the nerve," Lady Sketh muttered, enveloping Scala in a motherly hug. "You'll show him one day, Scala."

"Now, don't you tell him a thing about what you did, you hear me, girl?" Their voices faded as they retreated into the shadows of the Aisle. "Not until he treats you right . . ."

"Yes, Daddy." She glanced over her shoulder at Rudy. There was a look of scared uncertainty in her eyes.

In the sunlight at the foot of the steps, people were exclaiming over the deformed animals. Rudy looked down at the fang-gouges in his boot and worked his fingers into the slash to make sure it hadn't broken skin—Gil's illness, and Ingold's account of the poison sacs on the thing that had hurt her, weighed uneasily in his mind.

But there was no blood on the torn wool of his trousers. Rudy sighed, and took the porcelain water bowl from his pocket, turning it over in his hands.

*Are you saying my girl isn't a wizard?*

Thoughtful and very troubled, Rudy walked slowly back to his workroom, and wondered if any of the suspicions forming in his mind were, or could be, true.

That night, Rudy sat at the scrying table with the record crystals of magic and Gil's parchment notes, searching for the Bald Lady.

She appeared on two crystals, a total of six times. Rudy had been interested to note, when first they identified the various mages, that in her demonstrations of the more powerful spells—including the one he and Ingold had never been able to figure out—she was younger. Rudy had even asked whether that indecipherable spell was a restoration of youth. But Ingold had shaken his head: "In my younger days, if asked to be on such a—a *video*, as Gil calls it—I'd have chosen a spell of great complexity and power, too," he had said. "Now, I'd do exactly what she's doing in those demonstrations when she's older: demonstrate the basic circles of power, the elementary formation of the Runes and sigils upon which all magic technique is founded. If those aren't learned properly, all one's later spells will be flawed with weaknesses that have a habit of manifesting themselves at the worst conceivable times."

In one long demonstration she cured an adolescent boy of madness—Gil had identified it as hysterical obsession, but added that she'd never been a psych student. Watching the Bald Lady now, Rudy could see her gentleness, her patience, the calm and luminous serenity of her eyes, which were the color of the ocean on the morning after a storm. Four of the six vignettes were performed in the same room, a circular white belvedere in what appeared to be a town garden. The shelves between its many tall windows were stacked with record crystals and scrolls, the pickled pine table neatly piled with wax note-tablets and bits of slate. Movable blinds of what appeared to be plain white linen, like Chinese sails, modified the windows' light. Ingold had no idea what her name was.

This was the room in which she appeared in the last, and longest, vignette. Silent, as they all were silent, the Bald Lady sat at her table with a great armillary sphere of jewels and gold before her, explaining something with a desperate earnestness in her sea-dark eyes.

A sliver of night was visible around one of the window blinds. The room was drenched in witchlight, glittering in the interlocking circles of the armillary, in the jewels that marked the positions of certain critical stars. The stars deemed important differed in some cases from those in Ingold's armillary or the ones he had worked with in Quo—he and Rudy had yet to determine why. The woman moved the various concentric rings, the long arms that showed cometary courses swinging free, catching light like nervous fireflies. The intricate workings of gyroscopic wire and gears rearranged themselves, showing now this configuration, now that.

She pointed, explained, gestured with those long, delicate, sigil-traced fingers, and her eyes were filled with a most terrible fear.

*This is important,* pleaded the sea-dark gaze.

*You have to believe me.*

*You have to believe.*

She picked up a scarf of gray silk, no thicker than a breath of smoke, and drew it between two circles, demonstrating . . . something.

*You have to believe.*

*I believe you,* Rudy thought helplessly. *I'd believe you if I could.*

The image ran its course and faded, and he found himself staring into the central crystal of the scrying table, at the small purplish glow that lived at its heart.

And he thought, *The Cylinder in the center of this table is the same as the Cylinder Ingold found in Penambra.*

He didn't know why he hadn't seen that before.

He removed the Penambra Cylinder from the pocket of his vest and set it on top of the slick black stone of the scrying table. It was precisely the diameter of the drumlike table's central crystal, which was, in repose, clear as glass.

*Well, I'll be buggered.*

After a moment's thought Rudy stood, his bones aching still with the exertion of the magic he had called upon that day. Tiredness pulled at him, whispering to him that what he really wanted to do was lie down on the bed and pass out. He felt hungry, but not as hungry as he had been last week.

*Not a good sign.*

He made himself cross to the cupboard, fumble apart the Ward-spells, and put away the record crystals. It seemed to take him a long time to remake the guards. He put his head through the doorway of the watch-room and saw, as he'd hoped, the Icefalcon practicing his knife-throwing, using as a target Melantrys, who was waxing her belts and scabbards. "There's still nothing," the woman was saying as she reached to the hearth to daub up another ragful of wax, and the Icefalcon's dagger buried itself in the wall where her back had been half a second before—not bad, Rudy thought, considering the only illumination in the chamber came from the hearth and a couple of torches. She pulled it out and slid it back hilt-first across the floor to him. The plaster was chipped and pocked with a thousand cuts, old and recent, knife and ax and Patriot missile for all Rudy knew. "How long does it take for animals to come back to the woods after an ice storm?"

"Sometimes a few months." The Icefalcon threw the knife at Rudy without turning his head; it stuck in the doorjamb six inches from his nose. "Sometimes a year. The grass is only just growing back, though yesterday I found mushrooms. The berries were killed in the blossom, the nuts in the bud. Can we serve you, shaman?"

"You can quit doing that." Rudy slid the knife back to him across the floor. The Icefalcon scooped it into the top of his boot in one almost-invisible movement. "I need somebody to take a little walk with me."

Like Ingold, Rudy had long ago slipped into the habit of moving through the Keep by its most untenanted passageways, taking the unlighted, jerry-rigged backstairs, the long black stretches of corridor along the outer edges, in preference to the village-square bustle up closer to the Aisle. Now more than ever he relied on spells of misdirection to keep himself safe, Look-Over-There cantrips and the warnings of his own extended senses about who was around the corner.

For five years, he had known the Keep as a place of refuge. But now he felt uneasy in its darkness, troubled by the soft scurryings and scufflings he thought he heard around every corner, always wondering if it were his imagination, or whether in fact he smelled beneath the pong of wood smoke and humanity the queer, alien sweetness of the slunch. Everywhere, he seemed to encounter the benign rotundity of the smiling Saint Bounty. And when he turned away, he felt on the back of his neck the gaze of unseen eyes.

The corner chamber where Gil and Minalde first found the scrying table was on the third level south, concealed by a trick of shadow. The room still held an air of waiting, of expectation, like an indrawn breath. He doubted anyone had entered the place since he and Ingold and a small troop of Guards removed the table, rolling and manhandling it down to the workroom in the enclave of the Guards.

Rudy left the Icefalcon in the corridor and settled himself on the rough circle of stone on the floor where the table had been, holding the Cylinder in his hands. He breathed in and let it go, sinking his mind into the Cylinder, into the dimness of the room.

Breathe, release. Reaching toward the power.

Breathe, release. Memory.

As always, he had the sensation of being somehow within the Cylinder, embedded like a bubble in the glass.

The Bald Lady was alone in her white marble belvedere, the blinds up, the tall windows open into the garden and the night.

There was no light within the room, though beyond the matte cutouts of the trees just visible past the windows, lights of some kind could be seen: lamplight, glowstone-light, domestic fires. The reflected radiance winked and flickered in the gems on the armillary sphere that stood motionless, all its calculating arms and gears and springs and wheels stilled, suspended, as the stars were suspended like diamond fruit in the hollow velvet of the sky.

The chirping of crickets was clearly audible, and the deeper drum of cicadas. Carts clattered by with dimly jangling bells.

In the garden, a nightingale sang.

In the chamber someone moaned, very softly, a tiny whimper of pain, then the slow sob of ragged breath.

The Bald Lady bowed her head.

Rudy was aware of the low cot on the other side of the room and the emaciated herd-creature lying on it. Its wide eyes were open, glazing; its breathing stertorous. Now and then its small hands picked at its mouth, its hair.

*It's dying,* he thought.

He remembered a girl he'd dated—how old had she been? Fifteen? Sixteen? He'd ditched school and gone over to her parents' place to neck and found her pet parakeet dead of starvation in its filthy cage. No one in the household, it seemed, had thought to feed the poor thing for days.

He hadn't remained to do what he'd gone there to do.

The herd-things ate moss, he remembered. Moss that didn't grow on the surface of the ground. At the foot of the cot were trays containing bread, mushes of fruit, pulps of meat, a vessel of milk; a vain attempt to find anything that would keep the poor, wretched creature alive.

While he watched it, the sluglike white chest sank and did not rise; the lard-colored face went slack. At the table, the Bald Lady looked back and closed her eyes, hearing, knowing. Pity, grief, compassion traced their lines in her face, and the unbearable knowledge that there was nothing that she could do. She had done everything.

*All for nothing . . .*

After a moment she unwound the scarf from around her hands and dragged it again over the armillary, until the crystalline brightness of its gems was veiled, as if in a cloud of dust. Then she got to her feet and crossed to the window. She was still so young, standing there like a queen, but the youth was gone from her face, and Rudy knew that it never came back. The dark, strangely colored eyes were terrible to behold.

He had seen that look in Ingold's eyes. She had knowledge that she would give anything to unknow, had seen what she could never unsee. Closing her eyes, she folded her fist into a white-and-blue hammer and beat it slowly, angrily, on the flawless white wall. As if that could change what she knew would come, could break the wall of what must be.

In time she returned to the table, and laying her head down beside the veiled stars of the armillary sphere, she wept.

# Chapter 16

Swordsmen, Guardsmen, and other professional warriors are always on the lookout for new teachers and new techniques, and Ingold was a welcome addition to the staff of the St. Marcopius Gladiatorial Barracks. Once the men got used to Gil's presence—and the Alketch men were for the most part astonishingly shy of being less than completely dressed around women—she worked as a sparring partner, too, and learned a good deal about different methods of combat. She learned, among other things, how to deal with men who resented the presence of an armed woman and felt called upon to teach her a lesson, but at least two—the Boar and a bouncy, perpetually cheerful Delta Islander called the Little Cat—welcomed the chance to learn about Guards' technique and would push her hard in a bout without malice.

Gil and Ingold had arrived at the tail end of the Hummingbird Games, dedicated to one of the thirty thousand obscure local Alketch saints and financed by Generalissimo Vair na-Chandros to the tune of several hundred thousand silver crowns. There was a certain amount of talk about this in the noisy and garlic-smelling tenement behind the Arena, where they got a room through the good offices of the Boar, a big, inarticulate man with a mustache the size of a sheep. His ring-name in the c'uatal language, Bizjek—the monster red pigs of the deep southern jungles—was pronounced almost the same as the ha'al word for eggplant—bezji'ik—and within a day Gil and Ingold were calling him Eggplant, as everyone else had for years.

Niniak, an eleven-year-old thief who shared the room next to theirs with several of his younger sisters and brothers, explained to Gil as they toted water from the nearest fountain one night that Vair na-Chandros was trying to buy popularity after forcing marriage with the old Emperor's daughter Yori-Ezrikos.

"She sent out letters to every other general and nobleman in the realm offering marriage when her da and her brother croaked, but na-Chandros, he just camped out with his army and told 'em he'd kill all comers." The boy shifted his chewing gum to the other side of his mouth. Everyone, Gil had found, chewed gum, except for the very high nobility, who smoked opium in quantities that would have embarrassed nineteenth-century Chinese mandarins.

"Esbosheth, he came up with some second cousin or something of the old Emp who happened to be *his* nephew, and why didn't Yori-Ezrikos marry this brat and everybody would live happily ever after, and they been fighting ever since."

He shrugged. He had been six at the rising of the Dark, Gil thought. He'd lived through four major wars, plague, and a fire that wiped out a good quarter of the city; he would not remember much of the world before that time.

She felt ancient, and—with her nervousness about crowds, her increasing desire to remain out of sight, and her longing for the silence of the empty lands—extremely provincial.

"Hell, me, I don't see what the problem is," the boy went on cockily. "It don't really matter who she marries—the generals gonna run the country anyway. *I'll* marry her and live in the palace and eat meat every day and do whatever they say."

Gil, who had met Vair na-Chandros when he was in charge of the Alketch effort to assist and conquer the remainder of the Realm of Dar-wath, had her own reflections on how long anyone would last who shared even the illusion of power with that treacherous gentleman, but she kept them to herself. Niniak would have bristled at the merest sug-gestion that he couldn't take care of himself in any situation, and when Ingold wasn't around, had adopted a protective attitude about her as well. He'd given her a tin demon-catcher—a sort of filigree ball with a bit of col-ored glass inside—and a couple of strings of saint-beads, but when they reached the stairway that ran up the side of the tenement, he bounced up ahead of her as a matter of course. He was the male. He might have no shoes on his feet, but he had an honorific diacritical on his name.

Of course he'd go first.

Gil smiled and ascended the stair in his wake. At least Niniak hadn't noticed—or hadn't mentioned—anything strange in her appearance. But in a world where all women went veiled, she reflected, that was no guar-antee he'd notice even a major mutation.

She guessed, too, that Ingold had other reasons for lingering in

Khirsrit. The journey south had been an exhausting one. Scarce as food was in that cruel summer, with starvation walking openly in the lower quarters of the town, those connected with the half-dozen gladiatorial schools ate well. In spite of teaching and sparring eight and ten hours a day—hard physical training against men a third his age—Ingold looked better than he had when they were living off the famished countryside. The wounds on his back and arms were healing, the new scars fresh-red and shocking among the older marks and weals when he stood, half stripped, booted feet apart, in the sand of the ring. Most of the time he didn't even draw his sword until halfway through the bout, contenting himself with effortless dodging and sidestepping and a spate of mild commentary.

In a way, Gil knew, he was enjoying himself. This was his vacation. He was resting, gathering himself for the meeting with the mages under the ice.

There was never a time when Gil was not conscious of them. She feared sleep, for her dreams were foul, and the visions spilled over into waking memory. But such was her exhaustion—or the effect of the poison still working in her blood—that she was tired all the time, sleeping in spite of the heat in their chamber on the uppermost floor, and in spite of the noise of the families who had rooms all along the gallery, who fought and fornicated and shouted deep into the brief nights. She slept in the daytime as well, with the rickety wooden shutters bolted that led onto the gallery—the room was suffocating, but her instincts as a Guard would not permit anything else. In her dreams she sometimes saw the pool of heaving mists shimmering in the blue nonlight of the glacier's heart, heard the singing of the ice-mages as they wrought their spells.

Sometimes she would know what they were singing and would wake with hammering heart to see Ingold, sitting in the opened half of the shutters, gazing out into the starry night.

The day after the end of the Hummingbird Games there was a rumor that Esbosheth's army was going to make a try on the Hathyobar walls. Gil and Niniak walked down to the Southgate quarter and sat on the parapet overlooking the jewel-blue darkness of Lake Nychee and the half-burned counterpane of gold and green and black that were the fields visible beyond. No army showed up. Vair na-Chandros' men waited in gold-and-black, phoenix-headed barges drawn up around the watergates, painted holy banners stirring in the sullen breeze, and the generalissimo himself put in a brief appearance in his renowned cloak of peacock tails, but by that time people were getting bored and leaving.

On the rose-red walls themselves, Gil felt queerly exposed, visible to the looming shape of gray and black and green and killing white that was the Mother of Winter, a crouching monster reared against the sky. During the journey south, Ingold had spoken of the tombs cut into the complex of canyons at the mountain's feet, spoken with an edge of distant anger in his voice and the memory of some old pain in his eyes. "Most of the wadis of the necropolis parallel the ridges, just beyond the olive groves, but one of them leads straight back into the mountain itself."

There had been fighting in the necropolis when she and Ingold had first approached the valley, turning them aside into the city. There were mountain apes up there, too, Ingold had said, and almost certainly gaboogoos. She wondered now about how Ingold planned to reach the place at all, much less find where the entrance to the ice-mages' cave lay. If there were gaboogoos, or mountain apes mutated by eating slunch, no spell of concealment would cloak him long.

From the wall she could see the dark smudges of the trees that marked the mouths of the mortuary canyons, the ruined aisles of obelisks, statues, funerary steles.

She asked, "Was one of the Old Emperors blind, Niniak?"

The boy shrugged. "Me, I ain't no egghead. I dunno." He perched on a crenellation with his feet dangling over twenty-five yards of straight drop to the rocky strip of the shore. "How come you want to know that?"

"I heard a story about how one of the tombs up there—" She nodded toward the mountain. "—has a statue in it of a king with no eyes. I wondered who that might be."

"Oh," Niniak said. "Him." He'd bagged a handful of dates from a vendor, had considerately given Gil one and was unselfconsciously consuming the rest. A man needs his strength, after all.

"You know him?" Gil regarded the boy in surprise.

"Sure. At least Old Haystraw, he knows him. Haystraw's the old cripple who begs on the St. Tekmas pillar—that's on the landside south corner of the Arena porch." Landside was west; lakeside was east. Nobody in Khirsrit ever said west or east. Every pillar of the Arena porch was named for a different saint, and everyone in town knew which was which.

Niniak spit a date pit over the precipice of the wall and craned his neck to watch it hit the pebbles. "Haystraw, he used to be a tomb-robber, till the bishop's guards caught him. But he talked all the time about this king and that king, like they was his family or somethin'. But anyhow everybody, they knows about the Blind King's Tomb. It's way up that third canyon there—see? The canyon splits in two and you push through the trees and go up the left way, and between these two big ol' pillars there's a door and that's the Blind King's Tomb. Haystraw, he says there's this statue inside of the Blind King sitting on his throne with no eyes and his dog laying by his feet. But the canyon's bad luck, and anyway, everything up there's been picked over already."

He shrugged and spit another date pit. "Your old man, he ask me about it yesterday. He crazy?" he inquired conversationally, simply for information.

Gil gave it some thought. "I don't think so," she said. "I'm in a small minority, though." *Two,* she thought. *Three, if Alde's feeling charitable.*

Niniak laughed. "You talk funny. What's a minority?"

"A small group. If five thousand people think Ingold's crazy as a coot, and me and one other guy think he's sane, we're a minority. Let's go," she added, seeing one of the sentries on the wall idling over in their direction. Why any man would assume that a skinny, mannishly dressed woman with a scarred face who made no effort to proposition them was a prostitute just because she was unveiled was a mystery to her, but they all did. About half of them started negotiations with Niniak rather than with herself.

She held out her hand, to steady Niniak down off the parapet. As she did so she was marginally aware of the sudden throbbing of wings in the seven-foot forest of reeds along the lakeshore: ducks, swans, egrets leaping skyward. Gil thought, *They're attacking after all . . .*

The next second the stones of the wall beneath her feet lurched hard, a grating jar that would probably have pitched the boy down if he hadn't been held. The sentry grabbed for the parapet, swearing, and Gil pulled Niniak down quickly, knowing there'd be an S-wave in a second or two.

The S-wave was gentle. The whole thing couldn't have been more than a 4.8 here, but Gil felt cold in her heart. In the streets below the wall she heard yelling, cursing, a woman's scream—it didn't take much these days to set people off. Church bells jangled in every tower in the town. A moment later smoke stung her nose, rolling in billowing white sheets from a tenement; Gil swore. A stove or a lamp—the tenements were all so flimsily built, they'd sway like hula dancers in a quake. Down the street she could see that a half-collapsed church, the residence of hundreds of squatters, had come down completely. A woman was digging at the rubble, screaming.

Niniak yelled, "Damn bitch-festering witches!" his silvery eyes wide with terror.

"What?" Gil said.

He looked up at her as if she were stupid, fear fading almost at once before the male impulse to pedagogy. "Witches. They been making earth-quakes all winter. They get demons to do it. Earthquakes and famines and—"

"Look," Gil said, "why the hell would witches want to make earth-quakes? Or famine, either?" She decided not to get into the issue of why wizards would be setting off volcanoes all over the world in order to cause the cold that caused the famine that caused the plague . . . Presumably they were talking about human wizards, anyway. "I mean, sooner or later if there's a famine, the witches'll starve, too."

"No, they won't." Niniak regarded her with puzzled anger. "They're *witches.* They just make demons bring them food. And they do this stuff 'cause they're evil, is why. Like that bitch witch Hegda that lives on Cop-persmith Market. She's the reason there's all those rats in the city. She makes deals with demons. They're behind all this, 'cause they hate every-body—they were the ones who raised up the Dark. C'mon," he added, rat-tling down the narrow steps that led to the square within the gates. "Me, I think that's all we're gonna get for now, but if my glass bottle's broken back home, I'm gonna go burn that bitch witch Hegda's house myself."

In the wake of the earthquake a dozen fires swept the city. Beggars and the all-powerful street gangs took advantage of the confusion as the precinct firefighters—who doubled as police—tried to quell the blazes themselves or recruit help, and Gil and Niniak made their way back to the tenement behind St. Marcopius through running men, blowing smoke, dust and shouting. The boy dutifully escorted Gil to the base of the stair and then bade her a bright good-bye—"There got to be pickings some-place"—and Gil climbed the rickety, endless flights to the sixth-floor gallery, which miraculously hadn't pulled loose from the wall.

Ingold sat cross-legged in the doorway of their room, tilting his scrying crystal to and fro against the light. He pocketed the stone and stood as Gil picked her way cautiously along the narrow planking, staying as close to the adobe wall as she could. "You did well to return quickly, my dear," he said. He didn't seem terribly worried, and Gil realized that the first thing he must have done when the shaking stopped was to scry for her and make sure she was all right. "Vrango's bullies from the Beehive and the Children of the Revealed Word"—street gangs in Khirsrit often split along the lines of minor heresies—"have already started fighting. It's a good day to stay where we are, I think."

An aftershock touched the building, giving Gil the sickened sensation of being in a tall tree in a high wind. She caught the jamb of the door and clung hard, hoping this one wouldn't bring the already stressed walls down. She saw Ingold staring out through the doorway, not even bothering to hang on; saw the unseeing anger in his blue eyes and the swift harshness of his breathing.

"It's them," she said quietly, "isn't it?" A little shyly, she reached to touch his hand. "The mages in the ice?"

She felt him tense and withdrew her fingers; she understood his caution of her and had kept her distance. In her most matter-of-fact voice she added, "Is it close? The volcano?"

He nodded, and a slight shiver went through him. "In the south," he said. "Deep under the ice. The dust cover is thick already over the poles. We were right to come here, Gil." His tone was that of a man seeking to convince himself, and he did not look at her as he spoke. Turning away, he set about righting his flower pots; they held slips and cuttings of roses, a dozen varieties, from yellow to nearly black. Under the rolled-back sleeves of his woolen shirt, his wrists and forearms were welted from training cuts, the old shackle galls white among the fresh blue-black of bruises.

"They are there." His fingers paused on the extravagant velvet petals of a blossom he'd found in the abandoned court of a plague-sealed palace. "I know they're there."

She said, "In the Blind King's Tomb."

He turned his head sharply, and at that moment, in the street below where it led off the Coppersmith Market, there was a tramping of feet and voices shouting. Forgetting all question of the structural integrity of the building, Gil and Ingold both stepped to the gallery's splintered and sun-damaged rail. In the lane below a small squad of na-Chandros' black-armored soldiers hurried, surrounded by a flying storm of broken cobble-stones, dirt clods, and filth hurled from windows and alleys along their route.

They weren't dodging or turning to fight the gaggle of men who trailed them like pi-dogs in the wake of a butcher's cart. After a moment Gil made out what the voices were shouting: "Witch-bitch! Demon whore!"

"Hegda." Ingold stood with folded arms at her side, the extravagant green-and-purple chain of saint-beads he wore when not in the Arena glistening in the afternoon sun. He made no move to check his theory with the scrying stone, for the vicious-tongued old countrywoman who sold spells in the Coppersmith Market had sufficient mageborn power to prevent being scried by another mage. Ingold had spoken to her on a number of occasions—she'd spit on him yesterday for disagreeing with her—and Gil considered her no loss. "They've only been waiting their chance."

"The local Church authorities?" The height of the building and the narrowness of the street made it almost impossible to see down, but as the armored squad turned into St. Marcopius Square at the end of the lane, she recognized the bent, drunkenly staggering figure among them, arms and neck banded with mingled layers of chains of all weights and lengths, steel and copper, silver and lead. Runes of Silence, Runes of Binding, Runes of Ward, were hung on them, lead plaques that made a curious muffled clashing, spell-ribbons fluttering like dirty pennons, fur-ther numbing her power.

"Why would they care? It isn't like she's working for one of the warlords."

"Yet." Ingold led her back, gently, to the door of their room, the boards of the gallery swaying queasily under their feet. For a moment his hand, resting in the small of her back, had the old warm familiarity, the ease that had always been between them; then he seemed to remember that she could not be trusted, for he carefully took his hand away. Looking quickly at his face, Gil saw the expression in his eyes that she had seen there so often these four days in Khirsrit: not wary so much as questioning, uncertain. His eyes met hers for a moment and turned quickly away, and anger went through her, a sickening weary rage at the mages in the ice.

Ingold was already within their bare little room, gathering up her spare shirt and his from the table where they had been drying. "It isn't only the other warlords they worry about, you know," he went on. "The Church has never liked the idea of people going to wizards to solve their problems—or what they perceive to be their problems—instead of using the more difficult methods of faith, self-examination, and trust in God . . . accompanied, in many cases, by the advice of the Church. In good times the Church can afford to rely on their contention that magic erodes the soul and all illusion is the work of the Evil One or Ones. But in days of famine, when everyone is afraid, people think less of saving their souls than they do of feeding their children. And bishops are only human," he added softly, folding the worn garments and laying them on the small stack of rucksacks and spare clothing in the corner. "In these days, they're afraid as well. I warned her to leave town."

Gil remembered the children in Niniak's little band, country children with haunted eyes and ribs like barrel hoops, risking their lives to steal bread. "Maybe she didn't have anywhere else to go."

At sunset Niniak appeared in the open shutters of their doorway with the news that the woman Hegda would be burned in the Arena at noon the next day. "She was the one who started the earthquake, you know?" The boy had his brothers and sisters around him, like filthy little feral puppies; Ingold always kept a few scraps from supper to give them. The Eggplant and the Gray Cat, who lived on the lower floors of the building, did the same.

"Oh, come on!" Gil said impatiently, very conscious of Ingold, who was dozing on their blankets. "Why the hell would anyone want to do that?"

"Because she's evil," Niniak retorted, baffled by the question. He shifted his gum to the other side of his mouth. "Or maybe some rich guy, he paid her to. But she started it, all right. She confessed."

"How very astonishing," Ingold murmured without opening his eyes. "A woman who has the power to raise earthquakes, living in a hovel all these months and begging her bread in the marketplace."

The thief looked doubtful, then regarded him with narrow suspicion in his silver eyes. "She confessed. And she's a witch. Witches do weird stuff."

Ingold sighed and folded his hands on his breast. "You have me there," he admitted.

He went with Gil to the auto-da-fé, in a crowd of men from the gladiatorial school. The Arena was packed to its topmost tiers, and a line of Church soldiers, shaven-headed in their loose crimson uniforms, demarcated the end of the long, narrow combat pit where the stake was set, the rest of the sand being taken up by an impenetrable jam of spectators. The show was free, even to the nobility, the bankers, the corn-brokers and landlords. Ingold winced when two red-robed Church functionaries threw a couple of seedy scrolls and a codex or two on the head-high pile of brushwood and logs: Hegda's books, such as they were. Other Church soldiers led the woman out, weaving unsteadily and still laden with chains, her long white mare's tails of hair snagging in the bloody weals that crossed her naked back.

"Yellow jessamine," Ingold said quietly to Gil. His voice had a distant quality, and he was withdrawn into himself, with pain or shame—though a woman like Hegda had owed no allegiance to the Council of Wizards, its Archmage, Ingold, still felt he should be able to protect her. "The Council of Wizards usually uses bluegall root, which numbs the ability to use magic but leaves the prisoner otherwise unharmed. The Church favors jessamine. In a way it's merciful, under the circumstances. She won't be more than half conscious."

Gil shivered. She had seen death—had killed men and women herself, coldly and without thought, though later the reaction had sometimes been devastating. But it had always been in combat, and always quick. As a medievalist, she'd read about burnings, but had never seen one. She didn't know if she could deal with the reality.

The soldiers assisted the reeling figure up the ladder and lashed it to the stake. A crimson ecclesiastic stepped forth from among the guards, slim, straight, terrible as a bloodstained stiletto, and with uplifted white hands cried ritual words. At the sound of that harsh alto voice, Gil gasped and tried to peer past the massive forms surrounding her. "Want a better look, Gilly?" the Eggplant asked, and huge hands clasped her waist, lifting her effortlessly to a shoulder like a park bench. They were down in the reserved gladiators' section, close to ringside but near the center of the field. Someone yelled, "Down in front!" and Sergeant Cush turned around and yelled something about the protester's mother.

"Set me down," Gil said to the coiled, beaded braids next to her elbow, and the Eggplant glanced up at her.

"Stuff 'em, Gilly, they're just rubes." The Eggplant cracked his gum. He was very fond of her and had recently broken four of the King's ribs

after His Majesty had made a rather rough pass at Gil in the Arena's pil-
lared porch. Cush had given him five lashes for putting the King out of
action on the last day of the games, and the King had gone around ever
since saying that Gil was a girl-lover anyway, and ugly. Gil knew she
shouldn't care, but that hurt.

"No, it's okay." She'd seen what she needed to see. In a way, she had
known from the moment she heard the voice of the Prince-Bishop of
Alketch, speaking the words of eternal cursing upon the condemned. As
the Eggplant swung her down from her perch, she cast a quick final glance
at the Prince-Bishop, ivory pale among the ebony faces of guards and lesser
clerics. She could almost feel the bonfire heat of those hooded dark eyes.

The Prince-Bishop of Alketch, officiating prelate at the witch Hegda's
execution, was none other than Ingold's old nemesis Govannin Narmenlion, quondam Bishop of Gae. "Ingold," she said breathlessly, "Ingold, it's—"
She looked around for him among the gladiators.

He was nowhere to be found.

There was a literary tradition in the world where Gil had been brought
up—and in fact in the less respectable fiction of the Wathe, to which
Minalde was addicted, as well—that any heroine worthy of her corsetry,
upon finding herself in a situation of peril, should promptly run away
seeking her hero, endangering both herself and everyone else in the
process. Having searched for people in the woods, and knowing Ingold
fairly well, Gil remained with the gladiators, which was where she
guessed he'd look for her when he decided to reappear. In any case it was
useless to search for the old man if he did not wish to be found. He had
his scrying crystal, and would rejoin her when he had either ascertained
what he'd departed to ascertain or when whatever danger he perceived
approaching had passed.

In the end Gil did not see the actual burning, owing to the thickness
of the crowd. Pressed on all sides by a mob of sweating bodies, she heard
the old woman's slurred cursing turn to screams and barely smelled the
wood smoke and charring flesh above the stench of sweat, pomade, and
dust. A boy came by and tried to pick her pocket; another tried to sell her
a stick of fried bread. She managed not to throw up, but the Icefalcon
would be ashamed, she felt, of her squeamishness.

The Eggplant walked her back to St. Marcopius, his face a study in
inarticulate worry when a rush of faintness swept over her in the market-

place. He insisted she sit on the corner of a fountain until she felt better, and pushing his way off through the crowds, returned a short time later with a brightly colored coat of the kind fashionable among the gladiators' molls just then, adorned with bits of mirror and patches of leather and steel. He waved off her startled thanks. "You're cold," he said, helping her to her feet—and indeed, though very bright, the day was turning chill. "Your hands are freezing."

She put her hands out of sight in the wrapped front of the coat as quickly as possible, suddenly overcome with humiliation. She had dreamed last night about a ruined villa they'd passed through, in the near-empty city of Zenuuak—dreamed of the mirror she'd found in an inner room, and the transformed horror reflected in it. All day she'd been surreptitiously checking her hands. The gladiator seemed not to notice, however; he escorted her up all six flights to her door. After she thanked him, she bolted the shutters, knowing Ingold to be perfectly capable of working the bolts from the other side. She lay down on the mattress and fell into sleep as if drugged.

She woke to blue darkness and the sound of knocking. "It's me, Gilly," came Niniak's voice.

"I knocked earlier," the boy added when she opened the shutters. The sky over the red-and-yellow city's parapets was dimming, all the bells of its churches speaking their incomprehensible rounds. The smell of charred timber hung heavy in the air. Farther along the gallery some of the men who lived up there, a tailor and a shoemaker and a man who sold fish off a barrow in the street, played pitnak while their wives talked and sewed.

Gil scratched at her heavy mane of unbraided hair. "It's okay." She still felt queasy, and wondered a little at her own exhaustion. "What can I do for you?"

The boy's pixie face twisted in an odd expression, and he held out a broken curve of potsherd, such as shopkeepers toted up their addition on, or sent notes to one another, provided they could write. "Ingold, he asked me to give you this."

It said:

*Gil—*

*Forgive me. It was necessary for me to flee, at once. How they knew I was here I do not know for certain, though Hegda may have seen more in me than she said and passed it on to them to spare herself more pain.*

*Stay off the streets as much as you can, and guard yourself. I am safe. Only wait.*

"He's left you." Niniak's voice was neutral, dead, but she could tell the boy was furiously angry.

She shook her head. "He's just had to go into hiding. It sounds like he saw someone in the crowd . . ."

"Or he saw you had your back turned." The pale silver eyes glittered with old memory, old rage. "Like just 'cause you're ugly and got a scar and all you aren't a hundred times better than all them stupid girls that flounce around the street after men. What an idiot!"

Gil realized, with some surprise, that the boy had a crush on her. She hid a smile at this piece of consciousness-raising and said, "No. Ingold has enemies . . ."

Niniak held out a second potsherd. "He said give you this three days from now, if he wasn't back."

Gil went cold to her heart.

*Forgive me. It is all that I can ask. Please, please understand.*

*They hear with your ears. They see with your eyes. This I guessed, leaving the Keep—but I also guessed that you would follow, against your own will, did I not bring you. It has been death in my heart daily, hourly, to do this to you.*

*Without you at my side I stand some chance of reaching the cavern of the ice-mages before they realize I am on the mountain and rally the gaboogoos, the dooic, the mountain apes who because of the slunch are theirs to command—maybe even the armies of the warlords, for I cannot know now how far their power has reached. They knew of me through the minds of the Dark, in their dreaming, even as the Dark knew of them. As the Dark took my mind . . .*

Gil turned the sherd over; the writing was worse on the back.

*. . . so the ice-mages saw. They know I am a danger, insofar as any can be. This may be my only chance.*

As if she heard their voices in the distance, she felt the outcry of them, realizing they had been circumvented, tricked—realizing he was on his way.

She felt them call out, drawing everything they could to them—gaboogoos, cave-apes, mutants. Readying themselves to crush him.

*No*, she thought, her heart screaming as she felt that frantic, furious call. *NO!*

*I love you, Gil. If I have not returned by this time, I will not return. I bless you, I free you. I only regret—and I regret with all my heart—that I cannot see you safe again to the Keep. But I cannot be two men. I fear that with you, I have not even been one.*

*Please understand, as a warrior understands.*

*Please do not despise me for what I had to do.*

*If I have not returned, it is because I met my death at the hands of the ice-mages; and I met it with your name on my lips.*

*With all that is in me*
*—Inglorion*

# Chapter 17

Cold jerked Rudy awake. Cold and pain, an overwhelming wrenching breathlessness. Then a sense of shock that he knew instantly was secondhand but was clear as a scream in his mind. *Ingold!* he thought, staring into the blackness of his cell, knowing immediately the source. *Ingold . . . !*

The feeling didn't fade, but grew. Dizziness, the swimming dots of fire that merged into a single, terrible light; the numbing of his left arm; the hammer-blow of pain over his heart.

*Ingold!*

Rudy's mind fumbled, disoriented, with his sense of time. He'd fallen asleep in a tangle of old books and Gil's notes after more vain hours of searching for the answers he knew had to be somewhere: to time and stasis, to the power that had come to him at call, the power he had never felt before. He wasn't as good as Ingold yet at knowing immediately where the stars were at any moment of the day or night, but reaching out with his senses, he heard nothing in the watchroom of the Guards but the desultory click of the single worn set of pitnak tiles, and from their barracks only the soft draw of sleepers' breath.

The cold, the pain, the breathlessness, were already pouring away like smoke into a hole in darkness. Rudy fumbled with trembling hands under his pillow for his crystal, body aching from the aftershock. *Christ, don't do this to me, man!* The witchlight he summoned flared in the crystal's heart. *Answer me! Tell me it ain't so . . .*

Nothing. The thick grayness of the ice-mages' malice seemed to choke the air.

*God damn it, God damn it, answer me!*

He lowered his hands, the witchlight fading. *No. No.*

*Don't make me be the only wizard in this godforsaken world! Don't make me have to go after the ice-mages myself.*

*I'm not any good at this, dammit!*

Pain. Breathlessness. Dizziness. Pain.

He couldn't sort them easily in his mind, but he knew it was Ingold's pain he'd felt. Knew it as surely as if he'd heard the old man's voice.

*It's three o'clock in the Christly morning!* Rudy wanted to scream. *What the hell are you doing fighting monsters at three in the morning?*

If Ingold were no longer alive, thought Rudy, he'd be able to see Gil even if she were with him . . .

But even that he could not do.

*He can't be dead,* he thought, whispering it to himself like a mantra, willing it to be true. *He can't be dead.*

It was an endless time until dawn.

Accompanied by Janus, Melantrys, and the Icefalcon, he left the Keep as soon as the Doors were opened, climbed to the high ground near the orchards, where the slunch was less, and drew a power-circle, Summoning to himself every scrap and whisper of magic to be had from the earth, from the streams, from the dawn-fading stars.

But whether Ingold was dead and Gil in some place where the influence of the ice-mages lay too thick to pierce, or whether Ingold lived and Gil were with him, he could get no shadow of either of them in his scrying stone's heart. Head aching from the exertion, he tried to contact Thoth, but all that appeared in the amethyst's facets were dim images of flabby, death-colored fungoid parodies of human and animal life crawling out of a wasteland of slunch to attack the patched, rambling pile of the Black Rock Keep.

Even that view was distant. He thought he could see men with weapons around the walls of black and gray stone, and brushwood stacked before the battered iron doors and along the north wall where the wizards had their little beehive hermitages, but he could not be sure. Cold wind blew down on his back, and behind him he heard a swift scuffle, a slithering and then the heavy chunk, like someone hitting a watermelon with an ax. Blood-smell stung his nostrils as he turned.

"Better get back." The Icefalcon struck his ax into the earth to clean it. Whatever had come out of the slunch-decayed woods to attack lay in bleeding pieces at his feet. "There's more on the way. See anything?"

Rudy shook his head despairingly. Gaunt and tired, Janus and Melantrys were closing around them. At the foot of the slope the woods were thick with slunch, hanging in dirty mats and clumps from the branches of the dying trees. Something was moving deep in the infected glades, and Rudy shoved the crystal into the pocket of his vest and headed for the Keep. Fast.

"If Gil's with the old boy, he can't be too bad off," Janus pointed out.

As they sprang up the shallow black steps of the Keep, Janus turned back to scan the woods, shifting his sword in his bandaged hand; the wound he'd taken three weeks ago from a mutated dire wolf hadn't even begun to heal. This wasn't like the rip in Gil's face, attributable to some gaboogoo venom. Nobody's wounds were healing these days.

The dark line of hemlocks that fringed the high woods shuddered suddenly, shook and parted. Rudy gasped, "Mother pus-bucket!" and Janus only said, "Pox rot it, but it had to happen sooner or later. Get inside. We'll take care of it." Melantrys was already yelling for the rest of the Guards.

The thing plowing down the slope, head lolling and limbs and pseudo-limbs churning the white slunch to scraps and powder, was a mutated mammoth.

Scala Hogshearer was in the workroom when Rudy got there. The Guards' watchroom was a flurry of activity as he passed through it, men and women catching up weapons, heading fast for the door. He saw the girl's shadow moving back and forth in the dim lamplight that was the chamber's only illumination, heard her furious sobbing in the corridor, and at the sound, his own anger rose in him, a poisonous, breathtaking heat.

He stopped in the doorway, fighting to keep calm.

She'd ripped to pieces the parchment on which he'd been remaking the *Black Book of Lists*; had emptied boxes, scattered and broken the ivory rune sticks, smashed the porcelain scrying bowl and ground its pieces to dust under her wooden heels. The cupboard in which he locked all the truly precious stuff bore signs of ferocious battering, the hinges and lock surrounded by white, ripped wood where she'd tried to hack them free of the doors.

There was blood under her fingernails from the effort. She was clinging to the edge of the table as if on the verge of being sick, her dark, dirty hair hanging lank around a face bloated with tears.

"I can't do magic!" she screamed at him when he finally stepped through the door. She picked up his astrolabe—or what was left of it—and smashed it again and again into the surface of the table, the edge of the dial leaving huge scars in the wood. "I can't do magic anymore! I tried! I tried!"

She flung the metal circle into the corner and hurled herself at Rudy, pounding his chest with her fists as he grabbed her wrists and held her off. Even as heavy as she'd gotten recently, she was less strong than he expected.

"Scala, you can," he said gently, a little surprised at his own patience. Part of him wanted to smash the spoiled little bitch's head up against the wall, but that wasn't the part in control. *Son of a gun,* he thought detachedly, in the back of his mind. *I must be growing up . . .*

"Whoa," he said, as she began to hack at his shins. "Whoa, whoa, whoa . . . Take it easy, kiddo."

Her anger wasn't personal. And underneath it, underneath the fear of losing the attention of important people like Lady Sketh, was the horror of a loss that only he, of all those in the Keep, could comprehend.

"You're not teaching me right!" Her voice was a hysterical wail. "You're not teaching me what I need to know! Daddy says you have to! Daddy says he'll make you sorry if you don't! Daddy says—"

"Do you believe I'm not teaching you?"

"I can't do it!" She pulled against him, the unexpected reversal breaking his grip. She staggered back against the edge of the table, slapping at him and missing. Her face was a pulp of tears and snot, looking almost black in the dim, wavery glow of the lamps. "I tried! I tried all morning! I've done all your stupid exercises and your stupid meditation and everything you said and I can't do magic at all! I used to! I used to and now I can't!"

She blundered past him, shoving him out of her way. He heard her smacking into the walls of the corridor as she fled, sobbing, into the dark.

Rudy made a step to go after her, then gave it up. "Swell," he sighed. "So now I get a visit from Daddy. Just what I needed to top off the day. How lucky can a guy be?"

He rubbed his face, the ache of sleeplessness in his bones. *Ingold,* he thought. There had to be some way of learning what had happened to him. Of learning if he were still alive. He stopped to gather the torn parchments, the broken pieces of the ivory sticks. At least she hadn't burned the parchments this time.

He paused, the parchment in his hand.

*Anger?* he wondered. *Or something else? The voices of the ice-mages whispering in her mind?*

*Are you saying my girl isn't a wizard?*

His mind replayed the scene. Scala falling. The gaboogoos bounding past her, tripping over her, while she clutched her hair and screamed.

*They only attack the mageborn,* Thoth had said.

"Rudy? Master Wizard?"

Tir was standing in the doorway.

He still wore his cool formality, the stiff pose of distance, hands folded over his belt knot. Rudy straightened up, brightened the witchlight that flickered on the wall spikes, and inclined his head. *This will pass,* he told himself, to quiet the hurt in his heart at the boy's wary aloofness. *Whether he ever ceases to blame you for the death of his friends, this coldness will one day pass.*

"What can I do for you, Tir?" He brought up a chair—by the look of it, the one Scala had used to pound on the cupboard doors. Tir gazed around him at the carnage but didn't comment. He'd probably passed Scala in the hall.

"Rudy, there's people disappearing." He climbed up into the chair and sat with feet dangling. Like nearly everyone else in the Keep, he'd lost a lot of flesh, and in the frame of his black hair, his face seemed all eyes.

"Disappearing?" His fears for Ingold—his terror that he'd be the one, now, who had to deal with the ice-mages—vanished before the memory of the locked doors on the fifth level, the stink of the newly deserted rooms.

The child licked his lips, gathering his thoughts. "I didn't think . . . You know how sometimes you don't see somebody for a couple days, like they're doing something for their mamas or something?" His voice was soft and scared. "But I got Linnet to make me a calendar, and I marked it, every day, who I saw and who I didn't."

*He's too young for this,* Rudy thought, looking into the lupine darkness of those eyes. *Too young to have to deal with this.*

"There's people disappearing, Rudy. They really are. Brikky Gatson, and Noop Farrier, and Noop's papa and his papa's brother Yent and Melleka Biggar, and Rose White and both her brothers and their mama, too. Those were all the ones I started with. I hadn't seen them and I've been keeping marks for three weeks, Rudy. Old Man Wicket and Rab Brown and a couple of others, they stopped coming around, too. Only I didn't want anybody to know I've been asking about how long it's been."

"Fifth level north," Rudy said softly. "All of them except the Farriers, and they're fourth level north, right under the Biggars."

"And there's a stairway that leads from the Biggars' warren down to there. They go up and down all the time. It can't be plague because you're a Healer," the boy went on. "The other Healers would have told you, or Mama. And nobody called the Guards or the Hunters to go look for them in the woods, and nobody talked to Mama about them being lost or asked you to find them with your crystal, did they?"

"No," Rudy said softly. "Nobody asked." He fished out his crystal, though he knew he wouldn't be able to see anything. The slunch within the Keep, magnified and concentrated by the Keep's walls, held inside the malice of the ice-mages. In any case it was sometimes difficult to see gaboogoos by crystal.

"Old Man Wicket, the Noops, the Whites," he said, half to himself. "Koram Biggar's the head man in that section of the Keep. He can't not know. He can't not have seen . . ."

"Seen what?" Tir asked. "That they've disappeared?"

"Seen what they're turning into. Seen why they can't go out in the open anymore." He pocketed the crystal, got to his feet, knowing coldly, clearly, with hard-etched certainty in his heart that what he suspected was true.

"Scala, too," he said softly. "Poor kid . . . Thanks." He extended his hand, and after a doubtful moment Tir took it, eyes still wary and withdrawn. "You keep a good eye on things." He released his grip after one quick clasp, making it thanks only and nothing else. "Whatever else they tell you, keeping an eye on things is a king's job. I think it's time to tell your mama about this, and about some other stuff that's been going on. One more thing."

Tir paused, having scrambled down from his chair. Cautious, not ready to give.

"Don't look for these guys yourself, okay?" Hands on hips, Rudy regarded the boy, heart wrung at how fragile he looked, how vulnerable. "You've told me, so now it's my job. I'll get some Guards and go visit Biggar and Wicket and that whole section. You're not walking around the back halls of the Keep by yourself, are you?" Kids did, he knew.

Tir shook his head. "There's bad places there," he said softly. "Spooky places. They smell weird. It's safe where people are."

"Good," Rudy said. "After I've talked with your mama, would you be willing to take me around the Keep and show me where these bad places are?"

The boy hesitated, tallying in his head whether this familiarity would constitute a betrayal of his dead friends. Then he nodded. "All right." His voice was barely a whisper. As he disappeared into the dark of the corridor again, Rudy saw a king's duty in his eyes.

*People disappearing.* Rudy thought the matter over as he finger-nailed up the tiniest slivers of enchanged ivory and porcelain from the floor.

*You eat the slunch and pretty soon Los Tres Geezers start talking to you in your head, and you don't notice that Uncle Albert is turning into a pus-colored eyeless monster—or else you think, Hey, it ain't so bad.*

And meanwhile the noose around the Keep was tightening. For the past four days he and his bodyguard had had to fight off at least one attack daily by mutated wolves or eagles or wolverines on the way back to the Keep from the circles of power drawn under the watchtowers. It was becoming almost impossible for him to go outside of the Keep to scry.

There'd been another temblor yesterday, and the daylight was noticeably wan. After a long search in the scrying table he'd found the culprit, a dark cone of ash and lava pouring fire and blackness from the bleak marble white of the southern wastes.

*Cripes,* he thought, sitting back on his haunches now, staring sightlessly into the shadowless pale light of the workroom. *What the hell are we gonna do? What're we gonna do if Ingold's dead?*

He got up, unfastened the locks on the cupboard and cleared away the spells of Ward—which didn't seem to have stopped Scala's attack—and looked at the half-dozen little black knobs of protospuds, the tinier reddish beads.

He hefted one of the potatoes in his hand. Smooth, like polished hematite. He could just see the little eyes on its hard black belly, as if someone had taken the true essence of a potato, the genetic coding of what it actually was, and condensed it into this shorthand facsimile, designed to withstand all of time.

But it was alive. Deep within its heart, buried under all those spells of stasis, he could feel the unmistakable glow of sleeping life.

*It's the answer,* he thought. *Goddammit, I know it's the answer. Why'd I have to be the one to stay here? Gil should be doing this. She's the scholar.*

But he was the wizard. He was the one who understood magic. Gil might be able to decipher hidden clues from the record crystals—from

Tir's memories—from the visions he'd had through the Cylinder, all of which he'd meticulously written down. But he was the one who should be able to know what to do with the information.

And he didn't.

Without Ingold, they'd never survive.

He thought back on the hideous sensations of last night. An attack? Somehow it had felt more like something else—heart failure, maybe. A few days ago, by exhaustive efforts at weaving a power-circle, he'd managed to contact Ingold for a few minutes, enough to learn that they'd made it safely to the Alketch capital of Khirsrit, where they were working as gladiators, of all things: Ingold with his hair bound up in a topknot and looking like an overage thug.

But after that, nothing.

Scala's footfalls shuffled in the hallway. There was no mistaking that full-bodied sniffle. She was alone, thank God.

He closed the cupboard door and locked it, casually draping Ward-spells all over it again as she sidled into the room. Her face was puffy and blotched and he saw again how her gown strained over her plump shoulders, and anger tweezered him again, remembering the fragile pointiness of Tir's cheekbones, the way Alde's shoulder blades seemed to be coming out through her colorless skin.

Scala was holding a covered pottery dish about the size of a mixing bowl, and her eyes slipped furtively from side to side.

"Rudy, you've got to teach me right." She sniffed again; her voice trembled with desperation. "You've got to find out why I can't do magic anymore. You've got to help me, Rudy, please. Daddy . . ." Her mouth worked briefly, then she got it under control. "You don't know what it's like with Daddy. He says I'm not trying, but I am trying. I just—I just can't do it." She wiped her nose on her sleeve, then her eyes. "Please help me."

The pleading in her eyes was genuine. He wondered what Dear Old Dad's reaction would be when it became clear that he couldn't make good on his promises of future services to those who were counting on having a mage on their side. He could almost feel sorry for this spoiled, angry, self-important child, who faced for the first time in her life something she couldn't do and couldn't get anyone else to give her.

The fact that she had once had magic made it all the worse.

"Scala," he said quietly, "I'll do what I can. But—"

"I promise you I won't use magic against you, whatever Lady Sketh and the others tell me," she whispered. "I'll tell them I can't, that you're too strong. I'll do whatever you say. Only please, please give me something I can show Daddy."

She set the bowl on the table. "I brought you this." Her words were a bare breath now, and she glanced over her shoulder again at the door. "We're not supposed to tell, because then everyone in the Keep will want it and there isn't enough. Master Biggar and Old Man Wicket only give us so much. But if you teach me, I'll make sure you always have some. You and whoever else you want, Queen Minalde or Prince Tir or anybody. I'll steal it for you. Just help me. Please teach me something I can do. I don't want Daddy mad at me again."

Rudy uncovered the bowl. The smell of it rose around his face, familiar and chalky-sweet, like medicine half recalled from childhood. In the cool bright witchlight the stuff had a waxy glimmer, and Rudy looked up from it to his pupil's bloated face.

It was a porridge made of slunch.

# Chapter 18

*K*oram *Biggar and Old Man Wicket.* Rudy's shadow poured itself out of the darkness behind him like a monster ghost, ran along the wall as he strode past the glowstone in its iron-strapped niche and streamed ahead of him to darkness again. *"Whatever Lady Sketh tells me" indeed!*

He wondered whether Lady Sketh and her hapless lord were followers of Saint Bounty's gluttonous cult, or whether they were just allied with Biggar and his ilk because Biggar was hiding his illicit chickens in the Sketh enclave and giving them a cut; whether Lady Sketh—or Lord Ankres—even knew where those people went, who "disappeared."

He shivered, thinking about the deformed bones Gil had showed him, and the things that attacked him in the woods. The deformed mammoth that was even at this moment throwing itself against the impregnable doors of the Keep.

Alde would be in her chambers at this time of the morning, resting. She rested as much as she could these days. She was due in a month, maybe less. Rudy had assisted at a birth last week; Lythe Crabfruit, a woman taller and sturdier than Alde, even accounting for the malnutrition endemic in the Keep these days. She had died, in spite of everything he could do, and her baby with her. Not all the magic he could summon could breathe strength into her, could prevent the slipping away of those two lives from beneath his hands. Afterward he'd gone to the watchroom and gotten drunk on Blue Ruin. Now, with the grain shortage in the Keep, there wasn't even much of that.

*Ingold can't be dead,* Rudy thought desperately. *He can't be!*

Every time he saw Minalde he was filled with fear. He literally couldn't imagine what he'd do without her in his life.

Something skittered, scratching in a cell somewhere behind him. A cat fled yowling and Rudy swung around, listening, stretching his senses to hear . . .

Nothing. Or almost nothing. He'd taken the Royal Way, the wide main corridor on third south, glowstones all the way—they *couldn't* be pursuing him straight into the Royal Sector. He moved on, uneasy, his soft boots making little sound on the black stone floor. As usual in daytime, the Keep was nearly empty, the weavers and scribes attached to Minalde's service having taken their work outside.

*Saint Bounty. Patron saint of slunch.* No wonder the gaboogoos hadn't touched Scala the day of the attack on the Hill of Execution. No wonder she'd gradually lost the ability to work magic, as greediness—and almost certainly the stress of her father's expectations and demands— had driven her to gorge herself on Saint Bounty's magical abundance.

He wondered if it was something that would work itself out of her system eventually. She hadn't begun to change physically, though some people obviously had. If anything had happened to Ingold, if Wend and Ilae bought it, they'd need another wizard bad.

*There!*

He swung around again, his whole body prickling with the sense of being followed, of danger, of pursuit. He shifted his staff in his hand, and ball lightning flickered on the horns of its crescent. He rubbed his fingertips, summoning the power to within a breath of reality, until he could feel it crackle beneath his skin.

Minalde had two rooms tucked away behind the Council chamber, close to the Bronze Bird Fountain, in the warmest and most protected portion of the Royal Sector. Her door was open, a trapezoidal throw rug of amber lamplight lying on black stone floor. The other rooms along that corridor were closed off with shutters or heavy curtains. She sometimes sang as she sewed, but there was no sound, not even the scratching of her stylus on the wax writing tablets.

"Alde?" he called out, quickening his stride. "Alde, it's—"

Something in the room fell with a crash. A table toppled over, glass or a dish broken . . . *(And still no reaction?)* Rudy stopped in his tracks. Given the scarcity of glass, even the soft-spoken Minalde would have sworn at that one.

So he was already bringing up his pronged staff for action when the gaboogoos flung themselves out the door at him as if they'd been shot from a gun.

Lightning lanced from the metal of the staff head, splitting the thing that looked like a blubbery, flying squid as it flew toward his face; he cut and slashed off the hand of another with the razor crescent, then impaled the thing, shoved it back, called down ball-lightning that half blinded him in a roar of purple-white glare. The corridor stank of smoke and what smelled like burned rubber, and with a scratching grate of claws two things that had started out genetically as rats sprang at him from behind. He turned, cutting, slashing with lightning, terrified to use it in these confined quarters; the rat-thing rolled over and over, burning, and then lay still.

Rudy was already in Minalde's room. She was just stumbling out of the wardrobe whose heavy black-oak door was ripped and chewed and holed in a dozen places, black hair in a streaming tangle down her back, sobbing with shock and relief. The maid Linnet was stretched on the floor against the wall, throat a mass of sucker marks and bruises—Alde collapsed to her knees beside the body. The table Linnet had kicked over as a warning lay on its side amid smashed glass and spilled ink. Rudy dropped beside the woman and felt her hand.

Cold. Pulseless.

The life was there, though; he pressed his hands to her throat, to her chest, to her temples, calling on her—calling her to return. *Linnet! Linnet, dammit . . . !*

He thought he heard her whisper her daughter's name. The name of the man who had been killed by the Dark on the long road from Penambra, leaving her with child in that awful time.

*Linnet, come back!*

*Alde needs you, for Chrissake!*

Though his body did not move, crouched over the bruised and waxen tangle of flesh and hair, in that gray otherworld he held out his hand.

The gaboogoos were coming. He heard them.

Not gaboogoos. Mutants. Voices and footfalls, and the soggy thump of bodies staggering into corners and walls. He smelled them, like dirty rubber and ammonia mixed.

*Linnet . . . !*

He saw her, with the same queer doubled perception he had known through the Cylinder, as if the experience with that ancient magic had taught him to see more clearly. Saw Alde's friend standing alone in the gray country, looking much as she had when he first saw her on the march up from the river valley, her dark hair unstitched with gray and her young face unlined. She knew him, and for a moment anger passed across her face, anger and grief. Behind her there were shadows—a man and a little girl. Waiting, he thought.

Alde was calling his name. Warning . . .

Linnet turned from the man and the child, stretched out her hand to take his.

It all seemed to happen in seconds. Linnet's hand clutched convulsively at his sleeve and she began to gasp like a landed fish; Alde swung back around from the wall where she'd taken down the halberd Gnift the Swordmaster made her learn to use three years ago, when there'd been danger of a bandit attack on the Vale. Her night-dark eyes flooded with tears in the unsteady lamplight, but she didn't leave the door of the room.

Rudy snatched up his staff and called the lightning again, called it to within inches of his fingertips. The room was a trap and the footfalls were closer, coming down the corridor. He was a wizard. They'd follow him, leave Linnet and Minalde where they were . . .

"Stay here!" he yelled at Alde. "They'll follow me!"

She grabbed his wrist as he passed her, hanging on hard. "They tried to kill me! Linnet stopped them."

He didn't pause to reason it, just grabbed her hand and ran.

He flung a blast of white witchfire almost in the mutants' faces as he pulled Alde down a cross corridor, heading for the stairs, threw it to blind them, as something light and swift and deadly snagged in the leather of his coat. In that light he saw them clearly: Koram Biggar and the fifth level north devotees of Saint Bounty.

Rudy recognized some of them. It wasn't easy. In the worst cases it wasn't possible, the ones whose heads had mutated into bizarre blank parodies of gaboogoos, with eyes trying to mimic gaboogoo headstalks, and other little pendules protruding from what had been mouths and ears. No wonder they'd retreated behind locked doors. They were all armed—scythes, clubs, lengths of chain. Those that still possessed eyes were without expression, except for a sort of drunken, self-absorbed glassiness.

Like the gaboogoos, they attacked without a sound.

Rudy threw fire at them, everything he had, knowing that at least one had a dart-gun or a birding-bow or something that flung missiles steeped in poison. The heat of the incendiary spell was a thunderclap in the enclosed space. He didn't dare pause to look behind him but only plunged on, ducking as others came out of doorways before them.

A faceless thing dropped from a false ceiling overhead and cut at him with a scythe; he didn't try to figure out who that had been. It bled, so it had to have been human once. It was like a crazyhouse, like a nightmare, plunging through darkness illuminated with the flash and glare of witchlight, lightning, fire. Gaboogoos only two or three feet tall skittered out of cells, flew at them like rubbery birds, clutching with improbable hands. Rudy slammed a cell door in front of them, threw lightning down the trapdoor of a stair to the level below to make sure the way was clear, then dropped down first, helping Alde after. Winding stairways, corridors, the slapping of feet and dragging gasp of breath through orifices that had ceased to have any resemblance to nostrils. Dodge, dodge, turn . . . Empty blackness and echoing halls, and the snail-shell curve of a stairway ceiling overhead.

Rudy thought, *I've been here.*

He caught Alde's hand and they plunged down, heading for the crypts.

*The Bald Lady . . .*

He couldn't remember which dream it had been, when he'd stood in this chamber, deep in the crypts now, had seen her descend this stair. But he remembered the wall niche she'd passed and knew that he'd never seen such a thing in his waking knowledge of the room.

Hoping his memory was correct—calling down blessings on Ingold, who had chivvied and all but beat him into improving his memory—he fell against the blank black wall, gasped out the spells of opening the Guy with the Cats had used . . .

And the niche opened.

Five feet by five feet and as high as the chamber's lofty ceiling, it was still there, hidden behind a panel that was invisible from the outside.

The panel slid shut behind them, enclosing them in the cold black chimney—no false ceiling, no shelves, no spiderwebs, even. He summoned witchlight, so that Alde would not be frightened, and saw that from the inside the panel had exactly the same appearance as the walls. Then he thought, *Idiot, what if there's a crack under the door?* He didn't think it possible, but to make sure he scaled the light down to the barest thread of foxfire, just so that Minalde would not be sitting in the dark.

Whatever it had once contained was gone now, or maybe it hadn't been designed to hide record crystals or ur-food or weaponry. Maybe it had been designed for just this purpose: to conceal fugitives who knew magic, by the strongest spells possible, from people like St. Prathhes, with his cup and his lash and his crimson noose of spell-cord.

Maybe the wizards that raised the Keep knew they'd eventually need someplace to hide from people like him.

Minalde sank to the floor, hands pressed to her belly—*Christ, don't go into labor on me now!!!* He fell to his knees beside her, clutched her hands. "Alde, are you okay? What's the matter? Will you be all right?"

She shook back her dark ocean of hair, a glint of exasperation in her eyes. "Of course I'm all right, Rudy. They just tried to kill me—tried to kill Linnet . . . tried to kill your child."

Rudy whispered, "Oh, Jeez." He hadn't thought of that.

She managed a smile. "I'm not going into labor now, you know."

He swallowed hard. "Uh—sure. Of course not. I didn't think you were. I was just—you know."

Their voices were barest whispers in the utter dark. Mage-sighted, he could see her smile widen, though she tried to conceal it. "I know." She was taking in her breath to speak again, but he pressed his fingers to her lips. Someone was in the crypts. Searching.

A scrape of boxes. The bumbly smack of bodies against the walls. Even through the wall he thought he could smell them, that nasty, sweetish stink that had been in Scala's sweat.

In time the squishy pad of their footfalls faded.

"Linnet can get down to the Aisle." His lips were touching her ear as he breathed the words, praying the gaboogoos—the mutants who were trying to transform into gaboogoos—didn't hunt by hearing. He had no idea how they did hunt. He didn't think they could break the door, but didn't want to risk it. Radar in their heads? "The Guards will search for us. All we have to do is wait."

The silk of her hair tickled his nose as she nodded. In the enclosed space the scent of it, of sweetgrass and candlewax, permeated the air.

She sank against his shoulder. "Thank you," she whispered. "Thank you." Whether that was for rescuing her or for saving Linnet, who had vilified him, or what, he didn't know. Her arms went around his ribs and within moments she was asleep.

She'd been seventeen when she bore Tir, he thought, the sweet, obedient daughter of the ancient House of Bes, married to the cold-faced hero she loved from afar. But for the deep creases in the corners of her eyelids, she didn't look much older than that now.

Maybe it was the memory of Eldor Andarion, the recollection that the House of Bes also carried its memories, that made Rudy dream what he did. Maybe the fact that the tiny chamber, like a crystal within the greater crystal of the Keep, was a place wrought of magic. Maybe he didn't dream at all. He was certainly aware that he listened all the while for the Guards' voices, for the clank of their weapons.

Curled together in the darkness, he dreamed—or saw or remembered—two figures within the glow of lamplight, little but shadows around them. A man and a woman—to his surprise he recognized the man as he who had ridden to the Keep in a welter of blood and spoken to the Bald Lady amid the webs of light and magic.

He understood then, suddenly, who the man was. Who it had to be.

"You'll be all right?" Dare of Renweth asked.

"I should be. If the High Lord knew, he'd have closed in on us before this. Since your father's rebellion, he's never trusted your line." Their hands, Rudy noticed, were unmarked by tattoos—he supposed this was a thing only wizards did.

"I know he still thinks the Dark Ones are something you and Brycothis have cooked up between you, to wrest our inheritance back. Did Brycothis reach Raendwedth Valley in safety?"

"With about half the wizards." Rudy had expected Dare of Renweth to be six feet tall and look like Gary Cooper—if anything, he bore a slight resemblance to Ernest Borgnine and was far older than Rudy had imagined him to be at the time of the Rising of the Dark. Fortyish, stocky, and gray-haired: his own hair, too, though almost everyone else in that era, including Dare's lady, seemed to wear wigs. Hers was red, elaborately plaited, and caught up with white roses no bigger than a circle formed by a child's fingers. Past the centuries, Rudy could smell them, a pearly sweetness unlike the scent of any flower he had known.

"The fool," Dare went on softly. "He's been told. A thousand times he's been told they're our only hope."

"It's not easy to believe." She shook her head, the delicate braids swinging. He saw that under the wig she was older than her slim build and fresh complexion first showed, life and humor in the painted creases of her eyes. "I have trouble believing it, and I know you wouldn't lie—she wouldn't lie. But to say that these deaths aren't being caused by sickness, but by these . . . these things from under the earth, things that fly in darkness, that are invisible. It sounds like madness, Dare. Like an evil dream."

"Would that it were, Gisa." He took her hands, pressed them hard to his lips. "Would that it were. Bring them to Raendwedth," he went on. "Everyone you can gather, any who'll come. The fortress they're building should hold everyone, should contain food for all . . ."

"And that's what the High Lord fears." She rose from her chair—a chair Rudy could only dimly glimpse, but the shape of it was as unfamiliar, as alien to him, as their simple, gauzy clothes. "Be careful, my prince."

They kissed, gently, with an old passion whose heat had settled to a steady, cosmic core that would outlast darkness, death, and time: lives shared, children birthed and raised and set on their own roads, minds and hearts inextricably entwined. They were people nothing could separate.

Like candleflame they were gone.

Gently, so as not to wake Minalde, Rudy drew the Cylinder from his vest and looked into his darkness. He wanted to see Dare again and the Lady Gisa, but the image that was there—that seemed to have been there waiting for him forever—was that of the Bald Lady, in the black-walled chamber he recognized clearly this time as the crypt chamber.

Thin traceries of silver light still marked the walls, like thaumaturgical scaffolding, but he sensed that the Keep above them, though whole now and complete, was deserted, filled only with a vast emptiness almost more frightening than the night outside. The Bald Lady sat in the center of a huge diagram of power, a sphere rather than a circle, wrought of silver and light and blood and moving lightning that hung in the air, penetrated the black stone underfoot, the whole of it pulsing and whispering with the radiance of unseen starlight.

A small porcelain bowl was cradled in one hand, and as Ingold had said, she was performing the easiest, the simplest, the most basic and elemental of Summonings, the one he had tried to teach Scala.

She was Summoning water.

But it came to her through the great web of power. The water ran and trickled down traced threads of lightning and starlight, passed through the flames of the candles burning on the periphery of the diagram and through the ochre earth and silver of the sweeping power-curves. It was the simplest of Summonings, but it was done through the web of Life.

When the vessel was full, she let the diagram fade and from the glass dish at her side took something like a little black bead, which she dropped into the water.

"Making soup?" inquired a good-natured voice, and the Bald Lady turned, the ghost of what had been a smile flickering to her eyes.

"In a sense."

Standing in the workroom doorway, the Guy with the Cats looked a little younger than Rudy had seen him on fifth north, though he still looked about a hundred fifty and leaned on his staff. It was before he'd grown his hair out, the scalp tattoos faded like much-washed denim. One of his cats lay over his shoulder, the big gray Rudy had seen snoozing on the table next to him in one of the videos.

"Prathhes would have it you've gone off to commune with the Evil Ones."

She sighed and leaned her forehead on her illuminated hand. In a small voice she whispered, "I'm not far from it, my friend."

"My dear child . . ." He stepped forward quickly and put his hands on her shoulders, eyes filled with concern. "My dear child, we did everything we could. We worked the spell on the cusp of the stars' movement, when the planets were aligned with moon and sun—of all this century, the single night where the whole sky was a reflecting glass of power . . ."

"And as a result, Gisa and all the folk coming up from the valley—" she began, and the Guy with the Cats tightened his grip on her, shook his head.

"It wasn't our fault," he said softly. "It wasn't your fault. There was nothing you could have done. And there was nothing we could do about the other wizards whose help you called on for the Raising of Power, whom the High Lord put under arrest. We did what we could."

"And it wasn't enough," she said softly. "It wasn't enough. The power in the Keep is not sufficient to preserve it, to keep it alive and working for who knows how long before it is safe to leave. Who knows what magic will be summoned against it, and against those within? Though we bound the power of the stars, of the moon and the Earth, into the stone of the walls, there were not enough of us. And we are doomed, and all our world with us."

She passed her hand along the high, bald curve of her head, and Rudy saw how old the lids of her eyes were and how the fine lines settled in the corners of her mouth. The old man said nothing, only stood looking down at her with grief and pity in his eyes, stroking his big gray cat.

"I had a dream last night, Amu Bel," she said. "A dream within a dream. A dream of holding guardianship, of binding the power of the stars and the Earth into spells that would preserve forever. A dream of cold, and waiting in the cold; a dream of three sleepers who turned in their sleep, thinking it was time to wake. Three guardians, dreaming of that which they guarded and preserved. Or maybe—I cannot remember clearly—the guardians were dreamed of, dreamed into existence, by that which they guarded. Is this familiar to you, Amu Bel?"

She rose to her feet, and her hand stretched forth. The shape of the gesture was familiar to Rudy, the angle and curve that old Amu Bel had used when he'd opened the niche on fifth north. But the woman sketched images, shapes that Rudy saw at once were figures of power, the ecto-plasm of concentrated magic, though as unlike the diagrams of the magic he knew as the night-gliding polyps of the primordial sea floor were different from a New York taxicab.

Alien shapes. Alien and frightening.

For a moment she let the shapes float in the air between them, glowing cones that pulsed and shifted and moved in a dance that was the paradigm of their power, changing size in a curious fashion, as if they were coming closer or moving farther away through a dimension that lay at ninety degrees to all perceived reality.

And yet, Rudy thought, in a way he understood that they were exactly the same as the circles of power that he drew, the sphere of light and shadow that the Bald Lady had formed. They existed for the same purpose and delineated the same things.

She let the images fade.

Amu Bel shook his head. "This is something of which I have never heard. I cannot even imagine how to call forth power from such . . . such configurations. This is what you dreamed?"

She nodded. "I hoped it might mean something to you. That it might help us to find a way to—to connect the Keep directly into the power of the Earth, the power of the stars. To call it into a life that would hold it in magic forever."

"There is no such thing as forever, Brycothis," Amu Bel whispered.

"Then until the world changes and we can come forth again. Surely," she said softly, "that is not too much to ask?"

"For the wounded and the sick, the breath of life between their lips is all they dare ask," the old man replied. "We can only do what we can and trust that we will be guided when the peril is worst."

She lowered her head to her hand again and did not turn around when he departed, he and his cat. In time she sighed, a deep and bitter breath, and looked up again, and Rudy could see the tears on her face.

She murmured, "You sent that dream to me, didn't you? You who dream of your three guardians; you who are the living guardian . . ."

She shook her head. "I can't," she whispered, her voice almost below hearing, and she closed her fists tight and pressed them to her lips, as if fearing lest any see how they trembled. "I can't."

But in her voice Rudy heard that whatever it was she said she could not do—whatever it was that she would descend all those levels of stairways to the heart of the crypts to do—she knew that she could, and she must.

Kneeling again beside the pottery bowl, she reached inside and picked out the little black bead that she had put into the water. She shook the drops from it and laid it on the floor beside the bowl. Then she stood and gathered up her midnight-blue wool cloak, wrapping it around her, the tears starting again from her eyes.

She whispered, "Dare, my friend, forgive me. And farewell."

Turning, she walked from the room—to descend to the crypts, Rudy thought. To pass through all those rooms, touching the hydroponics tanks, the wyr-webs, the walls—bidding them farewell, before she passed into darkness.

On the floor beside the pottery bowl he saw the black bead, still wet from the water that had been called through the Sphere of Life. He saw that it had swelled to twice or thrice its original size, and put forth a threadlike white root and a green leaf.

# Chapter 19

It was full morning when Gil reached the Blind King's Tomb.

As she climbed the narrowing canyon in the flank of the Saycotl Xyam, it seemed to her that she wandered deeper and deeper into a dream, into an alien world; the terrible thing was that this world did not seem strange to her anymore. White slunch patched the canyon walls, then covered them, thin over the rocks, thick in the pockets of soil, enveloping trees, fallen logs, screes, in a rubbery shroud. Things stirred in the gutlike convolutions, creeping forth now and then, creatures she guessed were simulacra of life-forms unspeakably ancient: shelled things with translucent legs and feelers, slubbery mats of moving protoplasm; things that glided along a foot or so above the wrinkled surface and thrust jointed proboscises down into it to feed on what crawled within. Hatlike things that spit at her from hard round mouths. As a dream within a dream Gil remembered Thoth walking in just such a slunch bed on the plains of Gettlesand, a stranger in an alien world beneath a livid yellow sky.

A river of mist flowed down the canyon, knee-deep, obscuring the wet mat underfoot; she knew its source was the cold of the ice-mages' cavern and followed it, the music very clear now in her mind. Songs of guarding. Of waiting. Of holding all things in trust, until they could make the world right again.

She kept seeing Ingold's blood in her mind, red and hot over the lifeless lard of the slunch.

She kept seeing the statue of the king who had no eyes.

He was familiar to her when she saw him. A black basalt image, floating in a lake of mist in the cut-rock cave of the tomb's antechamber. Slunch grew all around it, up the walls, over the ceiling, a dirty oatmeal river spilling over the steps to the outside. It had put out immense stalks that groped weightlessly in the still air or crawled about on the ground, fat tubulate hoses that opened and shut, looking for something to touch. Gil waded through the mist, the unseen, sloshing, crawling slunch, into dimness lit only by the queasy glow of the alien stuff itself.

The inner door was visible only as a smoldering bluish square, as it had been in her dreams, and the Blind King, robed in lichen and slunch, gazed at her with a sad serenity; a glowing thing of a shape Gil had never imagined in her most fevered nightmares perched silent upon his head.

Gil saw Ingold's footprints, leading through that blue doorway, and the footprints of other things following after. Blood streaked and gouted the slunch, and it was torn here and there where he had turned to fight. She wasn't aware of how long she'd been hurting but knew she hurt badly, and all the voices in her mind sang songs about rest.

After she took care of one final thing.

She'd walked all night. She had avoided Esbosheth's patrols, and those of Vair na-Chandros, and the armies of bandits in the burned farms and wasted fields of the most fertile valley of the south, without much trouble. Though she'd taken considerable weaponry from the decaying corpses—including a recurve bow and a quiverful of barbed arrows—she found no horses and had been forced to go the whole way afoot.

A dark hump grew clearer in the mist as she approached it—a pair of dooic, dead, mutated almost unrecognizably: heads swollen huge, arms impossibly long—there were vestigial arms, and other things, growing out of their backs. The cuts were clean and few, Ingold's work, neat as ever. He would have been reconnoitering, she thought, until her awareness of his plan triggered an attack by every gaboogoo and mutant on the mountainside. Whether he'd retreated or been driven to this place made little difference now.

She felt uneasily at her own face and arms, telling herself for the thousandth time that her own mutations were only an illusion, then strung the bow and nocked an arrow. Ahead of her came frenzied rustling, movement without outcry, without so much as grunts of pain. The short Alketch bow was unfamiliar, lighter than the six-foot northern longbow. She guessed she wouldn't get many shots.

The passageway curved to the right. Directly before her a crack gaped in the stone wall, opened by an earthquake, perhaps. Ghastly slunch-light flowed through it, seeming bright in the mist-filled darkness, and a dead thing that had probably once been a mountain ape lay in the gap. It was burned all over its body and one arm was a stump; the blood smoked in the cold. Gil stepped over it, her breath a thick cloud now, light-headed with pain and with the singing in her mind.

*The pain is his doing. His doing. He ran out on you, left you to be* raped and killed by the gladiators . . . *You were* raped by them . . .

For a shocking moment the pseudomemory engulfed her mind: the Boar, the King, the Leopard . . .

She thrust it aside. Thrust aside, too, the false image that not only had it happened, but Ingold had been there.

The cavern she entered was perhaps fifty feet in length, that and more in height, narrow, like the nave of a Gothic church. Webs of attenuated slunch dangled from the ceiling, and long kelpy fronds writhed and twitched on the walls. Smoke as well as mist filled the cave, the fetor of burned slunch underlain by the harsher stink of charred flesh. In a dozen places balls of what appeared to be lichen burned fitfully, and dooic, mountain apes, and bloated things were trying to climb the slunch along the far wall to get at a shallow niche about halfway up, where a statue might once have stood, reached by a slender flight of stone steps.

The steps had been blasted away. Fragments of rock lay everywhere, fresh and bright, and pieces of gaboogoo, patiently crawling toward the wall below the niche.

Ingold stood in the niche. In places, the rock beneath and the slunch all around were scorched and charred with fire. Streams of blood glistened blackly in the slunch, on the stone, all around on the walls, where some had succeeded in climbing up. A lot of them lay dead at the foot of the wall, or were trying still to climb, hemorrhaging their lives out.

The wizard's arms were black with blood, as if he'd dipped them in a vat of it—the light of the dying fireballs caught red gleams of it when he raised his sword arm like a man exhausted, to strike at some flapping, toothed monstrosity that struck at him from the air. His movements had the blind deliberation of a warrior at the end of his strength; and blood ran from the cuts on his face and scalp to gum beard and hair to his skull. Gil saw him put his hand to the side of the niche to steady himself as the creature, whatever it was or had been, fell in two pieces with a spongy plop to the heap of dead things below the niche, twenty feet below his boots—a swamp of gore and cave-roaches and slunch.

Gil shot two dooic in the back before she was thrust aside by a gaboogoo nearly her own height that came out of the tunnel behind her. It ignored her as if she weren't there. She set down her bow and stepped lightly forward, hacked its reaching forelimbs off—it had no head—and then cut it off at the knees. It kept crawling through the slunch toward the yammering scrim under Ingold's niche, but probably couldn't do much damage. Ingold didn't seem to notice; a thing that had once been a saber-tooth was clawing its way up the slunch toward him, and in the gritty light Ingold's face was like a dying man's.

Gil picked up her bow, nocked an arrow, and fired at the thing on the wall.

Later she told herself it could have been the light. There wasn't much in the cavern, and what there was, from the burning fireballs he'd earlier flung, was fitful, flaring and dying . . .

So it really could have been the light.

Or it could have been that, at the last moment, her arm moved.

The barbed arrow buried itself in Ingold's chest, high under the collarbone. The impact slammed him back against the rear wall of the niche, shadow hiding him as his head leaned back for an instant to rest against the rear wall. Then slowly his body buckled forward, left hand groping to catch himself on the edge of the niche—he still kept a desperate grip on his sword. Gil's mind stalled in horror on what she had done, but her body and her heart kept working. Without, it seemed, any conscious volition whatsoever, she nocked another arrow, and that one she did put through the throat of the huge thing that clung beside the niche, snatching at Ingold; she thought, *He's going to fall in a minute and it'll drop on top of him.*

The creature fell first, dead or dying. Gil was halfway to the howling pack of dooic and apes and mutant things, sword flashing in her hand, when Ingold's knees gave and he crumpled forward out of the niche.

What followed was a vile business, a massacre. Gil cut stone-cold at the backs and necks of the dooic, the apes, of everything in sight as they fell upon the wizard's body. She severed arms, heads, hands as if she were chopping at vines, fighting the berserker fury that kept trying to rise in her, fighting the wild urge to start cutting madly at everything and anything regardless, hacking until there was nothing alive, then to turn the blade upon herself.

*Cold,* she thought. *Stay cold.*

None of them defended themselves against her.

When she was done, she threw the sword as far away from her as she could, lest she use it on him.

Before she turned him over, she saw the barbed arrow point sticking out of his back. She moved him carefully, hands foul with blood, trembling.

His eyes were shut, but he whispered, "Gil?"

*It will be with your name on my lips.*

*No.*

"You're all right," she said.

His voice was a thread. There was no blood coming from his mouth—the arrow hadn't pierced a lung. He said, "Oh, come now."

Cold as death, his hand moved on her wrist. "The priests in the ice . . ." he said.

"Did you see them?"

He moved his head, yes, and coughed. She felt the freeze of his muscles as he tried to suppress it, to lessen the pain.

"Did you fight them?" Once they'd known of his coming, he'd have had no choice. What she had seen, she realized, in this nightmare cavern, was only the tail end of the battle that had taken place while she was hiding and scrounging weapons through the trampled fields, the burned vineyards of the Valley of Hathyobar.

"I'm sorry," she said softly. "I'm sorry you had to leave me behind. I wouldn't have knowingly betrayed you."

*In spite of the fact that I just put an arrow through you.*

He shook his head and tightened his fingers on hers. "No," he said. "No."

*Cut his throat.*

*No.*

*Open his veins.*

*NO.*

*He's used you, raped you, mocked you, sold you . . .*

She could hear something moving, turned her head. There was a farther tunnel, leading inward still—a mouth of dim indigo hell that vomited forth mists. A shadow, a sense of cold more bitter than anything she had felt. A smell of acrid sweetness.

Something there.

An amorphous shape, and the sound of flutes that turned the diamond flecks of poison in her blood to lengthening knives.

Ingold flinched, as if he, too, could hear the sound.

"They crushed me like an insect." His lips barely stirred over the unvoiced words. "I could not touch them, nor would I have had the strength to overcome them if I had. They will do . . . as they will do. There is nothing further for us. The Mother of Winter . . ."

His eyelids creased in pain, and he turned his face aside.

"Come on," Gil said softly. "Let's get out of here."

He made a move that might have been denial, but he didn't resist—she wasn't sure that he could—when she put her arm under his shoulders, dragged and pulled him half to his feet. His whole weight, nearly half again her own, was on her, but he did what he could to walk. He did not try to speak as they dragged themselves slowly up the long corridor. She suspected he had not even the strength for that.

Behind her, she heard them. Deep in the mountain, where the rock ended and only ice remained—where light that wasn't light smoked sapphire in the glacier's heart, flashed on the slow-churning liquid in the pool they had guarded years past counting—their shadows flickered like pearlized dreams in her mind.

Only once Ingold said, "You don't have to do this, child."

"Screw you. I may go back without hope, but I'm not going back without you."

A square of light in the dark ahead. Stale smoke still burned her eyes, and she thought the copper stench of blood would never leave her nostrils, her hair, her clothing. Her body ached as if she'd been hammered with clubs, and an exhaustion she had never known before seemed to be drowning her. And in that drowning, in the edges of that dreaming, those silvery voices whispered to leave him where he lay, for the insects that crawled in the slunch to eat. It would only serve him right.

*Screw you, too. You've defeated him. Isn't that enough?*

Evidently it wasn't. He collapsed a few yards short of the glaring sunlight of the entrance, slipping down without a sound, and she dragged him, cursing, toward the light, a filthy and exhausted Orpheus hauling Eurydice out of Hell, with a trail of muttered profanity in their wake. From the dark behind her she felt their watching eyes.

Unlike Orpheus, she knew better than to look back.

Light surrounded them—chill and bleak, but light. Gil blinked in it, shading her eyes as she laid Ingold down on the stone, then straightened her back to look around.

A semicircle of men stood on the one shallow step that remained below the door. Others held the bits of horses, gathered in the canyon immediately behind. Armored and armed, most were black Alketch, though there were a few brown or bronze borderers and Delta Islanders among them. Their swords were drawn, a flashing hedge in the pallid light.

The badge they bore upon their crimson armor was the white circled earth-cross of the Church.

In the end Gil thought that it was only bureaucracy that spared her. That, and the bureaucratic mind that could not compass decision. Their orders concerned the wizard Ingold Inglorion, and they had no instructions regarding anyone else. When Gil stood above his body and said, "Take me to the Lady Govannin," they looked at one another uneasily, not knowing what to say. She refused to give up her weapons when asked; refused, also, to let them ill-treat Ingold, putting her hand on her sword hilt when the bloated, squint-eyed captain made to kick him in the ribs.

"He's all but dead, anyway," the lieutenant of the troop pointed out, stepping quickly between the captain and Gil when the man likewise made to draw his sword. "You can see we'll have to get him a horse, if he can sit one. There's no way he can be made to walk."

The captain's mouth puckered up at that. There was something wrong with the shape of his face, Gil thought—the position of his eyes. With a shudder of recognition she remembered the dream of the mirror, thought, *He's been eating slunch, like the animals. He's starting to change.*

And there were a dozen men of the guard who bore the same signs.

"What happened to him?" the lieutenant asked, a small, lithe elderly man with a Churchman's clean-shaved head.

Gil said, "It's something I must speak of to the bishop." The captain was still looking down at Ingold as if he were trying to figure out how to kill him without interference from his troop. Gil wondered what voices he heard speaking in his head.

They chained him, finally; the metal of the various loops and manacles, and the rune plaques that clattered dully from every spancel and cord, was all black with charring. Red spell-ribbon glared among the chains, red as new blood. Gil realized it was in those chains that the witch Hegda had been burned the previous afternoon. Lieutenant Pra-Sia ordered his men to make a litter for Ingold out of lances and spare harness, for there was nothing growing in the canyon, and the men were looking around uneasily at the unclean things moving in the slunch. Above the tomb's low door, worn away by weather and nearly eradicated by lichens, Gil saw a battered bas-relief of three forms bent over a cauldron, out of which grew something that looked like a tree. For some reason the carving frightened and repelled her, and made her want to hide.

Lieutenant Pra-Sia also cut the shaft and feathers of the arrow and pulled it through the wound and out of Ingold's chest, afterward binding on a soldier's dressing. The wound bled heavily, but the wizard made no sign of feeling anything. Gil walked beside the litter as the men carried it down the wadi, cold fog flowing around their feet, her hand resting on her sword hilt. The middle-aged lieutenant dismounted and walked beside her. Perhaps Khengrath, the captain of the troop, despite the influence of the ice-mages, understood that she would kill whoever tried to separate them, and die herself uncaring in the attempt: he didn't want to have to explain an extra skirmish to the Prince-Bishop. Perhaps he had other reasons.

In the dungeon corridor of the bishop's palace, which stood just within the watergates of Lake Nychee, the lieutenant said to her, "You must give up your weapon now," and when she stiffened, Ingold whispered, "Do it, Gil." They removed an iron grill from the floor and lowered him into the brick-lined pit beneath, but the captain let a ladder down for her. She thought, climbing down into darkness tessellated with squares of orange from the torches in the corridor, the man might still harbor hopes that she'd murder Ingold while he slept.

They left water and a little food, and brandy to clean Ingold's wounds. The cell was small but dry, every brick of its walls, floor, and groined ceiling marked with spells that were the death of magic, the silencing of power. By the light of the corridor torches falling through the grill twenty feet above their heads, Gil stripped Ingold and washed him as well as she could around the half-dozen manacles, the chains of all thicknesses that looped from arm to arm, throat and wrists and ankles. He no longer shivered, but his flesh felt deathly cold to her touch.

With the leftover water she washed the blood from her own face and hands and tried without much success to rinse it from her long hair. It remained, drying and sticky, in her clothing—the stink of it mingled with that of sewage in the cell. She sat on the edge of the low brick bench where they had laid him, and the weight of everything that had passed since leaving Renweth Vale seemed to descend on her shoulders, the icy smoke of dreams breathing through her mind again.

*Get out of my skull. Damn you, get out of my skull. Haven't you done enough?*

But it was all she could think about, and the thoughts consumed her. "Gil-Shalos?"

She thought he was only seeking reassurance and put her hand down to touch his shoulder. His fingers closed on hers.

"I'm sorry about your sword," he whispered.

"It's just as well. The captain wasn't real pleased. I think he hoped I'd ax you myself."

"Ah." He managed to smile, but did not open his eyes. "That's my Gillifer."

She tried to keep her voice steady. "He's been eating slunch, I think—changing. I suppose he told Govannin about you the minute the ice-mages realized you were at the door. Unless Hegda really did rat on you?"

He moved his head a little, no. Squares of lamplight lay over him, delineated by the grill overhead; they caught pale triangles where the skin stretched over his cheekbones, left his eyes in pits of shadow. "That was just . . . an excuse. Something to tell you. Forgive me, Gil. I couldn't—"

"No, you were right. They'd have seen you coming through me, and neither of us would have made it. Ingold, forgive me. I didn't aim that arrow on purpose. I swear I didn't. I hope you know that."

"I know it." A smile twitched one corner of his mouth, and he moved his hand as if he would touch her face; she took it in hers. "We might have saved ourselves trouble," he went on softly, weighing out his breath carefully, nursing the remnants of his energy even to speak. "There is nothing more that we can do against the mages in the ice, or against that which they guard. It will all come to pass now. There is nothing we can do to stop it; to stop them; to stop Her. It was good of you to come to me, good of you to guard me. Good beyond any words I can say. But I release you now, Gil. What we came here to do is done, or at least proven to be impossible. If they allow it—and Govannin might well, for old times' sake—return to the Keep."

"The hell I will," Gil said, still level, but her voice shook a little. "I'm not going without you. There's got to be—"

"Child, there is nothing to be done." His hand tightened on hers. "If they kill me—and I think they probably will—I can't prevent it. The battle with the ice-mages took everything from me, everything and more." He hesitated for a long time, as if he would ask her something, then at length he shook his head, letting the thought go.

"Thank you," he said simply. "Thank you for remaining with me."

*"Thank you,"* Gil repeated, her voice shaking. "Ingold, I love you. I love you to the ends of the earth, to the end of my life. Without you there is nothing, not in this world, not in any other world." Panic filled her at the tone of his voice, detached, as if already putting aside her and all things of his life, slipping away into sleep. She clung to his hands, as if she could force him to stay. "To hell with what the mages in the ice are doing to the world, Ingold—I hate them for what they've done to me. For using me as a weapon against you. For twisting me—taking me—but it won't last. I swear to you it won't. And it has nothing, nothing, to do with my love for you. I swear it."

His eyes opened and looked up into hers from sunken rings of black. There was a terrible sadness in them, and she thought, *I've lost him.* Desolation swept her; she could not imagine what she would do now.

"Don't send me away."

"And the father of the child?" he asked.

Time seemed to stop, like a plane stalling midair, held only by the grace of the wind. Later she wondered why she didn't jump to the conclusion that he was talking about Rudy and Minalde's child. But she knew this was not what he meant.

"What child?"

For the first time there was a flicker, a change, a life returning to the blue eyes; doubt, the rearrangement of something he had believed and acted upon. His white brows drew together a little. "Your child," he said. "The child you carry. I thought that was what you spoke of when you said it was better that you remain at the Keep."

Her voice sounded like someone else's to her ears. "I'm not pregnant."

But even as she said it she knew she was. Everything she had attributed to the poison of the creature that had scratched and bit her came back to her now with changed significance: dizziness, nausea, the constant need for sleep . . .

Even the conviction that her body was changing, twisted as it had been by the ice-mages' songs . . .

Boots clashed in the corridor overhead. Ferruginous lamplight jarred over them as the grill was thrust back. A ladder was lowered.

"Inglorion?" It was the bloated captain.

Gil caught Ingold's hand again and asked softly, "Why did you think it wasn't yours?"

He looked absolutely nonplussed at that, and Gil understood that it wasn't because wizards customarily laid barren-spells on their consorts—spells that had ceased to work the moment the ice-mages' poison was in her veins. He'd told himself this was the reason, she knew, but she knew, too, that this was not all.

It was because he was old. And because, deep in his heart, it had never really occurred to him that any woman would want to conceive and bear his child.

"Inglorion!" The guards came down into the chamber in a dry ringing of armor, and Gil stood, smashing the end off the fired pottery brandy bottle and holding the jagged neck like a knife. The spilled alcohol made the cell smell like a taproom. Ingold reached to touch her wrist, but his hand fell short, dangling from the bench with the weight of the chains.

"I'm coming with you." She didn't even look around at him as she spoke.

"That rather depends on where I'm going." She heard the jingle and slide of metal links, leaden rune plaques as he tried to sit, and the tearing gasp of his breath with the effort. Her eyes were still on the captain, the lieutenant behind him, and the others, counting who bore the signs of the eaters of slunch and who looked clean. Working out who to go for first, once she killed the captain and got his sword.

Through her teeth she said, "No, it doesn't."

The captain said, "The bishop has sent for you, old man. Give us trouble and the girl dies."

"My dear captain." Rather carefully, but with a perfectly steady hand, Ingold was pulling straight the rags of his blood-crusted robes, as well as he could under the drag of the chains. "Although I assure you of my complete cooperation, I don't believe I could make any trouble for you if I tried."

# Chapter 20

"**I**ngold, where are you? Pick up the phone, man!"

Cold mountain shadow fell across him, the sky above the Hammerking insanguinated with garish light. Downslope, near the track left by the mammoth that morning, the Icefalcon and Melantrys stood guard again. All they needed, Rudy thought, was black suits and sunglasses.

"You gotta answer me," he whispered, hopeless. "You gotta hear this. I know the shape of the ice-mages' magic. I know the spells they use to raise power."

*It can't be too late.*

The shape he had seen in the vision was still clear in his mind, the floating cones of what looked like glowing water, preserved as the Bald Lady had reproduced it from her own long-ago dream with a trained wizard's eidetic memory. The precise arrangement of large and small shapes, and the way they seemed to move nearer and farther away. The pattern of their dance. Ingold had to be able to do something with that. It had to tell him something.

If he still lived.

"My lord wizard."

Rudy looked up. The Bishop Maia, Lank Yar, and Lord Ankres stood just beyond the edge of the power-circle, a couple of Ankres' white-clothed troopers and three or four of Yar's hunters in the background. They looked grim, and rather white around the mouths.

Maia said, "I think we have them all."

The Guards were holding them on the training floor, one of the largest open spaces within the Keep to which access could be limited. Even those who had made the biggest fuss about searching the Keep for gaboogoo—Lady Sketh and Enas Barrelstave—were silent in the presence of the eyeless, mewing things that had been Clanith White and Old Man Wicket.

Koram Biggar, who had not begun to change, was blustering, "When all's said, they don't look so bad." He waved at Noop Farrier, whose wife had cut holes in his jerkin to accommodate the pseudolimbs growing from his chest and back. "You can't say that's really bad, my lady. What's the way you look, anyway, compared to being full-fed?"

He glared defiantly around him. The Guards and Lord Ankres' soldiers, who'd helped them in the sweep, looked a little queasy, but kept their weapons at the ready. At the sight of Rudy, Varkis Hogshearer pushed to the fore of the prisoners. "You have no right to name me as one of these!" he yelled. "You wait, Master Know-All Wizard! You wait till my girl's powers come in strong!"

Beside him, Scala was silent, tears running down her red, swollen cheeks.

"It's we who're full-fed, you know," Biggar went on, as the Guards began pushing and chivvying the shambling mob toward the stairway that led down to the makeshift prison in the first level of the crypts. "You lot are fools for not taking Saint Bounty's gifts! Look at her!" His finger stabbed out toward Minalde, still as marble with her dark hair disheveled, holding Tir's hand. Linnet stood beside her, throat mottled with bruises. Tir's eyes were somber, unsurprised, like water miles deep.

"Look at her, with her bones staring out of her flesh, ne'er mind the wizard's child she carries! It's we who'll live!"

"Aye," Janus of Weg said softly as the fifty or so mutants—and those unchanged others whose names Tir had given Rudy—were led away. "Aye, you'll live. But in what form?"

"It isn't all of them," Rudy said as the watchers emptied slowly out of the training floor, murmuring uneasily to themselves.

Minalde moved her head a little, no.

The small group closed up around them: Ankres, Maia, Janus—the core of Alde's power. The lines of her face seemed deeper in the brittle light, more drawn.

"It's a dangerous precedent to set," the bishop said gently. "We can't simply say that those who have been against us must be under the control of these ice-mages."

"Should be easy to tell," Rudy said. "Thanks to a man named John W. Campbell and a little story called 'Who Goes There'?"

Alde's morning-glory eyes widened in alarm. "You mean people in your world have to deal with this kind of problem?"

Rudy grinned, and just barely remembered not to kiss her, out of respect for Maia's position and Ankres' scruples. She'd regained a little of her color and looked not much the worse for their chase through the vaults, but he wished she'd pack up for the day and go to bed. She was just too damn pregnant for him to relax.

"All the time, babe," he said. "All the time."

The Old Testament Hebrews had used the pronunciation of the word "shibboleth." The fictitious fighters against Antarctic alien intruders had used a hot wire and samples of everybody's blood. Rudy used illusion, which gaboogoos walked straight through without seeing.

Lord Ankres jumped and flinched when Rudy summoned the illusion of a large and highly colored insect walking up his leg. That particular image did it for most people. For stoics like the Icefalcon, who wouldn't have reacted to a giant squid doing Groucho Marx imitations, Rudy simply drew a line of Ward across the empty cell he was using as a testing chamber and casually said, "Come over here, would you?" The young Guard stopped, baffled that he couldn't come more than halfway into the room.

He tested all the Guards, all Lord Ankres' men, and all of Yar's hunters first. He tested everybody who lived on fifth north.

Rather to his regret, Lord and Lady Sketh both passed with flying colors. But as Maia said, you couldn't arrest those who simply disagreed with you.

"You know why they interfered with the searches?" Alde said tiredly. It was deep in the night, and Rudy had been testing people for hours. Melantrys and her work party had just locked up the Doors after hauling out the last loads of slunch, room after room of it, tucked away in the mazes behind the Sketh and Ankres enclaves.

"My guess is Biggar and his boys hid their chickens with Sketh."

Alde nodded. "And stolen food. They simply swore fealty to Ankres, in the old style, and for Ankres that was enough to extend his protection to them." She perched awkwardly on the stool that Rudy had relinquished the moment she and Tir entered the training floor—Gnift the Swordmaster sometimes used it for demonstrations. The iron cages in which the glowstones hung overhead threw faded lattices of shadow over her face and across the worn wood of the raised training floor.

"They knew he was never going to let any of my troops go poking around in even the deserted areas behind his storerooms. He was livid when he learned Biggar had also sworn fealty to Sketh."

Rudy rubbed his eyes. In the squirming, glowing masses that he'd seen dragged through the Aisle to the doors he saw things like squamous fruit: half-formed gaboogoos taking shape. Dozens of the things of various sizes had been flushed out of the corners of the fifth-level mazes, out of the deserted storerooms and corridors that were officially the enclaves of the Keep nobility, though nobody ever went there. Just the thought of trying to destroy those foul heaps now piled in front of the Keep made Rudy tired.

"We'll have to kill them," Tir said very quietly, pressing his cheek to the back of Alde's hand. "Won't we?"

He looked as tired as they, his eyes years older than they had been that morning. *Once upon a time there was a boy,* Rudy thought, looking down at the hollowed face, the sad, steady blue-violet gaze. *Oh, Ace, I'm sorry.*

Alde brushed her thin hand over her son's hair. "We don't have to make that decision tonight, darling."

Tir looked up at her, saying nothing. Rudy wondered if the boy was thinking what he himself thought, what he knew Alde thought: *If Ingold's dead, and the ice-mages aren't gonna be killed, how long do we go on feeding people who're gonna have to be gotten rid of anyway?*

The Bald Lady had drawn a sphere to Summon not only water, but life. Reproducing it would be an all-day job, and the thought of Summoning the power to do so made his bones ache. But the memory of that single leaf, that single root, made him shiver. *Tomorrow,* he thought. *Tomorrow.*

Tomorrow he'd have to go back to testing. There'd been thirty-five mutants, maybe half a dozen who'd been with them—like Biggar and Hogshearer and Scala—and another ten or so who hadn't changed physically but upon whom the slunch had worked to the extent that they hadn't been aware of illusion. And the vast bulk of the Keep's population remained untested.

And there were still the other problems, the hydroponics tanks that didn't work to capacity, the power-circles by the Tall Gates from which— according to Lady Sketh—he should still be sending out his summons to all and any sorts of edible livestock.

*Probably some band of White Raiders is sitting at the bottom of the pass getting fat on the cattle and horses and sheep that come ambling up the trail.* "By golly, Slaughters-Everything-in-Sight, this's the best hunting spot we've had in years!"

Under the cool, brittle white lights Alde looked worn to the breaking point, and he remembered Biggar's stabbing finger. *Look at her, with her bones staring through her skin . . .*

And Ingold maybe not coming back.

*Christ, I wish I could just go out with a goddamn sword and kill a goddamn monster and have goddamn done with it! As methods of saving the world go, this one really stinks.*

*No wonder old Ingold has white hair, being responsible for everyone and everything around him.*

And then he thought, *If Ingold really is dead, I'm gonna have to try to kill the ice-mages myself. Oh, Christ.*

Alde slept that night in Rudy's small chamber, unwilling to return to the room in the Royal Sector that the gaboogoos had torn apart. Surrounded by Guards, she said she felt safe, but woke two or three times in the night sobbing and trembling. Given the fact that no one knew how many others in the Keep the ice-mages might be whispering to, not even Lord Ankres had anything to say.

Tir slept in the barracks.

At dawn, when Alde seemed to be resting more deeply, Rudy slipped from beneath the blankets, bathed in the long, deserted chamber off the Guards' watchroom, with its worn black tubs and the aged copper boilers old King Eldor had had sent there when he'd ordered the Keep regarrisoned, and padded down through the silence of the Keep to the crypts.

Turning a corner, he glimpsed Seya and the older of Lord Ankres' sons standing guard outside the room where the mutants were kept. Dimly, he caught Varkis Hogshearer's voice, ranting, ". . . all a trick, a cabal, an effort to turn this Keep into a Warlockracy . . ."

Another corner muffled the sound, unless he cared to reach out his senses to listen.

The long workroom where Ingold did his tinkering with machines, the low-ceilinged crypt whose floor was scratched and stained from apparatus that had vanished three millennia ago, was silent, dark, curiously comforting in its familiarity. Leftover bits of the ancient flamethrowers lay on the black stone wall-benches, the pine table that he and the wizard had hauled down. Wheels and pulleys and intricately jointed chains dangled from the ceiling. Water murmured softly in a black stone basin let into a niche in the wall.

From his belt Rudy took a packet of powdered silver mixed with herbs, another packet of incense, and a couple of burning-stones. He was exhausted from yesterday, and knew today would be nearly as bad. The sigils he marked, the circle of power he wove, he linked into the rhythm of the Earth and the phase of the moon, drawing power from those to lessen the drag on his own resources. He laid out stringers, as Ingold had once shown him, to tap the veins of silver and copper he knew lay deep in the ground, and a curve that followed the watercourses through the floor that fed the still-deeper crypts below.

Anything to help him get in touch with Ingold. Anything.

For a time he was afraid that if he relaxed to meditate, cross-legged in the circle's heart, he'd fall asleep. But when he breathed deep, his mind drifting down into the Now of magic, the weariness eased and the magic strength of the Keep seeped like a balm into his flesh and his soul.

*I live, and that is enough,* he thought as he drifted like an errant feather into the chasm where magic dwells. *I breathe. I'm here.*

Power flowed into him, dark rising up out of the earth and brightness soaking into his lungs from the air. In that sweet calm he collected strength and funneled it through the scrying stone, casting out his thought like a rope of light, calling Ingold's name.

Nothing came to him.

Nor could he summon any image of Gil.

What he saw of the Black Rock Keep—dim, faded, horrible—was only smoke and slunch and ash-hued monstrosities, glimpsed far off.

Dimly, he was aware of the sun rising above the Keep, of the great Doors opening for the workers in the fields, of other Guards in the bath-chamber. Of all life stirring and waking.

When he looked up, he saw Tir in the doorway of the crypt.

The boy had been around magic all his life and knew not to interrupt, or to step on the Weirds. He'd brought a pine-knot torch with him, probably swiped from the Guards' watchroom. Even that dim, grubby light seemed bright beside the pinlights of the incense fires, the bluish chains of light shining softly along the lines of the power-circle.

"S'okay, Ace. I'm done here." He started to rise, and Tir held up his hand, staying him.

"Do you need to go find him?" the boy asked.

"Ingold?" He'd never journeyed south, but Gil and the Icefalcon had told him of the road along the river valleys, the jungles of the border coasts, the brown hills around Khirsrit.

"If you turn yourself into a bird, like Ingold did," Tir said, a small figure forlorn against the darkness of the corridor outside, "you could get down there and kill the bad guys yourself. You said you know their secret now. You told Mama you saw it in your dream."

Tir carefully propped his torch into an empty jar, thin in his bright blue jerkin. Rudy saw that under the jerkin he was wearing a scarf of dulled reds and browns, which had belonged to Geppy Nool.

"What about you, Ace?" Rudy asked gently. "You and your mom? C'mere . . ." He held out his arms. "I'm not gonna be using this thing again tonight."

Tir ran across the lines of power to him, and Rudy felt them swirl away into the protecting shadows of the crypt. Tir put his arms around him, and Rudy hugged the compact little body close.

"He let them all die, to save the world," Tir said, face pressed to Rudy's shoulder, voice barely audible. Rudy felt a trickle of hot wetness in the bison fur of his collar, and against his cheek the sudden tightening of the boy's jaw. "I saw him. I was him. They were all coming here, to get away from the Dark, and the King was mad at him—at the man—at Dare. All the wizards were making a spell to make the Keep, so people would have someplace to hide, and Dare didn't tell them, didn't ask them to come with him when he went down to stop the King from hurting his family."

His voice broke, a thin treble breathless with remembered pain. "The King's men caught Dare's family down by the river where the Settlements are, and there was a battle. Everybody was killed except Dare and a couple of his men. Dare's wife, and his oldest son, and all them. But if the wizards had gone with him, the Keep wouldn't have been safe for people afterward."

Tir looked up at him, face streaked with tears, eyes desperate with the darkness of the memory he had seen. The woman with the white flowers in her red wig and decades of loving in her eyes. The blood-covered man riding to the Keep at the gates of dawn.

"He couldn't save everybody," Tir whispered, and hiccuped. "If the ice-mages live, we'll all die, won't we?"

Behind the child's voice was the King, asking an opinion of the colony's only mage, and the mage had to give it. "I think that's right, Ace."

Tir's breath fetched hard, then let out; he stepped back and wiped his eyes with his sleeve, and sniffled. "Can you turn yourself into a bird?" he asked. "Could you get down there and find Ingold and help him?"

Rudy shivered, remembering yesterday's desire for some definite action, something besides the slow grind of responsibilities for which he wasn't strong enough. "Does your mom know you came here to tell me this?" He remembered her anger at Ingold's departure, the ferocity with which she had fought Barrelstave and Bannerlord Pnak when the question arose of abandoning the Keep.

Tir shook his head. His voice was level now, but very quiet. "She wants to save the people here, to keep everyone here safe," he said softly. "But it's more than just people here. I'll help you get past the Guards, out of the Keep at night. And after you leave I'll tell her I said it was okay. She'll be mad, but I'll tell her I told you to go."

Rudy sighed, and put his arm around the boy again. "You won't have to do that, Pugsley," he said. "If I turned myself into a bird—if I could manage to turn myself into anything better than a turkey—"

Tir giggled at that, the King disappearing into the child.

"—I'd probably forget how to turn myself back once I got to Alketch, and get myself eaten for dinner. Birds are pretty stupid. I can't do it, kid. I don't have Ingold's power. You're brave for telling me I should go—braver than me. But you and your mom need me here. You understand?"

The boy regarded him for a moment, the elusive quality of ancient memory flickering in his too-thin face. His father's memories. Dare's memories. The memories of the pestilent brat who'd shot the egret, whoever he had grown up to be. Remembering half-comprehended choices, decisions made on grounds he did not yet understand.

Finally he whispered, "Okay. Thank you." He put his arms tightly around Rudy's neck.

Ten years ago, Gil guessed, the audience chamber in the palace of the Prince-Bishop of Alketch would have been an oasis of cool in Khirsrit's semitropical heat. Like most of the rooms Gil had seen in the south, it was nearly bare of furniture, the walls of ornate tile and plasterwork flowing upward into a hanging fantasia of pale-tinted stalactites—free of spiderwebs, a tribute to the palace servants and the fear that kept them at their jobs. Two walls consisted mostly of windows, latticed with sandal-wood and opalescent stone that was just visible past a heavy shroud of oxblood velvet, to hold what heat could be held.

The room was icy now.

Govannin Narmenlion folded narrow white hands and regarded the old man who stood before her—ragged, barefoot, in chains, and gray with exhaustion—with speculation in her serpent gaze.

"My lady." Ingold inclined his head.

"So." She touched a corner of the square of brown parchment on the granite desk before her, and the dark jewel of her ring glinted like a demon's thoughtful eye. "You have come south, Inglorion. I wondered how long it would be."

"Before what, lady?"

Her eyelids lowered, creased with age and chronic insomnia. In the north, after the fall of Gae, Gil had guessed her to be in her fifties, though shaven-headed as she was, after the custom of the Church, it was difficult to tell. She looked older now, more than five years could account for, and there was an edge to her harsh voice.

"I'll give the Lady Minalde credit for more intelligence than this. When she sent you here, she can't have known about this idiot Pnak who presented himself at na-Chandros' court the eve of St. Kanne's Day, he and his little band of fools, with their offers to negotiate for lands. Negotiate forsooth. Do they really think na-Chandros would deal in good faith for such lands that will still grow wheat?"

She held up the parchment and read, "The Vale of Renweth is useless now. Even the fields along the river will grow no crops to support us, and we must cast ourselves upon the mercy of the Emperor." She opened her fingers. The parchment dropped like a great sere leaf, skated across the polished prairie of the desk and turned over once in the air before it slid to the floor. "He would be well served if that hook-handed hellspawn bade them all come, with their children and their wives. But it is clear to me now, the direction of my Lady Minalde's pretty blue eyes. And lo. Here you stand."

Ingold shook his head. He was struggling to breathe, his face like wax from the effort of simply remaining on his feet; Gil had guessed by this time that the battle with the mages under the ice had badly strained his heart. He stood with arms folded, fingers toying gently with one of the several manacles around his wrists. "This is not why I came south, lady. I knew nothing of this."

"Then the Lady of the Keep is a fool." Her voice was soft and sharp as the scrape of a blade tip on stone. "Why did you come?"

Gil wondered, in Ingold's silence, if he would say, *To save human-kind*, and what Govannin's reply would be then. There were two chairs at the rear of the chamber, behind the Prince-Bishop's desk. In one sat a girl of fifteen or sixteen, with the curious top-heavy look of a fragile-boned girl whose breasts fill out large and early. Her forehead was wide and low—the milky dip of a widow's peak visible even beneath the pearl fringe of her veil—and her eyebrows a single line of white, unpretty against the ebony luster of her skin. In the other chair sat a white man who was probably only a few years older than Ingold, bald with age, who had once been tall but sat hunched, shrunken, as if drained of life and will save for the spite in his dark eyes. Though his robe was red, like those of the servants of the Church, unlike them he wore a beard, a river of per-fumed milk lying on his knees.

It was he who spoke. "They say that the Blind King's Tomb is a place of great magic, my lady." His voice was beautiful, a trained light tenor with an almost theatrical modulation, and as he spoke he straightened somewhat, gesturing with an actor's grace. "It is a place abrim with strange power, where dreams are dreamed and visions seen. Were I attempting great acts of magic, either to rally local warlords to rebellion against their rightful rulers or to cripple and damage the forces of the Empire by means of spells, it is the place that I would choose to work."

"I'm sure you would, Bektis," Ingold said kindly. "Every little bit helps those whose power needs that sort of amplification. I take it you haven't been there yourself? Of course not." He turned back to Govannin, leaving Bektis fuming.

"My lady, I came south for reasons which have nothing to do with the fighting among your lords. I came despite Lady Minalde's command, and believe me, I regard Bannerlord Pnak as a fool for even thinking he can negotiate with na-Chandros or Esbosheth's puppet Yor-Cleos—or with Her Highness here." He bowed his head in the direction of the young girl in the chair beside Bektis, but she only regarded him with silvery eyes, one shade darker than frost and expressionless as a snake's. She was one of the few people Gil had seen in the south who didn't wear a demon-catcher. Presumably no stray imp would dare invade the Prince-Bishop's sacrosanct halls. She wore saint-beads, however—carved butter-amber, and very costly.

Govannin, she noticed, wore neither. Nor was the Prince-Bishop veiled, the only woman she had seen so other than prostitutes. Were women in the Church here, then, legally considered as men?

She wondered how Govannin had managed to seize and hold power enough to dispense with the weight of custom—not that she didn't think she could.

To the girl, Ingold went on, "The cold of advancing winter—the winter of the world—has gripped this land as it has gripped others. Such crops as survive cannot feed your own people, my lady, much less thousands of interlopers from the north. I'm not sure that you could even feed them as slaves, though I'm sure some of the warlords might promise to do so."

Still she made no reply, and there was no warming of the bleak eyes. Gil remembered her name, Yori-Ezrikos—"Daughter of Ezrikos," who had been the Lord of Alketch and the Prince of the Seven Isles, *and no honorific diacritical for* you, *cupcake.* Boys in the deep south received names at the age of six, though the poorer families just numbered them—Niniak meant "third-born." Girls were never named. Vair na-Chandros, she recalled, had married the Emperor's daughter against her will: *wicked and rebellious,* the steward in D'haalac-Ar had called her.

It was Govannin who replied. "We are all tested." Knives of evening light, spearing through openings in the velvet draperies, crossed the ivory hands, the parchment on the floor, then faded from brass to copper to dirty bronze as Gil watched. "It is like you, Inglorion—like all wizards in their arrogance and their ignorance—to attempt to cheat Fate, to circumvent with will and illusion and this most subtle of snares called Magic, the fires intended to anneal the soul."

She settled back a little in her chair, and her eyes were a shark's eyes. "But a woman who brings drugs to her husband rather than let him suffer the pain of cleansing still sins. And for all your delusion of playing savior to the world, you are still the Hand of Evil and deliver all those whom you save over into Hell."

"And you know better?" He spoke without irony, ashen-gray and swaying slightly.

"I know the law." The calm self-satisfaction in her voice made Gil's heart sink. "The law says that all things proceeding from magic proceed from Evil, no matter how good their seeming or how beneficial their ends." It was the voice of one who will not be moved, who knows herself to be utterly right, killing others or dying herself without the smallest flicker of doubt as to her duty. From his low chair of ivory and rosewood the mage Bektis watched her, and Gil was struck by the whole-souled absorption in his face, and his utter loathing and hate.

"Evil is Illusion," Govannin went on. "Evil is Will. What else is magic but illusion and the action of a wizard's will upon the laws created for the physical world?"

"As is art," Ingold replied softly. "As is medicine. The first woman who struck fire from steel and flint circumvented the laws of the gods of winter, lady; the first man who shaped a branch into a spear to hurl into the saber-tooth's mouth defied the shape of naked flat-faced clawlessness which he had been given. But I will not argue."

He shook back the long white hair that had straggled down from his topknot, his eyes seeming very blue in the hollows of fatigue. "Those same gods of winter have defeated me. I came south and sought the Blind King's Tomb, in hopes of working a great magic, a magic that would arrest the killing frost that spreads across the world. It would keep matters from growing worse, even if they could not be bettered immediately. In this I failed."

He put a hand out quickly, trying to catch his balance; the guards pulled Gil back when she tried to go to him. Where the chains crossed his back she could see a slow-spreading spot of red on the bandages.

"My lady, what I came here to do, I could not do. I had not the strength, and now I do not know what can be done. I can only ask your mercy, and your leave to go out of these lands, to return to the North, and help my own people there as best I can, until darkness falls."

Govannin tilted her head a little, and there was something ophidian in her movement, as if she were gauging distance for a killing strike. "So learned," she said softly. "But ignorant, like a precocious child. I acquit you of malice, Inglorion. I know that you are beyond that. Had you a true soul, instead of only the self-blind shadow left you by Evil, I would say that your intent was good. You are indeed the greatest of the mages—"

Behind her Bektis stiffened indignantly and opened his mouth to protest.

"—and your fall, therefore, is the farthest, entrapped by the subtlest of the Evil One's snares: the will to save those marked by God for testing to the uttermost. Take him away."

Her eyes moved to Gil. "You stay with him still, child?"

Gil thrust her hands through the knot of her sword belt. "I don't think God has a problem with either loyalty or love."

"Don't you?" Govannin said conversationally, like the Devil at tea. "That is your error, child, and your sin. Take them both away."

She folded her hands upon her desk, the parchment on the floor stirring as the door was opened and the guards led Ingold through, Gil soundless in his wake. As soon as it closed behind them, he reached out for her, quick and desperate; the guards pulled her back once more. Ingold groped for a moment, leaning against the tiled wall, like a man struck blind. Then he put his hand to his side and slowly slipped unconscious to the floor.

# Chapter 21

"They're gonna attack the Keep." Rudy shaded his eyes against the dim glare of the morning sun, squinted up at the black face of the wall that rose above the Doors, dwarfing them to a small square of blackened bronze. "Sooner or later, they're gonna attack the Keep."

He ached in his bones from testing men, women, children—*Come over here, will you?*—and if he saw one more illusory mouse or bug, he was going to go after it himself with a stick. His head throbbed from experiment after experiment with the sphere of Life in the crypts, trying this source of power and that: the sun, the moon, the strange source that had saved his life on the fifth level. He was ready to smash the unresponsive, unaltered black ur-potato to pieces with a hammer—*There! Instant mashed potatoes! How about that?*

The woods around the Keep whispered and crawled with gaboogoos. He could feel them whenever he stepped through the Doors.

"They can't get in, can they?" Alde glanced over her shoulder, across the stream and the fields toward the diseased and dying trees.

"I don't think so . . . Your Majesty," he added, in deference to the fact that Enas Barrelstave and Lord Ankres were with them, and a mixed gaggle of both black- and white-clothed soldiery. "So I don't think there's any need for us to put brushwood around the walls, like they seem to be doing in Gettlesand. Gaboogoos aren't real flammable, anyway." He squinted up at the walls again. Utterly smooth, unpierced by any kind of defensive ports—no arrow slits, no pipes to pour out hot lead, no posterns for little surprise sorties—they were designed for protection against an inhuman enemy of variable dimensions.

He added, "But it'll mean we can't get out."

Barrelstave's eyes seemed to bug slightly from their sockets. He looked down across the fields, where work crews were weeding the new green corn and wheat, which to everybody's surprise had come up and seemed to be doing well. Rudy had studied everything in Ingold's library

about weather prediction and wondered if any of it would help him
should another ice storm come along.

"But it's just you they want, isn't it?" the tub-maker demanded wor-
riedly. "I mean, they won't harm the rest of us."

"Yeah," Rudy sighed. "It's just me they want. But even for the sake of
letting you folks get on with your gardening uninterrupted, I kind of hesitate about letting them tear me to pieces. I know it's selfish of me, but—"

"I'm sorry to correct you, Lord Wizard," Alde cut in gently, "but I'm
afraid I must. *You don't know* that it's just you they want." Her hand stole
for a moment to her gravid belly, speaking to him without words: *You,
and our child.* Her blue eyes moved to Barrelstave's, cool and without
anger. "None of us knows, truly, what the gaboogoos want. Not they, nor
those who have eaten the slunch whom we haven't yet found—"

"Oh, surely we've gotten them all!" Barrelstave protested uncomfortably. He bore on his hand the stain of ensorcelled walnut juice that
marked those who'd been tested from the many who hadn't, to keep
Rudy from wasting his time with retests, and had been genuinely horrified when, yesterday, the thoroughly respectable second-level matron
Urania Hoop had failed to recognize the spell-line across the testing cell's
floor. "I mean, we've tested everyone who dwelt in that area of the fifth
level—"

"And are you certain there aren't simply some people who are proof
against the illusion of wizardry?" Maia asked. Some of the people who had
been taken to the crypts, raving and swearing they had never in their
lives touched the slunch, troubled him deeply. "The way some people
cannot hear the difference between one tune and another?"

"You ever met any?" Rudy shot back.

The bishop was silent for a moment. He wasn't much more than ten
years older than Rudy, but his experiences leading the survivors out of
Penambra to the Keep had aged him prematurely, and his long hair was
almost completely gray. Like Ingold, he had the air of a man for whom
the vagaries of human conduct held few surprises. "No," he said at length.
"But I know Urania Hoop was a good, pious woman. And you must admit
it is scarcely fair to have susceptibility to illusion be the sole criteria of
losing one's liberty and being locked in the crypts with monsters?"

Rudy sighed. "I'm sorry about that, pal, I really am," he said. "But I
can't reach Thoth, and I can't reach Ingold, if the old boy's still alive, even.
For all I know, I'm the last friggin' wizard alive in the friggin' world, and

the gaboogoos are out to get me, too. So if you can get in touch with someone for a second opinion—" He pulled his scrying stone from his vest pocket, caught the bishop's crippled hand and slapped the crystal into the cleft hollow of the palm. "—you be my friggin' guest, and I'll thank you from the bottom of my heart."

"But until you do," Alde said softly, stepping forward to Rudy's side and laying a placating hand on Maia's wrist, "or until someone does, I'd like everyone to remember this. Eliminating Rudy—eliminating wizards—may only be a first step. With Ingold dead, with Thoth dead, with Wend and Ilae and the Gettlesand wizards dead, *we have no idea what else the gaboogoos will want.*"

She turned, and with the graceful serenity of a gazelle in unthreatened pasture, walked back up the shallow steps of the Keep, the others following in her wake. Catching up with her, Rudy said softly, "I wish you hadn't said that, babe. That's something I'd rather not even think about."

"Leave us."

Gil didn't recognize the voice, deep and surprisingly gritty, but she saw the red-clothed Church warrior who had lowered the ladder into the cell hesitate, and she knew who it had to be. A moment later the girl Yori-Ezrikos climbed down the rough steps, holding her gown of yellow-and-green painted silks up out of the way of her feet. Very much to Gil's surprise, she was followed by Govannin's tame mage Bektis, who peered around uneasily at the heavy brickwork, the dark groinings of the ceiling, and sniffed disapprovingly at the sour stink of spilled brandy. Ingold hadn't even commented on the fact that the room was spelled against the working of magic—had he not just come through a mangling by the ice-mages, he still wouldn't have been able to use his powers—but the erstwhile Court mage seemed to be trying not to touch any of the air.

"Stay at the end of the corridor," the girl said over her shoulder to her guards and looked up inquiringly at Bektis.

The old man listened a moment, then nodded. A wizard, whether or not his spells were under restraint, still possessed the trained senses and perceptions of a mage, and would be able to hear the retreat of even the quietest footfalls out of normal earshot.

Gil had risen to her feet at the younger woman's entrance and inclined her head awkwardly in respect of her rank. Ingold, lying on the wall-bench, made a move to do likewise, and Yori-Ezrikos signed him with a tiny, gold-nailed hand to remain where he was. This was fortunate, Gil reflected, since she guessed he would pass out again if he tried to stand.

"How is he?"

Gil bit back a spate of furious sarcasm—how the hell did she think he was, after Govannin had dragged him up, reamed him over, and passed sentence of death on them both?—and replied quietly, "Better. The battle with the mages under the ice . . . hurt him. Crippled him inside. He'll be better if he can rest."

"I'll be better still with a little food," Ingold said. The chains on his wrist clinked softly on the stone as he moved his hand.

The girl's cold eyes regarded him for a moment over her jonquil silk veil, then returned to Gil. "Is he your lover?" she asked. Her mode of speaking was very slow and deliberate, as if words caused her effort. Her hands remained resting on the amber saint-beads where they hung at her belt. Gil nodded. "How did you know about the priests under the ice?"

Ingold's eyes widened. "I was unaware that any legend in the South touched upon them. Or anywhere, for that matter. I would invite you to sit down, Majesty, except this bench is not particularly salubrious, and of course it would be presumptuous of me to imply that you could not be seated anywhere you wished, at any time. Would you offer our guest some water, Gil?"

The gray eyes did not change, disregarding Ingold's persiflage as if he had said nothing. She accepted the gourd of water from Gil's hands, however, and dipped her fingers into it, all that a woman of good breeding was permitted to do in the presence of a man who was not her family. She brought them up behind the concealing veil and touched her lips.

"It wasn't legend, exactly," she said, after a long period of consideration. "My nurse came of a mountain village, where faith in the saints is strange. There are three devils instead of one in all her stories, and they're frozen in ice. They work all their evil by making people do bad things with songs they sing in their minds. One of them plays a flute. Only mountain people tell those tales anymore."

The milk-white bar of eyebrow pinched in the middle, and for the first time the gray eyes lost their chilly hardness, looking into some depth beyond the dark stone pit of the room, the squares of grimy light.

"I thought that's why I saw the things I did in the dream I had," she went on. "That it was only Nana's tales coming back on me when I was cold and afraid."

She glanced around her, then sat on a lower rung of the ladder, Bektis standing respectfully at her side. Gil remained standing also, in respect for the presence of a ruler, her hands tucked into her empty sword belt. They'd replaced the pottery vessels of food and drink with gourds and wood, but Gil was already mentally dismantling other objects in the room, in case she needed another weapon in a hurry.

"What did you dream?" Ingold asked gently. "And why were you cold and afraid?"

Yori-Ezrikos did not raise her eyes from her hands, where they lay upon her knees; a storyteller would have put more expression than she did into her deep, rough voice.

"Four years ago my father died," she said. "He survived the rising of the Dark Ones by having the slaves pile wood all around the summer pavilion on the other side of the lake and keep fires burning through the night. Mostly the Dark Ones haunted the city, where there were more people. But afterward there was a plague, and Father died of that, and my brothers also. I had been betrothed to Stiarth na-Stalligos, my cousin, but he perished in the North. Vair na-Chandros, the general who led the army to help the Realm of Darwath, came back and made me marry him so he could be Emperor like Father.

"I know now that it isn't always like that between men and women." She raised her eyes and looked steadily at Ingold, then past him to Gil, and what was in them was more terrible than tears, more terrible than anger. "My ladies tell me that men aren't all what Vair is. If they were, I suppose women would crush the heads of all their male babies as they come from the womb, as I did with mine. Is he good to you?" Her voice had not changed pitch or level once. She might have been speaking of laundry. "As a man, I mean."

Gil reached down to touch Ingold's hand. "Yes," she said. "He's good to me. He taught me to wield a sword, so that I could protect myself."

The gray eyes brightened, curious, interested, and young for the first time: "Truly?" She regarded Ingold again, and for that moment Gil felt the vitality of this girl, the energy buried beneath the controlled and vicious calm. "I didn't think—" She stopped herself—she was a woman who had learned early to weigh each and every word that passed her lips—and simply said, "It is good." The cold returned, a steel visor clanging shut, and after a few moments she went on.

"As soon as I could walk again after the wedding, I ran away. I stole a horse and rode out from the Hathyobar Gate. I don't know where I thought I was going. I was only twelve. At that time all my uncles wanted the match, though later they changed their minds. Vair came after me himself with his men. I was so frightened of what he would do that I rode up into the hills and let the horse go and hid in the tombs. It was night. That was the year it first grew cold enough to kill the cane and the papyrus. I dreamed about the three priests in the ice."

"And how did you know," Ingold asked, in the scratchy velvet voice that seemed itself a part of dreaming, "that they were priests? Your nurse called them devils."

"I don't know," the girl said softly. "Yes, I do, though." She closed her eyes, remembering, the eyelids creased with powdered gold. "They worshiped . . . they worshiped . . . Her. They were magicians, but their magic was a song of worship, a song of power, for Her, in the pool."

"Yes." The word itself was the breath of white smoke, rising from the seethe of that gelatinous pool; the dark shape visible under the surface, dark and huge and waiting.

"They had worshiped in that single spot for so long, drawing up power out of the earth for her, that the rock was all worn away," she went on. "Every now and then their magic made the rock itself ooze creatures, dreadful things, things that crawled a few feet and died. I think I dreamed," she said. "I went through rooms, through corridors—through a crack in the wall. Through ice. I must have fainted but I don't remember. It was cold."

She brought up her hands, crossing them over ripe, upstanding breasts; she looked frail, sitting there on the ladder-step with her gold-slippered feet not quite touching the floor. "They were keeping her alive with the power they drew from the earth. Singing songs to her, worshiping her; waiting for her to awaken, to speak. I thought that when she waked she would know my name—I was afraid of what would happen when she spoke. I don't know how I knew that." She looked up at Ingold again, the frozen calm gone from her eyes. "Who is she? Did you see her when you fought the priests beneath the ice?"

"She is the Mother of Winter, my child . . . my children." He managed to stretch out a finger to touch the side of Gil's hip. "When the gaboogoos and the servants of the ice-mages drove me inward into the tomb—when I knew that I had to confront them then or die—I heard them singing of her. To her. She is the Life Tree of a world that ceased to exist when first the sun shone warm enough to admit the growth of green plants in the seas. In her body lie the seeds of all the life that world knew. She is Wizard Mother, the sanctuary of the flesh, her magic the repository of the understanding of the final shape, the destinies, the essences, of those creatures, that world. Hers is the magic of the heart and the flesh, not of the mind. The magic of mothers, of seeds, of the future imprisoned in a thought. She has waited a long time."

"For what?" Yori-Ezrikos' deep voice sounded loud in the gloom.

Ingold did not immediately reply. Gil wondered that she felt no surprise at what the wizard had said. It was as if she had known it all along, as if her blood understood—the poison of quicksilver and diamonds that ran with the human blood in her veins. Maybe, she thought, she had dreamed it.

Gil said softly, "She's waiting for the Winter of the Stars." When he still did not speak, she went on, "The world goes through phases—eons—of warmth and cold. You'll find reference to that idea in the books of the Old Gods sometimes, or the fragments of them that remain. I think it has to do with huge clouds of stellar dust passing between the Earth and the sun, blocking off the sun's heat—probably changing the color of the stars. At least the Scroll of the Six Gods speaks of it."

Yori-Ezrikos shook her head. "These things are forbidden in the South."

Gil bit back another tart remark and said only, "That book speaks of cycles—some of the most ancient magical texts do, too. From everything I can guess, these clouds can stay in place for thousands of years, sometimes tens of thousands, before they pass on again." *Let's not get into the subject of celestial mechanics—it works just as well this way as saying the sun passes through dust clouds, trailing its planets behind it.*

"That's why the Dark rose—because the world got colder, their herds died, and they had to hunt on the surface of the Earth. But before the Dark, before the birth of humankind, there were other things on the Earth when it was cold and dim—things that had minds and could work magic, though the magic is not magic as we understand. When the world got too warm for them, they retreated, hid themselves away in the heart of the glacier to wait until the cold returned again."

"Is this true?" Yori-Ezrikos looked up at Bektis, who cleared his throat, stroked his white beard, and looked solemn.

"Your Munificent Highness, Ingold Inglorion is the greatest lore-master living, with the possible exception of Lord Thoth Serpentmage. But I, too, was educated in the City of Wizards; I have studied as deeply and as widely as he. And never have I heard or read a word of what he says, much less of the fantasies dreamed up by this deluded young woman. Giant clouds of dust floating between us and the sun? Where does this dust come from? Why aren't we all choking and sneezing on it? I grant you—" He spread his hands with practiced expressiveness. "—Lord Ingold clearly encountered something out of the ordinary in the Blind King's Tomb. But you yourself know there are wild dooic in the hills, mountain apes and creatures fiercer still in these degenerate days. The notion that something magical dwells up there, something evil, some-thing whose destruction will reverse what seems to be a completely natural cycle of colder winters—"

"But it is not natural." Ingold opened his eyes. His voice was faint and infinitely weary, that of a prophet speaking from the dust. "Neither will it abate until all the world is covered in ice, locked under a mantle of slunch upon which feed such creatures as the Mother of Winter holds within her body and can summon from her memory, can create and can control."

He drew himself up a little against the wall, his blue gaze now crystal hard. "By that time, I assure you, Bektis, you and I and everyone in this city—every human being in the world—will be dead. But that point is moot."

He turned back to Yori-Ezrikos. "The answer to the question that everyone is so politely refraining from asking me is no. I am not mad. I thought I was for a long while—the time it took to journey here, the days Gil and I spent at St. Marcopius Gladiatorial Barracks. I had no way of knowing whether my visions were anything but lunacy at best or some complicated trick or trap. And I can't pretend that having my sanity confirmed yesterday by what I saw in the Blind King's Tomb comforted me much. I would infi-nitely prefer madness to the knowledge that my suspicions were true."

He was silent a moment, the orange light that fell upon him from the torches in the corridor lying in strange patterns along the differing links of the chains, like the encrypted message in some unimaginable genetic code.

"But they are true. And because the mages in the ice—the children of the Mother—and the Mother of Winter herself—are of a substance and an essence unknown to me, my magic cannot touch them. When I was driven into the tomb, I put forth all my strength, all my power, against them, and it was as if I fought shadows.

"My lady." He stretched out his hand to the young Empress, the bandages stiff with blood, and Gil saw the tightening of his jaw muscles under the weight of the chains. "I beg you, let me go. Even if you will not believe me—and there is no reason that you should—please, let me return to my home. My people need protection against what is coming. I swear to you I will not meddle, nor spy, nor interfere in the affairs of your people or your lands, unless you come against us. And if things go on as they are," he added quietly, "in a year, or two years, you will be in no position to do that."

"What of Bektis?"

Ingold looked momentarily nonplussed, his hand dropping to the bench again; he turned to regard his brother wizard with mild inquiry. "Oh, I doubt he'll be in a position to come against us, either."

"Do not jest with me," the dark girl said soberly. "I meant, did I release you—did I ask you to go again to the crypt of the Blind King to meet these children, these priests, of the Mother—would it aid you to have Bektis fighting at your side? For all that my Lady Bishop has done to him, he is still—"

Bektis hastily framed counterarguments, but Yori-Ezrikos spoke over his mellifluous objections.

"—he is still a man of power."

"Your Most Gracious Majesty, surely you cannot believe the ravings of a man who is clearly deranged! My position in the household of the Prince-Bishop is indispensable! Though I regret most exceedingly that I am unable to accompany my Lord Ingold—"

"You will accompany him."

Bektis shut up as if she'd turned a faucet or tightened a garrote. Gil didn't blame him. Yori-Ezrikos was not anyone she'd want to mess around with.

"I know everything about your position in the Prince-Bishop's household," Yori-Ezrikos said, "and what you have done in her service."

"Your Highness is kind." Ingold inclined his head; his hair and beard were damp with the sweat of the sheer exertion of the conversation. "But I fear—"

"My Highness is nothing of the sort." Her small hands had returned to her knees, the hieratic position reminiscent of the Blind King himself within his tomb. The silken veil moved eerily with the movement of her lips as she spoke, the gold flowers embroidered on its hem glinting in the torchlight from above. "But I believe you. I owe the Prince-Bishop a great deal, including my life, I daresay. Perhaps I do wrong in the sight of God by freeing you, by using your power to defeat this evil. I know not what this will do to my soul in God's eyes. But I am not stupid. I know that the cold causes the famine and the famine causes the wars. And if there is anything I can do to turn this tide, or to stop its flow, that I will do, though it cost me my hope of heaven."

She rose, a tiny woman not yet seventeen, with an eerie frost in her eyes. "Under this condition will I let you free, Ingold Inglorion. That you go with Bektis, and you try again with your combined powers to defeat the wizards under the ice. I shall give you whatever you need, whatever you ask for—protection, a time of rest and food to regain your strength, the best physician in the city. But you must swear to me that you will make the attempt. If not, you, and Bektis, and your wife here, will all die."

"Your Beneficent and Beautiful Majesty," Bektis said, "I beg you not to be hasty—"

"I said be quiet." She didn't even look over her shoulder at him. "Will you swear? I know wizards have no God. Swear to me—" She hesitated, searching her mind, and a curious expression glimmered in the silver-gray eyes. "—swear to me on the head of your firstborn child."

Ingold shivered. His eyes went to Gil for a moment, then down to his hands, lying chained and broken across his middle. If he thought about telling Yori-Ezrikos that it was useless—that no matter what aid she gave him he could not touch the mages in the ice—the sight of even that handbreadth of her face between the veils, Gil thought, would have changed his mind. It passed through Gil's mind that in another year or two, the man who raped her when she was twelve—the man whose child she had killed as it emerged from her body—Ingold's old enemy Vair na-Chandros the One-Handed—was going to be very, very sorry he had done what he did.

"I swear to you," Ingold said in a voice so soft as to be nearly inaudible, "on the head of my firstborn child, that I will attempt once more to destroy the Mother of Winter, though I die in the attempt."

"**I**ngold, this is ridiculous!" Bektis paced furiously back and forth across the gold and lapis tiles of the chamber Yori-Ezrikos had installed them in, his white beard and crimson velvet robe giving him the air of an agitated Father Christmas. "My Lady Govannin will never stand for it! We must make plans!"

The chamber, though comfortable in the spare southern fashion, was, Gil gathered, also proof against the use of magic therein, as were the other two rooms of the tiny suite at the rear of the Empress' wing of the episcopal palace. Gil thought she recognized the Runes of Silence ornately calligraphed into the goldwork of the tiles, worked into the plaster, probably graven on the stones beneath the tiled floor, as they had been graven on the bricks of the cell. A marble lattice looked into a garden, but heavy wooden shutters were folded over it on the inside, and there was no way through.

"Oh, I'm making plans." Ingold propped himself a little on one of the pillows that lined the wall-bench, seemingly the only type of furniture, except for the occasional pedestals or desks, that southern buildings boasted. In number of pieces, the room differed not the slightest from Gil and Ingold's chamber in the tenement behind the St. Marcopius Arena: only the mattresses and sheets on the wall-bench were of indigo linen, and the desk ebony and pearl. Where a leaf of the shutters was folded back, a few pigeons-blood roses grew through the marble fretwork, touching the air with their scent.

"And I suspect that since your powers and your position in Her Holiness' household are kept very quiet, she'll wait for some time before making inquiries after you."

The physician sent by Yori-Ezrikos—and escorted by two of her personal guards—had just departed, after telling Ingold that his heart had been badly strained and he must have at least two months of absolute rest. Gil suspected this was not what either Ingold or Yori-Ezrikos had in mind.

"I'm planning just exactly how I'm going to make sure of your assistance when we return to the Blind King's Tomb. Though I suspect I won't need to do much," the mage went on, refastening the breast of his borrowed ecclesiastical robes. "I'm sure our escort will have instructions to carry us thither in chains, and considering the population of gaboogoos and mutant dooic on the lower slopes of the mountain, I think you'll find it safer to accompany me than to make a run for it under a cloaking spell. I doubt you'd get far."

"Really!" Bektis sputtered, trying to look indignant at the implication instead of merely scared out of his wits.

The servant who accompanied the physician had brought a hammered copper platter containing lamb, doves, some kind of spiced aubergine mush, and a pie of honey, almonds, and rice, famine not having reached such proportions as to affect the Prince-Bishop's table, evidently. Or maybe it had, Gil thought, pouring herself a cup of mint tea. Maybe these were poverty rations, as Yori-Ezrikos and Govannin understood them.

"Can't you see it's hopeless?"

"Of course it's hopeless," Ingold replied around a dried fig. "My strength should return in a day or two—never mind what that charlatan said—but even at my strongest I was not a match for them, and I doubt that your assistance will improve the situation much. It would make no difference had I the entire Council of Wizards at my back burning incense and chanting. Without a . . . a thaumaturgical paradigm for the essence of the ice-mages, without an understanding of the central essence of the Mother of Winter, without a word of command over that essence, I cannot use my magic to combat theirs. It becomes, as it did before, a contest of strength between me and the gaboogoos. Even with the Empress' guards protecting us, we shall be hopelessly outnumbered before we even reach the tomb."

"Then why go?" Bektis demanded. He strode to the wall-bench, crouched beside it so that his handsome, pale face was level with the other man's. "Listen, I've never known a guard who wouldn't take messages out, at least." He pulled from his finger one of his many rings, a cabachon diamond caught in the grip of an emerald-eyed golden lion. "Govannin would never let me go if she knew of this outrageous plan of Her Highness'. She'd never let me be put in a position of danger. I'm too . . . too valuable to her. And I know too much. She could never spare me. And there are any number of warlords who would welcome your services enough to intercept us on the way to this lunatic mission at the tomb.

"Oh, you don't have to actually *serve* him!" he added, seeing Ingold's face. "Once they take the Rune of the Chain off you, you can take Gil-

Shalos here and flee! Govannin would be delighted to see the back of you. There would be no pursuit. You could—"

"You display a startling optimism about what people in this land would or would not do," Ingold remarked. "Could you get me a little of that aubergine paste on some bread, my dear? As for there being no pursuit, I should say that as long as—"

He stopped, as if suddenly listening, trying to catch some far-off sound, then turned to Bektis with sharp anger in his eyes and held out his hand. "Give it here."

"What?" The tall wizard made to rise in haste. But with surprising speed for a man whose doctor had just told him to take two months of absolute rest, Ingold's hand darted out and fastened to Bektis' wrist. Bektis made a move to wrench free, and discovered, as others had before him, that Ingold had a grip like a crocodile's jaws.

"My scrying crystal," Ingold said mildly.

"Really," Bektis blustered, "how would I have come by—"

"Gil." Ingold nodded at the other mage, an unspoken *Frisk him* in his eyes.

"I was keeping it safe for you." Bektis fished with his free hand in the velvet purse that hung at his hip, produced the thumb-sized fragment of smoky yellow quartz, and put it into Ingold's palm.

"That was exceedingly kind of you." Ingold used his leverage on Bektis' wrist to haul himself to his feet and walked, shakily, to the long wooden shutters that covered the lattice wall. Gil strode ahead of him and pushed them farther open; they were enormously heavy and she didn't like the way the old man's eyebrows stood out suddenly dark against his bloodless face.

A thin splash of sunlight fell over Ingold as he pressed his body to the lattice and thrust his arm through so that his hand, with the scrying stone in it, was outside the ensorcelled boundaries of the room.

He angled the central facet to the light.

"Rudy," he said mildly. "It's good to see you well."

# Chapter 22

It was late when Rudy finished talking to Ingold, late when the old man pronounced himself satisfied in seeing the shape of the ice-mages' power. Rudy had been horrified at his friend's appearance, and by the fact that toward the end of the conversation Ingold was quite clearly keeping himself on his feet only by hooking his arms through the stone crossbars of his prison—but damn, he thought, it was good to know the old dude was alive.

*He's got to live,* he thought. *He's got to make it through this one.*

God knew whether he'd be able to use what Rudy had told him, but at least he, Rudy, could tell Maia that no, *nobody* was born exempt from seeing wizards' illusions, so there.

*The Mother of Winter.* He shivered. *The Mother of Winter.* The mother of her world, holding all life and all that had been within her. And all that would be, if her three servants had their way. Tapping the roots of the earth's magic, deep within her unfreezing pool.

Like Alde, holding new life within her . . . And Gil, for that matter, how the hell about that? He grinned for a moment, then his smile faded. Not the greatest time in the history of the world to find yourself growing new life. Gil, he recalled, had always been wary around babies, sentimental as hell but never really comfortable.

No wonder Ingold had had that beaten, wary look when they'd left, knowing he'd placed on her all the customary spells to keep her from conceiving by him.

*Holding life,* Rudy thought. Like the Keep.

He remembered the Bald Lady again, the wizards sleeping all around her in the stupor of exhaustion. We will fail, she had said.

And yet they hadn't failed.

For the first time, he began to understand why: began to understand what she had learned, in her far-off dream of alien power.

In his mind he saw her, curled on the plinth amid the vast web of light whose perimeters defined the half-constructed Keep. Closing his eyes, leaning his elbows on the workroom table, he called to mind the whole scene again, visualizing the half-built walls, the shadowed pit of the foundations, the scaffolding with its glittering machines, the lines of starlight and fire that stitched between them, holding the energies of the Keep together. Defining what the Keep would be, in a future beyond what any of them would ever know.

In his mind, in that future, he located the niche where Amu Bel hid the food; the chamber where Gil and Alde found the scrying table and where he later saw the vision of the Bald Lady; the knoll of execution with its enigmatic pillars; the room where he and Alde had hidden, six levels down but, he now realized, exactly beneath the plinth where the Bald Lady sat . . .

"It's a grid," he said aloud. "The Keep is a power grid." He got to his feet, made sure the Cylinder was in its accustomed pocket, slung his coat around him and hurried out into the corridors, his footfalls a whisper in the Keep's dark heart.

"I'm coming with you." Gil closed the shutter on the thick gold moonlight that flooded the garden. Ingold had spoken to her, on their way south, of the lavish insect life of those warm lands, but even at midsummer the crickets cried slowly and the booming whir of cicadas was only rarely heard. Most of the lamps in the wall-niches had been put out, the remaining few strewing wavery arcs of amber flecks through their pierced brass bellies along the patterned plaster walls.

"No."

"Bektis will betray you."

"Whether Bektis betrays me or the sky falls makes no difference." He had returned to the wall-bench, where it deepened into a decorated sleeping niche, and was invisible save for the blur of his hair and beard and the glim of eyes. His deep voice sounded endlessly tired. "Whether we ride forth tomorrow or next month makes no difference, though I'm inclined to believe it will be the former, since God knows what our hostess told the bishop about Bektis' whereabouts. Even that . . ."

He gestured, and despite the spells laid on the room, for a moment the ghostly, flickering simulacrum of an illusion shimmered in the darkness, the precise arrangement of advancing and retreating cones that Rudy had shown him through the crystal. "Even that, illuminating—and astonishing—as it is, will make little difference in the end."

The moving shapes, like vast plasmic jellyfish, dissolved. Maybe they had only been in her mind. Gil heard Ingold sigh.

"It is more than power, Gil. More than understanding their substance. Their substance is alien, under the sway of alien magic. I understand a great deal now about how their power is raised, but I am not of them. I cannot command their central essence, what they truly are, which I do not understand. And without that command, my magic cannot combat theirs."

He drew her down into the niche beside him, and she rested against his shoulder, comfortable in the circle of his arm, in trust. Almost, she felt that it would make no difference now whether they lived or died, succeeded or went down in defeat. Only that they had this.

Quitely, she said, "You never were afraid of me because I might kill you, were you? Or because I'm . . . changing . . ."

"Changing?" He sat back a little from her, regarded her with surprise.

"Mutating." She could barely bring the words out, under the agony of shame. "Because of the poison. Sometimes I think it's illusion. Other times . . ." She held up her hands, not certain anymore if the fingers were longer than they had been, the joints more extended.

Ingold swiftly took the hand in his and kissed it. "It is illusion," he said, appalled, shaken. "Gilly, if I had known . . ." She turned her face away, but she could feel his eyes searching her. "No," he said, and she knew to her marrow that he spoke the truth. That his sight saw clear and his assurance could be trusted. "My darling, my child, that you had to go through that, along with everything else—"

"It's nothing," she said, brusque and awkward. "It was the least of it." There was a long silence, the warmth of his hands on hers strong and steady, real against the fading of the dream images of pain.

He was so shocked, so remorseful, that she made her voice light, to reassure him. "It's just that I couldn't tell. Like all those other illusions. But in the midst of it, I knew in my heart that even if it was true, it didn't make a difference to you. But you were so wary—and of course you had to be. So the only thing that really bothered you was you thought I'd lain with another man."

"In a sense," Ingold said slowly. "Although had I known . . . I didn't know how deep the influence of the ice-mages went in you, you see, or how deeply they could influence your mind. That you would try to kill me, yes; that you felt a great anger at me in the times when their influ-

ence was strong over you, yes—and you would have been more vulnerable at the beginning, before you learned to cope. What most troubled me
was the possibility that you had lain with another man under their influence and had found in the experience things that I cannot give you."

Gil said softly, "Oh."

"I would rather have left you at the Keep, not only for the sake of
your health and the child's, but to give you time to make up your mind."
He spoke hesitantly, choosing each word with desperate care. "I would
rather have dealt with the matter after the ice-mages themselves were
destroyed—if they could be destroyed—so that your mind would be
clear. But as I said in my note—and remind me to transform that brat
Niniak into a ferret to repay him for his misguided chivalry—the ice-
mages would have made you follow in any case, by illusion or compulsion
or whatever means they could. Though you would be their eyes and their
ears while with me, I would rather have had that than have you stalking
me, alone, through the wilderness and the cold. They have no care for the
physical well-being of their servants," he added bitterly. "And . . . for
better or worse, my dear, I wanted you with me."

She tightened her arm around his rib cage—carefully, for his left
arm was still strapped, to let the arrow wound heal. "Well, Ingold," she
said gravely, "despite the frenzied passion I developed for Enas Barrelstave, whose child I carry—"

Ingold pulled her hair.

Her voice sobered. "—I swear to you I'm not going to be the ice-
mages' agent on this trip. You know that."

"I know that." His hand stroked her hair in the dark. "But I cannot
let you lose your life in this cause. Not your life, nor the life of the child
within you."

"*They* are within me." Gil sat up and held out her arms, pulling back
the sleeves of her loose red tunic as if the veins beneath the flesh would
have turned color with the venom of the thing inside her. "*They're* as
much a part of me right now as your child, Ingold. More, because the
child is quiet, and these bastards talk to me, whisper to me, make me
doubt every word I say and every motion I make when I'm anywhere
within five feet of you."

As they whispered now, she added within herself. *He trusts you
again. Now is your time.* Her sword lay at the edge of the cushioned
bench, within the reach of her hand—a Guard reflex that she suspected

would be with her to the end of her days. Her knife was in her belt. That was the young Empress' doing.

"I've gotten more used to it now," she went on, carefully steadying her voice. "It bothers me less than it did. I can say, 'Oh, that's that darn such-and-such illusion again.' Like commercials on TV." She found she still could not name to him the visions she had. And in truth, she thought, there was no need.

"I feel like I've named the voices in my head, the burning in my veins; all those stupid lies and scenarios that play past me when I shut my eyes."

Ingold gathered her back into his arms, held her tight against him for a long time. Beneath her cheek she felt the tension of his pectorals and in his silence heard the swift flow of his thought. Then he sighed again, accepting something, releasing something.

There was infinite regret in his voice as he asked her, "And what have you named them, my dear?"

Gil sat up sharply, their hands still touching, their eyes locked; Gil understanding, knowing what it was she saw in the wizard's gaze. She thought, *Of course. There has to be a built-in compatibility in the poison if there's communication. Just as there has to be compatibility in the slunch, if it mutates human flesh and human thought.*

At the same time all the voices in her mind rose shrieking, crying to her that it wouldn't work, it would kill her, kill her child, kill Ingold. Half-seen visions of hideous terrors fleeted through her mind, the awareness of how easy it would be to pull her dagger from her belt and drive it into his heart, and beyond all other things, the clear awareness of pieces of a puzzle falling into place.

"You can use the venom in my blood as a magical interface," she said. "Can't you?"

A T Gil's request, the Lady Yori-Ezrikos sent to the St. Marcopius Barracks for warriors to thicken her bodyguard—the Gray Cat, the Little Cat, the Bear, the Eggplant, Sergeant Cush, and others whom Gil knew could be trusted. Ingold selected men from among the young Empress' regular bodyguard, using Rudy's criterion of susceptibility to illusion, and spoke to the Empress herself about preparations such as time and place, barges and equipment; presumably, Gil thought, to get at least some jump on the ice-mages. She was still deeply conscious that whatever she learned, they would know, and retired to the other room of the suite when Ingold dealt with such matters.

There was a mirror there. Sometimes she saw the deformed face in it, the hammer-jut of chin and the alien forehead, the horror that had become her eyes. Other times she saw only her own face. She could not tell which was more familiar, or which was the lie.

She couldn't tell either whether her overwhelming desire to eavesdrop was the ice-mages' or her own native nosiness. She rehearsed Dante in her head until the impulse went away.

She was aware that on the day before the first night of the full moon, Yori-Ezrikos manufactured a summons that would take Govannin to the town of Yeshmi All-Saints, a day's barge-ride downriver, the young Empress promising to hold Ingold for execution upon Govannin's return. Gil would have given a great deal to know what she told Govannin about Bektis' absence. A sudden attack of measles?

If, as Gil suspected, Govannin had used Bektis as a pawn in her climb to power in the South, she'd be hesitant to go head-to-head with her pupil over what might simply be a don't-ask-don't-tell request for services.

There were preparations that could not be hidden from the ice-mages, and those were difficult for her. As she and the two bodyguards assigned her brought the bishop's wizard to the small ball-court of the Empress' wing of the palace, which Ingold had begun ritually cleansing and stitching with Ward-lines against Bektis the moment Govannin was safely on her barge, Gil wondered whether the panic that rose in her, the ghastly sense that she would not survive the ritual Ingold was devising, was in fact her own common sense or her three pals under the ice.

Cold horror swamped her as they entered the ball-court, a long, marble-sided pit open to the sky, and she saw the lines of power Ingold had drawn in the sand, the Weirds that circled the walls. For a moment Ingold, in his red-and-black novice's robes, seemed a stranger as he ritually sealed the Wards behind them, then signed her to remove the spellcords and chains from Bektis' wrists.

"This entire project is ridiculous," the bishop's mage muttered through his teeth as Gil set the chains aside and Ingold returned to the measurement of an enormous circle in the court's smooth-combed sand. "Of what conceivable use can it be to attempt what will only destroy two of a precious and dwindling corps of trained wizards? Much better to study these . . . these whatever they are, if they even exist . . . from a dis-tance, to ascertain whether they are in fact priests or monsters or what-ever. They aren't even human."

"And while you're studying," Gil said softly, her eyes on the old man in the center of the court, "they're gaining strength. And men and animals are driven to eating slunch out of sheer starvation as the world grows ever colder. And those who eat the slunch eventually begin to hear voices in their minds saying, 'Kill that guy over there with the magic wand in his hand.' "

"There is no proof whatsoever of that!" Bektis practically spit the words at her. "And what proof has Ingold that the cold is the result of these . . . these things he says live in the heart of the mountain? In all my years of dwelling in the Alketch, I've never heard of such a thing!"

"Bektis," Ingold called mildly. "I need your help."

"Hmf." The tall wizard stalked stiffly away toward the center of the court, fingering little waves into his new-washed beard. "First time Lord High-and-Mighty Inglorion has ever admitted he needs anyone's help . . ."

Gil remained where she was, in the smaller circle Ingold had traced around her, joined to the larger, central design by a narrow Road traced in ochre, silver, and hawk's blood in the sand. Unlike Rudy, who claimed to see the lines of magic written as light in the air or, in some cases, reaching down into the earth like roots, she could only see the two wizards them-selves, sketching patterns with their fingers or the ends of their staffs above the growing maze of Runes, sigils, and power-tracks that grew about them on the dust. But either they could see something there, she thought, or they were the best mimes she'd ever encountered. All the invisible lines met at the same points, over and over; Bektis ducked one as a tall man would have ducked a stretched clothesline.

From the small ebony chest Yori-Ezrikos had sent to him that morning, Ingold removed silver dishes to hold the water necessary for the rite, silver braziers to burn the incense specific to the raising of power from noon sun on the day of the full moon. At the Keep, Gil knew, Ingold and Rudy frequently had to postpone spells and Summonings because they lacked materials that were, for thaumaturgical reasons, time-specific.

Fortunately, Govannin was the trustee of a quite astounding amount of treasure, handed over to the Church in the course of centuries by nobles and Emperors anxious to curry the favor of the saints. She'd seen the same thing in the ruined treasure vaults of Penambra, only Govannin's hoard made the Penambra trove look like a five-and-dime. Govannin would hemorrhage if she knew the use to which the Church's wealth was being put now.

Gil smiled.

At the lift of Ingold's hand, nine flames sprang to life in the braziers, nine cones of the finest incense flickered with brief coals, then sent up thin columns of smoke into the still air of the sunken court. The wan afternoon light flashed on the nine shallow vessels of water. Ingold and Bektis began to speak, words of power and light, and from the bronze-strapped chest beside him, Ingold lifted the pride of Govannin's gem collection: a cabachon diamond more than half the size of Gil's fist.

The Crown of Khirsrit, it was called.

Six hundred seventy-five karats of pure carbon.

"Can you do that?" she'd asked Ingold the night before last, as they sat talking and planning in the dark. "Alter the atomic valences of pure carbon so it will bond with the liquid oxygen in the pool the ice-mages guard?"

"You're sure the pool is oxygen?" For a number of years now, Ingold had been questioning Gil on as much elementary chemistry as she could remember, and laboriously devising his own experiments, for no other purpose than to satisfy his utter fascination with how the universe was put together. He had, to his own great surprise, made sense of two or three very ancient textual fragments by dealing with magic on chemical terms—something that told Gil a little more about the mages of the Times Before.

"Not a hundred percent." It had been pretty late then, the lamps, like elderly relatives at a party, one by one calling it quits. She and Ingold had pulled the blankets up over their knees, for though stuffy, the chamber was cold. Everything they said was being relayed immediately, she knew, to the ice-mages, but that couldn't be helped. All the gaboogoos in the world were going to be out there anyway.

"I'm guessing it's oxygen because oxygen's more stable than nitrogen," she said slowly. "Those would be the easiest to pull out of the air, the way you and Rudy can pull water vapor. Oxygen would require less magic over the years to hold in stasis. If it was something with a higher liquification temperature, like fluorine or bromine, you would have suffocated when you went in there to fight them. But if you charge a solid lump of pure crystallized carbon to be automatically open, to bond with the oxygen in the pool . . ."

"It will disrupt the thaumaturgic equilibrium," Ingold finished softly. "It will set off a chain reaction."

"And the thing in the pool will be destroyed."

"The thing in the pool," Ingold said. "The Mother of Winter." He touched the tangled night of her hair, traced with his thumb the print of the scars on her cheek. There was an endless sadness in his voice, a world of deep regret, as he spoke of their unseen enemy. "The guardian of the essence of all that vanished world."

"Do we have a choice?" Gil's voice came out taut and stifled, fighting against the waves of screaming rage that pummeled her mind, the nausea and splitting headache. Hands trembling, she curled her right thumb into the side of her index finger, where Ingold couldn't see it, and drove the nail into the flesh as hard as she could.

Ingold must have sensed the sudden strain, for he drew her closer to him, his strength a reassurance, like a lifeline in a storm. "If we have a choice, my dear," he said sadly, "it is one I cannot see."

"Gil-Shalos." Ingold beckoned from the greater circle, above which the shapes he showed her two nights ago had begun to take form. In the sunlight they were different, transparent, as if wrought of clear water, less like jellyfish and more like some kind of eerily glowing elemental plasm. Gil assumed the pattern of their movement to be part of their power— Ingold had observed it in the crystal for slightly over an hour, the night Rudy showed it to him, before Gil half carried him back to bed. In the open air the forms were huge, changing size and shape and position. They seemed to breathe, though Gil wondered what elements of the air they sought.

Bektis, eyes closed, hands outstretched, appeared to be in charge of maintaining those plasmoid shapes. He stood statuelike, garnet robes hanging in shining folds about his slender body, breathing deeply within his own small traced circle in the dust, the very picture of a great mage deep in the concentration of his sacred art.

Altogether less impressive, Ingold met her at the main circle's heart.

In his hands, the Crown of Khirsrit glittered with secret fire, the reflections from within it cast up onto his face.

"Gil-Shalos." He addressed her again by the name she had been given among the Guards. "Do you truly wish this? I have not the faintest idea what the spell will do to you, either in the charging of the crystal or when it breaks the greater spell of the pool. But the crystal will be linked to you. It will become—it has to become—in a Platonic sense a part of your body and your blood. To the best of my knowledge and calculation, you will be unharmed by this, but we are dealing with an unknown magic, and with a spell that I myself have invented. There are things about this that I do not know. I cannot tell what may happen, to you or to your child."

Gil had seen Minalde make a certain gesture many times, that of laying her hand on her belly, as if to protect the life asleep within. She made it almost without thinking, then self-consciously hooked her hand instead behind the knot of her sword belt.

"He's your child, too, Ingold," she said. "But one thing I do know: if the ice-mages are around seven months from now, he'll be under their control, if he's alive at all. If anyone's alive."

He stepped close and kissed her, and set the diamond in her hands. Using his right hand, he drew his left from its sling and put it on her shoulder, his right hand then on the other.

"Do I need to do anything?" Gil asked. "Meditate or say Om or something?" Her voice was a light, half kidding, covering genuine fear and a thousand screaming illusions in her mind.

He smiled into her eyes. "It would make no difference if you stood on one foot and recited 'The Shooting of Dan McGrew,'" he said. "Do their voices still trouble you?"

"I'm used to them." Which wasn't entirely the truth. "Will this hurt?" It occurred to her she hadn't even thought to ask before. Not, she reflected, that it made the slightest difference.

He only shook his head. "That's another thing I haven't figured out, my dear. I'm sorry."

She closed her eyes, conscious of the weight of the Crown of Khirsrit in her hands. Conscious, too, of the sun's thin heat on her face, of the stillness in the ball-court and the smell of incense and of the dust underfoot; of the sudden fierce rending pain in the scar on her face and the screams knifing through her mind, telling her to step over the power-lines, to hurl the diamond away, to whip out her sword and . . .

She remained still. She knew how spells were done. Pain rose through her like an illness, but she knew it was only the illusion of pain, sent by the ice-mages. She formulated it into a TV commercial in her mind—*Oh, that crummy thing again . . .*

Ingold was speaking, a long way off, the voice she would recognize and know in her dreams when she was an old woman—the voice it seemed she had known all of her life. The pain redoubled, and she wove words in her mind to cling to:

*I wonder, by my troth, what thou and I*
*Did till we loved; were we not weaned till then . . . ?*

Fire passed through her, a colorless torrent of heat. There was no pain. She felt odd and light-headed, and short of breath, and there seemed to be an enormous silence in her mind. The Ward-lines could not exclude the voices, because they were a part of her, a part of her blood, her essence—but that link would be, she knew, their undoing, for they could be reached by her name.

Far off she saw her dream vision again, of diamond dust and quick-silver flashing in the thick red surge of her bloodstream, and through it saw mists, and blue pulsing light, and three shapes half glimpsed that were not human, performing again and again rites that had worn stone away.

They were shouting something at her, but their voices made no sound. The diamond fire in her bloodstream seemed to flicker and flow into a new limb of her, a new part—diamond also, and surprising: flesh of her flesh, blood of her diamond-laced blood.

It seemed to take a long time. All of Donne's poem, and another of Shakespeare: *Like to a lark at break of day arising . . .*

At length Ingold said, "Gil?"

She opened her eyes. The light in the court had changed. It had the dense, glittery quality of the turn of the afternoon into evening.

The great, cone-shaped lights were gone. The nine fires in their silver dishes were smoking ash. The air smelled of the waters of the lake and of cooking from the city beyond the palace walls. A lake-bird squawked. She wondered what Sergeant Cush was teaching in the Arena tonight. Her hands, clasped around the diamond, were numb.

"Are you all right?"

She nodded. Sweat was dried in Ingold's hair and on his strain-lined face, gray with exhaustion. Bektis, visible past him, was combing his beard with a scented sandalwood comb and looking put-upon.

"Can you speak?"

She thought about it for a time, then shook her head. She wasn't sure why she couldn't, but it was as if the nerves that communicated from brain to tongue were paralyzed. *I'm all right, though,* she said with eyes and brows. Ingold nodded and went to a sort of vacuole drawn in the rim of the great circle, where a silken bag lay. Gil clutched at the diamond when she thought he might take it from her hands; he slipped the long strap of the bag over her head, his touch a reassurance that the bag was her property, part of her. She slipped the stone into the silk herself, feeling strangely unwilling to have anyone save Ingold even see it. She felt odd, as if she'd just waked from strange dreams.

"It's a common side effect of certain spells," he said comfortingly.

Gil nodded, accepting, almost indifferent to it. Considering what they were riding into tomorrow, it seemed like such small potatoes as to be microscopic. She flexed her fingers, winced at the pins and needles. Then she knelt quickly and traced in the dust of the ball-court, *It didn't hurt. I love you.* As quickly, she brushed it over, lest anyone see.

He knelt beside her, drew her against him, held her with a tightness that said everything he hadn't dared speak aloud: *I could have lost you; you're brave; I admire you; I love you beyond what words can say.*

Bektis said sniffily, "I would deeply appreciate it if you confined that type of demonstration indoors. If we're quite finished here, I certainly need rest, particularly if you are set upon this insane course of action for the morrow."

"Certainly, Bektis." Ingold got at once to his feet and crossed to the taller wizard, exerting all his warm charm to make him understand that his contribution to the rite had been invaluable and enormously appreciated, even if the whole ball-court had been carefully Warded to prevent him from running away while he made it. Guards, summoned by Gil knew not what method, were waiting in the entryway, chains in hand, and Bektis, who had shown every sign of unbending at Ingold's lavish thanks, pokered up at once and turned haughtily away from his colleague as he was manacled once more.

Ingold and Gil, hand in hand and innocent of chains, followed him back along the corridors to their ensorcelled suite, Ingold with an air of deep humility and apology that Gil knew to be completely spurious, and Gil, to her own surprise considering what waited for them all tomorrow, deeply amused.

Through the silk of the sack around her neck she could feel the diamond, a second heart against her chest.

The voices in her mind were silent. But she knew they did not sleep.

# Chapter 23

They left Khirsrit before the dawn in barges with muffled oarlocks, and the marsh-birds lifted in startled ribbons from the head-high forests of sedge and mist along the lakeside walls. Wrapped in the gaudy coat the Eggplant bought her, Gil watched them; behind her in the barge, a mare that bore food or weaponry or armor or whatever it was, wrapped under oiled sheets, blew softly and shook her head, the clinking of bridle-rings like the distant tap of a hammer in the morning still.

Her head ached. The ice-mages had whispered to her through the night, to slip the dagger from beneath her pillow and cut the throat of the man who sat awake at her side. The effort of silencing them, of telling them to go to hell, made her feel as if she'd spent the night at hard labor.

Whenever she awakened, Ingold's hand had touched her hair, her shoulder, her cheek. The brown velvet voice had whispered to her, words she no longer recalled. And she had slept again, the diamond safe in its silken bag beneath her hands.

Only now, looking across to where he sat huddled in his red-and-black robes of novitiate in the prow beside her, did it occur to her that he had not slept at all.

He politely hid a smile as a small contingent of Sergeant Cush's gladiators brought Bektis down the yellow sandstone steps of the bishop's private watergate—extended by newer wooden ones, for like all water, the lake stood lower this year than it had in centuries—his wrists heavy with spell-chains and amulets of Silence, and his back rigid with the indignity of it all. Ingold got to his feet and went to welcome him, nimble in the floating craft, so that it barely moved on the water's surface. The water made Gil profoundly uneasy. The opal brightness near the city walls changed within a dozen feet of embarkation to deeper and deeper tourmaline, then the otherworldly blue of the darkest morning glory. The barges were passing over the heart of the old volcanic funnel. Gil was not much of a swimmer. If they capsized, she thought, they would never reach bottom, only sink forever into the heart of that azure world.

She fought the desire to seize Ingold around the throat and fling herself overboard.

*What the hell*, she thought. *He probably* can *walk on water.*

She had to loop the throng of her knife hilt tight around her fingers and twist it hard to keep the thought at bay.

Before them, the Mother of Winter shimmered, nacre-crowned coal.

No smoke darkened the rising colors of the sky. Niniak the Thief had done his work well, spreading rumor among the city's various gangs—all of whom had connections to the warlords—that a shipment of food was due from the distant coast, though it was never specified which pass this fictive train would use or who had sent for it; some credit, Gil thought, should be left to the imagination of the generals involved.

Her hand strayed to the silken bag again, and she thought, *If I dropped it overside now, there would be no retrieving it.* For a moment the thought of the ensorcelled diamond flashing in the water amused her, fascinated her; how the water around it would be first brilliant, then darker and darker, colder and colder, as it sank away toward the world's heart.

But her mind recoiled from the thought of losing that second heart, that blood of her blood. A warm hand fell on her shoulder, and she looked up into Ingold's face; standing behind her, feet spread to take the roll of the boat, haggard in the growing light.

She took her hand away from the silk latches of her coat and put it over his.

*I will bear his child.* It was as if she were thinking of someone else. *If I live.*

They reached the Blind King's Tomb shortly after noon. The gaboo-goos were waiting for them.

"St. Bes' drawers!" Sergeant Cush dragged at the spiked bit in his stallion's mouth as the terrified beast wheeled to flee. "What in the name of the Seven Hells?"

"Oh, very good." Ingold smiled with genuine pleasure in his eyes at the things that crawled, spiderlike, squidlike, squatty and scuttling and barbed and toothed like scorpions, down the rocks in a pulpy white gush.

"*Good?*" The gladiators were backing their horses fast; Bektis was screaming invective that could have been heard in Penambra. "What the bloody demon-festering hell is goddamn good about it?"

None of the things was bigger than a cat. A bodyguard of five hundred couldn't have dealt with them all.

"It's always gratifying when one's communications are received and acted upon." The wizard dropped lightly from the saddle of his own mare and tossed the reins to Gil. She was one of the few holding her horse rock-steady, knowing it was no part of Ingold's plan to flee. She didn't even wonder how she would cope when the scuttering things reached them.

"I must beg your forgiveness, my dear," he went on, and ripped the oiled cover from the pack-mare's burden. "But when one's enemies are so obliging as to give one a line direct to them, they have no business being surprised when one uses it to relay information about plans—even if that information is misleading."

The mare was carrying four tall terra-cotta vessels about the size of butter churns, each equipped with a pump and a leathern hose pipe.

Gil laughed, the first sound that had passed her lips since last night. "You bastard!"

He smiled up at her, like a sleepy and mischievous elf. "Well—I try."

Gil—who'd been given charge of the pack-mare's lead upon disembarkation that morning—wheeled both her own horse and the mare, holding them in position as the squid-things, spider-things, scorpion-things wavered, hesitant, their advance already broken by the knowledge flooding from her consciousness into that of their masters. The Eggplant had dismounted already and stood at Ingold's side as the wizard unhitched the metal nozzle of the hose.

"Pump it."

Anything big enough to be proof against vitriol was big enough to be cut to pieces with a sword—and therefore dealt with by a bodyguard. But the reverse was also true.

"Where'd you get the sulfur?" she asked as the first stinking wave of it sprayed over those small, foul, and wholly undefended bodies.

"My dear, you ask that in a country that lives by the mining of copper?"

"Do we take it in with us?"

The smell was astonishing as the gaboogoos blackened, curled, fizzled on the stone steps like slugs under a drench of salt. Gil realized why Ingold had insisted everyone wear thick-soled boots.

"When you've fought as many renegade wizards as I have, my dear," Ingold said, wrapping his scarf over nose and mouth, "you learn one thing: never take as a weapon anything more complicated than a sword. And never take *anything* that can be blown up, or splashed back, or whipped around in your hand. Bektis, are you coming?"

"Have I a choice?" Sergeant Cush and Lieutenant Pra-Sia had already pulled the bishop's mage from his saddle, were stripping the chains of Silence from his wrists. A gaboogoo that had only been spattered with the acid staggered drunkenly out of the blackening mess on the tomb steps and snapped with its pincers at the hem of the old man's robe; Cush smashed it under his boot heel. It made a horrible noise as it flattened. Bektis looked as if he would willingly have scrambled up on the training director's shoulders had no one been watching.

"No." Ingold's blue eyes were suddenly icy under the scarred lids. "You haven't. I'm only going to say this once, because I'm sure the ice-mages have reserves of creatures large enough to be proof against vitriol."

He stepped close to the taller wizard, his sword in his hand now and power radiating from his dusty, sweat-streaked face. "If you flee, or betray us, or so much as flinch back, Bektis, I lay upon you a death-curse of pain, of humiliation, of cold, of filth, of regret. I lay upon you a body devoured before your mind departs it; a mouth filled with worms; flesh given over to ants and roaches. Do you understand?"

Bektis swallowed hard. Gil thought, *Ingold is the Archmage.* It was something she seldom had cause to remember. *Ruler of the wizards of the West. His words are the words of command.*

As through a mouth filled with dust, Bektis managed to say, "I understand."

"Gil's life is to be protected above my own. At all costs."

The bishop's mage nodded again. He stared as if hypnotized into what lay beyond the mist-filled gate of the Blind King's Tomb. Things reached and snapped at them from within, drawing back from the puddles of stinking acid smoking on the steps. Within the vaporous, glowing dimness, the very walls pulsed with the movement of the slunch.

Bektis looked about to throw up.

"If you flee," Ingold continued in a voice as soft as the darkness of summer night, "I think you're going to find that curse awaiting you about two strides away from the steps. Now come. It is time."

The voices filled Gil's mind, like the roaring of the sea, the flute crying birdlike above them.

They waded forward through the mist, into the dark.

In her dream last night she had seen the Mother of Winter. Unhuman and beautiful, flashing greens and blues and violets, she had risen from the heaving pool of stasis and cloud, and Gil had thought, *If she looks at me, I will die. If she looks at me . . .*

Mother-Wizard and guardian of the world long past, she had floated in her enchanted pool that stretched down, down the volcanic vent into the world's heart. Beautiful and alien as a snowflake, she had held out her arms, her three acolytes bowing at her feet. The life-forms of all that vanished world had waited in her shining body, peered from the forest of her blue mane, from the contents of her prodigal, scintillant memory.

She was back from her long sleep, with all her children singing in her train. Joyful to be living again.

And in Gil's dream the beautiful eyeless gaze had fallen upon her, from those spreading wilds of ferny cloud, a flashing of jewels in mist. The Mother of Winter had spoken her name. And she had died.

They shrilled in her mind. *You will die. If you do not kill him, do not stop him, you will die, and your child, your single egg, will die with you.*

Gil closed her mind. There was a reason she followed Ingold, through the ground-fog streaming around their boots, through the writhing slunch that sizzled under the spattering blasts of ball-lightning that hissed from the ends of his staff and Bektis'. She could not remember what it was, but she made that not matter.

Creatures unimaginable flopped and whistled, struck at them from the air or flashed snakelike from crevices in the rock. Simulacra wrought from the slunch, she thought, striking at them with her sword, decapitating, slicing off legs and tentacles and pincers. She was a Guard, and Ingold her teacher. Only that existed, like a steel sphere within the red shrieking maelstrom of illusion and visions in her head.

She thought the Blind King turned his head and watched them, eyeless, as they passed.

She thought her own hands were white as the slunch, and that she bore two swords—maybe more—in several sets of hands: one to fight the gaboogoos, but another to decapitate Bektis, who walked close before her, clinging almost to Ingold's red-and-black garments in horror and revulsion. To decapitate Bektis, and then Ingold himself.

And then she could rest.

The slunch was knee-deep in the inner chamber where Ingold had fought, shoulder-deep where it ran into the walls; heaving, moving, quivering with pseudopods and stalks. Ingold plowed ahead, cutting a way to the entry to the ice tunnel itself, and the bloated, mutated insects that had fattened themselves on the decomposing cave-apes and dooic Ingold had slain came roaring at their heads. Bektis spattered at them with lightning and fire: Bektis against whom she had rather foolishly pictured herself protecting Ingold. The tall mage looked grim and scared and furious, but showed no disposition to turn tail.

He understood, as Gil understood, that Ingold was the only thing protecting them from death.

Cold smoke poured at them from the tunnel that led to the glacier's heart, smoke and pallid light. White snakes of lightning ran from Ingold's fingers, skating along the slunch and running before them into the blue eternity of the ice, and Gil heard—maybe in reality, maybe only in her head—the flute that she knew from dreams. The ground stirred beneath them, and Gil caught at the rock of the wall, willing herself not to feel terror—willing herself to feel nothing. Bektis hesitated, and Ingold said, "They're bluffing. They know perfectly well a cave-in will make it impossible for the Mother of Winter to seed."

Movement in the mist. Ingold leveled his staff, fire pouring from its tip, and something like a plasmoid flounder struggled out of the burning slunch underfoot and threw itself at him. He cut it down automatically with his sword, slicing it in half and crushing it underfoot as he led the way down the inferno of charred matter and dim, brain-hurting glow.

Yori-Ezrikos had taken refuge here, Gil thought, with the small corner of her mind still capable of thought at all. It hadn't been as bad then, granted; but it was a gauge of her terror and loathing of Vair na-Chandros that she had come this far at all.

Or had she only fallen in sleep on the feet of the Blind King and dreamed of the music of the ice-mages and the beautiful, eternal thing sleeping in the pool?

The blue light deepened, dense as the bottom of the sea on the glassy curve of the walls. The white swirl of mists around them dimly defined the heat-spell in which they all now walked. Phosphorus shimmered, and all around her the glacier ice picked up eerie ghosts of their movements; she felt cold, cold unto death. Streaked with smoke and grime and blood where two or three gaboogoos had made it past the lightning, Ingold's face was serene, calm with concentration, witchlight seeming to flicker in his beard and hair and along the blade of his sword.

They had left the slunch behind. They were within the glacier, walking to its center as if into the heart of a geode, and the dense blue light grew colder, thinner where it hid within the ice.

The ice-mages were not anything like they had appeared to Gil in her dreams, not even at the end.

Maybe they weren't anything like she saw them now: Gil was no longer certain how much of what she saw was real. The floor underfoot—ice, not stone—was worn away with their magic, and a little slunch grew in the pit, but it might not have been real slunch, just something conjured out of the wanting of their minds. Things crawled up out of it now and then; one of them attacked Bektis' foot, and he crushed it, horrified loathing on his face.

The mages were waiting, crouched together. Aware. Shapes of light like vast jellyfish drifted and danced over the smoking waters of the pool that filled most of that enormous cavern, and in all that chamber there was no single sound but the thick slurp and heave of the liquid in the pool, and the breathing of the three who stood within the cavern's entrance, their breath smoking hard in the heat-spell's despite.

Ingold said, "Protect her." Gil could just see the protective shapes he called into being as he walked forward, boots squeaking; cones and spheres and curious, moving rods of power that glimmered and vanished in the air all around him, tenuous beside the shining power-shapes of the priests.

Gil heard them screaming something at her, but shut it out of her mind.

Nothing existed. Nothing. Nothing.

Only that she was a Guard, and when something happened to let her, she would react.

From her tunic she slipped the silken bag and felt within the jewel that was her flesh and blood and heart.

The smaller two ice-mages circled sideways to surround the small red-and-black figure walking toward them. The central mage, the great enchanter, reared like a rising black cloud above the pit. Gil couldn't even find an analogy to describe the domed shielding—if that's what it was—of the head—if that's what that was; the covered orifices; the long muddle of tubes and striking heads or hands or whatever they were, probing in and out like eels from rocks; and cold nonlight pouring from every crack and crevice of it, ultraviolet, pallid, searing. It spread itself out, bubbling, and Ingold stood before it with the quicksilver light glistening along his sword blade, gazing into its heart. Waiting.

Then moving lightly, he circled past it, and the thing turned to watch him as he stepped to the very brink of the oxygen pool. White fog frothed around his feet as he stood, staring into the depths with the shapes of the alien magic moving like living sails almost invisibly over his head, strange reflections of blue and green and rose passing over his face and hair.

Slowly, the shapes dwindled, faded, and died. An old man with a stick and a sword, in borrowed clothing, he stood among his enemies unprotected, his left arm held stiff where he'd taken it out of the sling. His face was sad as he raised it at last to the dark, shining thing that hovered above him.

"I'm sorry." He spoke soft, but in the utter silence his flawed, beautiful voice carried to the farthest ends of the cave. "I didn't realize. She's dead."

The great mage-priest crouched lower, tentacles shortening, thickening, shifting. The other priests seemed to shrink in on themselves, readying like cats to spring, and Gil felt malice and fury, a heavy pain pounding in her belly and head. The voices in her mind fell still. Their anger had no time for her now, no time for anything, drawing in on itself, denser and denser, an imploding universe of time and power and rage.

Ingold went on, very gently, "I didn't know it when last I came here, because I could not see the shape of your magic. Things were hidden from me. Maybe from you as well. But I think she's been dead for many centuries now."

His hand shifted a little on the worn wood of his staff, his sword lowered, tip touching the ice at the very brink of the pool. "She lasted a long time," he murmured, almost to himself. "But all seeds perish, if they lie unquickened in the womb of time."

*(not dead)*

Gil felt/heard like a hot grip on her vitals the leaden rage of their denial. The dark volcanic heat they had called in the earth was nothing more than a clanging echo to this refusal and fury and grief.

*(not dead back alive if back alive if)*
*(world will be the same)*
*(back alive if world will be the same)*
*(make it all the same put it back put it back)*
*(not dead)*

Ingold had to have heard them, had to have felt the swelling of that poison-storm of rage, and Gil could not understand why he didn't flee. Could not imagine standing there in front of them, under the growing horror of that rage, unflinching, only sad.

But he said, "She is dead," and his voice was the voice of a relative breaking the news to a grieving child. "You did your duty well. She could have asked for no better children than you, no better gift than your love. There was nothing you could have done to prevent it, nothing you could have done to bring that world back in time. It was only time that out-lasted her. I'm sorry."

And the dark condensed, spread and thickened through the blue thin unworldly dimness of the ice-shimmer. Anger. Denial and anger. Hammerblows of rage.

*(not so)*
*(not dead)*
*(not failed not failed not failed)*

Ingold turned away from them, and they fell upon him like nuclear storm.

Gil screamed warning, throat burning, and he turned with staff out-flung in a searing explosion of nova-scale light. They struck him in bursting sub-purple glare, like the colors in the back of the brain when the eyes are closed, saw him fall to one knee, raising his sword. She saw no more, though she heard him cry out. But she was moving already, run-ning, the carbon stone bursting fire in her hand.

Mist filled the chamber, surging up from the shapes of dark and X-ray glare, lightning and weighted rage. Mist whirled around her as

Bektis shouted, touched her with thrown spells of warmth that could not seem to shake free of the searing cold slicing her mind.

The pool was before her somewhere, covered in cloud—she saw Ingold brace himself, stabbing and thrusting with his staff, saw darkness encompass him at the same moment her foot caught on something under the drowning swirls of mist.

She fell, panting, the diamond bruising her palm. The clouds heaved up around her, and the next moment the heat-spells shifted, caught the cold air in an eddy of wind that swept aside the mist. For one instant she saw before her bare rock, black ice, and purple depths going down to infinite darkness, the slow cold liquid of her dreams heaving and churning with the rage of the mages whose spells had so long held it intact.

And in the dark of the pool she saw it, that floating, drifting wonder in its ferny universe of mane, like a shadow, suspended in what had once been its dream.

In her dream it—She—had spoken Gil's name, called forth the life from her body. Now Gil raised the diamond heart, the blood of her blood, the life of her life, while her own blood dripped to the rock and ice underfoot. The weight of the ice-mages' fury slammed down on her mind, crushing her consciousness toward darkness, but for some reason the pain in her hand, the sight of her blood trickling like thin red snakes, kept her mind focused. She heard Ingold cry out again and turned, arm upraised, to see him throw himself between her and the three shadows as they reached out for her.

The flash and crack of lightning seemed to split the world, and Gil threw the diamond with all her strength.

*Bektis, I hope that spell of protection's a doozy.*

The world exploded in a holocaust of smoke and light.

Too much had altered in the Keep over the course of the years to have left the crypts unchanged. What had been, Rudy guessed, the small chamber at the heart of the grid, had long ago been incorporated into one of the less efficient hydroponics vaults, which had then itself been let go to dust. *Thank God we didn't decide to lock the devotees of Saint Bounty in here,* he thought, coming through the rough doorway—which Gil had dated at late in the Keep's original period of habitation, whatever that meant. Most of the tanks had been taken out, and those that remained had been converted to storage of grain and dried fruits.

Studying the floor, he could see where three chambers had been joined into one. And the central of those three chambers had been round, small . . . and had contained, he saw now, brightening the light and kneeling to more closely examine the dirty black stone underfoot, a scrying table. Only the fact that the room was so little frequented let him see anything at all, because no one cleaned here. But in spite of the thin coating of dust and grime, there was no mistaking the round patch of roughness where it had been taken up and moved.

Moved where? Carried away from the Keep entirely, when the place had finally been abandoned? Maybe to Gae, to the palaces of the Kings of Dare's line? Maybe broken up, during some upsurge of antiwizard sentiment?

From the pocket of his vest he took the Cylinder and set it in the center of the rough stone circle on the floor.

"Brycothis?" he said. "You here?"

He shut his eyes. He was inside the Cylinder, inside the dark small circular chamber in the heart of the Keep.

"I'm here," the Bald Lady said.

He wasn't sure what he expected. Not this.

At times it seemed to him that he was standing beside the ocean on a January morning, the world an opal of pewter and cold; or that he was in a garden on a summer night, just outside a white marble belvedere through whose blinds light streamed golden, looking at the shadow of a woman bending over an armillary sphere. Sometimes he had the impression of looking at her sleeping—on a couch? In a cylinder of glass?—though oddly, he could not tell whether she was young or old.

Sometimes he didn't know exactly what he perceived.

The smell of vanilla and cinnamon.

That bone-deep sense of trust, of caring, of friendly peace.

He wasn't sure how to address her, or which way to look. "I, uh— I'm Rudy Solis. I'm the Keep wizard this summer. But you probably already know that."

He felt her smile and understood that after all this time, the core of her was human still.

He'd been about to ask about the spells of stasis, but that smile made him ask instead, "Are you okay? Have you—have you been alive all this time? Trapped?"

But he knew as the words came out of his mouth that she was no more trapped in the walls of the Keep than he could be described as trapped within the armature of his bones.

She was the heart of the Keep, transformed into it as Ingold had transformed himself into a peregrine, and for the same cause—to save those whom she loved.

But she thanked him for asking—it was like the warmth of still midsummer.

Memories stirred and swirled, as if she were trying to bring them into focus: fragments of consciousness drifting in the light, scenes that flickered through Rudy's mind as if he had been there, as if he remembered someone else's memories, or dreamed someone else's dreams.

A cat that had liked to sleep curled up on her hip, one paw over its black-and-white nose. The way the needles had stung when they tattooed the sigils of power and focus, the Runes and patterns of force, on her hands and arms. Someone's laughter. The color of her daughter's hair.

And then, very clear, he saw the Mother of Winter, sleeping in her pool. Sleeping truly, for she would move in sleep, dreaming of the eggs all safe within her body, dimly illumined by the soft glow of her living heart.

*Only the living will use magic to preserve those they love.* He didn't know if this was his own thought or hers, this woman's, in whose heart/dream/memory he now stood; he didn't know whether it was himself, or she, who wondered if it was for that reason that the Mother of Winter had sent the dream to Brycothis, to show her what she must do.

"Did it hurt?" he asked, desperately wanting that it had not.

He was reassured by the whisper of her laughter and the touch on his arm, palpable and immediate, of her warm fingers, though he saw nothing. A little sadness, when Amu Bel died, and Dare, and others, mages whom she could no longer protect.

The heart remembered. He was glad she was all right.

"Look," he said diffidently, "we've got this problem I wondered if you could help me with. How do you get them spuds to grow?"

And he felt around him again the summer joy of her smile.

The following day the gaboogoos attacked the Keep in force.

Knowing that thick concentrations of slunch—or the creatures that grew out of the slunch—interfered with communications by scrying crystal, Rudy had ensorcelled a ball made of leather stuffed with grass, such as the children played with, laying on it spells to turn first blue, then red, then green, then black, then white. He'd driven three stakes in the ground a few yards before the Keep steps, to form a tripod, and had set the balls on them; every morning, before the doors of the Keep were opened, he looked into his crystal, to see whether the ball could be seen by such means and whether it was the color it was supposed to be.

This latter guard against the possibility of illusion was in fact doing the ice-mages too much credit. When he checked on the ball that morning, with the first stirrings of light outside, he saw nothing. There was only the dense gray anger of the ice-mages, faded shadows within the facets of the stone.

"Whoa!" Shoving the crystal in his pocket, he hurried to the Aisle, where the farmers had already begun to gather, chatting with the Guards and waiting for the opening of the gate.

"Sorry, folks, can't be done," he said, striding to the front of the crowd, where Caldern and Gnift stood before the inner doors. "They're out there, waiting. I don't know how many."

"Are you sure?" someone inevitably demanded.

"That's ridiculous!" another declared, equally inevitably. "We need to get to our work! The season's going to be short enough. If we're not to starve—"

"And how do we know what you're seeing out there is true?"

Rudy planted himself before the doors, hands on his hips and the witchlight that burned above his head glittering on the locking-rings behind him and in the shadows of his eyes. "You don't believe me?"

There was silence.

"You're the people who made all the screaming fuss about me not being here to use my magic to protect you back when there was no way I could have protected you. Well, I'm here now. And I'm telling you: don't open those doors."

Without a word five of them flung themselves at him, hoes and knives and billhooks raised. Rudy was so astonished—though he realized later he shouldn't have been—and the quarters were so close that they were on him, tearing his staff from his hands, slamming him against the doors behind him before he could raise a finger in his own defense. He lashed out automatically, with fists and boots and elbows, hurling also the vicious spells of pain and suffocation that did, of course, absolutely nothing—Caldern wrenched a billhook away from one man and threw the weapon in one direction and the man in the other; Gnift beheaded a second farmer without an instant's hesitation; and the others in the fore-front of the group, Barrelstave and Lapith Hornbeam and a couple of the Dunk clan, fell on the attackers and dragged them back.

The attackers turned on their erstwhile friends and relatives and fought like demons, screaming and slashing. Yobet Troop had his fore-head opened almost to the bone by a hoe before he disarmed the man who'd been trying to bludgeon Rudy to death. At the same time, one of the attackers flung himself at the locking-rings, wrenched them over and plunged down the dark passageway between the two sets of gates. Rudy rolled to his feet and pelted after him, gasping. The farmer was already wrenching and twisting at the rings of the outer gate. Rudy seized him, and was thrown back by a strength almost superhuman; rolled to his feet and grabbed him again . . .

The door opened. Gaboogoos poured through the gate in a pallid, filthy tide. Rudy screamed, *"Shut the friggin' gate!"* and behind him heard the slam of iron, the snap of the locks, sealing him in the passageway with the mad farmer and the monstrous horde.

Rudy shouted the Word of Lightning, levin-fire spangling around him in sizzling bursts, cracking back and forth from the black stone of walls and ceiling and floor. Mutant animals were mixed with the gaboo-goos, snarling and shrieking as the bolts hit them; the air in the close-cramped tunnel was filled with the stench of charring matter, the stink of smoke, the reek of his own hair and clothing singeing.

Someone was by the light of the gates, men's forms struggling. Rudy saw the flash of a sword against the predawn gloom outside. Guards had slipped through the gate behind him. Janus was dragging the outer doors shut even now, while the Icefalcon hacked at the dog-sized gaboogoo spiders that struggled to come through even yet. The farmer lay head-less underfoot. Rudy called a flare of witchlight as the outer doors slammed shut, and a moment later the commander strode back to him through a reeking ruin of carcasses, coughing, "You cut that a mite close for comfort."

Rudy was slumped back against the wall, panting. The floor was car-peted with dead gaboogoos, most of them tiny, pincered, too small for a man to kill with a sword. "The crypt!" he gasped.

"Ankres is on his way."

By the time the inner doors were opened again, and Janus had sum-moned a heavy enough company to hold them, Rudy was halfway across the Aisle, running for the corner stairway that led down to the crypt. Even so, he reached the place almost too late for the battle. After the initial shock of being attacked by fourteen or fifteen men and women armed with makeshift weaponry, Seya and Melantrys, who'd been on guard, had been able to hold their own and hold the doors behind which the mutants were locked. The attacking slunch-eaters, none of whom had been tested yet and none of whom lived on the fifth level north, had fought like mad things, refusing surrender, as if they had no concept of anything but the death of those who kept them from opening the doors. Half were dead by the time Lord Ankres and his men got there, the black stone of the crypt corridor puddled with blood. The other half had died fighting, while the mutants in the crypt itself flung themselves against the door, screaming and pounding and cursing. Rudy arrived, breathless, in time to see the last of them die.

"Devils take them," Lord Ankres whispered, turning one of the attackers over with his foot. It was one of Lady Sketh's sewing-maids, with a scythe from the Sketh storerooms in her hands.

The day was a nerve-racking one, of meetings, of plans drawn up, of anger and rumor and fear. "What are we going to do about them?" demanded Barrelstave, Ankres, Janus, everyone, in Council. "We can't just stay behind locked doors. We have to farm."

But the answer was always the same. "If we open those doors, we're screwed," Rudy said. "Half those gaboogoos are the size of mice, and everybody in this room knows the problems we have with mice in this Keep. Their goal isn't just to destroy me. It's to destroy the core of this Keep, which is made of magic, living magic. And if the core goes, everything goes—the ventilation, the water, the magic in the walls."

"But we are, as you say, screwed as it is," Lord Ankres reminded him, from his position at the foot of the Council table, a slim small man, seventyish and dark-browed, with a bandage from the fighting on his brow. "Are we not?"

"Not if Ingold can kill those things in the South," Rudy said quietly. "And I think that's what's going on now. I think that's why they're attacking."

"And if he can't?" Maia asked.

Rudy sighed. "Then we're in real trouble."

All over the Keep, throughout that day, fights broke out: over food, over shoes, over fancied slights; fights between men who were rivals for the same woman or whose opinions had long differed about how food and power and space should be allotted; fights that had nothing to do with the squirming, yammering things that waited outside the doors, and everything to do with them.

After the Council meeting Rudy returned to the old storeroom at the very heart of the Keep, mounting paranoid watch over the great Sphere of Power he had wrought there the night before. Its long traceries spread over walls, ceiling, and floors once again, the influences of its power filling the air and sunk deep into the stone underfoot, calling on the stars, the phase of the moon, the position of the sun, readjusted for certain changes in the atmosphere as Brycothis had shown him. Drawing all power into the clay vessel of water at its heart.

"The gaboogoos don't care about the food, do they?" Tir asked, sitting cross-legged on the floor outside the Sphere's perimeter, a tuft of magefire floating over his head.

Rudy shook his head. "They just want to get rid of magic, Pugsley."

He looked down into the clay vessel at the earth-apples, grown now to three times their original size. They were still dark, but from every eye a thread of white had sprouted. The tinier beads, filling out slowly to their intended size, appeared to be rose hips.

Ingold would be pleased. Maybe more pleased, Rudy thought wryly, than he'd be about the potatoes. He could almost hear the old boy saying, *One can always get food.*

*A lot you know, pal.*

But he did hope they were the tiny white ones Gisa of Renweth had worn, which even in dream had smelled so sweet.

In a day or two, depending on what happened outside with the gaboogoos—depending on what was happening, what he was positive was happening, somewhere in the South—he'd ask Brycothis how to alter the hydroponics tanks to produce the quantities of food needed to carry the Keep through autumn and winter.

Always supposing somebody or something didn't kill him first. The screaming of the mutants in their crypts, audible even in this chamber like a faint, terrible whisper of wind, got on his nerves. He didn't *think* they'd be able to break the door of their prison. Still . . .

"And they only want to get rid of magic because we're using it to keep them from putting back the world the way it was when they were alive."

"Are they not alive?"

"Not really." Rudy sighed and rubbed his face, decorated with two or three days' worth of beard and the scabs and welts left by the gaboogoos who'd gotten through the gate. Looking back on it, he was astonished he hadn't managed to kill himself, or Janus, with the lightning. "It's just that we can't live in the world they need, and they can't live in ours. It's like we're taking turns on the planet, and it's our turn, and they want their turn back again. That's all."

"Oh." Tir studied the portions of the Sphere visible to him, the traced lines of silver and blood on the floor, the incense vessels filling the air with dreamy, pungent smoke. "Will Ingold kill them?"

"We're in deep trouble if he don't, Ace."

Toward evening Minalde came down the curving stairs that Brycothis had walked long before her, exhausted and pale and moving as if in pain, but clad in what Rudy privately called her "Royal drag," her hair dressed to make her appear both taller and older. Not that she needed the latter, he thought uneasily, studying the thin face within the loops of pearled chains. She carried a covered clay dish and a vessel of water—Tir leaped up at once to help her, and Rudy quickly "unsealed" the opening to the Sphere and hurried out to the small unmarked portion of the chamber to fetch her a chair.

"Do you think you could come to tomorrow morning's Council meeting and do that trick of yours with the lightning again?" she asked, sinking gratefully down and handing Rudy the dish with hands trembling with fatigue. "When Barrelstave rounded the turn of his first hour of speaking, I found myself thinking of it . . . longingly."

Rudy laughed and hefted the dish. "Yummers—carrion and peas. My favorite." He realized he was starving. *Probably literally*, he thought after a moment, pulling his horn spoon from a pocket of his vest. *But let's not go into that* . . . "What do they want?"

"They don't know." Alde sighed. Her thin fingers fumbled with the elaborate braids, the gold pins that held them, shaking her head to loosen the heavy midnight cascade. "They want to be told everything's going to be all right, though that isn't what they're saying."

She shivered, and in the silence the mad howling of the mutants in the crypt could be heard again. After a time she whispered, "Is there nothing we can do? I've just come from there. You hear them pounding on the doors—they're using enough force to smash their own bodies, break their own bones. They haven't had food since yesterday evening, and now nobody can take them any, or water."

"I don't think there's anything anyone can do." Rudy came over to her chair and took her hands. "How are the rest of the people taking it?"

"They're scared."

"Hell." He knelt beside her and pressed his face to the velvet of her worn red dress. "*I'm* scared."

She put her arms around his shoulders, and there was somehow infinite comfort in that slight grip, the warmth of the unloosed swags of her hair, and the smell of sandalwood that permeated clothing and flesh.

"You can't be scared." Tir spoke up from her other side, where she held him, also, in the circle of her arms. "You're a wizard."

"Don't you believe it, Ace," Rudy mumbled. "*That* scares me worse than all the rest of it put together. If you—" He straightened up, his head snapping around to listen. "What's that?"

Alde shook her head. "I don't—"

He lifted his hand for quiet, got to his feet and opened the door. The Icefalcon had stepped a few feet from the wall, face expressionless, the dirty yellow torchlight that barely illuminated the outer vault a wavery line along the edge of his drawn sword.

Like the eerie wail of wind—like the shrieking of the ice storm—the noise was audible through the farther door.

Screaming.

# Chapter 24

il woke up cold, with something crawling across her leg. She reached to brush it away and drew her hand back fast—a gaboogoo the size of a large cat staggered from her touch on crablike legs. Something warmer grasped her fingers. Ingold's hand.

Nausea swamped her.

"Isn't this where I came in?"

"I beg your pardon?"

She realized her speech was slurred, nearly unintelligible, but didn't bother to repeat her comment. She didn't recall what she meant.

Impenetrable white mist curtained the chamber, still as death. The blue glow around them had waned, and only the single dim magelight burning above Ingold's head reflected on the fog. Gaboogoos continued to crawl in and out of the hazy ring of light, claws skidding and clicking on the ice, which had become slick around them from the heat of Bektis' sphere of protection.

By the way the mists didn't come near them, Gil guessed the spell of protection included a self-contained atmosphere. Given the amount of carbon dioxide now in the chamber, they'd have been quite dead without it.

Both wizards looked like a couple of teaspoons of warmed-over death. For once Bektis didn't look indignant, or irritated, or anything but bone-tired. He reached out to help Ingold to his feet, and Ingold helped Gil.

"Come," Ingold said softly. "You have a right to see this."

Hurt arm hanging at his side, leaning heavily on his staff for support, he led her to the edge of the pit, where the pool had been.

The liquescent, half-frozen oxygen was gone. Only shreds of smoke remained, curling from the black throat of the volcanic vent. The Mother of Winter lay on a ledge some fifty feet down; the chasm plunged beyond her to endless night in the bowels of the earth.

There was no contortion in the great, glistening shape of gelatinous flesh, no sign of struggle, of anger, of resistance. The treelike head lay turned away from them, the long mane of blue fern trailing wetly over the edge, mist-wreathed and phosphorescent in the witchlight, the whiplike, spiraling tail losing itself in the fathomless black. Where the flesh hung like a wet tent from the chitin that shaped her back, Gil could see what might have been the shape of eggs within her, millions on millions of them, a hard black roe beneath translucent skin.

"She's beautiful." She didn't know why she said that, except that in its own weird way it was true. Mother-Wizard. Heart of the vanished world.

Ingold had been right. She had quite clearly died in her sleep, a very long time ago.

"That?" Bektis was recovering. His voice was an angry squeak. "Well, to each their own. Good riddance, I say."

"Yes," Ingold murmured, leading Gil away from the edge. "Yes, I suppose you would." He paused and, holding carefully onto her arm for support, bent to retrieve his sword, which lay half under the decomposing black things whose whole duty for eons had been to keep the Mother of Winter alive at any cost, to await the day when the world would return to what it had been. The world would never, Gil thought, return to what it had been. Not for anyone.

Sergeant Cush, Lieutenant Pra-Sia, and the Eggplant met them in the tomb's outer chamber, coughing and cursing, their torches burning sickly in the barely breathable gas emerging from the passageway. "Don't come any farther," Ingold called out, and limped more quickly to meet them in the knee-deep slunch of the chamber around the Blind King and his patient, wise-eyed dog. He brushed the slimy strings of his white hair out of his eyes. "I take it the gaboogoos are gone?"

"Gone?" Cush made a noise in the back of his throat that could have been a gag or a bitter chuckle. "Like sayin' a chap with the yellows is poorly, friend. They're as gone as it gets in this world."

He led them out. During the battle with the ice-mages, more—and larger—gaboogoos had attacked the tomb, and either lay in pieces or wandered aimlessly about below the steps. Only a few of the mutant dooic were still alive, the ones who had been least changed, and they were clearly in extremis, lying in the corrosive goo underfoot with blood slowly leaking from their mouths as the slunch-permeated organs of their bodies dissolved. Ingold shivered in the lurid gold of the slanted evening light, grief and pity in his eyes.

Gil turned her own hands over. They were perfectly normal. She put her fingers to her face. The scars were only scars, healing, and rather small.

Her veins no longer itched. The constant backtaste of metallic sweetness was gone from her sinuses. With the enchanted diamond, the poison had been drawn from her, cast back to its originator. Her flesh was free. The silence within her mind was like winter morning, with all the world wakening to peace.

"The gaboogoos themselves just wandered off," the Eggplant reported, scratching his bead-braided head. "Like they just got word nobody was payin' 'em. You all right, Gilly?"

"Fine," she said, meaning it, and the big lunk's eyes warmed as he pulled her to him in a hug.

"And speakin' of pay . . ." Cush took Ingold's arm in one huge hand, Gil's in the other, and led them down the foulness of the tomb's steps, picking their way through the filthy zone of burned slunch and vitriol, to the great rocks that half hid the tomb from travelers in the canyon below. Among the blue shadows of the more open ground behind them, the Empress' guards were fetching the horses back from their place of safety, their voices low and distant, the only sound in all that dreadful, wasted place.

Cush lowered his voice to exclude the others. "It true what you said? Now it'll get warm again, and the rains'll be back, and famine and plague'll go away?" His sharp, pale gold eyes flickered back toward the guards where they gingerly inspected the decayed and blackening gaboogoos, the dead mutants, with gestures and cries and demon-signs drawn in the air, and he chewed quicker on his gum. "I don't hold with magic, of course, but . . . can you tell me who's going to take power then? Which way it would pay a man to jump?"

Ingold sighed and shook his head. "That I cannot," he said softly. "I only said that if we accomplished what we set out to accomplish, the weather would grow no worse, or in any case not much. Slowly, things may improve, or they may not. There's no way of knowing."

"Hm." The director of training surveyed the ruin behind them, the smoke drifting from the chemical-blackened doorway of the tomb, the strained and blood-streaked faces of the old man and the girl. "You did all that for 'no way of knowing'? You need a good manager, you do, my friend."

The wizard smiled slowly and scratched a corner of his beard. "Well, I've been told that before."

Cush shrugged. "Hardly worth your trouble, seems to me. Still . . . that saint-kisser Pra-Sia he tells me we're to bring you back to Her Highness when you're done here. Somethin' tells me . . ." He lowered his voice. "Somethin' tells me she ain't one to take 'no way of knowing' for an answer."

"No," Ingold sighed. "No, and since she didn't send enchanted spancels along, I suspect she may be counting on me to do exactly what I'm going to do."

"And that is?"

"Not come back to her for a reward." Ingold closed his eyes for a moment, visibly gathering his depleted strength, then made a small sign with his fingers. Almost in the same movement he stepped forward, uninjured arm held out, and caught Sergeant Cush as he fell, easing him unconscious to the ground. Past them, Gil saw every guard and gladiator simultaneously collapse, leaving Bektis, who had been haranguing Pra-Sia, standing by the horses with an expression of offended shock on his narrow face.

"Well, *really*, Inglorion!"

"Don't." Ingold raised his bandaged hand to stop the bishop's mage as Bektis prepared to gesture the men awake again. "Think about it, Bektis." He strode down the sloping ground from the rocks where he'd left Cush, hands tucked in his sword belt, as if the deed to the entire mountain and half the plain of Hathyobar were sticking out of his pocket.

"I have no idea what Her Highness intended for us once she got us back into her power—neither us, nor you. She's a calculating woman, and a ruthless one; Govannin's pupil, and like Govannin, not averse to using forbidden magic for her own ends. Nor averse to lying to her preceptress. She may consider having a tame wizard at her beck an advantage when she raises an army against her husband."

He stepped over Lieutenant Pra-Sia and came to a halt, surveying the field of battle as Gil neatly hitched the reins of all the horses to the pack-mare's lead.

"Now, I can assure you she won't have me." He hesitated for a moment, then asked gently, "Will you come with us, Bektis? I understand why you remain . . ."

Bektis' handsome face worked at his words, and he backed away, trembling. "You understand nothing!" he hissed. "Nothing!"

Ingold only looked at him, sadness in his face. "It isn't worth it, you know. You have your chance now to leave her, maybe the best you will ever have."

Bektis turned white with rage. "You, Ingold Inglorion, are an unscrupulous scoundrel!"

Ingold's eyes changed—resigned, Gil thought. Whatever hold Govannin Narmenlion had on the wizard was beyond Ingold's power to break.

"But in need of a manager," Ingold sighed, shaking his head and casting a regretful glance back at the peacefully sleeping Sergeant Cush. "I suppose he's right. Is there any vitriol left in those tanks, my dear?"

"Not a drop." Gil unhitched the last one from the pack-mare and dropped it to the ground. "But we're in luck. Every one of the guards' horses is a mare. I knew Cushie rode a stallion, and the Gray Cat, but . . ."

"Why do you think I asked the Gray Cat to be part of our party?" Ingold caught the rein of Cush's stallion and swung lightly into the saddle. "As for the mares, luck had nothing to do with that. I told Her Highness that it was part of the spell. And Govannin's seedling roses, of course, which are in my saddlebags. Give the Eggplant's gelding to Bektis—we'll trade the other two for cattle on the way north." He held out a folded and sealed scrap of papyrus. "Would you be so good as to tuck that into the good sergeant's tunic, my dear?"

"What is it?"

"Instructions for removing the Wards around the Penambra treasure. We'll stop by and load up on the rest of the books and enough silver to replenish our supplies, and to remove the really magical parts of the Wards, but I think our friends deserve some remuneration for what is, I fear, a rather scurvy trick. Bektis . . ."

He turned back to his sputtering colleague and raised his hand in blessing. "If you will not come, I can only say, may the shades conceal you from your foes and the stars lead you home."

"And may you break your leg the moment you step off that horse!"

Gil came running back from her errand, her whole body light, as though she could run for days untiring. Every muscle in her ached as if she'd been beaten with chains, but the pain within was gone. "You can't leave the geldings for Cush and the boys?" She cast a guilty eye on the sleeping gladiators. The Eggplant had been a good man to work with and had had, she suspected, a little bit of a crush on her. The Gray Cat had taught her how to use a net and trident.

"Pra-Sia's guards would only take them and leave our friends to walk in any case. A poor reward for Cush's warning, but we've given them all the best possible excuse. I think he'll understand."

He wheeled Cush's big bay stallion as if he'd ridden in the cavalry for years. "If we ride fast, my dear, we should make the other side of the hills by morning."

They camped toward the end of the short summer night in a burnt-out hill-fort in the southern spur of the old volcanic wall. Through the tail end of the predawn light, Ingold labored to obscure their tracks and hide the horses, and Gil realized only then that the old man had spent the last of his magic putting the sleep-spell on the Empress' guards. It would be hours, perhaps days, before he could protect them with illusion against bandits, warlords, and the vengeance of the Church.

Until then they would have to ride carefully, by night.

She hoped to hell Niniak's rumor had drawn the warlords away from their route.

She thought about the little thief as she assembled a meal from the contents of the saddlebags, while the dove-blue air of the east stained pink, then apricot, swelling to white with the growing overture of the sun. A little throwaway, she thought, as likely as not to die in the next plague or be killed in the next food riot . . . wicked and bright and angry for her sake that Ingold had deserted her because she had a scar on her face.

Pain tightened hard in her chest. She'd known him four days and would never see him again.

Or the Eggplant, big and inarticulate, with little jeweled chains decorating his ankles.

Or Sergeant Cush. Or even the formidable and terrible Yori-Ezrikos.

She leaned her back against the broken stone wall behind her and let the sorrow rise through her, telling their names over to herself, as if they died the minute she'd ridden away out of their lives.

She missed them. She would always miss them.

"Gil?" Ingold was standing in the doorway, a sackful of wild corn and beans and a few tomatoes slung over his shoulder, white hair bright in the rising of the sun. "Are you all right?"

She nodded. It had been a long time since she'd thought about her mother, or her sister, or the few friends she'd had in the history department of UCLA. She wondered if any of them were still trying to find her.

*The incredible disappearing woman,* she thought. *Step through the wall of fire—the wall of magic—the wall of Somewhere Else to Go—and you're gone.*

He knelt beside her, and she reached out blindly and took his hand.

After a time he asked her softly, "What do you want to do about the child?"

She didn't know why she understood so immediately what he was asking, but she did. She raised her head, looking into his face; it was carefully blanked, but there was deep concern and a haunted doubt in his eyes.

She realized she'd only known she was pregnant for three or four days. And hadn't had two spare minutes together, with her mind clear, to truly consider the thought, *I'm going to have a child.*

*I'm going to have a child. I'm going to be pregnant for nine months—well, more like seven, now—and at the end of it I'll have this . . . this little peep in my arms, like Tir when I first saw him. Like my sister's kid.*

She didn't know what she felt, a hot strange tightness in her chest, an overwhelming desire to cry.

But she didn't want to confuse the issue with tears. Didn't want to hurt him with them.

Carefully, she asked, "Is there a law about it? I know they frown on wizards marrying, but Church law is pretty iffy at the Keep these days. What do you want to do?"

"The Church frowns on wizards marrying," Ingold said slowly. "This is partly for the sake of its own power, but partly out of consideration for the woman and the child. Wizards . . . don't make particularly good parents."

Gil folded her hands over her knees and smiled. "You mean they head off to parts unknown to save the world because of weird visions they have in caves?"

"Er . . . precisely." He scratched at a corner of his beard. "I would not

. . . harm you for the world, Gil." The words came carefully, picked and chosen from all possible words, and it came to Gil for the first time that for all his glibness, Ingold was terrified of speaking about the things that meant the most to him. Like her, she thought, he feared that he would say something wrong, something that would lose him the single thing he most needed in the world. And it would be all his fault.

"I would not . . . ask you to do anything you would regret, or . . . or be angry with me for, later. With me, or with my memory. For I could have been killed today, Gil. I could have gotten us both killed, without compunction and without regret, doing what needed to be done or what I perceived needed to be done. Today, or any day in the past five years."

"You could," Gil agreed softly. She touched her belly again, wonderingly, understanding why Alde made that gesture. There was somebody in there, she thought. Somebody who wasn't her.

"My judgment isn't that good."

She smiled a little. "Whose is?"

"It's your life, Gil." He drew a deep breath. "And you have chosen how you want to live it: as a warrior, as a scholar, as a woman free of any bonds that she cannot lay aside. A child is not what you wanted. I know that."

"No." She shook her head and pulled the leather thongs free that bound her hair, shaking it down to lie loose over her shoulders. She saw for the first time there was gray in it, though she was not thirty. So she hadn't gone completely unchanged after all, she thought, without rancor or annoyance.

But then, who ever did?

She thought about Niniak again, and the Eggplant—and her sister, her professors, her friends.

She went on, "No, it wasn't. But you know . . . we change. I've never wanted to find myself in bonds that I couldn't lay aside, no; in a situation I couldn't just walk away from. I never wanted to be trapped the way I was trapped by what my family expected of me, the way I was trapped whenever I argued with my father or when my mother started quoting how much things would cost. I was with you because I wanted to be, because I chose to be. If I let the Icefalcon or Melantrys or Janus or the Eggplant beat the hell out of me with a training-sword, it was to get where I was going—like lost sleep or ink stains or a headache from looking in a record crystal too long."

She fell silent a moment, turning her hands on the much-worn leather bindings of the sword hilt.

"But what we want changes, too. That's something I never understood before: the kind of love that can come to you when you stick around through really thick and really thin; the kind of love when you put yourself on the line, when you give it time and stay long enough to learn to care. When you make someone—and I don't just mean you, I mean the Keep, and Rudy, and Alde, and even doofs like Enas Barrelstave—when you care enough about people to make them a permanent part of your life. It's different from what I knew before."

"That's what I'm saying," Ingold said. "That I cannot guarantee that I will be a permanent part of your life."

"I can't guarantee that your son will be, either," Gil said softly. "But I'd like to have all the time with him that I can. And this may be the only chance I get."

Minalde's child was born a month later, two weeks before the equinox of fall.

Rudy sat on the steps of the Keep watching the coagulating twilight blacken to night, dyeing the glaciers, staining the slunch beds below them, black-veined by dying fruit trees. The glaciers, he supposed, would continue to grow—though from Brycothis he was beginning to learn the spells by which they could be turned aside from Renweth Vale and convinced to flow down the other side of the ridge. With any luck, the slunch would stay pretty much where it was, until a warm year killed it, who knew how far down the road. Gaboogoos still grew out of it, but they didn't attack anybody, just wandered around the woods in their fanciful shapes, weird souvenirs of a forgotten world. They didn't eat anything or harm anyone, and eventually died of starvation or heat prostration, or gaboogoo distemper, for all he knew. Some animals still ate slunch, but they puffed up and died pretty fast, and most of them avoided it now. After seeing what had happened to the devotees of Saint Bounty, nobody in the Keep could even be brought to touch the carcasses of either gaboogoos or mutants that died in the woods.

Rudy sighed. The surviving members of the Brown, Wicket, and Biggar clans had carved a stone stele to place on the mass grave in which were buried the ashes of Koram Biggar and Varkis Hogshearer and all those others who died screaming when Gil broke the final complex of spells that kept the Mother of Winter in stasis. Maia had spoken a blessing over them, asking God to accept the clean parts of them and to forgive them for what they could not help.

Scala Hogshearer was buried up with the herdkids, in the orchard behind the Keep.

Without mentioning it to anyone, Rudy kept an eye on both graves. So far, no slunch had grown on either one.

He leaned his back against the Keep's black wall, let his head tip back to rest on the ensorcelled stone. Alde was all right. The baby was fine.

He'd delivered the child himself.

He'd done it himself because neither of the Keep's two new wizards—red-haired, silent Ilae and quiet little Brother Wend—had ever delivered a baby. In the Black Rock Keep, Tomec Tirkenson's hagwife mother-in-law Nan was in charge of that—and virtually everything else. And in any case the newcomers arrived only days ago, escorted by Old George the dooic and his band, stumbling and filthy, exhausted after weeks of flight and hiding from the gaboogoos. Wend was still laid up with fever and fatigue, but Rudy was reasonably sure he'd make it.

It was good, he thought, not to be the only wizard around anymore.

Good to know that Tirkenson, Thoth, and the others at the Black Rock Keep had likewise survived.

He had a daughter.

Blue-eyed, black-haired, and beautiful as a perfectly ripe peach . . .

He closed his eyes again.

He had a child.

Down the valley he heard them singing, in the direction of the pass.

"*Yippee-ti-yi-yo, git along, little dogie,*

*It's your misfortune and none of my own . . .*"

He thought absently, *Gil must be in a good mood.*

It was as if she'd only been gone a few days. As if Ingold had only been gone a few days.

It would be good, he thought, to have them back.

"*Yippee-ti-yi-yo, git along, little dogie,*

*You know Wyoming will be your new home.*"

What they were singing didn't sink in for a minute; only that Gil couldn't carry a tune worth sour apples, and Ingold had a very nice baritone.

Then he opened his eyes.

They were riding across the meadow—*riding*—he on a bay horse, she on a long-tailed black, driving before them a small, mixed herd of mares, sheep, and a dozen or more scrawny cows. Four of the mares bore packs on their backs, and from somewhere Ingold had gotten two scraggy yellow dogs, who trotted gamely along through the short, hesitant grass, nipping at the heels of stragglers.

Ingold had told him via crystal that they were coming back. He had neglected to mention this.

"Cool." Rudy got stiffly to his feet and came down the steps of the Keep to greet them, hands in the pockets of his vest. "French fries *and* burgers."

Gil tossed the reins down, sprang from the saddle; skinnier than ever but somehow better than she'd looked in a long time. Peaceful, he thought. Something had changed in her eyes. She wore a gaudy-hued silk coat and still had her hair up in a gladiator's topknot. "Sorry it took us this long, punk," she said, and hugged him, for the first time ever. "We did hurry. Is Alde okay?"

"Alde's fine," Rudy said, returning the embrace with a slow, tired grin. "You didn't need to rush. Everything, uh—came out okay."

Ingold dropped from the saddle like he'd ridden trail herds all his life; all he needed was a ten-gallon hat to go with his red-and-black Church wizard robes and the bearskin coat that looked like he'd looted it off somebody who'd been dead for a long time.

"Rudy, I congratulate you . . . I congratulate you deeply." People were running down the Keep steps around them; the two herd dogs barked furiously, but stilled at a gesture from Ingold, sitting in the grass and watching suspiciously while Bok the Carpenter and Lank Yar and others exclaimed and argued and put ropes around the animals' noses and horns.

"My apologies for not mentioning the herd. Frankly, with the Raiders as thick as they are in the valley, I'm astonished we weren't bushwhacked a dozen times on the way up here. We purchased the cattle along the way—two of those calves are male, by the way, so we really will have a herd again—but the sheep were an entirely fortuitous find."

"They were on the road up here," Gil said. "Look at 'em—they look like they've been wandering around in the wilderness for years. What they were doing up here . . ."

Rudy laughed. "Well, I'll be buggered. Nedra Hornbeam's idea worked after all. I've been trudging out to that frigging circle at the Tall

Gates every day and Summoning All Useful Animals. I never thought it'd pay off."

"I thought they seemed in an unlikely hurry to get up here." Ingold scratched the corner of his mustache, which looked as usual as if he trimmed it with a sword and no mirror. "It will be good to sleep in a bed again, not to mention speaking to one of the wizards from the Times Before. And I'm delighted you were able to make the roses viable—there've been no single-petal white roses in the world for centuries. Really, Rudy, you—"

He was stopped on the steps by Enas Barrelstave, who bustled out and caught his arm in an eager grip. "Inglorion!" He shook his finger in remonstrance, stepping out of the way of cattle, sheep, and horses being led up the steps around them and into makeshift byres in the Aisle. "Now, it's all very well of you to disappear on a cattle-buying trip, but you really should have consulted the Council about it before you left. It's not that we don't respect and value your services, but you can't simply . . ."

"You okay, spook?" Rudy slung his arm around Gil's shoulders as they mounted the steps in the wake of the chattering mob.

She glanced sidelong at him and smiled again. "Yeah," she said. "I'm okay." The scar seemed a part of her features, as if she'd always had it, like the dark smoke-rings around the pupils of her eyes.

"I guess you won't be training with the Guards for a while."

"The hell I won't," Gil said. "There's no reason a woman can't train up until the month before she delivers—though I'm not going to get into any death-fights unless I have to. You think I can't deal with it, punk?" She gave him her old cold stare, and Rudy dropped his arm and backed hastily away.

"No—I just meant . . . I know you can deal with it." Between Ingold and Gil, he thought, that was gonna be one tough kid.

Cold wind blew across them from the glaciers above; in the doors of the Keep the Guards beckoned, wanting to lock up for the night, black forms silhouetted against the gold lamplight inside. "There gonna be much of a harvest?" Gil asked.

"Some. We'll send out an expedition to the marshes down by Willowchild for hay. But we've got the hydroponics tanks up and running the way they were originally designed, so even if we get thwacked by another ice storm, we should be fine. I don't think we'll have any problem talking Barrelstave and Company into okaying some kind of underground stables.

It might be that until the weather evens out we have to give up outside farming completely, except for things like the orchard. Even at that, we got more apples than we thought we would, growing in late . . ."

They paused on the steps, looking back at the bleak landscape. Somewhere down the valley a mammoth hooted; a small herd of squid-like gaboogoos flapped slowly from the slunch beds, palely glowing like otherworldly birds. Rudy shook his head at the alienness of the scene.

*Until the weather evens out. However many centuries that might take.*

But they had food. And they had books. And they had roses, for when the weather warmed up again.

"So what'd you name her?" Gil asked. "Your daughter?"

*My daughter.*

"Gisa," Rudy said softly. "That was the name of Dare of Renwerth's wife, who died on the way up to the Keep . . . died because Dare wouldn't pull the wizards off raising the walls. Gisa of the Flowering Hands. She's been a long time on her way here."

"Gisa," Gil said softly, turning over the word in the tongue of the Wathe, and Rudy nodded.

"The old word for spring."

## ABOUT THE AUTHOR

At various times in her life, Barbara Hambly has been a high school teacher, a model, a waitress, a technical editor, a professional graduate student, an all-night clerk at a liquor store, and a karate instructor. Born in San Diego, she grew up in Southern California, with the exception of one high school semester spent in New South Wales, Australia. Her interest in fantasy began with reading *The Wizard of Oz* at an early age, and has continued ever since.

She attended the University of California, Riverside, specializing in medieval history. In connection with this, she spent a year at the University of Bordeaux in the south of France and worked as a teaching and research assistant at U.C. Riverside, eventually earning a master's degree in the subject. At the university, she also became involved in karate, making Black Belt in 1978 and competing in several national-level tournaments. She now lives in Los Angeles, California.